The Twilight Hour

NICCI GERRARD

PENGUIN BOOKS

PENGUIN BOOKS

Published by the Penguin Group
Penguin Books Ltd, 80 Strand, London WC2R ORL, England
Penguin Group (USA) Inc., 375 Hudson Street, New York, New York 10014, USA
Penguin Group (Canada), 90 Eglinton Avenue East, Suite 700, Toronto, Ontario, Canada M4P 2Y3
(a division of Pearson Penguin Canada Inc.)
Penguin Ireland, 25 St Stephen's Green, Dublin 2, Ireland (a division of Penguin Books Ltd)
Penguin Group (Australia), 707 Collins Street, Melbourne, Victoria 3008, Australia
(a division of Pearson Australia Group Pty Ltd)
Penguin Books India Pvt Ltd, 11 Community Centre,
Panchsheel Park, New Delhi – 110 017, India
Penguin Group (NZ), 67 Apollo Drive, Rosedale, Auckland 0632, New Zealand
(a division of Pearson New Zealand Ltd)
Penguin Books (South Africa) (Pty) Ltd, Block D, Rosebank Office Park,
181 Jan Smuts Avenue, Parktown North, Guateng 2193, South Africa

Penguin Books Ltd, Registered Offices: 80 Strand, London WC2R ORL, England

www.penguin.com

Published in Penguin Books 2014
001

Copyright © Joined-Up Writing, 2014

All rights reserved

The moral right of the author has been asserted

Set in 13/15.25pt Garamond by Palimpsest Book Production Ltd, Falkirk, Stirlingshire
Printed in Great Britain by Clays Ltd, St Ives plc

A CIP catalogue record for this book is available from the British Library

ISBN: 978–1–405–91983–8
OPEN MARKET EDITION: 978–0–241–95010–4

www.greenpenguin.co.uk

To Michael, friend in all seasons

I

Eleanor woke to what was not there. Outside, the wind still roared, dashing pellets of rain against the windows; inside it was too silent, not a breath or a heartbeat save hers. The darkness felt uninhabited. Before she reached out her hand, groping past the water jug and the vase of dying flowers to touch the bed and find it empty, the blanket thrown back and the pillow dislodged, she knew she was alone. She let fear seep through her, into every space in her body. She could taste the muddy, metal ache of it in her mouth; feel it in the palms of her hands and the base of her spine and in her throat like a rippling, oily snake; she could smell it on her skin, sour as spoilt milk.

She was awkwardly curled up in a chair and her left foot was numb, her cheek creased from where it had rested against the wood. When she moved, her skirt rustled and she remembered that she had not undressed the night before, only loosened her hair and kicked off her shoes. Too tired and full of confusion, she had sat down in this chair in the darkness and let sleep end the dreadful day.

For a few seconds, she stayed quite still, listening

to the erratic thump of her heart, waiting to know what she should do, and then she pushed herself out of the chair with a violence that made her stumble. Her cramped foot caught against a mug and tipped it and she felt her ankle give; she heard herself let out a whimper of pain. She could barely remember the shape of the room and held her hands out blindly to find her way to the door, knocking against the end of the bed, the corner of the chest of drawers, feeling around for the door knob, the banisters that would lead her down the narrow, creaking stairs. Pitch darkness everywhere, however much she strained her eyes to catch a chink of light through the blackout curtains, until she stumbled into the kitchen and saw the dull glow of the dying embers in the hearth.

There was a pair of boots by the settle, and she fumbled her feet into them and opened the front door. The wind met her full on, slapping her wetly in the face, whipping her hair around her cheeks, taking her breath away. Even from the shelter of the porch, the sound of hundreds of thousands of leaves in rippling motion was extraordinary, like a sea in a storm or a train bearing down on her. No one should be out on such a night as this, not a stray dog or a flung bird. She didn't give herself time to consider, but stepped out into the streaming wildness and clumsily started to run. The boots were much too big for her; she could feel their thick rubber chafing her shins. The wind gusted against her as if trying to force her back. Lifted twigs scraped her skin and out on the lane a branch bounced past her, then a dustbin lid in a hurtling clatter. She was soon soaked to the skin, her shirt clinging to her ribs and her damp skirt tangling in her legs. She tried to call out, but the wind snatched the name from her mouth before it made a sound and gulped it up.

The houses on either side of her were unlit, huddled shapes. She ran on. There was a pain in her side, and her ankle where she had turned it sent pinches of pain up her leg; her toes slammed against the end of the boots. She had painted her toenails red two nights before, while he watched her. Burning eyes. She could feel the bruise he had left on her arm; the love bite she had wrapped a scarf around to conceal throbbed on her neck. He had pressed his fingers into her flesh and ground his mouth against hers until she tasted blood, and he had said that she could never leave him. Not now. They had gone too far.

She sensed rather than saw the path and turned off the road. Overhanging branches clawed at her hair; there were brambles in the hedgerow that tore at her wet clothes. The wind thundered. There was a smell of ploughed earth and wet bracken. Then she was out on to the open meadow and running down the slope. The sound of the rushing waters met the sound of the leaves and the rupturing sky. At last she came to a halt and stared wildly around, making out the massed shapes of trees, the brown surge of foam. A blind certainty had impelled her here, and now what?

Even as she stood there, at a loss, the rain stopped and the moon flew clear out from the clouds for an instant – and in that instant she saw, she thought she saw, a face. A white face in the dark waters, like a petal, like a broken reflection of the light. Then the moon was swallowed back into the clouds and the face, or the phantom, was gone and all that remained was the roiling blackness.

Eleanor kicked off the boots and then pulled off her skirt, feeling it rip. Even now, at this moment of extremity, she recollected how he had unhooked it, very slowly, crouching at her feet, his hand between her legs, his eyes fixed on her, looking into her. Memories have their own pace; they exist in their own world where the rules of time do not operate. For as she ran downstream and then – arms spread wide and hair streaming out behind her in a banner – as she jumped high and wide towards the water, she found herself remembering the first time she had laid eyes on him and it was as if she was seeing him again with that stab of terrible desire. And she found herself thinking, almost with rueful amusement, that this was really a very stupid thing to do. She wondered if she was about to die, but felt no fear, only a sense that she had not had the life she had planned. What would people think? What would they say? Shaking their heads: poor them. Who would have thought, who would have guessed, how did it all come to this?

Time stopped and she hung in the air like a great bird. The rain had ceased, the wind was dying down, the wildness blowing itself out and leaving a ruined landscape behind. Too late, too late. She saw herself suspended there, looking down at the dislocated face of the moon, and then she saw herself fall.

She hit the water and became her flailing, desperate body again, no thoughts or memories left. The current buffeted and rolled her, sucked her under. Her lungs were bursting and there were bright spots exploding behind her eyes. Something – a rock, a log – scraped at her thigh; she felt her skin split. She imagined blood clouding in her wake. Then suddenly she surfaced, exploding into the wind again, sobbing air in, howling it out. Down once more into the liquid rush of grit and pebbles and mud, river weeds wrapping her, but for a shorter time and the next time she came up she drew in a deeper and more sustaining breath and managed a few strokes, carrying her with the filthy flow of the water. She flung her hand out to clutch at an overhanging branch and felt it burn along her palm, and her fingers closed on air. Everything was too fast, a grainy rush of sensations: rocks and stones and trees and the roar of water and the faint-est flicker of the half-moon that occasionally nudged out from behind the clouds.

She hit a rock and pain needled through her; her

body was thrown sideways like any other piece of river garbage. This time she managed to grasp a root and hold on to it, her body swirling sideways. And then, as if in a dream, she saw the face once more – or was it? – just upstream and surging towards her, tipped up to the moonlight; like a sleeping child, she thought, like a water lily peaceful in the floods. She reached out with a howl and clutched, found hair that slid through her fingers, found a handful of cloth that she tugged on. And the body followed like a great fish, pale and glinting under the water, until it was there beside her, rubbery waterlogged flesh and closed eyes, all stoppered up with mud and slime.

'You fool,' she said above the noise of the river. She heard her voice, almost conversational, matter-of-fact. 'You will not. You will not.'

Eleanor took the upper arm and pulled again and now they were in the slipping shallows, protected by the embrace of the roots while the river rushed past. A bit further up, she saw that the bank dipped right down, and she heaved and bumped the weight until she reached it. Holding on to one wrist, she clambered backwards on to the bank. The body started to slide from her.

'No,' she said, as though words could stop it escaping. 'I'm not going to let you go.'

And she hauled at the arm until she thought she would pull it from its socket, and now she could put her hands under both armpits and she pulled with all her strength, feet sliding in the muddy grass and her spine crackling with effort. She let out gasps with each tug. It sounded like sex, she thought. Like a ferocious climb towards climax.

'Come on,' she said. 'Please come on. Please.'

With agonizing slowness, the weight shifted, moved towards her until, with a lurch that made her topple backwards, it was out of the shallows and lying on the grass on top of her. For a moment, she lay quite still, staring up at the soft bowl of darkness above her, holding the moon and the white sprinkle of stars, and looking at the dim pattern made by the branches of the trees. Nothing cared about these two bodies spread out on the wet earth; nothing saw. Then she scrambled from under the weight and knelt beside it, leaning down to put her warm lips on the cold ones, blowing breath steadily into the mouth the way she had been taught. Breathe in, blow out, breathe in, blow out. My life into yours. My life for yours. My love. Selves dissolve. Pump the chest. Again, then again. Like a machine. Like bellows. A memory of being a child and watching the fire puffed into life. And at last there was a gasp, a groan, a gush of watery bile escaping the mouth. Eleanor stopped. She lay back down again on the bank and closed her eyes. She could feel the earth turning beneath her. Her body was seized by a violent shivering; every muscle was jolted by cold and grief. Hot tears seeped out from under her muddy lids.

'I will never forgive you,' she said. 'Can you hear me? Never.'

She opened her eyes and stared up at the great black sky hanging over her, blazing now with stars. It was over.

2

Eleanor Lee stood in the library that smelt of things that were musty and decaying. The wind rattled at the loose panes and curled its way in down the chimney. It had been many weeks since she had set foot in here. Dim shapes had become even dimmer; objects melted back into the shadows. Darkness was setting in, and she had waited too long and come too late to hide the past from the present.

She pointed her cane in front of her, feeling for the edges of chairs, stray items on the floor. Brushing against the old rocking horse, she set it moving, cantering on the spot, white eyes staring wildly. Her stick met an object and she bent to touch it: it must be the dolls' house that her children and then her children's children had played with, yes, with a roof that lifted up to reveal a miniature, orderly world. A pile of books toppled as she passed. A silk scarf that someone had left was lying there like the discarded skin of a snake. She lifted it, rubbed it thoughtfully, and hung it round her own neck. Her feet moved softly through the debris; her long skirt swished; the bangles on her wrists chinked. She reached the pair of tall steel cabinets standing side by side against the far wall and slid the top drawer of the taller one open. Her fingers scrabbled over the contents, feeling the tightly packed cardboard and plastic folders, the stray papers underneath. Where could they be? She pulled out a random folder and held it in front of her for a moment, squinting her eyes as if suddenly everything would become clear again, just for an instant. It was quite hopeless of course. There was drawer after drawer of filed papers and then she knew, without seeing, that there were boxes on the floor as well, and she couldn't even remember now where she had put what she had come to find. She should never have kept them all these years.

On an impulse, Eleanor plunged her hands into the drawer and drew out folders, scattering them around her, swishing at them violently with her cane before bringing out the next handful until there was nothing left. She yanked open the second drawer, but suddenly stopped and gave a deep sigh.

'Don't be a fool,' she said out loud, in a soft, cracked voice. 'Think.'

She made up her mind and tapped her way out of the room, moving more quickly once she was in the familiar hallway and then the living room where a fire crackled in the hearth and a bottle of wine stood open on the side table. There was a piano near the door, its polished wood gleaming in the soft light and on its top a copper bowl brimming over with its own rich, shifting colour. Eleanor felt around on the mantelpiece for the box of matches, which she took back with her into the library, shutting the door behind her. She moved with purpose towards the two filing cabinets, her cane zig-zagging swiftly in front of her, and when she got there pulled open the bottom drawers, feeling to make sure there were folders stored in each of them. She struck a match, felt it flare, and dropped it into the first waiting space; then she prepared to strike the next.

She had thought that a metal drawer would be the perfect receptacle to hold its own small and self-contained bonfire. She could burn the contents of the drawers quite safely, one by one, leaving only a soft dissolving heap of ashes. She was wrong. Almost immediately, the flames shot out of the first drawer, tall and orange, and caught the bottom of the velvet curtain. They started to gobble up the material, greedy and bright. Eleanor stood for a moment, transfixed; the shapes of the flames printed on her eyelids, the acrid smell in her nostrils and throat. Then the heat hit her and she stumbled backwards, tripping against the dolls' house. She took the thick embroidered shawl that Gil had given her years ago from her shoulders and tried to drop it over the drawer of fire to stifle it, but it simply fed the flames, which had taken on a life of their own, leaping away from the cabinet of secrets and running up the wood of the windows. Sparks flew at her and she felt a myriad of tiny blisters bubble on her skin. It was like being stung, she thought, maddened wasps darting from the furnace.

As she backed out of the room that was full of flickering lights and a busy crackle of destruction, it occurred to her that this would be a brutal and grandiose way to die – sending the old, beloved house up in a mighty bonfire simply in order to conceal secrets from seventy years ago. But at least no one would ever know. Destroy the building but keep the self hidden away and safe.

She came to slowly. She could smell something burning and then realized she was smelling herself. Burnt hair and burnt skin. A pillow under her aching head, stiff sheets. She lifted her arm and found it was wrapped in a thick bandage. She opened her blind eyes and caught the artificial brightness of strip lighting.

'Where am I?'

'What the fuck were you doing?' a voice boomed into her. She wished she was deaf as well as blind, so she didn't have to hear them all telling her, asking her, scolding her as if she was so old now that she had become a child once more.

'Hello, Leon. I'm in hospital, I take it?'

'Of course you're in hospital. You're very lucky you're not in a morgue. How could you have been so stupid, putting a match to the house?'

'It was an accident.'

'Of course it was an accident! What else would it be? You could have died.'

'But I didn't. I'm quite all right, Leon. Just a few burns. Do I look a fright?'

'What?'

'Hello, Gran,' said a voice on her other side.

She moved her head cautiously, feeling the muzzy pain in her skull. Her mouth tasted of ashes.

'Jonah!' She smiled towards him. 'You're here too.'

'I am. You don't look a fright. Just a bit smudged and a few patches are missing from your eyebrows and some of your hair's a bit frizzy. How are you feeling?'

'I don't know really. What happened?'

'Don't you remember?' Leon was pacing back and forward now; three steps took him to the curtain and then he swivelled round on his heel and charged off in the other direction. Back and forward, pushing his hands into his pockets then pulling them out again. Like a smouldering fire himself, thought Eleanor, as she watched his bulky shape pass by at the bottom of her bed. Jonah, by contrast, sat placidly on the moulded plastic chair. She could smell his aftershave and when she put out a hand, could feel the softness of his overcoat.

'I remember the fire starting,' she said cautiously.

'Luckily for you, Adrian's son was up playing some computer game,' said Leon. His shoes squeaked as he spun round. 'He saw the fire out of the window and

13

came running and put it out. He called us once he'd called the ambulance.'

'Was much destroyed?'

'Hardly anything, apparently. The curtains and some of the window frames. It'll be a mess of course.'

'What about the filing cabinets?'

'Those steel things? I've no idea, but I imagine they're built to withstand a bomb. Don't worry. All your papers and letters will still be there.'

'Oh.'

Leon sat down at last.

'Listen now, what would have happened if Adrian's son hadn't been awake and seen the blaze from their house and come running?'

'But he did see it. And if he hadn't, I would have rung the emergency services and they would have put the fire out.'

'How long do you think it takes for them to get all the way to you?'

'I don't know.'

'And by the time they arrived the whole house would have gone up in flames, and you with it.'

'Perhaps.'

'This can't continue,' said Leon.

'What does that mean?'

'I knew something like this would happen, but you'd never listen. Living alone in a big falling-down house in the middle of nowhere. You're old and almost blind.'

'I'm well aware of that.'

'It's not safe. I can't let it go on like this.' She could imagine his face from his voice: heavy-jawed, with that slightly pompous expression he wore when he was anxious. He'd been the same as a little boy, when he was angry and upset and needed comfort but couldn't bring himself to ask for it.

'Leon,' she said, her voice cool. 'I know you mean well, but I'm not a child and I'm not of unsound mind. It's not up to you, it's up to me.'

'That's quite true.' Jonah pulled a bright green apple from his coat pocket like a magician, rubbed it on his sleeve and then took a crunching bite. 'Tell us what you want, Eleanor.'

'I want to go home.'

'Home!' Leon gave an exasperated snort.

'Yes.'

The door opened and a tall woman with a mane of long grey hair rushed in, breathless, her cheeks pink from the night air.

'Mother!' she said, half-sobbing, sitting heavily on the bed. She reached out with a hand but did not touch the old woman, who looked tiny beside her, fragile but indomitable and somehow very alone, like someone perched on a life raft on bucking seas. 'Oh darling Mum! You've given us all such a fright. Are you all right? Your poor arm! What have you gone and done now?'

'Hello, Esther. How nice of you to come.' As if it

was a tea party, thought Jonah, grinning to himself and pleased by her.

'She says she wants to go home,' Leon put in. 'She says—'

'I am here, you know,' interrupted Eleanor tartly. 'I can speak for myself.'

'You can't just go home, not after this. You must see that,' pleaded Esther.

'I see nothing of the sort. The fire was obviously put out before it could do much damage.'

'That's not the point.'

'Then what is the point?'

'For the time being, at least. Come and stay with one of us while we think of what should be done.'

'What should be done,' repeated Eleanor, sitting up straighter in the narrow bed. 'That sounds ominous.'

'I just mean—'

'I know what you mean. You mean I can no longer be trusted to take care of myself.'

'You could have died,' Leon said once again, as if it was his trump card.

'Who cares? Why does that matter so much? I'm ninety-four. I can die if I want to!'

'Do you want to?' asked Jonah, sounding interested.

'Not particularly. But I want to choose how to live. And I certainly don't want to sit in a waiting room for death with a blanket on my knees and nurses calling me dear and feeding me sloppy shepherd's pie and rubbery scrambled egg and trying to make me play bingo and have my hair done and my relatives dutifully visiting me on wet Sunday afternoons, making polite conversation.'

'But—'

'Sing-alongs!'

'That sounds somewhat exaggerated,' said Leon, stiff and upset.

'Does it?'

'Anyway.' Esther put her hand out once more and did touch her mother this time, tentatively, as if she was still hot from the flames. 'You don't need to go into a home. You can come and live with one of us. You know that. Me, for instance. Or I'm sure Quentin or Samuel—'

'No. I would rather die.'

'Are we that bad?' asked Jonah.

'I would rather die,' repeated Eleanor, 'than be looked after by my children.'

'Have you considered that this is not fair on us?' said Leon. 'We worry about you, all alone there. We worry about going on holidays or leaving you unattended for days at a stretch. We race up and down the motorway to visit you, and you're constantly on our minds.'

'Ah,' said Eleanor. 'I think that's called emotional blackmail, Leon.'

A woman screamed in the ward, a repeated wail of distress. They heard the clack of heels over linoleum and a calm voice speaking to her, but the wailing continued.

'Why won't you live with me?' asked Esther. 'We could have a nice time together. God knows, I could do with the company.'

'I won't live with you, Esther. I won't live with any of you.' She hesitated, gave a long sigh. The three round the bed saw her bony shoulders tighten and then sag under the hospital gown. 'Please would you all leave me now.'

'I've only just arrived.' Esther sounded as though she would cry. 'As soon as I heard I jumped in the car and—'

'I know. Come back in an hour or so. I'm tired. I want to sleep.'

But she was very far from sleep. She closed her eyes as they left and then opened them as soon as she could no longer hear their voices or footsteps, only the high whine of the lights and the faint creak of the hospital trolleys, and outside the windows the sound of ordinary life continuing: the slam of car doors and the hum of voices. It was a relief to be alone. She sat up in bed, and took several mouthfuls of water from the plastic beaker beside her, although the ashy taste in her mouth remained. Her children pressed in on her with their anxieties and their needs. They made the air feel tight and hot and still, like a gathering storm.

She tried to see herself through their eyes: ancient, stubborn, burdensome, hanging on to life long beyond her time. Sometimes they talked about her as if she wasn't there. 'Like a mule,' they would say under their breath. 'You know how she can get. There's no reasoning with her.'

She was ancient and she was stubborn but she had no intention of being a burden. She took a deep breath and set her jaw.

'Very well.'

'Very well? What?'

'I will go into a home. I know how you all worry. It's not right. None of this is right.'

'Don't do it just for us,' said Leon. 'You know I didn't mean—'

'I know exactly what you meant. Nobody should be ninety-four. It's humiliating.'

'But surely—'

'Put the house on the market. I will move out at Christmas.'

'Really? You do see it's for the best – for everyone.'

'I will move out at Christmas, but before that I'm going home. Alone.'

'We'll do everything.' Leon was speaking rapidly, guilty and trying to placate her. 'You don't need to do anything. Sell the house, find a nice place, not like the kind of place you were speaking of, sheltered accommodation—'

'It's all right, Leon.'

'And we'll sort out all your things. We can do it bit by bit.'

'No. That's my condition. I want to go home alone and I want someone else to sort through my possessions; all my papers and my mementos.'

'Why?'

'Because I do.'

'But we'd like to do it for you; it would be no trouble.'

'I want a stranger.'

'As you wish.' Leon sat down on a chair that wobbled under him. He rubbed the side of his jaw, hand rasping against the silvery stubble. 'If that's what you want, I'm sure that can be arranged.'

'It is what I want.'

'As a matter of fact,' said Jonah, 'I think I might know the very person.'

3

Peter biked from the station as the day was fading into a smoky dusk. The street lamps dwindled as he left the town and soon there was no pavement, only a damp grass verge and a narrow, pockmarked lane that the headlights of an occasional car would briefly illuminate. The light on his bike was thin and weak and didn't help him. Then there were bats; oily rags blown above his head before dissolving back into gathering darkness. Silence that wasn't silent when you listened, but inhabited by faint sounds: the wind like the sea in the trees; the faint shriek of an owl; a rustle in the undergrowth beside him — and once a tiny creature spun across the road just in front of him, like a leaf rolling, but he glimpsed its sharp eyes.

He stopped for a moment, just to listen to the sounds his body made in the creaking quiet of the night: the intake of breath and its unsteady release; his heart banging against his ribs; the faint clamouring in his head and in his ears. He smiled to himself, feeling a prickle of excitement. He wasn't used to quiet and he wasn't used to dark. He couldn't remember when he had last left London, or even the tiny grid of the city that he had occupied. For some time, he hadn't left the flat, or his bedroom in the flat. His bed, where he'd pulled the covers over his head and burrowed into his own warmth, cradling his pale slender body. Waiting, until gradually waiting became the thing in itself, intransitive – not waiting for anything or expecting anything, just a suspended state of being – following the clouds in the sky, the skeins of birds, the way the light fell on the garden. Click of door, tick of clock, patter of rain, murmur of pipes, his mother's contented snores at night. But now Jonah had summoned him to take care of his granny and he was on his way again. He realized that he felt interested, buoyant, alert.

The house was up a long, uneven drive. It was so dark now that he couldn't see his way and had to dismount his bike in order to avoid veering off the track and into the thorny hedge. His feet, cold in their thin shoes, crunched on loose gravel. The house was just a massed shape. He could see it was large, but that was all. There was one dim light on in the porch, but the windows were dark and it was hard to believe there was anyone inside. Had he got the day wrong? He slowed down, putting off the moment when he would be knocking on the door. The wind was cold on his face and he thought he could smell the sea. A long shiver of anticipation ran through him.

He leant his bike against a wall, lifted off the bulging panniers, unslung his small rucksack so that it hung off one shoulder – and then before he had time to change his mind, he knocked on the door, bold and hard, and listened. A dog barked from somewhere inside and then stopped barking. For a while there was nothing, but as he was about to rap again he heard the tap of a stick on the floor, and footsteps. They were very slow and deliberate, as if the person taking them was pausing between each step. Then the door swung open and he found himself facing the indistinct shape of a woman. He could see that she wore a long skirt and that her hair was quite white. She stood very still and upright just a few feet from him. Behind her was the dog: large and shaggy in the gloom, with a panting pink tongue. Peter took a nervous step backwards. He wasn't sure about dogs. Once when he was out running a whippetty creature had launched itself at him and fastened its teeth into his bare thigh, simply hanging there while its owner had moaned and said she didn't know what had come over it. He had the faint scar still.

'Hello,' he said. 'I'm Peter. Peter Mistley. Are you Mrs Lee?'

'Peter?' She held out a thin hand and, putting down one pannier, he took it. A clutch of bones and the slide of dry, warm skin. 'I didn't hear a taxi.' Her voice was soft and blurred, like worn velvet.

'I biked.'

'Dear me. That's quite a way. Is it dark?'

Peter turned his head to look at the night behind him, the obscure tumult of the sky.

'Yes,' he said uncertainly. 'It is really quite dark now.'

'Then I had better turn on the lights. Come in out of the cold. Your bike will be quite safe out there.' As if guessing his anxiety, she said, 'Don't worry about Polly, she's a very old rescue dog and she's even intimidated by the wood pigeons.'

She let go of his hand and he stepped into the hall and shut the door behind him. She reached for a switch on the wall. The gush of light revealed her to him and he had to prevent himself from gasping. She must have been one of the oldest people he had ever seen, except in photographs in magazines. *National Geographic*, he thought, as he gazed at her. She seemed to him like a landscape that had been battered and ravaged by torrents and winds and the erosion of decades. She was quite tall and very thin, and she stood as straight as a ruler, as if age, which bends most people, had pulled her upright. Her hair was a mass of silver-white cobwebs above the chipped mosaic of her face. She wore a long grey woollen skirt with a frayed, grubby hem and her body was draped in a tasselled shawl that had seen better days. One hand – bruised, shiny and liver-spotted, with swollen knuckles and a great ring on the fourth finger like an encrusted glittering knob –

grasped a cane. Peter couldn't tell if she had been beautiful once, or whether she still was: the sheer fact of her having lived for so long awed him. The dog that stood behind her seemed equally ancient and faded: a brindled shabby mongrel with a torn ear and beseeching eyes.

Then: 'Oh—' he suddenly murmured.

'What?'

'You're blind.'

'I know.' She rested her unseeing eyes on his face and smiled. Her neck, rising out of the folds of the shawl, was alarmingly thin. It felt rude to stare at her when she couldn't look back at him.

'Sorry. I mean, I'm sorry that I didn't know.'

'My grandson didn't tell you?'

'No.'

'So like Jonah.'

Jonah: mysterious, cosmopolitan Jonah, steeped in history, biblical and heathen, swallowed by a whale in his previous life. Jonah with his beautiful clothes and his dark eyes, whom Kaitlin was with now, stepping from the wreckage of her relationship with Peter into something more courteous, less stormy and intense perhaps. His email to Peter had come out of the blue and was as formally composed as a letter – he was looking for someone who could sort through all of his grandmother's papers, photographs and books, deciding which should be sold, which given to an interested university and which should be binned.

His grandfather had been some distinguished doctor, and his grandmother had spent a lifetime in education, as a teacher and then a teacher trainer. Was he interested?

'Do you have a bag?' the old woman said now.

Peter let his panniers and rucksack fall to the floor. He suddenly felt enormously tired. He wanted to sink down on the floor beside his luggage and rest his head on the wooden boards. Perhaps she was so blind that she wouldn't notice. She'd go on talking to him as though he were still standing beside her. He was wearing a thick overcoat and there were patches of cooling perspiration on his shirt. He felt graceless in front of this creature from another century, with her extraordinary face like a map of life – which was ridiculous, of course. She couldn't see him. He could make gestures at her, or turn from her, and she would go on facing him with her secret inward smile.

'I'll show you your room later. First, shall we sit by the fire? Have you had dinner?'

'No. Yes. That is, I'm not—'

'You haven't eaten but you don't want to put me to any bother? Especially since I can't see.'

'Well, yes,' said Peter.

'I can see shapes and sometimes make out faces. And when the sunlight is bright, it hurts my eyes. But I don't need to see.' She held up the arm that wasn't holding the cane; a clink of bracelets. There was something of a sorceress about her: a female Prospero. 'I see with my fingers and my ears and my memory. Follow me.'

He picked up his rucksack and panniers and followed her as she made her way down the hall, with her slow, delicate steadiness, Polly beside her. Her feet barely made a sound on the boards, whereas his sent small pulses through the house. He had an impression of dark, oppressive oils in gilt frames, of framed black-and-white photographs showing groups of people in strange garb, of a sudden glimpse of the two of them thrown up in the mottled mirror that hung – slightly askew – on the wall. She like a wraith and he laden and stumbling behind her.

'Here we are.' She pushed at the door in front of them and it swung open into a kitchen. 'Leave your bags here. Take care of the step. And the floor slopes.'

The kitchen was long, with uneven stone tiles and a table running along its length. There were windows set deep into the walls, and on the wide sills stood pots of salmon-pink geraniums. But one of them was dead, he saw, just a dry twist of wood, a few brown leaves. He looked around the room. There was an old-fashioned stove at the far end, and near it a small fireplace where the last embers glowed. There was a leather sofa, old and shabby, on which two ginger cats curled, one at either end, tails twitching in dreams. He took off his coat and folded it on the table.

'The time is nine-eighteen,' said a bossy female voice from underneath it.

'Oh!' He picked up the coat and saw the talking clock.

'The house is full of voices,' said the old woman. 'Sometimes they keep me company. They can have a mind of their own.' She put her hand out and tapped.

'Zero grams,' announced a different voice, deep and plummy. 'Zero ounces.'

'Now then, what will you eat? There's some cold chicken in the fridge, I think. And some nice cheese that my grand-daughter brought. But that was some time ago. Perhaps it's run away by now.'

She opened the fridge door and put her head inside.

'I can't tell,' she said cavernously. 'Would you like to look?'

Peter joined her by the fridge, which was spacious and almost empty.

'Is there bread in there?'

He pulled out a nub of brown bread in a brown paper bag and a plate of pale, spreading cheese.

'Yes,' he said. 'Bread and cheese is good for me. I'm not very hungry.' Though he was suddenly ravenous, almost dizzy with hunger.

'I used to make bread.' She straightened up. 'For many decades, I made bread twice a week, Mondays and Thursdays. It gave a structure to my days, when they had no other. Structure is very important, you know.' Peter noticed how she spoke in whole sentences, precisely, as if she were seeing them written down first, following the punctuation on the page. 'I used to love making bread: the sour bubbling yeast and the fine sifted flour; the elastic plumpness of the dough as it rose. Now it's just another thing I will never do again. I will never run down a hill, I will never watch the sun set. I will never swim in the sea, which was my great joy. I will never dance.'

'You could still dance,' said Peter boldly. 'You move like a dancer.'

'I will never make love again or share my bed with anyone.'

He blinked and was mute. That hollowed-out, stripped-down, flayed body.

'Eat your bread and cheese. There are knives over there.' She floated her hand. 'Then we can sit by the fire in the living room and we can talk about what you are going to do for me.'

Peter found the knives – blotchy silver with cracked bone handles – and sat. The dog sat beside him, hopeful. He put out a tentative hand and dabbed her upturned nose in an approximation of a stroke; her tail thumped gently on the floor. Then he spread some of the cheese on the stale bread and took a mouthful. She stood beside the dying fire and seemed to watch him. There were crumbs everywhere, and he felt scrutinized.

'How long have you lived here?' he asked.

'Oh. More than sixty years, though we had a flat in London as well, until we retired,' she said. 'This was where we came at weekends and during holidays. Especially the long summer holidays with the children. I know it by touch and by heart. I know instinctively how many steps there are on the stairs and how many paces it will take for me to cross the living room and stand by the bay window that looks out over the lawn. Many rooms I never enter any more. I live here and in the living room and my bedroom. Sometimes the library: I can smell the books. Paper, leather, dust, sunlight, wood. When I first came,' she continued, 'I was young and I had young children. Each room was full of noise – and the garden, too. Tomorrow you shall see the garden. I can tell you the names of all the roses, though I can no longer see them. I am very fond of roses.

'The tide comes in,' she was saying, quietly so that he had to strain to hear her. 'And the tide goes out again. The children left, of course, as children must, but then later there were often grandchildren here too. I hung their little clothes on the line and remembered what it was like to be a mother. But then they grew up as well and had their own lives. And my husband died. He died many years ago, you know, and although he was old when he went, I have lasted many years without him. I have outlasted everyone. Moss has grown over the gravestones of most of those I have lost.'

Peter gazed at her, knife suspended. How could she speak to him like this, when she'd only met him a minute ago? Perhaps when no one was there, she talked like this as well, her soft voice murmuring in the empty rooms, like waves on a shore. Was this what loneliness did?

'I'm sorry.' He didn't know what else to say.

'But now they think I can't cope here,' she continued, as if he hadn't interrupted. 'They worry about me. That I will set fire to the house and myself – well, I suppose I've already done that so they have good reason. That I will chop off my fingers with my sharp cutting knife, that I will fall down the stairs or slip in the shower, forget to take my pills, not wash, not eat, not drink, not look after myself.' Her voice was rising in strength. 'How old do you think I am, young man?'

'Call me Peter. I don't know. I can't tell.'

'I am ninety-four years old.'

He had thought her older, over a hundred.

'I am ninety-four years old and if I fall down the stairs, that's my concern. If I climb on the roof, then let me. There are worse ways of dying than falling from the roof. The world shrinks.'

'That's a sad thought,' he said.

'I'm sorry. Poor boy, you've just come to sort out papers. How's the cheese?'

'Very nice. Thank you.'

'Is it too runny?'

'It's runny, but—'

'You don't need to be polite, you know. I was far too polite when I was your age – but how old are you?'

'Twenty-five.'

'Twenty-five. I was married and a mother by your age. In my day, women were expected to be very polite when they were twenty-five. You could do monstrous things as long as you minded your manners. Have you finished?'

'Yes.'

'Put the plate in the sink and we'll go and sit by the fire.'

Peter, the dog at his heels, followed her out of the kitchen, and then up three broad steps and into another room, where there were sofas and, at one side, a piano. None of the lights were on but a fire blazed in the hearth and the old woman walked with unerring steps to an armchair and sat in it, laying her cane carefully on the floor beside it. The flames threw flickering lights over her creased and folded face and glinted on the keys of the piano. Peter felt as though he had walked into a strange dream, and waited for what she would say next.

'Would you pour me some wine?' She pointed to a

table in the bay window, on which stood a bottle of wine, half-drunk, and several glasses. 'And do please join me.'

'I'd like that; thank you.'

'They open bottles of wine for me when they come, though I think I can manage. I've had the practice. I don't like the idea that they can keep track of what I drink – not that I drink so very much and if I did, why would that matter? They know what I drink, what I eat. They open bills and official correspondence. They know how much money I have in the bank.'

'Here.' Peter handed her a glass of wine, touching its rim against her hand so that she could grasp it. 'Who's "they"?'

'Helpers, carers, call them what you will. You lose privacy when you're old and blind. People arrange your life for you.'

'That must be hard.' He took a sip of the red wine; ripe fruit. Old and dark. He watched the way she drank hers in bold gulps, as if she were thirsty.

'You're on display. Sometimes I sit here and I think that anyone could tiptoe in and just watch me. Watch me sitting here. Watch me walking from room to room, touching things. Watch me when I spill food or smash at things with my cane.'

'You smash at things with your cane?' A ripple of admiration ran through him.

'Wouldn't you, in my position?'

'Probably. I hope so.' He smiled at her, before remembering that she couldn't see it.

'Do you like fires?' she asked.

'Yes. Though I've never lived in a house with an open fire in it.'

'No?'

'I've always been in flats or modern houses. Nothing like this. I like it a great deal. It makes a room alive.'

'Mmm. You can spend hours staring into a fire. Listening to the bubbling, crackling noises, seeing shapes, letting thoughts drift through you. My husband, he used to make bonfires. He'd be outside all day, feeding branches into the flames. All day,' she repeated. She passed a hand across her face. 'When he died, I had to learn how to make a good fire. Now, someone else has to do it for me, of course. Like so much else. In the morning someone comes and makes sure I'm not dead and brings in shopping and meals, clears the ashes and makes up the new fire, and in the evenings someone comes in and makes sure I'm still alive and calls me "dear" and asks how we are. What do you look like?'

'I'm sorry?'

'What do you look like?'

'I don't think that I know exactly. It's not something that anyone's ever asked me before.'

'You know what I look like, although I can hardly remember my own face. I used to gaze at it. I used to stand in front of the mirror and stare into my own eyes and smile at myself and make myself ready for the world. It's hardly fair that you can see me and I can't see you.'

'I don't think I look very extraordinary.'

'Nonsense. Everyone looks extraordinary in their own way. What's your way?'

'I—' He reached up and touched his face. 'Well. I have reddish-coloured hair.'

'Ah. Red like a carrot or red like a fox?'

'A fox, I think. Or perhaps an apricot.'

'I'll take the fox. Freckles?'

'When I was a child. Not so much now. I have fair skin. My grandma used to tell me that I looked like an Irish sprite; something that lived in the woods.' He felt startled by the gush of happiness that ran through him.

'What colour are your eyes?'

'Green.'

'Green. That's good. Do you like the way you look?'

Peter considered this.

'It depends.'

'Depends on what?'

'I don't know. I think it depends on how I am feeling about myself: if I like myself then I like my face. There are times when I am a stranger to myself. Mostly I think that this is simply who I am. I don't see myself.'

'Mmm.' She nodded, considering this.

'Shall we talk about what I'm supposed to be doing here?'

She turned her face towards him.

'Of course. I'm asking you too many questions. What did Jonah tell you?'

'He said that you were moving house and that you had decades of papers, books, manuscripts and photographs that needed going through. Some he said you could give to a university since they might have cultural or historical importance. Some that were more personal to you would be distributed among your family. Some—' He hesitated. 'Some you might want to keep.'

'Even though I'm blind, you're thinking.'

'And he assumes there will be quite a lot of stuff you'll simply want to throw away.'

'Yes. I think that covers it. I'm not a very organized person, I'm afraid. Or at least, I've kept everything, for it's hard to throw away your past, and I've let it get into a mess.'

'That's all right.'

There was a silence and she stared into the flames, unseeing.

'There is a reason I do not want my family doing this for me.' Peter waited. 'Some things I would prefer to keep private.'

'I understand.'

'Funnily enough, I believe you do.' She passed her

36

hand across her face, then asked: 'Is this what you do?'

'Do?'

'For a living, I mean. Are you someone who catalogues things? A cataloguer of other people's lives. Well, why not? It's more important than packing up furniture and china, isn't it – packing up precious memories. The things you might find; the secrets you might spill and break.'

'I'll be careful,' Peter said. He took a mouthful of wine, spicy and rich.

'I'm sure you'll be careful. You sound like a considerate young man. Perhaps you are a librarian or an archivist?'

'Jonah didn't say?'

'No. He's a man of few words, isn't he?'

'Yes. But I'm not a librarian.'

She waited. Peter shifted in his chair.

'I'm not really anything at the moment,' he said eventually.

She looked with kindness at the space just to his left.

'I'm sure that's not true.'

'I'm between things.'

He expected her to ask what he was between, but she didn't. She simply nodded and said, 'The place in between is a very important place. You must be tired.'

'Not so much.' For he felt both weary and entirely awake. The journey, the bike ride through a misty darkness to this old house near the sea, the old woman all alone here like a creature, sweet but a bit sinister, out of some German fairy tale, filled his brain with shifting confusion and excitement.

'Well, I'm going to bed,' she said, feeling for her cane and rising with a surprising grace from her chair. 'Don't smoke inside the house. I know you smoke, I can smell it on you, but please not inside the house. You could lean out of the window, I suppose, like my grand-daughter Thea does, and she thinks I don't know. Or she climbs up on the roof.'

'Where am I to sleep?'

'Ah. I'm sorry. I was forgetting. You follow the stairs up to the second floor. Your room is the one with the sloping ceiling. I always liked it. I occasion-ally used to sleep there when I came to the house on my own. It feels rather like a secret place, an eyrie. You can see a patch of the sea from the window and sometimes you can hear it too. There's a shower and toilet next to your room, and they put a towel out for you. I thought it best for you to be self-sufficient.'

'I think I'll have a cigarette in the garden before I turn in.'

'Don't lock yourself out. Use the back door.'

'What time shall I begin tomorrow?'

'What time? Why, whatever time suits you. I am always up early and then I can show you where every-thing is.'

'Thank you.'

'No, thank *you*, young man.'

'Peter, please.'

'Peter. And I am Eleanor.'

'Good night, Eleanor.'

Eleanor reached out to check that her radio was at hand, for when she woke in the small hours. The World Service helped her through into morning. Wars, economic crashes, the farming news. Then she turned on her side to sleep in the position she had always slept in – knees drawn up, arms gathered underneath her chin, like a tiny child. Sometimes when she woke in the night she forgot who she was, or when; she thought she could hear her mother talking softly in another room, and tears of warm happiness would gather under her closed lids. In the night, memories flow back. You live in them. The future is short and the past is long.

He was very close to her tonight. She could see his face and feel his body, not far from hers. She could feel his eyes watching her and because he was watching her, she was beautiful again and full of fresh, fast joy. She talked to him. She told him the thoughts and half-formed impressions that drifted through her mind, like petals, like ash. She told him things that she had not known she was feeling. She couldn't have said if she spoke out loud or if they were words in her head. For years, she had been silent, silent as the grave; she had allowed him to leave her, or perhaps it was truer to say that she had left him. What else could she have done? She had once called him heart of my heart; she had once told him that she would die without him. But she had gone on without him. Only in dreams had he sometimes been returned to her and then she would wake with a heart that beat so loud she thought it must wake the whole house and boom out her secret to them all. Such treachery. She would lie in the soft darkness and listen to the sounds of the night outside her window and she would wait patiently, diligently, until the dream faded and her heartbeats calmed. That was one lesson life had taught her: all things pass. Sorrows pass, like dreams. Pain leaves centre stage and stands in the wings. You hold on to the self you have forged; lie in the bed you have made for yourself; wait for morning. The light that will creep through the curtains, the cockerel that will crow and the sounds of the ordinary day that will come again.

The clock in the hall struck the hour. The wind rattled in the window frames and outside, small animals crept into the undergrowth among the dry dead leaves.

She saw a face. It was always the same face nowadays: grey-green, wide-apart eyes, slightly hooded, mink-brown hair, thin lips in that curious half-smile that had always made her heart turn, sharp cheekbones; an agile, watchful, waiting face. Young, of course. The world ahead of him with suffering hidden in its folds. And she was young too, as she lay in the twilight world between waking and sleep, because old people are also young. She had tender eyes and elastic skin; her heart was foolish and full of hope and terror, her body flooded by longing. She wanted him so badly that a small cry escaped her parched lips. She wanted everything.

'My love,' she said. 'What a journey.'

4

She was up long before him. He woke to the smell of coffee and burnt toast. Music was playing from the kitchen. He passed by the living room, where a young woman was clearing out the ashes in the fireplace and re-laying it with fresh wood and kindling. He raised a hand and she looked at him incuriously and then returned to her task.

Standing in the hallway, Peter saw how the house was shabbier than he had realized the previous evening. The ceiling was stained, a suspicious crack running along one side. Damp flowered on the walls. The paint was fading and the paper blistering. Some of the boards under his feet had split; small balls of fluff had gathered in the corners. The curtains were bleached by decades of sunlight and a vast spider's web hung from the end of the pole. He examined the photographs that lined the walls, several of which now hung askew. A few of them were obviously recent – in colour, unfaded family groups, everyone lined up and smiling for the camera. There she was, a few years younger, in the centre of a crowd of descendants. How extraordinary it must feel to have been the source of all those people, who looked very different from each other – dark and fair, chic and grungy, each one a little world in themselves. Peter himself came from a tiny family: a mother but no father that he knew of or had ever cared to look for, one childless aunt, no cousins, no grandparents left – so paltry compared to this population of children and grandchildren and great-grandchildren. There was Jonah, a teenager but unmistakable with his sardonic smile and his blank sloe eyes.

He paused in front of another photograph, much older, in black and white. A collection of young people. The men wore hats and ties, the women had skirts below their knees. Was that her? He peered through the dusty glass at the face, slightly out of focus but still – it might be. Slender and upright, with narrow shoulders, her chin was lifted, as if in defiance. She had dark hair and high cheekbones. Her eyes were wide apart and her mouth was smiling. Her hand was on the shoulder of another woman, shorter than her. He moved on. This must be her, formally posed on a sofa with a baby on her lap. The baby looked too big for her; it was bald and round-headed with plump arms, dimpled fists and a mutinous expression on its face (Peter couldn't tell if it was a boy or a girl) – but Eleanor looked radiant, glancing sideways at the camera with her bright, searching eyes, a small smile on her painted lips. She had shapely calves and a sharp collarbone. So she had been lovely, he thought, this old woman whom he could hear in the kitchen, banging pans, burning toast, talking to herself above the music that was blasting out from the radio. He pushed open the door. Polly lifted herself, padded towards him and subsided at his feet, rolling over on her back and waving undignified legs in the air.

'Good morning,' he said.

She turned, holding a wooden spoon in her hand. She was dressed in wide-bottomed trousers and had a brightly patterned scarf wrapped around her head. She looked like a raddled Bohemian.

'Egg?' she asked, raising her voice above the soar of violins.

'Sorry?'

'Would you like an egg?' She gestured with the spoon as though it were a baton. 'Scrambled. Boiled. Or I could make you bacon and eggs. Emily brought my shopping in this morning.'

'Really?'

'You mean, really, did she bring the shopping, or really, can a nearly-blind woman make bacon and eggs?'

'Neither. I meant, would it really be all right to have bacon and eggs?'

'I like cooking for other people.'

'Then thank you.'

'Sit down.' She pointed her spoon at the table. 'I have a list.'

'Oh?'

'In my head, of all the things I need to tell you before you start. I've been composing it.'

'Should I write it down?'

'If you want. I don't think it's necessary. I'm going out later with one of my daughters. We're visiting a friend of mine whom I have known for nearly eighty years. Think of that. She's deaf and I'm blind. Still, we can poke each other with our sticks. You'll have the house to yourself.'

'I'll make a start on things.'

'Good.'

'The list?'

'Right. First of all, you must help yourself to food and drink. Someone comes with the shopping every few days. You know where the fridge is, and there is also a freezer, there—' Her spoon pointed accurately. 'You can have anything you want. There is wine in the cellar. Too much wine; it will outlast me, however hard I'm trying to outlast it. Have as much as you want. Maybe you'd like beer. I don't have beer, however, I hate it. So if you want some, you have to buy it from the village, which is two miles away. You could go on your bike.'

'Of course.'

'Coffee and tea are in here.' She rapped a cupboard with her arthritic hand. She was in a much more prosaic mood this morning, businesslike and almost curt. 'Washing: there's a washing machine in the scullery. You'll find it. It's perfectly easy to operate, and there's a line outside round the back. If it's wet, you'll have to drape things over radiators or chairs. I don't have a drier.'

'That's fine.'

'No smoking inside. But I said that last night, I think.'

'No; of course.'

'Jonah thought it would take you two or three weeks.'

'Until I see what there is, I couldn't say.'

'Would you like to have guests?'

'Guests?'

'Friends to visit?'

'Probably not. Thank you, though.'

'They would be welcome.'

'That's kind of you.'

'It's not kind. This house is large and the rooms are lonely.'

'But I think it will just be me.'

'If that's what you want.'

'It is,' he said firmly.

'In the evenings, we can perhaps have dinner together sometimes, should you wish it.'

'That's very—'

'But you can always say no. I won't be offended. I like people who say what they think. And there's no obligation: I like company but I never mind being alone. And in the day, I'll just leave you to your own devices.'

'I might have lots of questions; presumably there will be decisions that I can't make for you.'

'You're here because I don't want people I know going through my life for me. Ask me anything; it doesn't matter what you come across. You're just a stranger. Perhaps the best thing would be if we met at the end of each day, in the early evening. Then you can ask me what you want.'

'All right.'

'In three weeks' time, it's my ninety-fifth birthday.' Peter was about to wish her many happy returns, but she continued: 'You will probably be done by then. My family are all arriving. There are a great many of them, more all the time. There will be a large, noisy, exuberant meal where I will be bathed in everyone's tenderness and no one will talk about why this is happening, and then everyone can decide what they wish to take from the house. I think the grandfather clock is in great demand, though no one is actually saying so. It's as if I'm dead, living in my afterlife.'

'Because you're leaving this house?'

'Yes.' She sighed and opened the fridge, feeling around for the bacon, removing an egg from the holder in the door. 'We have a buyer. Some rich banker, I think, who snapped it up the day it came on the market and will renovate and decorate top to bottom. I will be gone before Christmas. I would like to have had one more Christmas here, but I will be with one of my sons and then—' She waved her spoon.

'Where will you go?'

'Where?' Turning the dial of the hob, where a pan already waited.

'Yes.'

'Where do ninety-five-year-old registered-blind women go at the end of their lives?'

'You're going into a home?'

'There should be another word for it. Say, a waiting room.'

She expertly cut a knob of butter from the pack and dropped it into the pan, where it sizzled.

'Couldn't you live with one of your children?'

'No! I don't want to. It wouldn't be right. I want no child of mine to be my carer. I would rather die.'

She sounded angry and passionate.

'But maybe they would like it?'

'No!'

'Maybe they don't want you to go into a home. Maybe you think you're relieving them of a burden and actually you're depriving them of a pleasure.'

'Young man—'

'Peter.'

'Peter. You don't understand.'

She peeled three rashers of bacon from the pack and dropped them into the butter.

'What don't I understand?'

'You do not understand – indeed, why should you

and how could you? – the gross indignities of old age.'

'Indignities?'

'Yes. Soon, I will very probably need someone to cut up my food. To wash me. To cut my toenails. To pluck the little coarse hairs from my chin. To wash my dirty clothes. To take me to the toilet. To wipe my bottom. I can't see if you are blushing but you probably are.'

'No, I'm not.' Indeed, Peter did not feel embarrassed by the old woman's words; he almost felt uplifted by them.

'Then I'll become incontinent. I'll dribble. People will spoon mush into my mouth.'

'This all sounds rather drastic, when you seem so strong, so self-reliant.'

'Ageing is drastic. It is very bodily. Maybe I'll start to lose my memory; very probably I will. We can't escape these things, you know. Bit by bit I'll go into the darkness. I won't be their mother any more, or their grandmother, their great-granny. I'll be like an ancient leaking baby.'

'But if they love you!'

'Ah, you're a romantic. You believe in the notion of a self – a real me, no matter how I decay into shrieking, burbling horror, no matter that I have no words and recollection of who I once was.'

'Well, yes. I do. Of course I do. You'd still be you, even if all these things happened, which they probably won't. The essence of you, Eleanor Lee, will remain.'

'You should see my sister.'

'You have a sister!'

'Yes. A stepsister. Don't worry, she's younger than me. A mere ninety-one. Perhaps she'll outlive me, but I don't envy her that. She'll come for my birthday. You'll meet her then.'

'But I'll be gone by then.'

'Perhaps. We'll see. Is the bacon crispy enough?'

Peter came forward and looked at the three blackened rashers.

'Yes,' he said firmly. 'They're just right.'

'You mean they're burnt.'

'No! I like them well done.'

'Very well.'

She cracked an egg assertively on the side of the pan and dropped it into the fat.

'Cut yourself some bread and toast it,' she ordered. 'Do you cook?'

'Some things,' he said. 'I make a good Greek salad. And I'm quite proud of my spiced aubergine. And my marmalade cake. And I'm a dab hand at a dry martini.'

'You'll have to teach me. We can cook together and drink together.'

'I'd like that.'

'I think your egg will be done soon. It might be better if you serve yourself.'

After, she took him to the room she called the library, though really it was more like a junk room at the end of the house, large and unheated, with draughts of cold air coming in through the ill-fitting windows and bare boards on the floor, covered here and there with small patches of brightly coloured rugs. Some catastrophe had taken place at the far end of the room, where a pair of long crimson velvet curtains hung in burnt tatters from the rail, and the window frames were scorched. Peter stared around him in consternation. He saw three tall metal filing cabinets on one side of the room, one of whose drawers stood open, full of sodden, half-burnt papers in a soup of black liquid. Near them, under the burnt windows, were two trunks and a battered cardboard suitcase missing its lock. There were piles of books on the floor as well as on the shelves, and boxes everywhere, splitting and overflowing with folders and papers. Drifts of ash mixed with balls of dust. At the end of the room were several teetering stacks of yellowing newspapers; in the middle, beside an old wooden rocking horse, were a couple of plastic laundry baskets – one blue and one grey – that were filled to the brim with photographs.

Those were the things that were to some extent stored. There was also a large amount of clutter – small objects and large, tat and things of value, miscellaneous, uncategorisable, bewildering. Peter, gazing around him, noticed a single woollen mitten, a small dolls' house with its hinged roof, a leather case open to reveal an old-fashioned shaving kit, a bundle of velvet curtains, a roll of carpet, a wooden painter's model of a hand with articulated fingers, a cracked porcelain dog, a red bucket half-filled with buttons, ancient stiff riding boots, a tin watering can minus its rose and with a broken handle, several biscuit tins, and a deck-chair on which sat a teddy bear with only one eye.

'Blimey,' he said weakly.

'Is it a mess?' she asked.

'There's a lot here.'

'I know. I always thought I'd sort it out myself but I never quite got round to it and then, well, I can't now. I've never been very good at throwing things away.'

'I can see.'

'Well. That's not your concern. You just need to look through the papers and books.'

'There are a lot of those as well.'

'I know.' She smiled. 'Sixty or seventy years' worth.'

'Was there a fire in here?'

'Of sorts,' said Eleanor.

'What happened?'

'I lit a match.'

'Oh.' Peter waited and then, when she didn't say anything, asked, 'Were you hurt?'

'Only my pride.'

'I could do with some guidance.'

'In what way?'

'Why does Jonah think that these papers' – he made a gesture at the overflowing boxes around him – 'will be of interest?'

'I have no idea. Maybe they won't be. You must be the judge. Now, I'm going to get ready for my daughter. You will be wanting to make a start. Help yourself to whatever you want. I'll see you this evening.'

And with that she was gone. Peter could hear her three-legged walk receding and then he was left in silence, in the cold, disordered, ash-smudged room. He gazed around him. He had gone to bed last night oddly elated, stirred by being in this shabby old house. Now he felt slightly dejected. He recognized the mood and its dangers, an ill wind blowing through him. He shook his head vehemently. He mustn't give in. This was his chance to return to the world he'd been avoiding. He had to give himself a chance. He should decide how he was going to set about this, and then just move through the mess like a mole through earth, nosing it aside bit by bit until he emerged on the other side. He would start with the books. They were straightforward. Most of them would have to go to a second-hand bookshop or a charity shop. Then he would move on to the photographs. Finally, all the papers.

He looked at his watch: it was nearly ten o'clock. He had to treat this like a real job, or he would be overwhelmed by it: every day he would work for eight hours. He would allow himself one cigarette each hour. He would try to get up at seven and have a run before breakfast – perhaps Polly would come with him, though he wondered if the ambling old dog could move fast enough. When he started early enough to give himself time, he would go for bike rides in the afternoon, before it got too dark. To the sea, perhaps, which he still had not yet seen except from his bedroom window as a faint sheet of dull grey, barely distinguishable from the wet grey sky. He could swim in it. He liked cold water and surging waves; they made him feel alive in the way that warm turquoise oceans never had. He loved lonely empty oceans.

Work. He ran up to his room lightly, taking the stairs two at a time, seeing as he did so a car draw up in a splutter of gravel and a woman with a dramatic mop of silver hair get out. She was tall and walked with long strides through the drizzle towards the house. That must be Mrs Lee's daughter. Maybe she was Jonah's mother – Peter had a very hazy idea of the family. He wanted to stay and see what she was like, but at the same time felt like an intruder. He took out his laptop, a notebook and a couple of pens, as well as his iPod. He would work to music, a steady, energetic beat. He would concentrate on the job at hand and would drown out his thoughts.

*

But as soon as he heard the car draw away and knew he had the house to himself, he left the dusty junk room and set out to explore it, feeling that he was doing something forbidden and yet unable to resist the rooms that stood empty behind closed doors. He had seen most of the rooms downstairs already. He went into the living room where they had sat the evening before, but which had then been lit only by the fire. He opened the drinks cabinet and peered in among the dusty bottles of liqueurs and spirits, and pulled up the piano lid, pressing his fingers down briefly on the ivory keys. The notes hung in the air. Polly padded softly into the room and stood beside him patiently, waiting to be stroked. She smelt of wet towels and had sad brown eyes. He looked at the pictures on the walls and the ornaments on the shelves, picking up a great satiny shell to hold against his ear for the distant sound of the sea. There were dozens of coloured-glass bottles lined up, brown and blue and cloudy green, like potions from an apothecary's store. He lifted one and pulled out its stopper, putting his nose to the opening to sniff, but it was empty. He lifted the lid of the piano stool and stared down at the sheets of music. Chopin, Debussy, Mozart, Saint-Saëns, but also music-hall songs and hymns. Some were browning and dog-eared. Perhaps she had had them since she was a girl. There was a carved little chest in the corner and inside that were board games and playing cards. Peter imagined Sunday evenings, rainy afternoons, everyone together in the laughter and squabble of a large, close family.

The kitchen he knew, but he pulled open the fridge door and peered inside, plucked a few shrivelled grapes from the bunch to eat, popped a cherry tomato into his mouth. When he heard a sound he started guiltily, but it was only one of the cats. Behind the kitchen was an old-fashioned scullery with a vast, cracked sink at one end. There were splitting Wellington boots in there, and ancient walking boots, several coats on hooks, a battered old trilby, a walking stick, folded deck-chairs, dog food and cat food, and a rusting birdcage. Upstairs, he wandered along the corridor, opening doors and peering into rooms: a bedroom with a high bed and cracked wooden shutters and a long rail of dresses that swayed like elegant women dancing, autumn light lying across its splintering floorboards; a smaller bedroom with a single bed in one corner, piled with old toys and smelling of neglect; a bathroom with a window reaching to the floor, so you could lie in your bath and look out on to the garden; a laundry cupboard stuffed with yellowing sheets and fraying towels. It was a house that creaked and rumbled, full of narrow doors leading to dark recesses, of corners for spiders.

He half-opened the door to her room but then

drew back, suddenly disturbed by his snooping, and returned to the junk room with a mug of coffee and a biscuit he'd found in a jar in the scullery. It was stale and bendy and stuck to his teeth. Outside, it was raining. Wet brown leaves lay like a rash on the lawn. He would start with the books: there was always something reassuring about books, their heft and the smell stored up in their pages, probably unopened for decades. But it quickly became obvious what a large job this was going to be. Shelves hold many more volumes that you'd ever think. He sat on the rocking horse and opened a file on his computer. He wrote down the title and author of each book, arranging them in alphabetical order according to author, noting the publisher, the date of publication and also the general category: fiction, history, biography, politics, philosophy; books on art; books on wildlife; cookery books going back decades; travel books; guides to hotels and bed-and-breakfasts from the fifties; gardening books and various out-of-date manuals. There were dozens and dozens of books about medicine. Peter put them all to one side, to go through later. Three were by Gilbert Lee – who must be her husband, or perhaps one of her sons. He should have found out all these things before arriving. He hadn't even googled Eleanor Lee. Probably there were hundreds, thousands of people by that name. Jonah, typically, had told him almost nothing. Peter didn't even know how many children Eleanor had, how many grandchildren. He wanted to linger over the books, smell their old and long-unopened pages, but restrained himself. He would take a few up to his room this evening and look at them at his leisure. First editions he put in a separate pile that soon became several piles.

Then there was the substantial number of children's books, large and battered, showing the signs of many readings. Nursery rhymes and fairy tales and stories with large writing and bright illustrations. He opened a chunky volume with a black cardboard cover that was coming loose (*Uncle Lubin and the Bagbird*) and saw a wonky drawing in blue crayon on its title page: house, puffs of smoke coming from its tall chimney and a vastly oversized cat made up of two circles and an enormously long tail by the front door, lots of birds in the shape of floppy 'm's in the sky. Surely the grandchildren would want them for their own sons and daughters. You can't throw out books you've loved as a child. How can you throw out books at all? He never had, not even his beaten-up copies of old thrillers he would never read again and that had sand between their covers, pages turned down.

He put all the children's books to one side. The family could go through them on the birthday weekend – when he planned to be gone.

*

Before lunch, when the rain was easing, he biked to the nearest shop in the village a couple of miles up the lane. There was a dog – a stringy creature – tied up outside and it lunged at him and barked furiously. Peter made cooing noises at it, but it went on barking and galloping on the spot, the bristle of fur at the back of its neck standing up. Inside, the woman serving was leaning across the counter in animated conversation with an old man – presumably the dog owner. He looked a bit like his pet.

'Good morning!' He spoke loudly and pleasantly. He had the idea of making a proper effort to integrate himself into the local community. No good being a snooty Londoner, a convalescent outsider wearing strange clothes.

They nodded, faces unyielding. He persevered, his voice ringing out in the small space.

'I'm new here. I arrived last night. I'm staying at Mrs Lee's house up the road. Beech End. Helping her out.'

'What can I do for you?' asked the woman.

'Oh.' For a moment he felt mildly crestfallen. A welcome would have been nice. 'Just twenty of those, please. And some matches,' he added.

He circled round the yelping dog and biked away, singing tunelessly against the wind.

At lunch, which he didn't take until well after two o'clock, he made himself a sandwich. The bread was fresh, presumably brought by the woman he'd seen laying the fire. There was clearly a system, a small team of people who brought in food and laid the fire and washed the sheets. In the spring and summer, someone must come and mow the lawn – or perhaps the family took it in turns. He went into the garden with his lunch. The rain had stopped and the grey sky had cleared into a miraculous blue. The trees glowed in orange and soft yellows. Peter went first of all to the front of the house, which had only been a shape in the darkness last night, his feet crunching over the gravel that was still wet from the night's rain and gleamed in the autumn sun. It was built in lovely dark red brick with large square windows, but though it wasn't as big or imposing as his imagination had made it, it was still too much for one blind woman to live in. Peter knew nothing about architecture, but he could see that it was a patchwork of old and new. It was asymmetrical, with tall chimneys and a buckling roof, a crack running up one side. There were weeds growing in the gutters, roses trained up the walls. The house had the air of struggling against age and decay. He saw that several roof tiles had fallen to the ground. The window frames were rotting.

He walked round to the side of the house, through the wooden door set in a low brick wall. Here there had once been a vegetable garden, but it had run amok. Nettles had invaded the rows of raspberry canes, ranks of weeds smothered the beds. There was a disintegrating fruit cage and a wooden bench that had lost half its slats and was green with moss. He snapped off a twig of rosemary from the bush that had thrived with neglect and sniffed it before putting it into his shirt pocket. Then he went to the back of the house, where he had smoked his cigarettes last night. The long lawn that ran down towards the glorious woods had been recently cleared of leaves, which lay in sodden heaps under the yew tree, but nothing else had been done to halt the march of nature. Dandelions pushed through the cracked patio paving stones; the hedge that marked the start of the lawn was ragged; the rose garden of which Mrs Lee was so fond was overgrown and full of bindweed and brambles, though a few late flowers still hung from their branches.

A path ran down the centre of the lawn towards the trees. Peter, finishing his sandwich and lighting a cigarette, followed it. The lawn petered out and turned to long grass and then scrubby undergrowth. He could smell mushrooms and dead, decaying leaves. Then he stepped into the woods themselves, and was in a different world, one that was silent, dim and cool, with light filtering down through the branches to lie in puddles and shafts on the ground. There were a few isolated notes of birdsong around him and, in the distance, a noise like a demented typist that he eventually identified as a woodpecker. The earth was springy underfoot, leaf mould and moss. What a place this must have been to grow up, he thought. A house full of secret corners and attics; a wood where you could have adventures and be lost; the sea nearby; at night darkness and a vast and starry sky. Peter shivered, feeling suddenly homesick – though not for home, wherever that may be, but for crowds, lamps, cars, streets where at each step you could look in through a different window and see another life framed there, the man at the cooker, the woman on the phone, a couple kissing. For the jabber and press of lives rubbing against each other.

With an effort, he turned back towards the house, rosy in the afternoon light. As he approached it, a car drew up and he saw Mrs Lee in the passenger seat, beside the woman he had seen that morning.

'Hello,' she said as she got out of the car. 'You must be Peter.'

'I am,' he said. 'Hello.'

'I'm Esther. Eleanor's daughter. I'm so glad you've come to help us like this.'

She shook his hand firmly, meeting his gaze. She looked formidable and faintly ironic.

'I'll do my best,' he replied.

'He seems nice,' said Esther, after Peter had left them.

'He reminds me of someone,' said Eleanor, so quietly Esther could barely make out the words.

'Who?'

'Someone I knew a very long time ago. In a different life.'

5

Peter pulled on his running things and stepped out of the house into the early morning, not fully light. The last of the frost was still on the grass that crunched as he walked across it, and there were spiders' webs glimmering among the roses. Polly came with him, trotting at his heels with her blunt muzzle lifted towards Peter and her tongue hanging out. He ran well this morning, he had known he would, and Polly moved softly and patiently at his side, never varying her pace. When he stopped to regain his breath at the top of the hill that looked out over the sea, she stopped too and waited. Her eyebrows were of a different colour from the rest of her coat, and bushy, and it gave her an enquiring look; Peter had never realized that dogs had eyebrows, or that they turn grey, just as humans' do. When Polly lay down, she had a silky grey tummy and her muzzle was grizzled. How old was she? And where was she going to go when Eleanor went into her home? How would she bear it? He knelt down and stroked her and she lifted her head up and let her tail thump softly on the grass. On the beach, she found a rotting dead fish and gave it to him and he thanked her as if she could understand him, and then buried it.

In the newsagent, the woman serving handed him a pack of cigarettes without asking, then said, 'You're staying with Mrs Lee?'

'That's right.'

'Mmm.' She put her head on one side; her eyes were bright with curiosity. 'It's good someone's with her, even if it is a stranger. To be living all alone there at such an age, and half-blind too. No one was surprised at the fire.'

'She's more competent than most people half her age,' said Peter, who was surprised at hostility that spurted through him. He wanted to lean forward and jab the woman in the eye.

'Is she – you know?'

'No. I don't know.' He waited for her to spell it out.

'All there.' She tapped the side of her head with her index finger. 'They say she talks to herself and hits things with her stick.'

Peter stared at her until she reddened and then said in a cold, polite voice: 'I have no idea what you're suggesting. But if you're asking if there's anything wrong with her mental faculties, no there isn't. She's sane and clever and kind and generous in her instincts. Which you can't say about most people, can you?'

He paid for the cigarettes, told her to drop the change into the charity box and sprinted back to the house, euphorically angry. Polly trotted at his side.

When he went back to work, she followed him and sat looking at him in a friendly fashion for a while, as if he'd passed some test.

It took several more days for Peter to finish going through the books. During the day, he saw little of Eleanor, although he heard her in the house – sometimes with a visitor, sometimes listening to audiobooks, occasionally knocking against things in the kitchen, dropping things. And every so often, he would look up from his work to glimpse her in the garden, her shoes wet in the long grass and drifting heaps of leaves, and her cane moving deftly in front of her, guiding her through the place she knew so well. He saw her stop by the roses and stand with her head lifted as if she were smelling the flowers, though few hung there now. One morning, she went down the path to the woods and her fragile figure was swallowed up by the columns of trees.

Each afternoon, she played the piano. He didn't recognize the music, but he liked the notes rippling through the old house like a stream, a river, skipping and merry and then sombre, meditative. He could almost see the light on the water. The same tunes over and over again, so that years later, hearing them, he was seized by an acute nostalgia for that time when he had been so adrift and so free. She got frustrated, though: he heard her crash her arthritic hands discordantly down upon the keys, bang down the lid. Once, in the middle of the night, he woke and heard the music rising faintly up towards him. He knew she slept little. She told him that she would sleep in her grave. She said it quite calmly. She said that death was a friend to the very old, who had already lost so many they had loved.

'My children say I'm a tough old bird, that I'll live for ever – but I feel like a feather just hovering on the surface. One breath of wind—' And she made a gesture. 'I would like to go like that, lightly. Not like my sister. She's a burr; she'll have to be prized off.'

Peter wanted to ask about her sister, but he had learnt that direct questions made her clam up. She told him things as and when she wanted, and then she talked in long paragraphs, following her thoughts easily, gathering them up like skeins of wool to plait together. So instead he said that the poet, John Donne, would sleep in his own coffin, to remind himself of death, and Eleanor nodded.

'There was a time when I used to want to die,' she said almost casually. 'But I don't now. I don't crave death and darkness, but I don't crave life either. Not the way I did, when I wanted things so bitterly.'

And she raised her head and smiled at the young man.

'Could you not have what you wanted so bitterly?' he asked, trying to speak lightly as if that would trick her into telling him.

She shook her head at him.

'It wasn't so simple,' she said. 'Beware what you wish for.' She stood up with surprising agility and tapped the floor with her cane. 'Tonight we will eat together, if you would like. You can help me make a lemon surprise pudding.'

'Great. I'm not very good at puddings.'

'I'll teach you. It's nice to pass things on.'

He had packed up the books into cardboard boxes that he had ordered on the first day, with her permission, and that were delivered as flat-packs that he assembled. Tomorrow, he would start on the photographs, and that evening, before they ate, they sat by the fire that Peter had lit and she told him about her family, while Polly laid her warm head in his lap.

'There's a photo hanging above the piano,' she said. 'Bring it here.'

Peter rose and lifted the large framed photograph from the wall, exposing a nest of cobwebs and dust behind.

'You hold it and I'll tell you who's in it,' said Eleanor. 'I think I can remember who is standing where. I might get some of the grandchildren wrong but that's all right.'

Peter put the picture on his knees and gazed at it. He saw Eleanor in the middle, old but not yet ancient, with clear eyes and her beautiful silvered hair gathered up in a knot. She made everyone else seem bright and impermanent. She was wearing a grey dress and she stood out from the group assembled around her, because while they were all smiling or making strange surprised grimaces, she looked serious and serene. She almost seemed as though she were standing alone, thinking about something, and the rest had been Photoshopped in beside her.

'Obviously the man beside me is my husband Gil,' she went on. 'Gilbert. That was one of the last photographs ever taken of him.'

Peter examined Gilbert. He was tall, and had the appearance of a solid man who had suddenly grown thin. He had thick grey hair and a high forehead and he was looking not at the camera but at his wife with an expression that was obediently smiling but also supplicating. And Peter now saw that Eleanor's hand was reassuringly on his elbow, as though she were steadying him.

'He had cancer,' she said. 'He was not far from death. Everyone came for his birthday.'

Peter murmured something.

'He was a good man,' continued Eleanor as though he hadn't spoken. 'Much better than me. I don't think I've ever met a kinder man than Gil. Everyone loved him. He died calling for his mother.'

'Oh!' said Peter. 'That's a fearful thought.'

'Many people do,' said Eleanor. 'Didn't you know? Gil said that in the war, he held countless young men's hands while they screamed out for their mothers. I don't think that I will, but you never know. Gil's mother wasn't a very nice woman, but I suppose that isn't the point. He was very fond of gardening. And he loved trees. That's why we bought the patch of wood down there.'

'I'm sorry,' said Peter.

'What for?'

'That he died.'

'He lived a long, full life. It's when people die before their time that you grieve the most.'

'Of course.'

Watching her face, he saw an expression pass over it like wind over the surface of the sea. Then it was gone and she was calm again.

'I hold him here,' she said, laying her gnarled hand over her chest. 'The dead go on living in our hearts. Now. Let's see' – briefly closing her unseeing eyes to make the picture out more clearly – 'the man on my left in the suit is my son Leon. You will meet him soon. He likes to come and check the state of my feet and my blood pressure. Very scary. He's a doctor too. He looks uncannily like his father used to. Dark hair and dark eyes and strong face.'

'I see that.'

'His wife, Giselle, is next to him. A Russian, and a very good painter. Love came to Leon like a thunderclap,' she added. Peter wondered again if she talked to other people like this, or just to him because he was a ship passing in the night. He looked at Giselle and thought he could see Jonah in her dreamy face, though her mouth was opened as if caught mid-sentence.

'Esther you know,' said Eleanor.

And there she was, in a long flowery dress with her mane of hair.

'Is she a doctor too?'

'No. She was an academic, teaching History of Art. She's retired now. She has several grandchildren who aren't all in the photo, or I don't think they are – it was taken too long ago. Beside her, her husband Luke. He left her for a woman half her age and half her worth and then had a heart attack and died. He was a weak fool,' she added. 'Men often don't like strong, successful women. Esther's never been malleable, never sweet and agreeable. She's sour and fine, like a good red wine. Then I think it's Quentin and Marianne. Quentin and Leon were very close but they fell out.'

'Over what?'

'Quentin became a born-again Christian and Leon's a pugnacious atheist. He lectured Quentin and Quentin kept tenderly forgiving him in a way Leon found quite intolerable. They barely talk now. But they'll have to at my party.'

'Do you believe in God?' Peter was surprised to find himself asking, but for once, she answered.

'No. Not me. Not at all. Not for a very long time,

if I ever did. Gil had some sort of respectable, civilized, undramatic faith – he was such an Englishman. Until the last months, that is, when he no longer believed in anything except pain and ending. And the ending of pain. You wouldn't let a dog go through what he suffered.'

'That's terrible,' said Peter. Then, 'Who's the man on his own?' He was looking at a slender figure with silver hair and a bony face. He was smiling, but to something out of sight of the camera, and one arm was half raised. He looked like an ageing dancer.

'Ah.' Her voice softened and fell. Her hand went up to cover her chest once more. 'That's my Samuel, my eldest. I named him after my father. Flesh of my flesh.' She corrected herself at once. 'They're all flesh of my flesh, of course, but he's the one I always worried about. Grief is like an arrow to the heart when you have children, straight and true. It doesn't miss its target.'

'Why have you always worried?'

'Some people seem to know how to deal with life. Even when they are going through difficult times, you feel they have a resilience and a sense of control. Samuel is not like that. There are periods of his life when I've feared for him.'

'Has he been—?'

'Now let me see.' She pointed at the photo in Peter's hands. 'The jumble of children and teenagers on the ground in front of us are the grandchildren of course. I won't tell you who they are. I can't remember who was where, and anyway they've all changed so much. Grown tall, left home, found jobs and partners. Some of them have children themselves. Some of them are still adrift; who'd be young nowadays? I think we will have a family photograph when they all come for my birthday. What a lot of us there will be then. I've almost lost count, but then I was never very good at maths, even though I had to teach it sometimes.'

'Teach it?'

'Yes.'

'Were you a teacher, then?'

'Why do you sound so surprised?'

'I just thought—' He remembered now that Jonah had told him she'd been something distinguished in education. Yet he had thought of her always here, in this big old house.

'You thought that I came from the dark ages when women didn't work – that I never did anything but wear dresses and have children and tend the garden?'

'No. I don't know what I thought.'

'I always had to earn my living. I was a teacher. And anyway, I couldn't have supported a life of idleness. I did my Highers and my teacher training and I taught in a London school in the East End until the war came and then—' She stopped abruptly. 'Well, almost all the children I taught will be dead now. I think we're done, aren't we?'

'Who's the small elderly woman?'

'Oh! Now isn't that odd; I forgot she was there.' She chuckled softly. 'A Freudian lapse, you might say. That's my sister Meredith. We always called her Merry. She used to suit the name. She was very pretty, with a soft round face and golden hair. Boys loved her. Men loved her. Everyone. She had a laugh like a bell tinkling, or one of those wind chimes my grand-daughter used to collect.'

'Does she have family as well?'

'She has a stepfamily. Her husband was older than her and is long gone. Well. You could say that she is long gone too. It has been many years since she remembered anything. She doesn't usually know us; sometimes she thinks I am her stepmother – my mother, that is. She still laughs, though. It makes my hair stand on end to hear it.' She grasped her cane and rose abruptly. 'Shall we go and make our supper? I could eat a horse. Old people are supposed to lose their appetites, but I find I am perpetually hungry. It's as if I've got a great hole inside me that I can't ever fill.'

6

Days took on a certain shape. There was the early rising, though she was always up before him; the run round the lanes with Polly, always the same circuit that took him down to the sea, and always shouting out a 'hello!' to the dog walkers and the road sweepers, the old man collecting whelks; the steady work that took him through to lunchtime in the woods to clear his head and stretch his legs. In the afternoon, after he had finished for the day and before their evening meeting, there was the sea again. He would bike there and walk along the beach, above the ragged hem of the tide-line. The wind was sharp and salty, making his eyes water, and on these autumn days the sea was usually brown and grey, though sometimes when the sun broke through it sent up diamond sparks. He loved to watch long-legged, sharp-beaked sea-birds whose names he never discovered, and loved to hear them as well – their piercing, lonely cries sent a shiver down his spine. They made him feel lonely and glad.

He no longer listened to music through his headphones when he worked; somehow the music seemed too insistent, stopping his journey back into Eleanor's past. And he had stopped checking his phone for emails or texts; recently, he hadn't even bothered to charge it. He only called his mother to reassure her. He hadn't bothered to shave for days, either – stubble was beginning to thicken into a beard that was darker than his hair. When he looked in the mirror he was taken aback by the face that stared back – the long hair and mismatched beard gave him a disreputable yet slightly dashing air. But no one could see him except himself, and strangers who didn't matter, and the owner of the corner shop in the village where he bought his cigarettes and who glared at him and pursed her lips. Eleanor didn't know that she sat by the fire opposite someone who looked like a pirate. She herself always took care over her appearance, wearing clothes that were soft and richly coloured, though often moth-eaten and shabby. She told him that even when she was alone, she would wear nice clothes and do her hair up. 'I'm dressing up for myself,' she said. 'I'm impressing myself.'

The world receded. He felt that the house was like a boat, stalwart amid the autumn winds, and he and Eleanor were alone on it together, even though there were days when they barely saw each other. He heard her footsteps moving round the rooms; listened to her at the piano; noticed when cars arrived to collect her or drop her back again. Sometimes there were other people in the house, but Peter rarely met them. He didn't really want to; they made him feel like a stranger in a place where, alone, he was starting to feel oddly at home, safely locked into a structure where each day had the same pattern.

He worked doggedly. Now he had moved on to the photographs. The medical ones had shocked him to begin with – in fact, made him feel nauseous and also ashamed of himself for his disgust. Gilbert Lee had specialised in facial reconstruction; Eleanor said it was because of what he had seen in the war. He had been an early pioneer, and they were invaluable documents, but when Peter picked up that first image of a face before surgery, he had felt such a jolt of horror that he had had to go outside and smoke a cigarette among the withered roses. It was like a face that was no longer a face at all but a caricature of humanity – the features rearranged, the mouth torn and displaying a shattered mouthful of teeth, a crater where the cheek should have been. How could any-one bear to be alive when they looked like that? He was disturbed by his repulsion – after all, he told him-self, a suffering person looked out of that blasted face. When he talked to Eleanor about it later, she nodded at him. 'You have to look into their eyes,' she said. 'See beyond.'

'Beyond?'

'Beyond superficial strangeness,' she said. 'Back to their humanity.'

'Yes. Yes, that's it.'

'People are often scared,' she said. 'Gil used to say

that children often wept or cried out when they saw some of his patients. Or ran away.'

'It is the stuff of horror,' said Peter.

'What are we horrified by?'

'I don't know.' He thought of the series of pictures he had leafed through. 'A face seems to express who we are. So it's like a disfigurement of the self or something.'

'Dangerous, isn't it, to moralize physical ugliness?'

'Yes,' said Peter. 'I know.'

And gradually he became inured to the primitive terror of those images and started to dwell upon what had survived: the smile behind the twisted mouth, the pain in the eyes. He understood too the acts of redemption that Gil and his team had performed – for there were also the 'after' photographs, where noses were reconstructed, skin grafted, jaws rebuilt and a recognisable person emerged again from the wreckage caused by guns, bombs, fires, and in one case a maddened dog.

There were other photographs, of course, hundreds and thousands of them; many blurred, bleached, stuck together in wads of unrecognisable images, but some clear, bringing back moments in the past. Some figures made brief appearances and then disappeared, but of course there were the faces that repeated, until Peter felt he knew them. Gilbert Lee was there, at first young, but then thickening, greying, stooping into old age. Peter liked him from the outset for the kindliness of his face and the clarity of his gaze under those heavy lids. Eleanor's children were there too – hundreds of them as babies and small children, then fewer as they grew up and left home; many seaside snaps and moments of significance such as birthdays, graduations, weddings.

Then there was Eleanor's sister, Meredith. Peter looked at her with interest because of the way Eleanor talked about her. A whole history lay behind the way she said her name, giving a weary sigh. Merry didn't look so complicated to Peter. As a young woman she was undeniably pretty: she was small and slight, with a heart-shaped, dimpling face and a delighted smile. She looked vivacious and expressive – the camera caught her gestures, her lifted head, her eloquent glance, her hand held out in greeting, her laughter. She grew plumper with age, but was still compact and pleasing. Her blonde hair turned a kind of primrose-grey and her pink sweetness weathered. She wore calf-length pleated skirts and good shoes and stood in family groups, her arm pushed through her husband's. She looked very unlike Eleanor, thought Peter.

For he was becoming fascinated by Eleanor – the old woman whom he met in the mornings and evenings, who talked to him so freely and yet so impersonally, and the woman of the photographs. He was half in love with her younger self, but intimidated by her as well, because she seemed tall and beautiful and free, quite beyond the adoration of someone like him. In the evenings, beside the fire, he would stare and stare at Eleanor's blind and creviced face to see the face beneath: the dark-haired, smoky-eyed one, with creamy skin and smooth throat and pure profile. Even in photos, Merry seemed to move and flirt and charm, but Eleanor was still. Her husband watched her and she gazed out at the world as if she were seeing something nobody else could see.

There were a few photographs he returned to. The first was one of her standing with her class. He didn't know the date but it must have been in the late thirties, shortly before the war. The picture belonged to a different world: dozens of peaky girls with scrubbed faces, about ten or eleven years old, all in neat pinafores with their hair tied back in pigtails or plaits, smiling hard and obediently at whoever was behind the camera. Under a cloth, thought Peter; that was how it was done – and everyone having to stand quite frozen for a while. Frozen in time, just before catastrophe rolled over the country. How many of them had died young? One girl near the end must have moved, for she was more out of focus than the rest. In the centre of the group, holding a pupil by each hand, stood Eleanor Wright, as she then was. Tall and slim in a plain, high-necked dress, with her lustrous hair pulled back, her face serious but a little smile just pulling at her mouth, and her eyes secret. Peter kept gazing at those eyes. He wanted to ask the old woman what she had been thinking about but didn't dare.

Then there was a much smaller one, of her looking over her bare shoulder. She must have been wearing some kind of evening gown, he thought. Her round white neck and her smooth cheek, the look of recognition in her eyes, startled him. He wanted to be looked at like that: dreamy and deep and sensuous. He wondered who she was acknowledging – Gilbert, perhaps, or perhaps just a stranger who had caught her unawares.

Finally, there was a photograph of her when she was several years older, presumably a wife and a mother; her hair was short, brushed behind her ears and she wore trousers and a white shirt. She was outside this house, sitting on a step with an empty glass by her bare foot; in the distance you could just make out a child running. But Eleanor didn't notice the child who would soon burst in on her consciousness; she was reading a book and Peter thought that she seemed utterly immersed in it, as if the world had fallen away from her and she was all alone. It was this quality of immersion, of removal from the busy, crowded life she lived in, that drew him.

He arranged all the photos into categories, neatly labelled files and boxes, but these three he took and put in his little attic room. At night-time, she gazed at him and she withdrew from him into her secret self.

He thought that she lay beyond him, a door to which he didn't have a key – until he came across the letters.

7

Peter was three days into sorting through the papers. He didn't know how he would ever get to the end of them: Eleanor seemed to have kept everything, and in no particular order. The metal cabinet's drawers – apart of course from the one whose contents had been set alight – were stuffed with bank statements, bills, receipts, school reports, drawings done for her by her grandchildren, letters, old essays by various of her children on subjects ranging from fluctuating asymmetry in behavioural ecology to Ibsen's treatment of social issues. There were postcards sent decades ago alongside birth certificates, surveyors' reports, contracts for Gilbert Lee's books, first drafts of articles in his carelessly elegant handwriting. Peter found a whole sheaf of recipes in spidery writing, the ink brown and the paper yellowing. It wasn't Eleanor's handwriting, which he'd come to know well, and could recognize even when she was using capital letters. Perhaps it was her mother's. It gave him a shivery feeling to imagine Eleanor's long-dead mother carefully copying down recipes to hand on, brown soup and jam roly-poly, which had been pushed into drawers and forgotten.

Eleanor had been gone since yesterday and wasn't due back until the following day, and it was striking how much difference her absence made to being in the house. It was quiet and somehow blank. There were no audiobooks being played at full volume in her bedroom, and no piano music rippling out from the living room. When Peter had woken that morning, he had noticed at once the lack of the comforting smell of toast and coffee that usually greeted him. He continued with his routine – making piles of paper, deciding what should be given to her children (their reports, for instance; their birth certificates and old passports), what should be discussed with Eleanor, and what binned (the bank statements that were over twenty years old, certainly, or those numerous scraps of paper which simply had figures jotted on them, or even shopping lists). There wasn't a great deal that he thought was worth giving to a university library, although it was amazing what some libraries would take.

At lunch he hurriedly ate a piece of bread and cheese and went down to the woods. It was a pale day, the grey clouds parting to show patches of opal-blue. There were several winter birds in the garden – robins, sparrows, a tiny plump wren. Peter liked small brown English birds that looked so plain and sung so sweetly. He had in his pocket a folded piece of paper that he'd lifted from the cabinet that morning. Now he took it out and unfolded it, re-reading the message on it, written in round letters: 'Dear Miss Wright, thank you for being our teacher. You have taught us a lot. We will never forget you and we hope you will not forget us. We hope you are very happy and that you will visit us. We hope you like your present. It was Miss Forrest's idea. She said green was your favourite colour. We hope the war will be over soon.' There followed a cluster of signatures. Beside one of them, in miniature letters, was written: 'I think you are very pretty.' Peter liked the painstaking formality of the note and thought he must show it to Eleanor when she returned – for how could you throw away something like that? And yet he had learnt that she was ruthlessly unsentimental in what she discarded; he wondered what had made her like that. There were several bin bags in the corner of the room of letters and drawings and messages that she said would feed the great bonfire they would have, when Peter had finished.

He smoked a cigarette and then returned to the house, where he made himself a pot of coffee and took it back with him to the room where he worked, to stave off the afternoon drowsiness that always overtook him. He reached into the cabinet for the battered cardboard file at the back of the drawer. It was unmarked but when he opened it up contained loose letters, and then a brown A4 envelope in which, he saw when he peered inside, there were several more letters, all in tight, angular writing on semi-transparent paper, so that the words showed on the other side. Peter sat on the floor beside the rocking horse and poured himself a cup of coffee. The sun shone through the large window and lay across the floor in blocks of dusty yellow light. He really was sleepy; his eyes felt heavy. He picked up the first letter determinedly. It was in a different hand from those inside the envelope; when Peter turned to the end he saw it was from Gilbert. There had been other letters from Gilbert that Peter had read, most of them warm but practical and to the point. They had been kept in a plastic folder, all together. This one was undated and quite short, and from the smudged scrawl, seemed to have been written in a hurry. For a moment, Peter considered not reading it – it seemed illicit, a betrayal of Eleanor's trust in him – and yet what else was he being hired for? Anyway, it was too late. Even as he was considering putting it aside unread, he had begun:

My dear Eleanor,

You're wrong: I didn't speak lightly or recklessly, and I am not particularly noble or even romantic, except perhaps where you are concerned. I loved you from the moment I set eyes on you and that has never changed, nor will it do so. I wouldn't be taking you on, you'd be taking on me: my melancholy, my cautious and solitary nature, my lack of charisma and eloquence. I am, as you know, a dogged kind of fellow, not a star. I am a doctor, not a hero. I am a rationalist and not a poet. Anything I have achieved has been done through patience and determination but I have come to believe that these are not secondary virtues. Their roots go deep. I believe you can trust me. I think you know by now how much I care for you and how I will never cease to work for your happiness.

I will call on you when I return next week.
Yours in hope and love, Gilbert

Now he really did feel like a snoop. Nevertheless, he re-read the letter, slowly this time. He admired this Gilbert – the man who reconstructed shattered faces to give them back their shared humanity, the one he'd seen in the photographs looking with such adoration at Eleanor, and also the one who wrote this letter, in which he both deprecated himself and yet put himself boldly forward. Gil knew what he had to offer: his solid kindness, his enduring love. He knew his limitations. And Peter gathered that Eleanor had perhaps resisted him; he'd had to persuade her to marry him. He imagined Gil the following week, waiting to find out whether Eleanor would agree or not. She would emerge from a doorway, pale and slender in her high-necked dress with the solemn radiance that Peter was so drawn to in the photographs he had gazed at, and Gilbert would step forward to greet

87

her, trying to see her answer in her eyes. And she said yes. Yes, Gilbert. Yes, I will. I do.

He picked up the next letter, in different handwriting – the same writing, however, as in the recipes.

Dear Ellie, how nice to hear your happy news. We all like and admire Gilbert very much and you probably know how long we have hoped for this! He is all you could want in a husband – and all I could want in a son-in-law. It is a happy day, and we need some happy days, don't we, with so much sadness and loss around? When will it be? Soon, I hope. I am already planning to wear my blue coat with the sable collar. Isn't it strange and perhaps a little shameful how superficial things like a coat or a treacle pudding can lift the spirits?

Robert joins with me in sending our congratulations and love,
Mummy

This letter Peter added to Gilbert's. He picked up the third, on thick cream card in a beautifully even sweep of italic writing, and scanned it.

Wednesday 21st
  My Dear Eleanor,
  Gilbert came to see me this morning. I would like to extend my congratulations and best wishes to you. As you know, I am a widow and Gilbert is my only child, and therefore it will not seem strange to you if I add the hope

that you will make him as happy and fulfilled as he deserves.

Yours sincerely,

Mary Lee

Ouch! Peter gave a sympathetic wince at the coldness of the letter. So: Eleanor's mother was delighted and Gilbert's mother was sour and disapproving. Perhaps Eleanor was too independent-minded for Mrs Mary Lee – not submissive enough for her taste, not eager enough to please and placate. Or maybe she didn't like the fact that she was a teacher in the East End. Or was it simply that no one could ever be good enough for her son?

The final letter before Peter looked at the contents of the envelope was on one side of a small piece of paper decorated with a row of flowers at the top and bottom. The few lines were in the exact middle of the page, in a large and looping hand.

Dear Eleanor, Your father would have been proud of the young woman his daughter has been turned into. With love from Winifred (Nan)

Now Peter took up the envelope and pulled out the thin wad of letters in different writing. But the first sentence made him lay them down again. 'Nellie, my beloved,' he read. 'What have you done to me? What shall I do with myself now that I know you?'

He poured himself another cup of coffee, though

it was tepid, and took it outside. He smoked a cigarette, sucking in the smoke urgently and tipping his head back to blow it above him in tendrils of ashy blue. His hands were trembling slightly. Nellie, my beloved. Who was it calling her that? Even Gilbert was slightly formal with her, addressing her respectfully as his dear Eleanor. But this person was intimate; his voice came fresh and urgent down the years. Peter smoked a second cigarette, putting off the moment when he would go back inside, feeling dizzy with the acrid rush he pulled into his lungs. He was glad Eleanor was absent; he felt he could not have continued reading those letters with her nearby.

Nellie, my beloved. What have you done to me? What shall I do with myself now that I know you? I feel quite wild, my darling. I cannot tell if it is wild with joy or with despair. How is it that no one can tell that my heart is bursting? I want to keep you secret and deep and I want to shout your name out loud (don't worry: I won't). I have to see you again and hold you again and feel the softness of your skin and smell your clean, beautiful hair and press you to me until I don't hurt with this terrible desire. Tell me you feel the same, Nellie. You must. I know you must.

There. Peter pressed his fingertips against his temple. Who was it? He didn't sign his name – or perhaps it was a she? No, he didn't think so. And how could he dare call Eleanor *Nellie*? Nellie was a sweet and slangy name, girlish and innocent, but the Eleanor he knew was grave, watchful, to his eyes beautiful, and a bit scary. Even when she was young, in those pictures he had purloined and which were now on the chest in his room at the top of the house, she had a mystery about her.

He picked up the next letter, if you could call a hastily scrawled few words by such a name.

Tomorrow evening, by the quince tree. I'll be there as soon after six as I can. I will wait for you until nine xxxx

And then a longer letter that he read slowly, hearing the words in his head.

My Darling, it began. *I write this at three in the morning, when it seems that the whole world must be asleep apart from me. But I can't sleep tonight. It feels that I will never be able to sleep again. I drink whisky and smoke and there is nothing that can calm me or dull the intensity of this moment, when all I can think of or see or hear is you . . .*

Peter read the letter twice and then laid the paper carefully on top of the previous one. He felt slightly sick, very agitated. And finally, now that he was actually prying into the secrets that she had kept for so long, the last scrawled note.

You have my heart. Keep it safe. I will be home again; my only home is you.

This time, at the bottom of the note, there was not a signature, but a single letter. An 'M', made with a flourish.

Peter stared at the words for several minutes. Then he lifted his head, a thick pain in his throat and behind his eyes. He felt – absurdly he knew – abandoned, as if everyone in the world had forgotten about him. The house seemed very large and very empty. Silence pressed in on him, and outside, the light was just beginning to thicken towards dusk, the huge sky fading. He must have been sitting over the letters for longer than he'd realized, time slowing down around him. He stood up and turned on the standard lamp, feeling stiff and sore, as if he'd stayed too long in one position.

This mysterious 'M' had written about feeling strange to himself; Peter knew what that meant. Perhaps everyone knew but never articulated it: the sense of not belonging to your own self, of life being like a great river that swept everyone up in its currents – but not you. You had let it drift into a small backwater, a little crevice by the shore, muddy and shallow from where you twitched and bobbed, watching other people passing by. He knew that Eleanor, whatever had happened to her and whatever she had done, had been in the great and purposeful river of life. You could see it in her magnificent ancient face and in the way she still held herself, erect, head up, hands firmly clutching her cane, great blind eyes fixed on her purpose. Peter had only known her a few days, but he believed that however she had suffered, she would have done so actively. If she had ever loved, she would have immersed herself in that love. If she had grieved, she would have let grief course through her, filling up all the spaces and holes. If she had lost, she would have lost bravely.

In this last year, there had been times when Peter had let go of hope and let go of himself. This didn't mean he had been in despair. Despair was too exact and cruel a word for the blankness of his mood. He had been absent, trying to empty himself of himself, until only a tiny flicker of vitality had remained buried in that torpid body. He had wanted only to breathe, in and out and in and out, lying in the warm darkness, life withdrawn to a great distance until it had no power to hurt or even touch him.

When he was at school, he had played rugby a few times, though never with the necessary conviction to stop him being slightly scared of the hurtling bodies, the massive shoulders, the hard boots and fixed grimaces of faces he had thought he knew. He could still clearly remember a day, in the middle of winter, when the ground was frozen and his breath smoked in the air. Rain had started falling steadily; he had lain with his cheek on the frozen, muddy grass; his fingers had been trampled on; someone had kicked his shin and a coagulating purple gash ran down it. Numb with cold, he felt nothing until he stood under the shower, when suddenly his whole body started to hurt. His face burned as though he had scrubbed at it violently with a wire brush; his cuts and bruises stung. And his hands – my God, how they had throbbed, pain pounding up his limbs and into his mangled fingertips. He almost screamed out loud, standing in the shower under needles of tepid water, waiting for the violence in his body to recede.

Returning to life was painful, of course, and exhilarating too. He had loved his days spent here because they were like his gateway back into the busy, messy, vivid world. Yet he had not expected a few letters, written by people who must be long dead to a woman who was old and blind, to cause him such mysterious grief. He paced the room, his footfall stirring dust from the boards. All along the walls were piles of photographs, manuscripts, books: the fruits of his labours. A life was stacking up here. But these letters – how should he file them? Who was this 'M', anyway (Matthew? Mark? Michael? Marmaduke?), who dared call Eleanor 'Nellie' and talked about moonlight and love?

Maybe he was in one of the photographs. Peter picked up a pile and started rifling uselessly through them – this man with a stupid moustache? Or this blond buffoon? All these awful Englishmen, well-fed and complacent, putting their meaty hands on the rumps of their wives as if they owned them. He liked Gilbert Lee and was prepared to imagine Eleanor with him, two people going through the world together, constrained and dignified. But not someone whose letters groaned with desire. You could almost feel him touching her when he wrote. Sweetest love.

Sweetest love. He had called Kaitlin that once. The memory sluiced through him. Leaning up on one elbow and looking down at her as she lay with her face on his pillow and her hair – the colour of golden treacle – spread out. He had seen the freckles on her shoulder and the crease marks on her cheek and her long eyes had glinted up at him from under those thick lashes.

Sweetest love. He needed to find out about M. Where had he gone? Who had he been?

8

Peter left the junk room, followed by the dog that had become his faithful shadow, and walked outside to light a cigarette, looking across the garden and over the woods. He was smoking too much, but that didn't matter. Things like that didn't count here. So he lit another and then he decided he should have a drink to go with it – that was another thing that didn't count. Not tonight, anyway, when he was all alone and the day was dying and he couldn't see a single light except for the ones from the house, standing behind him like a ship on an endless sea. He went back inside and made his way to the cellar. Eleanor had told him he must help himself to anything he wanted, and he wanted something alcoholic. The cellar smelt dank and musty, of things that were growing in secret. The walls were cold and slightly damp to his touch. He fumbled around for the light switch, and for a moment was dazzled before his eyes adjusted. There were so many bottles in here, in racks and in boxes, far more than she'd ever be able to drink, even if she lived to be a hundred and drank a bottle a day. Anyway, she was leaving; presumably her children and grandchildren and all the great tribe of her descendants would come and plunder this space and leave it empty at last. It was clear that someone had already starting putting bottles into crates.

He pulled a red out of a rack; its label was peeling off, but he could read the date. Twenty-two years old! Almost as old as he was. It was probably undrinkable by now. He tucked it under his arm, and then caught sight of several different-shaped bottles on one of the shelves that all contained amber-coloured liquid. Whisky. He thought of M drinking whisky and thinking of Eleanor. *Nellie.* By the light of the moon. He picked one bottle up, squat and half-full, and unscrewed the cap to sniff at it. The rawness caught him in the back of his throat, and he took an experimental sip. Probably someone like Jonah drank whisky like a connoisseur, peaty liquid slipping down his throat, his eyes closed. *Mm*, he'd say. *Iodine. Burnt sugar.* It made Peter's eyes sting. He felt that something was coming loose inside him, but in a good way. At least, he thought in a good way. He remembered reading about Keats dying of TB in Italy; coughing up blood; coughing up bits of his own body.

He took the whisky and the wine upstairs. He didn't want to sit in the living room, with its closed piano and cold hearth and no Eleanor in her high-backed chair. First, he went into the kitchen and opened the wine; he was tempted to drink it straight from the bottle, glugging it back so that dizziness rose in him like a mist, but he was going to do this properly. He took a glass from the cupboard and poured himself half an inch, a deep crimson. The two cats twisted around his legs, trying to get his attention: what would happen to them once Eleanor was no longer here? Would they stay in the house? It didn't seem right to take them away to a new home – and perhaps, he thought with alarm, they'd be separated. That would never do.

He swilled the wine round in the bottom of the glass the way he'd seen it done and took a sniff, then a delicate sip. If it was ruined, he couldn't tell. It tasted deep and spicy, just the drink for a dark evening in November. He put the cork back in the bottle and set it by the hob to drink later. First, he was going to sit in the garden with his whisky and his cigarette. He found a tumbler and sloshed some of the beautiful tawny liquid into it, then a bit more. He added a few drops of water and carried it out into the garden with Polly. The first sip attacked his heart and his head simultaneously. Thoughts and feelings ran together. His eyes were swimming and his throat clogged. He felt acutely solitary, and wished that someone would creep up to him out of the darkness and take him in their arms, where he could forget himself. For a moment, he let himself remember the feel of Kaitlin's slim fingers, such clever teasing fingers, the taste of her lipstick, the little hollow at the back of her neck and the blue veins in her wrists. That husky, sexy laugh. And

Eleanor's face – the one when she was young, looking over her bare shoulder at someone. Sweetest love.

Back in the kitchen, he rifled in the fridge for his supper. He cut a large wedge of the game pie he found there and warmed it in the microwave, then emptied a bag of salad leaves into a bowl and dressed it. It wasn't much fun cooking alone in this big, empty house. He had to resist the urge to eat it with his fingers, standing by the window. This is what Eleanor did night after night. She would cook elaborate meals and eat at the table, with her tarnished silver cutlery, and her chipped patterned plates that had probably belonged to Mary Lee or her own mother, wearing her moth-eaten gowns. Structure is important, he heard her say. The smell of the past in every room and the future dwindling. How did old people bear it? He poured himself a large glass of red wine and sat down, took the first forkful of pie. The clock on the wall told him it was nearly eight o'clock, but it had been dark for so long that it could have been midnight. He should have brought his book down here to read as he ate. He took another mouthful of wine. His glass was only half full now so he topped it up.

'That smells good,' said a voice from the doorway, and Peter leapt to his feet, knocking his fork to the floor.

'Eleanor! I didn't hear a car. I thought you weren't back till tomorrow.'

'I changed my mind. Giselle wasn't well and I was just in the way. I wanted to be at home. Is there any left? I haven't eaten.'

'Yes. Shall I put some on a plate? With salad?'

'Thank you. I'm very hungry.'

'Mustard?'

'Yes please. And will you pour me some wine, please?'

'Of course.'

'How's your day been?' she asked, sitting across from him, tapping her fork on the plate until she found the food, expertly lifting it to her mouth. She ate with appetite. He watched as a chunk of pie fell on to her lap, but she didn't notice.

'My day? My day's been – it's been fine. Good. What about yours?'

'I went to a lunchtime concert with my son.'

'That's nice.'

'Yes. Ravel piano music. He fidgeted. He wanted to be at work, I could tell. What's wrong?'

'Wrong?'

'Something's wrong with you this evening.'

'No. Honestly. I'm fine.' But he had to tell her sometime. That was his job. And after all, why was it so hard to say? 'I've been reading letters today,' he managed.

'Have you? Is there anything you want to ask me?'

'No. That is, maybe.'

'I see.'

'What?'

'You found some letters that have surprised you and you don't know how to broach the subject with me.'

'Kind of.'

'Love letters,' she said, 'I presume.'

'Yes.'

'And why should love letters that were sent to me seventy years ago be distressing to you, Peter?' Her tone was polite, distant, shrivelling him. 'After all, you're simply employed to sort out my affairs. Is it because I'm old and it's unthinkable that an old woman should once have been a young woman, with sexual feelings?'

'Of course not!'

'Or because you wonder if I was unfaithful to my husband? Perhaps you disapprove?'

Peter forced himself to speak.

'It's hard to explain. I felt like a spy. And then – and I know it's absurd – but I had this idea of you and your husband and family as pretty much perfect. Or at least, as good as. The kind I've only read about in books.'

'The happy family, you mean.'

'I guess.'

'Even happy families are complicated, Peter. That is to say, they are myths.'

'I know that really. It's just that I had a story in my head and it's been jolted.'

'I'm sorry about that.' Was she being sarcastic? He couldn't tell.

'What do you want me to do with those letters?'

'First of all, I want you to read them to me.'

'Now?'

'If you would. Pour us both some more wine and we can go into the living room. You could light the fire. Afterwards, you can burn the letters.' She pushed her plate away and rose to her feet, steadying herself with her cane. 'This is why you are here, Peter,' she said in a gentler tone. 'So that my family – my happy family – never have to read them. Where were they?'

'In the back of the smaller metal cabinet, in an old cardboard file.'

'I couldn't find them. I don't know why I waited until I was too blind to rescue them; it was stupid sentiment. Come along now. Bring the wine.'

'There's only a bit left.'

'Bring another bottle then.'

The fire was lit, more wine poured into their glasses. Eleanor took up her usual position in the armchair by the hearth. She was wearing a long velvet skirt that had rubbed thin in patches, giving it a fungal appearance. She folded her liver-spotted hands together in her lap and nodded.

'Go on then.'

'There are just four of them; is that what you remember?'

'So few,' she said softly. 'So long ago.'

Peter picked up the first letter and cleared his throat, loudly and unnecessarily.

'Nellie, my beloved,' he said. His voice cracked. 'What have you done to me? What shall I do with myself now that I know you?'

He looked up to see a smile playing across Eleanor's lips.

'I feel quite wild, my darling,' he continued. He heard the words fill the empty room, while the flames guttered and shadows deepened in the corners. He forced himself to read on until he reached the end of the first letter. Then looked up.

'Thank you, Peter.' Eleanor sounded quite steady. 'Will you throw it on the fire for me?'

'Are you sure?'

'Yes, dear,' she said. Her voice was tender. 'I can't read it myself, and I don't want anyone else to read it, although perhaps it wouldn't matter any more. So long ago. Anyway.' She pressed one hand against her frail ribcage. 'I think I can keep the words inside me. They will be quite safe there now.'

For a moment, Peter considered keeping the note for himself. He could put it with the photographs that were still in his room; she would never know. Then he leant forward and placed the paper on the fire, watching it until it crumpled, blackened, turned into ashy petals.

'It's gone,' he said at last.

'Thank you. Will you read the next?'

'It's just a couple of lines. Tomorrow evening, by the quince tree. I'll be there as soon after six as I can. I will wait for you until nine.'

Eleanor nodded. 'The quince tree.' She spoke softly to herself. 'I have always loved quince trees. They are very special. I planted them here when we came. They have floppy pale pink blossoms in the spring and their fruits are downy globes with a fragrance like honey.' She sounded dispassionate, as though she were on a gardening programme and was answering a question that had been sent in. 'And I met him by the quince tree. Yes, I did. Put it on the fire.'

Peter obeyed and picked up the third sheet of paper. He cleared his throat and began. His words rang out in the dusky, fire-lit room. 'My Darling, I write this at three in the morning, when it seems that the whole world must be asleep apart from me. But I can't sleep tonight. It feels that I will never be able to sleep again. I drink whisky and smoke and there is nothing that can calm me or dull the intensity of this moment, when all I can think of or see or hear is you.' He stopped for a moment to gaze at Eleanor's face, but it was blank.

'I can see the moon from my window,' he continued, with an uncanny feeling of speaking with the voice of a dead man, pleading his case all these years later. 'Moonlight makes everything familiar seem strange – I feel strange to myself. That's why I am writing this now; I have to talk to you, say something; anything. As soon as I end this letter I'll have to begin another. I used to mock all the clichés of love, Nell, the sentimental things that old fools say because they don't have the wit to find their own words – but I realize now that they are true and I can't find better ways to speak what I feel because I'm an old fool now as well. I'm sick with love.'

He stopped. His mouth was parched so he took a deep mouthful of red wine. The flames guttered and crackled. Outside the wind strengthened.

'My heart is breaking with love,' he said into the flickering hush of the room. 'I'm born again with love. Burning up with love. Deep in love – so deep there's no way back. That's what you said to me, that first time. There's no way back.' He stopped and waited.

'Thank you,' Eleanor said politely.

'Do I burn it?'

'Please.'

He did so and picked up the final letter to read. 'You have my heart. Keep it safe. I will be home again; my only home is you.'

Eleanor put her hand up and touched her cheek with the tips of her fingers.

'Yes,' she said.

'Should I—?'

'Please.'

He crumpled the last sheet of paper into a ball and tossed it into the flames. 'That's the end,' he said, when the last sheet had withered and burnt.

'Yes.' She lifted her head. 'Perhaps I should sleep now, though I feel far from sleep. Or I can play the piano awhile. It won't disturb you?'

'No. It won't disturb me.'

'Thank you,' she said. 'I am glad we have had this evening.'

'I am too.' He hesitated, trying to find the words. 'Eleanor, won't you tell me the story?'

It was out. He didn't know how he dared, but the thought of never knowing what had happened made him reckless. Bit by bit, Eleanor's history, her youth and beauty, had come to haunt him. It was as if the present, with all its pressing anxieties, had slid away and he had stepped back into a different time. Beyond this house lay the insistent world; but inside its old and crumbling walls, amid the firelight, the piano music, the empty darkened rooms, the old woman's footfall in the sleepless night, the photographs of faces long gone and barely remembered, and now these passionate letters, was layer upon layer of the past.

'What?' She lifted her head. He thought how her skin looked like damaged silk, so thin it could rip at any moment.

'Your story. The one I've burnt. What happened? Who was he?'

There was a silence. Peter couldn't tell from her blank expression if she was angry with him.

'What a very strange thing to ask,' she said. He pressed his hands tightly together and waited. 'Why should it matter to you?' she asked.

'I'm your stranger. This is what you wanted me to find and destroy. I've done it. But I'd like to know.' I need to know, he wanted to add.

'It's an everyday story, Peter, one that could be told by thousands of women. And it was more than seventy years ago. I was a young woman, just starting out, and now I'm very old, the only one left standing. Everyone else has gone; I'm the only one who knows anything of it now, and soon enough I'll be gone too.'

'So why not tell me? Pass it on.'

'Pass it on? I'm curious why you should want my old, worn-out memories.'

'I don't know, but I do.'

'That's not enough.'

'All right.' He felt half-drunk and yet alert. 'I feel somehow it might be helpful for both of us.'

'You do, do you?' Her tone was dry; he couldn't tell if she was amused or angry.

'Yes. For me, my time here is like a kind of—' He hesitated but then forced himself forward. 'Healing, I suppose,' he said. 'It's as if I'm at a refuge or a halfway house, where I can ready myself for the next stage.'

'I'm glad, of course. But why does knowing about something that happened many decades ago help with that?'

'I don't know. It feels like – this will sound mad – something I've been given to do. Like a task or a gift or something.'

'Or like simple curiosity.'

'Maybe.'

'And for me? You implied it would be good for me.'

'Well. I thought if you were leaving here, putting your past in order, you might want to tell your story to someone; speak it at last.'

'If you say the word "closure", I am going straight to bed.'

Peter laughed.

'I won't say it then. In fact, it feels the opposite of that. More like something opening than closing.' An entrance to a hidden room, he thought; a gate in a high wall and beyond it some bright unfolding view.

'Do I want that?' she asked – although she wasn't asking him. 'I am old. Perhaps it's too late to open doors long kept shut.'

'You're not old.' Peter's voice rang out in the room. 'Or at least, not in the ways it matters. You are young.'

'Young at heart, you mean?' She was smiling at him, slightly mocking but affectionate.

'Yes.'

'The soul's changes.' Her voice was soft; she was no longer speaking to him. 'The happy and tumultuous dream of youth. I've never told anyone.'

'That's why you should tell me.'

'Your generation believes nothing should be hidden, that shame and grief are better spoken.'

Peter waited. The fire crackled and outside the wind poured through the rippling autumn leaves. 'Ah well, why not?' Eleanor said at last. She put her empty wine-glass down on the small table at her side and leant back in her armchair. 'Although with stories it is always very hard to know where to begin, where to set out from. When I was young, I thought my story would be tremendous. I wanted everything.'

9

Eleanor Wright had never known her father. He had died in the war when her mother was just three months pregnant. She had grown up with a photograph of him that was blurred enough to be generic: a young man in uniform, with a wide, unsteady smile and close-cropped hair. When Eleanor's mother, Sally, was a bit tipsy or tearful, she called him Sammy, but to Eleanor he was always Samuel. Samuel Wright, twenty-two years old and a joiner by trade, who had died on 2 July 1916, on the second day of the Battle of the Somme, without even knowing he was going to be a father. She would have nightmares about his death for the rest of her life: a young man with a wide smile walking towards the yammering guns with his comrades. Bodies piled together, some wounded and some dead, churned up in the mud and blood. How long did it take and did he have time to know as he lay there that he would never make it back home to his wife and his little plot of land where he planned to grow potatoes and onions? Or did he cry out for his own mother, as Gil had once told her men do? It was his smile that upset her; it was so young and so unguarded.

Every year, she and Sally would remember his birthday together, as if he were getting older alongside his wife and little daughter – but of course he was always twenty-two years old, and always unsteadily smiling. She wanted to know her father – as if by knowing him he was somehow also knowing her; as if she could make him proud – but she had precious little to go on. There were the few letters he had sent to Sally from France, which were kept in the little memory box in the front room like a kind of shrine, but they were short, almost dull. However often she read them, she couldn't extract his personality. There was also a photograph of her mother in a tarnished oval frame, a red mug that he had apparently always drunk his tea from, his school certificates, a cloth cap, a Bible with pages so thin they were almost translucent, with his name written at the front in stiff, careful letters.

Sally told her that he had played the upright piano in their parlour; jolly songs on a Sunday evening, carols at Christmas, everyone singing along and he leading them with his fine tenor voice. The music was still there in the piano bench, along with Sally's sewing things. So Eleanor had taught herself to play the piano as well, with the aid of her grandmother's friend who had given her the basics. She put her fingers on the stained ivory keys – a few of which were dud, making a dull clonk when she pressed them – and imagined her father's fingers there instead. She played 'Abide With Me' and heard his voice singing the words. She used to rifle through the wardrobe where a few of his clothes still hung: his one good suit, his jacket with the darned elbow, his best white shirt with the stiff collar. She purloined his cuff-links from her mother's pink jewellery box and put them under her pillow. They were her talisman. When she told Peter her story, she had them still, cheap and oversized, on her bedside table. She would take them with her into the home. One day she would die with them under her pillow.

Her mother made dresses for her living. She would take orders for gowns from women in the big houses and make them up in her front room. Bolts of silk and Egyptian cotton stood in the corner; tins rattling with a satisfying variety of buttons and beads stood on every surface. Eleanor would often open them and run her fingers through their smooth brightness, like the water-rubbed shingle on a beach. Sally was tall and her slimness had become gaunt over the hard years of her widowhood; her hands were roughened and red. She cut her thick dark hair with her pinking shears once a month and sometimes went too far. Her close work had made her short-sighted, and Eleanor noticed that when she was tired she would blink repeatedly. But when she talked of her husband her face softened and became like that of a girl, almost coy with her memories. She talked of how they had loved each other. She even went to a séance where she tried to contact him, and came back agitated but unsatisfied. Made glamorous by his death, he became the perfect lover, the idolized husband with everything commonplace removed: he represented the tender companionable life she would not now have. She would recall incidents from their brief time together with a fond smile and moist eyes. She said that not a day went by when she didn't miss him. But Eleanor missed someone she had never known. She mourned an absence and loved a ghost. Yet the ghost had never loved her. At most, she had been an unspecific hope. Sometimes she felt that she barely existed because he had not known of her.

She used to wonder why her father had fallen in love with her mother, who had large hands and wide shoulders and a bump in her nose, and who would lose her temper easily. Panicky, lonely, she would lash out at Eleanor and then she would cry and Eleanor would comfort her. She would watch her mother blow her nose and wipe her eyes, tidy her hair with her clumsy hands, and she would wonder at how undependable adults were. She grew up knowing that she had only herself to lean on.

Thirteen years after her father had died, Sally told her that she had met someone. A very nice man called Robert who lived in the neighbouring village and had a little haberdashery shop. She wanted Eleanor to get to know him, and so he would be coming to tea that Sunday. She hoped they would get on. Her expression as she said this was anxious and beseeching; Eleanor's was blank. She was bewildered and also forlorn. She had never thought that Sally would ever look at another man again; she had not thought that another man would ever look at Sally. She had just thought of her as a perpetual widow and mother, *her* mother: just the two of them together in a world suffused with the tragedy of the mother's past, but looking to the daughter's future. Now she realized with a sense of sudden loneliness that Sally had her own separate future, and that she was still young, and perhaps she was even attractive. Eleanor examined Sally and saw that she had allowed her hair to grow longer, and it looked as though she had even put curlers in it the night before so that it fell in ringlets. She was wearing a navy-blue skirt with a cinched waist. She had polished her shoes. Her lips were redder than usual and her eyes brighter.

'But—' she said, and then stopped. But what? Her eyes slid to her father's browning photograph on the mantelpiece. His smile looked brave and sad. Questions crowded to the front of her mind. ('Why?' 'How?' 'What about me?') 'Robert?' she asked instead.

'Yes. He's looking forward to meeting you. I've told him so much about you, how clever you are, and kind.' This last word spoken as a covert instruction: be kind to me. 'He likes reading too,' she added rather pathetically. 'You can talk about books.'

'We can talk about books,' repeated Eleanor slowly.

Robert Forrester was a few inches shorter than Sally; a bright-eyed, bustling, organising kind of man with a receding hairline, a moustache like a caterpillar, and a pink, plump, mobile face. He was, Eleanor came to discover, full of plans and always optimistic in the face of misfortune or loss. His brown eyes moved from the mother to the daughter, attentive and hopeful. He did everything quickly – whether it was taking off his coat, unwrapping the pound cake he had brought with him from its brown paper wrapping, or drinking his tea. His voice surprised Eleanor when she first heard it because it was low and rich, and seemed at odds with his jovial appearance. He struck her as plucky, and she was touched by him in spite of herself. He had an odd and sprightly charm.

He also had a daughter. Sally hadn't mentioned her; perhaps she hadn't dared. But the girl accompanied him to the house on that first visit and was standing beside her father when Eleanor went to the door. She was hanging off his arm, buttoned up in a woollen coat against the March winds, with a hat pulled down over her forehead and a muffler round her throat, so that it was only possible to see that she was small, with a pink-and-white face and cornflower-blue eyes. Eleanor looked at her and then immediately glanced away. It was too much to take in. Her mother had met a man and that was startling enough; the fact that she had met a man with a daughter rendered Eleanor momentarily mute with refusal. She saw the new life ahead of her – no longer her and her mother eating boiled eggs for dinner or sitting by the inadequate fire while Sally stitched and Eleanor read with a knitted brow, but Robert and this wisp of a girl who would presumably be her sister. She looked cute; her cuteness made Eleanor shudder. She took off her hat and her hair was long and the colour of lemons; it was tied into a single plait, with a bow at the end. Her father unwrapped her scarf and unbuttoned her coat and she emerged, a delicate, neat figure who turned her face up to Sally to be kissed on her cheek and then moved towards Eleanor as if expecting the same.

'This is Meredith. My little Merry,' said Robert, as if to know her was to love her. 'Merry by name and Merry by nature.'

He and his daughter laughed, and Merry's laugh was like a silver bell, tinkling and clear. Sally, after a pause, joined in. Eleanor tried to smile. She kissed the girl on her pink cheek, cool from the wind, feeling uncomfortable in her tallness and her darkness and her self-contained anger, and then held her hand out to Robert, who grasped it eagerly, holding it longer than she wanted while he told her that she looked just like Sally, while little Merry took after her mother, luckily for her.

'She wouldn't like to be fat and ginger-hued like me,' he said.

'She is a little slip of a thing,' agreed Sally.

The slip of a thing sat on her father's lap, and put the end of her plait into her mouth. Eleanor, facing her, felt savage but she kept her face inscrutable.

'Your mother tells me you love books, Eleanor? Or can I call you Ellie?'

'I prefer Eleanor.' She saw him flush slightly, and added hastily, 'I do like books', although she couldn't think of a single thing that she had read that she could mention. Merry squirmed on Robert's knees, wanting attention.

'You want to write when you're grown up, is that so?'

Eleanor stared at him. Rage itched inside her. She wanted to be cold and rude; she felt her mother's eyes on her.

'She's a very good writer,' said Sally. 'You should see her short stories.'

'I don't know,' said Eleanor. 'I just like reading.'

She liked escaping, that's what it was. She yearned now to be under her covers with a hot brick warming the sheets, in a different world: ice, fire, adventure, journeys across wastelands and through perils. Love. Walls fall down, worlds open. Her own house felt hot and small. Four of them couldn't fit in here. Robert and her mother on the other side of the thin wall; her cheeks flamed. At night, she could hear her mother snoring, or even sighing deeply in her sleep. And then she and this Merry would have to share a room. Stifling. She would never be alone again, but would be the responsible older sister to this winsome delight. She glanced at her father's photograph as if he could save her. He smiled and smiled, but not at her.

'Merry's mother died eighteen months ago,' Robert Forrester was saying to her.

'Oh.' Eleanor looked at the girl. 'I'm very sorry,' she mumbled. This made it even worse: she couldn't even be cool towards her without feeling brutal.

Merry sucked her plait even harder. Her blue eyes filled with tears. Eleanor saw that her nails were bitten down to the quick, her white socks were clean but threadbare. Sally leant forward and patted her on the knee and her father rested his chin on her yellow head for a moment. The three of them made a tender group.

Six months later, Eleanor was sharing a bedroom with Merry. The room was small and she only had to reach her hand across the space that divided them to be able to touch her new sister (stepsister was a word neither Sally nor Robert would countenance; they wanted to be one happy family). At night she could hear her breathing, sometimes murmuring in her sleep. In the first year, Merry would regularly wake with night terrors, sitting bolt upright with her blue eyes glazed and her face pinched to a narrow blank, her heart galloping beneath the brushed nylon of her nightgown. She would talk fast nonsense. Eleanor never woke Robert: she disliked going into her mother's bedroom, where the pair of them would be bundled under their blankets, snoring, a faint thick odour in the air. Instead, she would climb out of bed and sit beside Merry, take her by her shoulders, speak to her soothingly and lay her back down on the pillow, putting her rag doll in her clutching hand and wiping the strands of lemony hair off her sticky forehead. In the morning, Merry would remember nothing. Her face would be pert and fresh again. 'Did I really say that? Were my eyes really open?' She loved to hear stories about herself; indeed, her whole world was a story about herself.

Every morning Eleanor brushed her sister's hair and tied it into plaits or pigtails. She taught her how to play cat's cradle and how to crochet, and before long was giving her rudimentary lessons on the recorder and the piano. She helped her with her reading and her sums and watched her practise her ballet steps: first position, second position, third, fourth; flicking little jumps and pirouettes. They walked to school together, Merry's hand in hers, and back again at the end of the day. She altered her cast-off clothes, adding flounces and flowers to prettify them. She wiped Merry's eyes when she wept, which she did often; Eleanor never cried. She couldn't remember the last time she had done so.

She fooled everyone, and sometimes even herself. She was the big sister, the dutiful daughter; grey-eyed, watchful and grave. She never showed that she minded how the household revolved around Merry, who was vulnerable and trusting; who laughed and wept and danced and opened her blue eyes wide; who sat on her father's lap and whispered confidences into Sally's ear and knew how much everyone adored her, because she was, of course, adorable. Like a bouquet of spring flowers, like a sweet pea, everyone's cosseted pet. Eleanor's fists were clenched inside her pockets. Her face was blank with rage.

'The worst of it was,' said Eleanor to Peter, 'she really was sweet. I kept trying to catch her out, expose her hypocrisy, but I never managed. She was helpful and pretty and well behaved; complacent but not exactly spoilt. It was simply that she had to get her own way and if someone refused her or wasn't charmed it was as if the sky had fallen on her. She had no inner anchor; no real resilience. Her well-being depended on everything going the way that she wanted; when it didn't it was as if her whole sense of self collapsed. That must have been a very scary way to live. But she had a cheerful temperament, like her father, and she never doubted for an instant that I loved her and wanted what was best for her. It seemed to me that she lived in a picture-book world, with herself as heroine. The rest of us were colourful characters who had walk-on parts or were her audience. I was a make-believe sister. She behaved towards me the way she thought she should behave towards her older sister, and she expected me to do the same with her. And I did.' She frowned. 'Or at least, I did until that summer.'

'What summer?'

'The one this story is all about.'

Many years later, when she was in her late sixties and Merry's memory loss was becoming too obvi-ous to ignore, Eleanor went to see a therapist. She never told anyone about her sessions, not even Gil. She was slightly embarrassed by herself: an elderly woman wanting to finally face up to her feelings of shame and guilt. The therapist had suggested she lie on the green couch by the low window. Eleanor had to unlace her stout boots and rest her head on a ridiculous doily-like spread. She lay, limp and tired, dazed by the feelings that had brought her there, looking out of the window at the spring day, the sun sending shafts of light through the bud-ding trees, and thought of all the people who had lain there before her and would come after her, to weep out their secrets and their pain.

But she found it hard to say the words she had practised. The woman sitting at her head, invisible but breathing audibly and occasionally giving a dry cough, was too young, at least twenty years younger than her. Sometimes she asked questions that Eleanor found irritating or irrelevant. She wanted to talk about her sister and explain what had happened when they were both young. She tried to say something that would open the door into the room she had not entered for all these years, but she had kept the past a secret for so long that now it had become almost impossible to break her silence. She supposed she wanted to confess, but not to this woman, not lying on this couch. Perhaps a priest hidden behind a grille would have been better: to murmur to someone you cannot see, like Midas whispering into the rushes. I am not what I seem; I am someone else.

Images filled her mind, like snow settling, covering over the present with the past. Merry's soft round face and her own narrower one in the mirror together: the two sisters, blonde and dark, sweet and inscrutable. That day, the one she was really here to talk about, and Merry's innocent blue eyes staring at her. Had she seen anything? Had she known even then, and in her rambling forgetfulness and the foggy reaches of her mind, did she still know? Is that why she sometimes laughed with such silvery wildness when she saw her sister's face? Sometimes Eleanor wondered if Merry's guilelessness was really a profound deviousness: that she was so practised in her role that she never revealed herself to anyone, even herself.

'You were saying,' the therapist had reminded her at last, 'that you feel oppressed by something specific in your past.'

'In a way.' Eleanor stared at the tiny clouds sailing past in the blue, blue sky.

And yet she had never wished it had not happened, not even in the darkest days. How could she? Joy filled her throat, a thick desire that choked her words. She lay on the couch consumed by longing and loss, an elderly woman, a wife and a mother of grown-up children, with a ladder in her tights. She couldn't speak to this woman. She couldn't speak to anyone.

'Perhaps I began at the wrong place,' she said to Peter at last. 'Although I had to begin with Merry. Merry is where it started.'

He stood up and put more logs on the fire. They were slightly damp and they spluttered, sending up greenish flames. He thought Eleanor looked exhausted. Her mouth was a funny shape and it occurred to him that she might have had a stroke in the past, like his grandmother with her tugged-down mouth and slurred speech. 'Pether.' What should he do if it happened again, just the two of them in this remote place?

'Beginning is always hard,' he said, remembering those days of sitting at his computer, seeing the glowing blankness of the screen, unable to press a single key. He used to crouch for hours like this, in the grip of a monstrous boredom, while his mind twitched uselessly.

'I was going back too far.'

'Perhaps you needed a run-up.'

'Yes?' She smiled in the gloom – a smile back into herself. 'That might be it.'

'So what is the right beginning?'

Eleanor Wright always remembered the birthday of the father she had never met. She used to commemorate it with her mother, lighting a candle in their church, although of course he had no grave there. Later, she had made her own rituals, reading out poems by Tennyson in her clear, low voice, saying tender things to him and assuring him he was not forgotten. On this beautiful spring day, when the whole world was young, he would have been forty-six; his brown hair would be darker and perhaps receding; his smile would not be so white or so wide. But he was for ever young. Soon, she would be older than him.

She untied her apron, put on her hat and her light coat and left her schoolroom, nodding at the children who hung around the entrance. Two girls, who a few minutes earlier had been taking their weekly doses of syrup of figs from Eleanor, were bouncing a yellow ball between them, counting out loud in a high chant. It was a warm day, but they still wore scratchy jumpers, blue skirts, grubby white ankle socks. One of them had clogs on her feet and her face was unhealthily pale, almost grey, as if she lived underground. Gil was waiting across the road, standing in the shadows of the tall building. He didn't smile when he saw her but the angles of his face relaxed and he watched her as she walked towards him, so that she felt suddenly conscious of herself: the way her black shoes clacked on the cobbles, the brush of an escaped lock of hair on her neck, the touch of the rough fabric of her dress against her legs. The sun was low and calm. She tucked her hand into the crook of his hand, smiling up at him, feeling a faint quiver pass through him at her touch. They didn't speak and for a moment the busy street receded and it was just the two of them under a bright sky.

Was this love? Her friend Emma said that it probably was and her mother, when Eleanor mentioned Gil on the phone, hoped it was. Her class, who had seen her with this tall, dark-haired young man, giggled and whispered behind their hands. He was a medical student, following in the footsteps of his father, who had been an eminent doctor, but had died two years before in an unfortunate road accident (there were rumours he had been drunk at eleven in the morning when he stepped off the pavement into the path of a Ford).

Eleanor had met Gil at the house of a distant cousin on her dead father's side, Rosalind, whom she had got in touch with on coming to London and who occasionally invited her to small unpredictable parties that she called her 'dos'. Gil had come up to her while she was standing by the picture window, knowing nobody but quite content to stare out at the blossom in the square, while behind her voices rose and fell and someone wound up the gramophone and filled the room with scratchy love songs. Later, the carpet would be rolled back for dancing; Rosalind, loosened by gin, shimmying across the bare boards with her head tipped back and her hair rippling over her shoulders. Eleanor would normally have gone by then, although she had always loved to dance; her slender body would become sinuous and her face dreamy as she let the music flow through her. She had spent her teenage years dancing, in village halls and in friends' houses and sometimes in her own bedroom, to the music floating up from the wireless in the parlour.

Gil had introduced himself. He looked older than he was, more grown up than the rest of the men in the crowded room, and had a slow and easy manner, quiet without being reserved. In all the years of their marriage, Eleanor never saw him hurry or heard him boast. He hated being the centre of attention and never minded being outshone – indeed, he rather liked it, preferring to watch others.

Soon, she was telling him about her school in the East End, her class of girls with pinched faces who called her 'Miss' and ate boiled potatoes or cold bread and dripping for lunch, about her Islington bedsit, freezing through the winter months, and how she would go the cinema just to warm herself. She spoke about being from the countryside, and of the mud and darkness as the days shortened, of picking soft fruit in the summers to earn money. She told him how she had always known she would leave as soon as she was able to be independent, not adding that that was the only way she could be free and in control of her life. She didn't tell him about her father, or about loving books, or about her stepsister Merry – not for weeks, and then only bit by bit. Perhaps, even when he died and she folded his blue scarf beside him in the coffin, brushed the hair that had once been black behind his ears, laid her fingers against his cheek one last time, she still hadn't told him everything. She was a woman who liked to keep things back. There was a place coiled inside her that was secret and closed to almost everyone.

He bent towards her, attentive, curious, his brow wrinkled. He never patronized her. Older than her, better educated, better off, more successful, he always believed that she was cleverer than he was and in every way that mattered more important. A week later he wrote to her – a brief note asking her if she would accompany him to the theatre. They had met, drunk Martinis in a bar with small dark cubicles, where Eleanor had felt hot in her black woollen dress with its high neck and long sleeves, the zipper knobbly against her spine. Her lipstick left a mark on the glass that she tried to rub off with a finger when Gil wasn't looking because it seemed somehow suggestive. She felt pleasantly cloudy. Then they had gone to the theatre together and watched a poor play from the stalls. He hadn't held her hand or tried to kiss her, but walked her back home to Islington along dark streets and left her at the door.

He was solid, tall, with untidy dark hair, dark blue eyes and an absent-minded, benevolent air that came, Eleanor believed, from being the only child of comfortably middle-class and indulgent parents. She soon learnt that he always left a trail of possessions behind him. On that initial date, he had had to return to the bar to collect his scarf – the same blue scarf he was to have for the rest of his life and that she put in his coffin when he died. The first time he came to her bedsit, he left his keys on the table. He would leave his coat in the cinema, his hat on the table of the café where they often went for cups of tea and iced buns, not remember where he had parked his bike, put down his medical bag in foyers and then forget to pick it up. His absent-mindedness attracted women, who wanted to look after him, but he didn't seem to notice. When they flirted with him, he would look at them genially and then turn his gaze back to Eleanor. It seemed to her he had simply decided, from the moment he set eyes on her standing alone by the window, that she was the one. She felt that he saw something in her that no one else recognized and even she barely knew existed, a virtue that she could only aspire to, or resist.

Today they went to the small park, where there was still blossom on some of the branches and the birds were singing their hearts out. A sad Chinese man was sitting under their usual tree, so still that Eleanor wondered at first if he might have died there, with his eyes wide open and fixed on some mysterious horizon. He probably worked in one of the new factories that belched their smoke into the London skies. Terence, who lived on the floor beneath her in Islington, and who had a large belly and spindly legs and talked to himself in his poky room, said that she should avoid speaking to the Chinese at all costs. As if they could cast an evil spell simply by resting their brown eyes on her. She looked at this man's smooth sorrowful face and his neat hands folded in his lap. She imagined a vast country of rice fields and mountains and peaceful oxen and little temples, and then to be living in the East End, in a crowded room with his whole family, while pink-faced Englishmen smelling of beer and sweat muttered insults under their breath.

Gil laid out his coat on the bleached grass and they sat on it. He had bought some oranges, and he took the pocket knife with the mother-of-pearl handle he always carried with him and with great concentration cut circles into the skin and peeled it off, handing segments of the fruit to Eleanor who ate them slowly, feeling their tang in her throat, watching Gil's competent hands. Hair on his knuckles, strong wrists. Perhaps he had cut people open with those hands, certainly had felt their bodies, prodding, probing, feeling for pain and discomfort, finding hidden lumps. Her glands started to ache slightly. As if he could sense this, Gil took off his scarf and wrapped it around her neck, saying it was getting cold, now that the sun was low in the sky. She found his solicitousness both reassuring and vaguely oppressive, a soft, heavy blanket she could wrap herself in.

'Today', she said, 'is my father's birthday.'

'Is it?' Gil sat up straighter, waiting for her to say more.

'Yes.'

Gil waited but she said nothing more, just looked over at the man sitting by the tree. Her mouth, he thought, was like a flower. He watched as she opened it wide enough for the last segment of orange.

'Do you think of him a lot?' he asked eventually.

'I think of him on his birthday,' Eleanor replied. 'And on my birthday as well. And when anything momentous happens, I think of him and wonder what he would have made of it, and am sorry he's missing it all. With all this talk of war, he's in my mind a lot. That it will all happen again.' She shivered. 'You can feel the excitement in the air now that conscription has been announced. Young men, *boys*, wanting to be heroes. Young women wanting them to go, so they can wait with a white handkerchief pressed to their weeping eyes. Not the mothers, of course; mothers generally know better.' She turned to look at him and he felt the force of her gaze.

'Would you go?' she asked.

'Of course, if I was needed there and not here. I'm not a pacifist.'

'No.'

'But I would come back again.' His tone was pleading. 'Eleanor, I would come back.'

'Everyone has to think like that. You all have to believe you'll come back. You wouldn't go otherwise. Death isn't real to boys; war is a game.'

'I'm not a boy.'

'No, you're not. But you'd go nevertheless.'

'Would you care so very much?' he asked, and then stopped. She didn't say anything and he leant forward – very slowly, so that she could draw back at any time – and kissed her on her mouth that looked like a flower, and her white neck that reminded him of a stem.

He hadn't kissed her before, except on the cheek, when they met or parted. He had been so afraid of her pushing him gently, firmly, away. Part of being in love with Eleanor was his sense that she was out of reach: a grey-eyed, secret country girl. He put his hand behind her head and held her against him. She tasted clean and slightly salty, and he felt her lashes scrape against his cheek. A few yards from them, the sad Chinese man looked away politely, at the small white clouds and the green leaves that hung limply in the heat. Gil pulled away at last and looked at her and happiness coursed through him. She smiled at him, pushed his unruly hair back from his face.

'What are you thinking?' he asked, stupidly.

'I was thinking we could go to the church and light a candle for my father. It's what I used to do with my mother on his birthday. I'd like to do it with you too.'

Eleven days later, he went to her bedsit. He had a rubber in his pocket and a bottle of champagne in his bag. They couldn't go to his place; he still lived in his mother's house in Chelsea. Eleanor had been there for lunch once. Mary Lee had sat across the table from her, holding her knife and fork tightly like weapons, her elbows pressed against her corseted body, and asked her a string of questions she seemed to have prepared in advance: what Eleanor's father did, what kind of education she had received, what kind of school she taught in now, whether she spoke French or German. Eleanor felt that she was being interviewed for a job for

133

which she was woefully unqualified. She became cool and withdrawn, and only understood many years later that Gil's mother had been scared of her because she came from an unknown world and because her beloved son was so smitten and she dreaded losing him entirely. She had imagined a different kind of wife for Gil: someone petite, blonde and shy, who belonged to the old, disappearing order and was in awe of Mary Lee; above all, who wouldn't take her son away from her. Eleanor failed on every count: she was modern, astringent, resolutely independent. She taught children who had nits and TB and whose fathers worked in factories – or not at all. She read poetry that didn't rhyme and magazines that were left wing and vaguely racy. She liked TS Eliot and James Joyce and Virginia Woolf, and she probably smoked and wore trousers. She rode a bike.

Gil rang on the doorbell but before his finger was even off the button the door was yanked open and he found himself face to face with Gladys Bartoli from the ground floor ('call me Signora' she would say, winking excessively) whose Italian husband Eleanor had never seen and was pretty sure didn't exist except as a glamorous fiction that allowed Gladys to keep her chin up. In spite of the warmth of the day she was wearing a moth-eaten fur coat and had unmatching daubs of rouge on her cheekbones. She admired Gil, liked Eleanor, disliked Terence (who in turn called her a disgrace to the neighbourhood). She kept a cat in her rooms, which wasn't permitted by the landlord; she thought no one knew about it, though the animal's mewing could be heard through the night and in the day it fought with other cats in the small back yard, or caught mice and sometimes even rats and left them by the door.

'I was on my way out!' she sang. 'But you know your way.'

Gil felt his purpose must be obvious. The rubber in his pocket might as well announce itself, the cork pop from the champagne bottle. He felt tawdry and wanted to retreat.

'Thanks, Gladys,' he said. 'I do.'

'I know she's in because I heard the bath water. Getting ready for you.'

Gil made his way up the two flights of stairs. He could hear Terence in his room on the first floor. He felt that he was wearing too many clothes. His collar was tight. His shoes creaked on the bare boards.

'Come in.'

Eleanor was standing before him in slacks and a white shirt. When she turned, he could see the shape of her shoulder blades beneath it. Her hair was still damp and lay in coils against her neck (the neck he'd pressed his lips against, he thought); she wore no shoes. Gil stepped into the room and kissed her on the cheek, constrained by the bat of Gladys's heavy eyelids, by the smell of cooking coming from

Terence's room underneath them, by what was in his pocket. But Eleanor seemed quite relaxed, or at least unembarrassed. She took his coat and hung it on the chair. She offered him tea, moving easily round the table and the chairs of the kitchenette, telling him about the day she had had, mimicking a fellow teacher, pointing out of the window at St Pancras in the distance. He should have been putting her at her ease, but it was the other way round. The door that led to her bedroom was shut. He tried not to look towards it.

'How do we do this?' she said to him, smiling. 'You're the expert.'

'I'm really not an expert, Eleanor! Believe me.'

'Well, you know what I mean.'

'Perhaps we should have a glass of champagne.'

'All right.'

He took the bottle from its bag. It was warm, and when he eased out the cork it only gave a stifled pop. He poured some into a glass tumbler and into Eleanor's plastic toothpaste mug, which gave the champagne a minty taste, not unpleasant he thought, tipping it back, needing courage.

'You don't need to do this if you don't want to,' he said, half-hoping she would want to put it off.

'I know.'

'You only have to say the word and—'

'Gil. I know. It's all right.'

She came up to him, where he stood among the

hard-backed chairs feeling lost and foolish, and put her arms around him and kissed him on his mouth. Then she took him by his hand and led him through the furniture to the door of her room, pushing it open, stepping inside. He sat on the narrow bed, feeling it sag and hearing it give a groan, wondering if Terence could hear it too. He took off his shoes, pulling clumsily at the laces that he had double-knotted that morning. She undid the buttons on her blouse and slid it off, letting it drop in a puddle on the floor. He stared at her pale arms, paler underneath, almost blue, and at her shallow breasts beneath the thinness of the camisole.

'You're not like other women,' he said, holding one black brogue in his lap like a pet.

'No woman is like other women. You should know that.'

'You're right, I should know that. You have to teach me these things.'

He put his shoe down and she lifted off her camisole and undid her bra, turning away from him and then back again. The window was half-open and through the blowing folds of the striped curtain, voices floated up from the street. He felt heavy and blurred; the champagne still tingled in his nostrils. He pulled off the tie that had belonged to his father and let it dribble through his fingers on to the counterpane. He tried to undo his shirt, but his fingers fumbled on the buttons. It meant too much to him.

He was numb and sluggish with love and could barely move. He tugged and felt a button give. In the street someone was giggling. On the dresser the photograph of a young man in uniform was smiling commiseratingly at him.

Eleanor undid her slacks and stepped out of them, then stood before him.

'Is this all right?' she asked. She was being neither shy nor coy, simply asking for his advice.

He held out his hand and she took it.

'You're lovely,' he said thickly.

'And you are still dressed. I feel at a disadvantage.'

'Sorry.'

Her mother should have told her. As she lay on her bed with Gil beside her, lying on his stomach with one arm over her body, she said to herself that if she ever had a daughter she would make sure that she knew in advance what it was like. Was this what she had been holding out for? Blood, pain, sweat, sticky indignity, self-consciousness. The grunts and smells of another person, the unbearable nearness. The way he laboured determinedly above her, and she became an object, a task, a piece of earth he was toiling away at. His breath in her mouth and his stubble on her cheek, his sweat on her skin and his fingers where no one's fingers had ever been. Worse than that, his sudden importunate need. He became like a child, not a man, and she became like his mother, cradling and comforting him. But perhaps her own mother was saving the advice up for the night before her wedding. She smiled, imagining the strangled embarrassment of the conversation. She felt dull and tranquil, and didn't mind the sound of Gil's breathing beside her now that he had rolled away, and of the voices filtering up from the streets, where children were playing hopscotch along the paving stones, the thud of their feet beating out a rhythm that took her back to her own childhood.

'What are you thinking?' asked Gil, turning over, propping himself up on one elbow.

'Oh – everything and nothing.'

'Everything and nothing.' He studied her. 'You know that I am hopelessly in love with you, don't you?'

'Yes.'

'And do you——?'

'Ssh. Not now. This is now.'

'All right.'

'I will never lie to you,' said Eleanor, half-knowing even then that this itself was perhaps a lie.

'What makes you say that?' He sounded alarmed.

'I don't know. But it seems important to say it: I will never lie to you, Gil. I promise.'

There was a deep silence, broken only by the crackling of the flames.

'Did you keep your promise?' asked Peter eventually.

'What?' Eleanor sounded as though he had woken her from a dream.

'Your promise not to lie to Gil. Did you keep it?'

'What's a lie? I was very young, young and foolish as that song says. I thought that honesty was more important than kindness. I think that I never told him an untruth. But perhaps that is simply obeying the letter of the law and not the spirit. We all have to lie to each other, don't we, in some way?'

'I don't know.'

'The truth would send us all mad.'

Peter waited for her to continue but she said nothing. Her woollen tights had a large hole in them, he saw, and the collar of her blouse was frayed. One of the large buttons on her cardigan hung by a thread. She seemed to be coming apart.

'What happened then?' he asked, quietly because he feared that a direct question would shut her up.

'Then?' She blinked her unseeing eyes, then rubbed them with her knobbly hands. 'I am rather tired now.'

'I've kept you up,' said Peter, wanting to shout: 'Who was "M"?'

'We can talk tomorrow,' said Eleanor. 'Not now.'

'In the morning?'

'No. You have your work then, and Jonah will be here.'

'Jonah?' He hadn't met him since Kaitlin. Yet he

had known that he would probably see him here; indeed, it was part of the reason he had accepted the job. The day of reckoning.

'Yes. Everyone comes to make sure I'm still alive. Barely a day goes by; tomorrow it's Jonah's turn.'

'That's nice.'

'They're very kind.' She sounded ironical.

Eleanor fumbled for her cane and then dropped it so that it clattered across the floor. Peter picked it up and handed it to her, nudging her hand with the end of it so that she could feel it.

'Would you help me up?' she asked. 'It's been a long day.'

'Of course.'

He stood and bent over her, taking her upper arm, tugging gently. He was half afraid that she would break, her arm slide out of her socket. She came up easily though, light as a child. She smelt musty; her hair was white and soft and he could see the pink scalp beneath. He felt her skin slide over her bone under her clothing.

'Shall I help you upstairs?' he asked.

'If you would be so kind.'

Even utterly exhausted, she retained her manners.

He put one arm around her waist and the other beneath her elbow and steered her into the hall, bumping her against a wall, awkward on the stairs that wound round. They hobbled into the corridor, like a three-legged race gone wrong and he stopped before her bedroom door, then pushed it open.

He had never been in her room before and didn't know what he would find there; he hesitated.

'Thank you,' she said gently, dismissing him. Then: 'Oh. I left my overnight bag in the hall. Could you perhaps fetch it for me?'

Peter ran down the stairs two at a time and picked up the small carpet-bag, then flew up again. Her door was still ajar, but he knocked and waited for her to call him in. Eleanor was sitting on the bed with her hands in her lap. The room was large, with two windows that looked out over her rose garden. The walls were lined with books that she would never read again. There were even books in piles along the wall. Above her bed was a photograph of Gil as a young man and another of an even younger man, in uniform, faded over time so his outline was blurred. He was smiling very broadly. On her dressing table were a soft-bristled brush, a small jewellery box and a wedding photograph. He wanted to look at it more closely but didn't feel that he could start wandering around her bedroom while she sat upright and fatigued on her bed.

'Here.' Peter laid the bag at her feet. He saw a thick cotton nightdress on top, inside out, and quietly, so she wouldn't hear him, he took it out and turned it the right way round.

'Thank you.'

'Is there anything else you need?' he asked.

'I don't want you to undress me, if that's what you're worrying about,' she said. 'Go away.'

'Good night then.'

'Good night, Peter.'

'Sweet dreams,' he said.

Peter was up before Eleanor; despite the tiredness behind his eyes, he forced himself out on his daily run. The morning was dark and damp. Birds struggled against sudden gusts of wind, and leaves were thick and wet underfoot. Many of the trees were nearly bare now. On the return loop, he stopped at the village shop for a packet of cigarettes, cancelling out his feeling of virtue. He couldn't decide if he was healthier because of the exercise and good food, or unhealthier because of his sudden hike in tobacco consumption.

'Hello, how are you today?' he said on entering, as he always said. He was resolutely cheerful to anyone he met out here; he held on to the idea that it was a countryside duty: say hello to everyone you meet, strike up conversations, offer to help people whose cars have broken down. Above all, smile. He wrenched his wind-blown face into a grin.

The woman nodded at him suspiciously.

'It's hard to get up in the mornings, isn't it?' continued Peter.

'For some people,' she replied, and he trotted off again, clutching his fags, grateful to Polly for her persistent loyalty, longing for the first mug of black coffee.

Eleanor still hadn't appeared, though one of the helpers was there, Gail. She'd brought provisions that she was stacking in the fridge and cupboards. Her small son was with her ('Training day,' she said, shaking her head from side to side. 'Again!'), and he was keeping himself amused by climbing on to the stool with great difficulty, like a mountaineer traversing a ravine, and then jumping off. From time to time he would stumble, land on his knees, emit a howl, and then begin again. The window-cleaner had also arrived. He stood outside at the long window, rubbing on sudsy water and then sweeping his wiper down the panes. They could hear the squeak. It was faintly disconcerting, thought Peter, to drink coffee with a man staring in at you, making circling motions with his hands like a mime artist. He tried to smile at him, but the man didn't seem to notice or even know that there were three people a few inches from him, on the other side of the glass.

'I've taken coffee up to Mrs Lee,' said Gail. 'She's tired this morning.'

'She was up late.'

'Poor thing.' Gail gave a vast sigh.

All of a sudden, there were two people standing on the other side of the glass, staring in: the window-cleaner, with his wiper suspended, and someone else, gazing into the kitchen as if he were a visitor at the aquarium. The coffee trembled in Peter's mug and he set it down carefully.

'Well, fuck,' he said.

'Ssh!' Gail put her finger to her mouth and looked across at her son, who jumped from his stool and crashed to the floor.

'It's Jonah.'

'Who's Jonah?'

'He's early. I didn't think he'd be so early. I'm not ready.'

'Ready for what?'

'Just, ready.'

Jonah was still standing there, but the window-cleaner had sluiced the pane of glass with soapy water so that his face was obscured. He looked like one of those dodgy characters you see on television whose features have been smudged out. But his beautifully cut coat was clear, and his grey shoes with their blue laces. Then he was gone.

Peter stood up. He was still in his running gear, damp patches under his arms, down his chest, on his back. The sweat had cooled on him and he was clammily cold. He patted at his damp, tufty hair, trying to tame it, remembered his piratical beard; he'd been meaning to shave it off.

'Oh well,' he said. Why did it matter anyway?

Jonah glided in through the door. He was smooth and lustrous, light on his feet – those feet in their classy shoes. Peter remembered a game he used to play with his mother on car journeys: what animal did people resemble? Jonah was a panther – or perhaps something underwater, streamlined and making no sound.

'Good morning,' he said, as if they'd said good night the evening before.

'Hello Jonah.' His voice was steady. He was waiting to find out what he felt: anger or grief. But he felt neither of these, just a steely determination to do this right.

'Is there any of that coffee going?'

'There is. Do you take milk?'

'No.'

Peter remembered how Jonah had always used words sparingly. He took a mug from the back of a cupboard; it had writing spiralling round it. 'Shoo, clouds, shoo!' he read. He poured some coffee out.

Jonah took off his coat and hung it on the back of a chair. Under it, he wore a dark blue cardigan that looked soft and expensive. Then he introduced himself to Gail, who was partly obscured by the fridge door but looking out at him curiously.

'Hello.' He actually gave her what looked like a very small bow. Was it ironic? 'I'm Jonah, one of Eleanor's grandsons.'

'Gail,' said Gail, a lump of Parmesan in one hand and a bunch of celery in the other. 'Your grandmother is still in bed. I took her coffee.'

'And who are you?' asked Jonah. He squatted beside the little boy who was halfway up the stool, legs at a dangerous angle; his face was red with effort and he looked worn out.

'He's Jamie,' said Gail. 'It's a non-teaching day at school. He's in Reception. I had to bring him. She doesn't mind' – with a small jerk of her head, to indicate she meant Eleanor – 'she says she likes having young life in the house.'

'Quite right,' said Jonah. He took the boy under both arms and lifted him on to the stool, then took a seat himself. He had let his hair grow longer, though the back of his head was shaved, and he now sported a half-beard. He wore a single stud earring, and several rings on his fingers. Peter saw that his thumbnails were painted silver. On the inside of one wrist was a tiny tattoo that looked like a maze.

Gail left the kitchen, her son trailing after her. Jonah lifted the mug and took a sip. He nodded. 'Good,' he said. Then he looked at Peter with his eyes like sloes, and menacing and dark as a tunnel you'd never get to the end of. 'How's it all going?'

It could have meant anything: How are you? Is your life all right? Do you like being here? How's the work progressing? Peter paused, considering which of these questions he wanted to answer. He wanted to behave with dignity both in the eyes of Jonah, and in his own eyes. He had loved Kaitlin and for a while, she had loved him too. But in his darkest days he had abandoned her and for many months been bereft, guilty, undone. Now he wanted to leave this house restored and thinking well of himself. It had been his task and his pledge to himself.

'The job is going well,' he said at last. 'I haven't finished yet. But I've gone through all the books. There are some valuable first editions that I've put in boxes for you to look at. You'll have to come back later for any papers.'

'Good.' Jonah picked up a shiny green apple from a bowl in the middle of the table, rubbed it against his arm, and then took a large bite.

'And I like being here, with your grandmother. She's an extraordinary woman.'

'Isn't she. There aren't many like her left.'

'I don't think there were ever many like her.'

Jonah nodded approvingly. Peter took a mouthful of coffee, steadied himself.

'I've been wondering: why did you ask me to come here, Jonah?'

'Why? Well, for a start I knew you were at a bit of a loose end and also that you'd be good at it.' Peter didn't speak, but waited for him to continue. 'But also, perhaps, to make amends.'

'Ah. Did you do me wrong, then?'

'Didn't I?'

'I don't know. Kaitlin fell out of love with me, or at

least, she saw that we were doing each other no good, that we were wounding each other. And she fell in love with you. I'm not sure of the order of things and nor am I sure I want to know. What should you have done?'

'I thought I was supposed to say that to you.'

'Oh.' He put the mug down on the table and wiped the back of his hand across his mouth. He was starting to feel very cold now and needed his shower. 'I don't think I much care who says what to who any more.'

'I suppose', said Jonah slowly, 'that I wanted you to be all right.'

'So that you could feel all right as well?'

'Maybe. Also, I rather like you.' It was unexpected, as was the gladness that coursed through Peter when he heard the words.

'Do you?'

'Yes.' There was a pause. 'You don't have to say anything.'

'I don't think I was going to.'

They grinned at each other.

'So let me ask you the same question: why did you agree to come?'

'I wanted to face things, not hide from them. I'm tired of that. I want to get on with my life, that's all. I don't want to be in the grip of my past. Also, I thought it might be fun.'

'Fun?'

'Yes.'

'Is it?'

'It's satisfying and absorbing. So I suppose you could call that fun.' He looked down into his mug, then up again. 'Is Kaitlin OK?'

'She is.'

'Good. Will you tell her—?' He stopped. Tell her what? 'Say that I send my best wishes.' He had wanted to say *blessings*, but that seemed too much.

'I will. She talks about you.'

'Does she?'

'Yes. She tells me stories.'

'Oh.'

'Happy stories, mostly.'

'That's generous of her.'

'Yes. Things you did together; things you said.'

Jonah went over to the fridge and opened it. He examined the contents, seemed to decide against them, and shut it once more. Peter, watching him, was pleased with the way this was going. He felt open and clear-headed, full of a new kind of energy.

'I come here every two weeks or so and I read poems to Gran.'

'Oh. That's nice.'

'She loves poetry. She knows reams of it by heart, or at least, she used to. Perhaps she's starting to forget.'

'I don't think she forgets much. She still plays the piano.'

'Does she? Yes. And she'll always have that. Music is the last thing to go.'

'You're talking about her as if she's disappearing.'

'When I was a boy I used to come here in the holidays, while my parents travelled. They were always travelling, in spite of my father's position at the hospital. Conferences all over the world, I suppose, and my mother's homeland. I would turn the globe that stands in the living room and spin it, watching all the countries they went to turning round and round. Anyway, when I stayed here, every evening at dusk, my grandparents would take a walk through the garden together. None of us went with them; they didn't tell us not to, but we somehow knew that it was a private ritual; we wouldn't be welcome. They would always take the same paths and stop in front of the same shrubs and trees. They usually held hands, but didn't seem to talk much, just walked together in companionable, oddly courteous silence. They were always very polite with each other, very thoughtful. My father told me that it was the same when he was a boy as well. Every evening without fail – earlier in the winter because it gets dark, later in the summer – they would enter the garden together. Even when my grandfather was very ill and weak, they would go out, hand in hand, and stand among the roses they loved, or under the hornbeam there, a tree that is many times older than my grandmother.'

Peter said nothing. He had never heard Jonah talk so much.

'When he died,' Jonah continued, 'I used to think of her here alone, as dusk fell, and wondered if she still took those walks through the garden, and if she did, what she thought about. Did he still accompany her; did she feel him beside her, like she feels the memory of her music in her fingers when she plays? And how long does it take for someone to disappear at last?'

He stopped and looked at Peter, as if expecting him to provide an answer.

'I don't know,' said Peter.

'Of course not.' Jonah stood up in one easy motion. 'And I'm keeping you from your shower.'

'It's all right.'

'It's been good to see you,' said Jonah. And he put his hand – his long-fingered, beautiful scholar's hand – on the top of Peter's sweaty head and rested it there an instant, as if in benediction, then lifted his coat from the chair and left the kitchen.

'Wow!' Peter said out loud.

Later, passing by the living room door, he heard Jonah's voice, but he couldn't hear what he was reading. He wondered what Eleanor's favourite poems were, and imagined her sitting in the shade of the hornbeam tree with a volume of poetry, her dark head bent, her face wearing that faraway look he had seen in the photographs.

He met Jonah again as he was leaving. He and Eleanor came to the junk room. Jonah's arm was under Eleanor's elbow, but Eleanor looked surprisingly sprightly, after last night's exhaustion. There was a touch of colour in her cheeks; she wore a green silk scarf around her shoulders and ridiculous slippers with rosettes on them.

'Hello,' she said, smiling slightly to the left of him. 'We'll meet later, shall we?'

'If that's good for you.'

'I was saying to Jonah that we will have a vast bonfire on my birthday, a conflagration of the past. You should be there.'

'I don't think—'

'You should be there,' she repeated. 'You should meet all the people you've been studying and cataloguing.'

'I don't know.'

'Fireworks,' Eleanor said. 'We shall have fireworks. The grandchildren can arrange it.' She touched Jonah on his arm. 'Don't you agree, Jonah?'

'That we should have fireworks?'

'No, that Peter must be present.'

'Oh, certainly.' His tone was smooth, like polished marble off which meaning slides. Peter couldn't tell if he was sincere or ironic. 'And we should also have that great bonfire of the past. Send everything up in flames.' He raised his gloved hand. 'Goodbye.'

Peter and Eleanor sat beside the fire. Eleanor had a beautiful patterned shawl across her shoulders and a long necklace of amber beads around her neck; red wine glinted in their glasses. There was a little bowl of smoked almonds on the low table. Polly sat beside Peter and laid her head on his lap. He stroked her muzzle, hearing her heavy tail thump on the carpet.

'What happened next?' he asked.

Two weeks later, on a Friday, Eleanor took the train home. It was May, and the following day was Meredith's birthday. Because the weather was hot, Meredith had organised a picnic. They would walk across the fields to the river. People could bathe if they wanted. She had written to Eleanor two weeks before, saying she hoped she would be there – eighteen was a significant age, after all, even though it would be three years before she could vote. Her writing was round and neat. Eleanor could picture her writing it, the tip of her pink tongue on her upper lip, her forehead in a frown of concentration. She wrote that she hoped that Eleanor would bring her young man – those were her words, 'young man', as if she had lifted the phrase from Sally's lips – since she was very eager to meet him, as were her father and Sally. Eleanor's old friend Emma was going to be there. And, she added, there was someone she wanted Eleanor to meet as well.

At first, Eleanor had hesitated over inviting Gil and when she finally did so, it was grudgingly, although he accepted enthusiastically and he would join them the following day. There was a part of Eleanor, a large part, that didn't want to take Gil home with her. He was her secret life, the one she had made for herself in London. She didn't know if she wanted him meeting her family, and she didn't like the thought of them meeting him, approving of him, taking her to one side to congratulate her. Eleanor had told him about her family, but sparingly, just factual details: Robert owns a haberdashery that doesn't bring in much money; Sally sews dresses, but only for her favoured customers; Meredith has trained to be a secretary. Her thoughts bumped against the fact of Merry. She remembered the time, when she was still living at home, when a young man, a boy really, had come to collect her. They were to go dancing. She was coming down the stairs in her satin pumps, excited, but Merry had rushed to answer the door. The pair had stood at the threshold, Merry gazing up at him in admiration, agreeing, exclaiming, giving her silver peals of enchanted laughter. Eleanor had seen the expression on the young man's face: he was flattered and charmed; how could he not be? Merry was so agreeable, so pliant in her manner, hanging on every word. It wasn't consciously manipulative; she behaved in the same way to women as well. She remained like a small, indulged child, wanting to like everyone and be liked in return. Liked, loved, adored. Eleanor thought of telling Gil that if he flirted with her sister or was at all captivated by her winsome, dimpling charms, then she would never see him again. But she decided not to give him the benefit of an advance warning; she would just watch him and see how he responded.

It felt strange to be going home, she thought, as the train trundled through the green countryside, stopping at stations that stood empty in the golden light, rosebay willowherb growing at the end of the platform. Secret rivers and little back gardens. It felt as though she were being taken back to her childhood, the years reeling back, until at last she was stepping out on to the platform with her overnight bag and squinting through the dazzle of low evening light for Robert.

More than seventy years later, she remembered everything. She was wearing the clothes she had worn for teaching, for she had come straight from the school: a black skirt and a white high-necked shirt, plain black shoes that needed to be taken to the cobbler to repair, for the soles were wearing out. She remembered seeing her stepfather coming out of the shadows to greet her, plumper and balder than she had remembered. How his thinning hair, damp from the heat, stood up in clumps, like a bird's crest, and how he smelt of something that took her back to childhood times: wood smoke and pipe tobacco and bacon and a sour tang of sweat. The bristle of his cheek scratching against her skin. He was older, redder, more anxious. His quickness had become jerky, his cheerfulness like an insistent sprightliness that made her feel tense. She remembered the heat of the day, and how the road was dusty under the wheels of the little car, his pride and joy, and the leaves on the trees freshly opening in the dusky light.

Sally met her at the door, wearing a white apron over her clothes. She had a smudge of cold cream down one wing of her nostril. There were new lines on her face, a couple of tiny hairs on her chin, and Eleanor noticed how she blinked often, as if to clear her vision. Perhaps all those years of sitting over swathes of silk and muslin had ruined her eyes early. She reached up and kissed Eleanor on one cheek and then the other. Her hands were cool but her face felt warm, flushed from the cooking. She smelt of biscuits and the flat-iron, a dry, domestic aroma that took Eleanor back to her earliest days, before Robert and Merry had swelled their little family.

'Something smells good,' said Eleanor.

'I'm making us an egg and bacon pie. I know how you used to love it.'

Did she? Eleanor made an approving noise.

'And tomorrow you can help prepare for the picnic. Otherwise I don't know how I'll do it all in time. All the things Merry wants!' She made a sound that combined exasperation with approval.

'I'd be glad to.'

'What time is your young man arriving?'

'His name is Gil,' said Eleanor, as she did every time. 'At twenty minutes past midday. I'll take my bag upstairs, shall I? I've Merry's present with me; should I give it to her tonight?' A silver locket on a slender chain, satisfyingly coiled inside a silk pouch.

'Listen.' Sally, running her hands up and down her apron. 'I wanted to tell you, before you see her. We're a bit worried about Merry. Could you perhaps have a word with her? Merry's always listened to you.'

'I'm not sure that's true.'

'Oh, it is.'

'So why are you worried?'

'You know how she is. Stubborn.'

Yes. Eleanor knew how Merry could be stubborn.

'She's met a young man. She's set her heart on him.'

'Who is he?'

'Oh.' Sally sat down heavily in one of the chairs.

'That's the thing. We don't really know anything about him, except—' And here she dropped her voice, as though the thing were a secret scandal. 'He was one of those that took the Red Train.'

'You mean he went to Spain to fight?' Eleanor felt a thrill of excitement running through her. She had read so much about all the poets and artists and idealists who'd gone to fight Franco, but she'd never actually met any of them.

'Yes.' Sally gave an outraged sniff. 'And went and got injured of course. He doesn't have a job, not anything steady. He writes things for magazines.' She pulled a little face. 'He's here convalescing with some aunt or cousin. I don't know. He's not like any of the young people Merry knows. He has some strange ideas and just seems a bit, well, I don't know how to put it. *Odd.*' She looked beseechingly at Eleanor. 'And he hasn't got one coin to rub against another, though it doesn't seem to bother him. Robert doesn't trust him at all. He thinks he's unstable.'

'But Merry's in love?'

'She *thinks* she's in love. I call it infatuation. Will you talk to her?'

'What, tell her not to be in love? No.'

'Warn her.'

'Warn her against her own heart, you mean. No.'

'Eleanor! She's too young.'

'Too young for what?'

'We all thought she was going to get engaged to

Clive Baines. You remember Clive? He's been sweet on her for years and she likes him. He's such a lovely young man. He's been conscripted already and is off for his military training, and I'm sure he would like it to be settled before he goes.'

'You mean, she's old enough to marry Clive Baines, but too young to fall in love with this other man, because he's odd.'

'You make it sound stupid, the way you say it. We don't want her to make foolish choices that she'll regret for the rest of her life. This man, I don't think he's got the same values as us. But Clive would make her happy.'

'Why should she make any choices at the moment? Women don't have to choose between one man and another, as if in the end that's all there is.' She spoke too fervently, urging her own case, not Merry's, and made herself slow down, speak more calmly. 'There are other things in life, you know. Marriage isn't everything. Times are changing.'

'That's all very well for you to say. You've got yourself a well-off, handsome doctor.'

'Stop it! I haven't got myself anything. Except myself,' she added, softly.

'I thought you'd understand.'

'I think I do.' Eleanor heard and hated the coldness of her voice. She tried to make amends. 'I can talk to her about not rushing into things blindly. But I'm certainly not going to tell her to accept Clive Baines.'

'Merry's not like you. She's highly strung. I don't want her heart broken.'

It was the refrain Eleanor had been hearing ever since Sally and Robert had met: Merry's not like you; you are strong and resilient, able to look after yourself, while Merry is delicate, breakable – which was, of course, part of her charm and most of her power.

'You can't prevent broken hearts.'

Merry was in the room she and Eleanor had shared for six years. The walls were still papered by a pattern of ridged pink and red roses that Eleanor had always disliked, the beds were covered by the same patterned counterpanes, Eleanor's yellow and Merry's a pastel blue. There was still the oval mirror on a stand on the little chest between the beds, and a wardrobe in the corner. There was the same tiny crack in the top pane of glass in the window that looked over the garden, where even now Robert was pulling weeds, and the old stain on the carpet. And yet the room was now unmistakably Merry's. Her clothes lay brightly heaped on Eleanor's bed, her lipsticks were under the mirror, alongside a fashion magazine. It was her smell that filled the air: lavender and something musky. She herself was standing at the open wardrobe, wearing a slip and holding a dress up against herself, white with blue sprigs on it. Her arms were round and white; her yellow hair was tied in childish plaits that were coming undone. She looked absurdly young and pretty, a creature of the spring.

'Hello, Merry.'

'Eleanor! Oh darling Eleanor, I didn't hear you arrive.'

She flung herself into Eleanor's arms and rested there awhile, the dress rustling between them. Eleanor felt the soft press of her breasts, the tickle of her hair.

'Deciding what to wear for your picnic?'

'Yes. Isn't it silly? I'm so excited and nervous.'

'You're allowed to be excited on your eighteenth birthday, but why are you nervous?'

Merry gave a little laugh.

'I've never had a party before. And also—' She threw a quick sideways glance at Eleanor. 'Michael's coming.'

'Michael.' She would never again say his name so calmly.

'Yes. The person I want you to meet.' She grasped one of Eleanor's hands. 'He's lovely.'

'Is he?'

'Just lovely. You'll see.'

'I'm looking forward to it.' She hesitated. 'Are you very fond of him?'

Merry regarded Eleanor with suspicion, a little crease forming between her eyes.

'What's Sally been saying?'

'Just that she's worried. And so is Robert. They don't want you rushing into this before you're sure.'

'And what do you think?'

'Why don't you answer my question to you first — are you very fond of him?'

'Yes! He's so mysterious and brooding.' She gave a little shiver and hugged herself. 'Like someone out of a novel by Georgette Heyer.'

'Oh,' said Eleanor dubiously. 'And is he very fond of you?'

'He might not know it yet. But—' She gave her winning smile; a dimple appeared on her cheeks. 'You know me, Eleanor. If I want something, I'm going to get it.' For a moment, her face hardened, her lips thinned. 'Nothing's going to stand in my way.'

'But—'

'And I am *not* going to marry dull old Clive Baines.'

'I like Clive.'

'You marry him then — but you've already got yourself a sweetheart, haven't you? Your doctor.'

'He's not—'

'You'll be the favourite now, not me. Marrying someone like that; very grand. You should see Sally's face when she talks about him.'

'Merry—' began Eleanor.

'But don't worry about me,' continued Merry. 'They'll come round. You wait and see.'

*

Later that night, as they lay in their twin beds as if they were girls again, Merry said, in a whisper, 'Eleanor?'

'Yes.'

'Have you ever – you know?'

Eleanor did know, but she certainly didn't want to reply.

'Well? Have you?'

'Why are you asking?'

'Is it very painful?'

'I'm sure it depends,' Eleanor answered evasively. 'Now go to sleep. You've got a big day ahead.'

'I never would with Clive. Ugh. But someone like Michael – I bet he's had loads of women. You can just tell.'

'Listen,' Eleanor said, her voice low and clear. 'You don't have to obey other people. You have to do what *you* want – about work, about love, about sex, about marriage. About everything. But that doesn't mean simply giving in to immediate desires. It means you have to know what you really want – in a big, deep way. It's about freedom; the freedom to be yourself.'

There was a trilling giggle in the darkness next to her.

'Golly,' said Merry. 'I'd forgotten how serious you can be. I just want to be safe and happy and have fun.'

And she still remembered, too, what she put on for

the picnic seventy-five years ago: a sage-green frock with short sleeves and tiny mother-of-pearl buttons, the brooch that Gil had given her pinned on to the collar, and a little straw hat that her mother had trimmed for her years ago. She had risen early and helped Sally prepare the food while Merry remained curled up in bed, half-dozing. Then she put on her dress, tied up her dark hair, and went with Robert to the station to collect Gil. She remembered the car journey back to the house, Robert chatting on and Gil's amiable responses – and how she felt a swell of gratitude for his kindliness, his ability to be easy with everyone, making what was strange seem familiar and what was familiar seem approved of. Every so often, he would turn in the passenger seat to cast her a quick glance, and she put a finger against the back of his neck, under his untidy hair, and felt him stir under her touch. She knew the power she had over him and marvelled at it.

And the house, she saw it through Gil's eyes and it seemed suddenly small and shabby as they approached it, with the stove chimney, the blue door and the neat front garden; the lean-to water closet where as a child she had sat listening to the rain bounce like bullets off the corrugated iron roof; the upright piano with its missing notes in the parlour where she had learnt to play.

Sally greeted Gil, slightly stiff in her nervousness,

but he was warm and easy. Soon they were talking about Abyssinia, her volunteer work for the Red Cross (Merry was helping too, she said; everyone had to do their bit), the vegetables they grew in their back garden. Eleanor watched them. She was grateful to Gil but resisted the way he was taking her back into her family, when she had been so fixed in her determination to escape them. She had a clear sense of how he liked to make bridges between people, however separate they might seem. He did it in his work and in his personal relationships. He always and everywhere believed in connectedness, in tolerance, in seeing the other side, in discovering a common cause. He wanted everyone to get on and had about him an impersonal benevolence and sympathy that was deeply attractive. That solid, unwavering kindness was one of the reasons that Eleanor had fallen for him, and yet at the same time it made her pull back. It was too soothing.

The guests had not yet arrived and Merry was getting ready, Sally said, rolling her eyes fondly at them (these young women! she seemed to say). It was as if Merry were her real daughter, prettying herself upstairs, while Eleanor was the visitor. The two men went into the garden to look at Robert's garden. Almost as soon as they were out of the door, Sally turned and put her hand on Eleanor's arm.

'What a *nice* young man,' she said.

'Yes.'

'So good-looking.'

Eleanor didn't reply.

'And obviously dependable.'

'You can tell that from two minutes?'

'Oh. Don't be so matter-of-fact. I can tell he's in love with you. Don't let him go!'

She remembered what Merry was wearing too, when at last she came down the stairs: her pale yellow dress that Sally had made for her and that went with her yellow hair and her wide blue eyes, and that she must have put on thinking of what food would suit it. Little sandwiches with cucumber or lemon curd, and jelly if it would stand the heat of the day; early strawberries. The dress had a full skirt that ballooned out when she twirled. Merry was a girl who twirled. Did she know how lovely she looked when she skipped, danced, put her head back to laugh and her rippling hair fell behind her like ribbons of light? Of course she did. Turning to her dear old father, to her stepmother who had always treated her like her daughter, to her darling elder sister up from London, to her friends gathered for the occasion; a light hand on their arm, her mouth parted in a smile of delight. Never mind storm-clouds gathering. Never mind dread, the footfall in the darkness. Today was Merry's birthday and they were going down to the river, these young men and women, carrying the hamper and the tartan rugs that smelt of mothballs, to where the willows dipped their branches in the water, to have a picnic.

But there was something different about Merry that day. Eleanor noticed it at the time and remembered it later. She was ever so slightly jittery, jangled. Her sprightliness was thinned, with an artificial edge to it. Her eyes didn't stay on the faces she was gazing up at but every so often darted to one side. She hung off Gil's arm and told him in her beguiling voice how pleased she was to meet him at last, but her heart wasn't quite in it. She was waiting.

She was waiting for the young man who was late to arrive. They clustered outside the house, under the blue sky. Clive Baines was there. And his brother Jeremy who had also joined up the week before and already had bristle-short hair and an air of solemnity about him. Eleanor chatted a while with the people she knew, although they remained polite with her – she was the older sister, after all, come up from London with her doctor-friend. Then her friend Emma arrived, whom Eleanor had known since they were seven. Emma was fair, her hair a reddish-blonde, full lips, wide-apart eyes and a light dusting of freckles over her nose. She had an amused and sceptical air about her; she refused to take things tragically. Eleanor introduced her to Gil and then after a few minutes withdrew into the shade of the house, standing back from the group and watching them in the heat that was making her drowsy. Gil was chatting with Emma and another young woman, and after a while Robert joined them; she noticed how Gil drew her stepfather into the little group, putting him at his ease.

She should never have feared that Gil would turn out to be untrustworthy; the danger lay elsewhere. In the figure walking towards them now down the white road, quickly because he was late but with an uneven gait; one of his legs dragged. He was smoking a cigarette, the blue smoke curling in a wisp over his shoulder. Then he let it fall to the road and extinguished it with the heel of his sound foot. Merry saw him too. She detached herself from the group and went up the road to meet him, drawing near him, taking his hands in hers. For a moment, she looked like a woman, not a girl.

Because she stood apart, Eleanor saw him long before he saw her. She had the chance to look at him straight, before love transfigured him. He was slender, not particularly tall, with hair that was the colour of a mole: a soft brown that was nearly grey, and falling in a wing over his forehead. His skin was pale, like an Irishman's. His mouth, she saw as he drew closer, was wide. He wore a thin dark suit whose trousers were held up by a belt – or no, by a tie. Her first impression as he joined Merry's party was one of buoyancy. His smile was generous, he turned from person to person, responsive, quick, seizing hands, nodding his head in agreement. But she also sensed a contradicting sombreness about him, and a detachment that was at odds with his surface engagement. She thought – or rationalized to herself, later – that he was in the group but not of it, as if he were acting a part, although not insincerely. She never thought him a charlatan, but he was simultaneously urging himself on and standing back.

She watched as Merry, her arm still tucked through his, introduced him to Gil. The two men shook hands. She felt a small shudder pass through her, as though it were her hand this young man was pressing. Gil looked solid, handsome, safe, warm and real. She wanted him to come to her and take her back to their old life that all of a sudden seemed far off. Her clean, bare bedsit, with Terry coughing and creaking beneath her and Gladys lurking in the hallway, the schoolroom with its rows of double desks, their sunken inkwells and scratched surfaces, girls in pigtails and the chant of times tables, men in crowds down by the docks with their sad eyes and calloused hands and boots without laces. Sunday afternoon at the pictures, the trams and the buses and the sluggish brown river. What was she doing here? A picnic with lemonade and jelly, and this young man who had come back from the singed tip of Europe to attend pretty Merry's eighteenth birthday. She drew further back.

Of course Merry wasn't going to accept acceptable Clive Baines, who stood in the group clustered around her, trying to smile though his face was lumpen and defeated. Eleanor felt the hot surge of blood beneath her skin. She looked at Gil, so contented and at his ease, and then away again. Back at him.

Merry cast her eyes around, found her sister and gave a little exclamation of gladness. She pulled at the young man's hand and he stepped forward to meet Eleanor. The heat made her skin damp. She thought of the scorched landscape of Spain, cicadas and olive trees. Strong young women with swarthy skin laying aside their needlework and babies and standing at the barricades alongside their comrades. Layer after layer of respectability peeled back and all that was left was all that ever mattered: love and struggle, life and death. She had looked at the pictures with Gil but this young man had been there, travelling out on the Red Train from the Gare d'Austerlitz with others who would lay down their lives for a cause. She looked into his face and all of a sudden the smile that he hid behind disappeared, like a mask dropping from him, and for a brief moment his face altered, became stern and solitary. It could only have lasted a second but the look between them was too intimate, and she felt a door heaving open inside her, a cold wind blowing through her.

Later he used almost exactly those words. He

said: 'I felt that a door was opening.' Or did he say: 'I felt that an abyss was opening'? Or did she make that up as well, when it was all over and she needed to make a story out of everything, to carry her through? His eyes like a corridor, endless, but tunnelling through her as well. When Gil looked at her, Eleanor knew that he saw what was good in her, or imagined it; his love made her better than she could ever be without him. But when he looked at her, she felt that he saw everything she wanted to keep hidden and secret. The illicit self: anger, egotism, the spidery heat of desire, little coils and tendrils inside her.

'Ellie,' said Merry, turning from one to the other. Eleanor could feel the heat of her nervous excitement; she was like someone wound too tight. 'Meet Michael. Michael, this is my sister, stepsister, Eleanor. You two are obliged to get on! I insist.' And she gave her laugh, a thin ribbon of sound spooling out around them all.

'Hello Michael,' said Eleanor, her calmness a skin of indifference over her swelling apprehension, and held out her gloveless hand. 'I'll do my best.'

'I'm sure you will,' he said. 'And so will I.' He had a northern accent. Later he told her he came from a back-to-back in Leeds that had since been bulldozed to make way for the great tower blocks that dominated the city centre. His dad had been a drinker and violent on a bad day. His youngest brother had died of diphtheria. His mother was ambitious and fierce, urging all her children on to better things. He was a scholarship boy, a book-worm, an ardent autodidact. Of course Eleanor compared this to Gil's clean, high-ceilinged back-ground, silver cutlery and a car in the garage. 'Poor Gil,' she said to Peter, seventy years later, her face bright with tenderness and pity. 'My poor darling Gil. He didn't stand a chance.'

Now Michael took her cool hand in his warm, dry one (a musician's hands, she thought to herself, though in fact he didn't play any instrument and couldn't hold a tune; hands like her own; long thin fingers, bitten nails) and nodded his head over her knuckles, in a remnant of a bow that was perhaps mocking. She held herself quite still but felt that her body was thrumming, quivering. He said that he had heard a lot about her. His voice had the slight rasp of someone who smoked too much. She said (was that her voice, so light and careless?) that he had the advantage over her; she'd only just been made aware of his existence. And then Merry was whispering something to him, tugging at his arm, wanting them all to get going, and he turned from her. Or she turned from him.

Down by the river, it was a day of heat and heavy shifting light. The sky was turquoise and later vio-let, like a bruise. The sun shone through the new leaves. They all sat along the bank in groups. Eleanor laid out a rug under the willow tree that she used to climb. She remembered how she would drape herself along the length of the branch that stretched out over the river and lie like that for hours, the leaves like green streamers around her, gazing down into the eddies, dreaming, letting dreams drift through her.

Gil sat beside her, not touching her but near enough for her to feel his body heat. He took off his shoes and socks, and rolled up his shirtsleeves. His hair was slightly damp and she could see dark circles forming under his armpits. She thought of him lowering his body on to hers and gave a tiny, involuntary shudder. She could feel the sweat between her breasts and on her back, but at the same time she was cold under her warmth, goosebumps on her skin, as if she were sickening for something.

Emma joined them, lowering herself on to the rug, peeling off her stockings and stretching out her strong white legs luxuriously. She had freckles on her knees. She put her hat over her face and seemed to fall asleep. Eleanor slid off her sandals and curled her bare legs under her. She had her back turned to them both, facing the river. The voices behind her rose and fell. She knew she should make more of an effort, engage people in conversation: poor Clive Baines or that nice Lily Glover, who was Merry's best friend from way back and whom Eleanor had taught to play 'Sweet and Low Down'; and 'Don't Stay Up Too Late' on their out-of-tune piano at home. She drank lemonade and toyed with a sandwich. It was too hot to eat. Gil was saying something to her about childhood holidays he remembered, and about how the government had transported tons of sand into St James's Park, so that poorer children could play at being at the seaside. She let his hand slide over hers. Every part of her body was clear to her. She could feel the weight of her head on the stem of her neck, and the swell of her breasts, the way that the blood flowed through her and the rhythm of her heart. Heat pricking her skin. She turned her wrist under Gil's hand and looked at the blue vein there. It was as if she were someone else. She tried out her voice on Gil, tried out her smile. The shadows of leaves fell on her arms and on Gil's face.

Everything had been a mistake. She shouldn't be with Gil. The certainty lay like a cold shadow across her. She imagined saying that to him, now, as they sat here and the party went on behind them as if thrown up on a screen. She tore a morsel off her sandwich and pushed it into her mouth and chewed it, swallowed it, then another. Gil was speaking again and she nodded and smiled and her hand lay under his.

'Have some strawberries,' said a voice and pleasure splashed through her. She turned and there he was, his suit jacket off, his shirtsleeves rolled up like Gil's, but his arms were thinner and browner. The sun of the south, she thought, taking a fruit and biting into it. To her left there was the streak of a semi-naked body and a young man was leaping into the river, hanging in the air momentarily, pale arms and legs outstretched, and then falling with a splash into the water. He rose with a shout and thrashed his arms about in triumph.

'Are you going to swim?' Michael asked them, as another figure, a woman, raced towards the bank, clad in a tight-fitting black swimming costume and a rubber hat decorated with squishy plastic flowers, and already squealing in expectation of the shock of the cold.

'Shall we?' Gil was enthusiastic, boyish, kneeling up and reaching for the towel where it hung over a low branch. 'I need cooling off.'

Emma sat up abruptly. She hadn't been asleep after all.

'Me too,' she said, rising to her feet in one calm movement.

'You go,' Eleanor said. 'I might join you.'

Emma disappeared out of sight with her towel. Gil went into the undergrowth to pull on his bathing suit. Michael and Eleanor watched them go. They didn't speak for a while. She pulled at the fringe on the rug and felt his eyes on her like fingers touching her.

'Merry said you were the clever one.'

She was the clever one; Merry the pretty one. That was how it had been. She turned her head from him, irritated.

'I don't know,' she said. 'That means nothing. I just like knowing things. I like reading.'

'What are you reading now?'

'I'm tempted to tell you that I'm reading *To the Lighthouse*, because that's the novel I love above any other. But it would be a lie. I'm reading *Rebecca*.'

'Is it good?'

'Yes. It's tremendous.'

'But you prefer Virginia Woolf?'

'I love Virginia Woolf.'

'She's a great snob.'

'I don't know. She stands for women.'

'Privileged women.'

'I'm not a privileged woman.'

'Are you not?'

'No. I am not.'

'You're a teacher,' he said.

'Yes.'

'In London?'

'The East End, near the docks.'

'Yes,' he said, as if she were simply confirming what he already knew. 'Do you like it?'

'Yes,' she said. 'I like it a great deal.'

'Why?'

Eleanor considered.

'I like making children *see*,' she said.

'See what?'

'Sometimes things hook them. Often it's just drill and things by rote, chanting out multiplication tables. But then suddenly they understand it. Not just the clever ones. Not just the ones who are the easiest to teach. There's a girl called Mary, very poor, with a snotty nose and nits in her hair, a lumbering creature who wears hand-me-down clothes and hardly talks and keeps to herself. But she loves poetry. You can see it, a light going on inside her. Suddenly seeing there's a larger world. That's what I like. And,' she added, 'I like knowing I'm good at what I do.'

'You're a good teacher?'

'Yes. Though I don't want to be a teacher for the rest of my life; there's so much else. But the point is that I like working. The others often moan about it; they want to be a rich man's wife – but I like earning my own wage, even though it's not much. I like living in a city, on my own, nobody telling me what to do or where to go or how to think. I like freedom. I need it.'

He lay back, his head on his hands.

'Everyone needs it.'

'Yes. But they don't have it. Women have never had it. It's our turn.'

She said it as though he might disagree, but he didn't. He smiled at her and said: 'Of course it is. We men have run things for long enough and look what a mess we've made.'

They were silent. She gazed at the white bodies in the green water and wondered why Gil and Emma were taking so long.

Then she asked, abruptly, 'Does your leg hurt?' although what she really wanted to know was what it had been like, being shot, perhaps thinking he was going to die in a strange country. What had he thought about? Had he known he was in history at last, not just a spectator on the sidelines?

'Not so much,' he said. He gave a smile that wasn't really a smile at all, more a way of holding seriousness at bay. 'It doesn't tell me when it's going to rain or snow. It's not become my conscience.'

Eleanor glanced sideways at him. 'Were you there long?'

'No; an embarrassingly short time.'

'Was it very terrible?'

'No, Eleanor.' He spoke her name deliberately, separating it out into syllables. 'For others, it was terrible. For the Spanish it is a tragedy. But as for me and my involvement, it was a farce.' His face hardened; his smile was almost a sneer. 'I'm not a hero, you know. You mustn't be thinking that.'

'I don't think I was.' She considered. 'I'm not sure I believe in heroes.'

'No?' He scrutinized her. 'That's good.'

'I like to be on an equal footing with people, not better or worse or higher or lower than them,' she said, not really understanding what she meant by that, interested by her words and promising herself to think about them.

This time the silence seemed to belong just to the two of them while outside of it, the bright sounds of the party continued.

'I'm coming to London soon,' he said at last. 'I've been idling in the country long enough. Can I find you there?'

The sentence had an odd construction. *Can I*, as in, am I able to? Or *can I*, meaning, do I have your permission? And the way he said it made it sound as though he was asking himself, not her, the question. Eleanor didn't reply, but ate another strawberry and said, 'What to do?'

'This and that. I don't have a trade, as your mother has probably told you. There are people I need to see. And after all, we're all just waiting.'

'For the war.'

'Of course. Out of the frying pan and into the fire for me.'

'Perhaps waiting's almost the worst,' she said.

'Oh, I don't think so. No. We should make the most of this waiting time we have, before it all begins.'

He made a gesture towards her, palms upwards; on his right hand she saw a white thick line snicker down from the thumb's base.

Eleanor looked at his hand and felt slightly sick. She glanced away, at the swimmers in the water, several of them now, pallid wavering underwater bodies like transparent fish beneath the green-filtered light. She sheltered her eyes with her hand and stared at them. Gil came and laid his clothes, neatly folded, beside her, then bent and kissed the top of her head lightly before striding to the bank. His towel was wrapped round his waist and he didn't remove it until the last moment, as if he were shy. It was the first time Eleanor had properly seen his body. He had lain naked beside her but she hadn't looked at him and anyway, it had been dark, the curtains drawn, her eyes mostly closed against the insistence of his gaze. Now he looked back towards her from the bank, like a boy needing permission, and she raised her hand. He slid himself into the flow.

'Can I?' Michael asked again, and she felt as if she were on a swing, at the top of its arc. Everything standing suspended and clear, before the world comes towards you again in a blurred whoosh. Then Merry was on them, with her friend Lily behind her. They looked like two summer flowers, with their fair hair and bright-coloured frocks.

'Come on!' they cried, and Michael let himself be led away.

Later, Eleanor let herself down into the water alone. Emma went home, hugging her and saying they would meet in London soon; she had found a job there. Gil lay back on the grass, his hands behind his head and his eyes half-closed. Merry and her friends were clustered on the bank. Merry had her head on Michael's shoulder, her blonde hair loose and almost dry. Her skin was pink; she looked very young.

Eleanor swam upstream, beyond the group, and lay on her back in the dusky silence. She closed her eyes and saw the pattern of leaves against her eyelids. She must not. No, she must not. Monstrous, unthinkable. She must not think it. Or feel it or even let the thought touch her body. She swam further up the river, against the tug of the water.

13

The following day, two young women arrived at the house. Peter heard the car, the doorbell ringing, the sound of voices in the hall. About half an hour later, there was a tap on the door and immediately it was pushed open and they came in. One was carrying a large mug with coffee slopping over its brim, and the other a slice of cake on a small plate, holding it in front of her like an offering.

'Peter?' They advanced into the room. 'Coffee?'

He got to his feet. He had been leafing through a bundle of letters sent from grateful patients to Gil.

'Yes,' he said. 'Thank you.' He thought he recognized the one with hair the colour of burnished conkers from the photos. She had the remains of freckles on the bridge of her nose and a wide, generous mouth. All the clothes she wore were loose and colourful and she had a bright bandana in her hair. The other one he didn't recognize – but then, she was obviously in disguise. Her hair was cut very short and dyed a violent red; her face was artificially white with smudged black eyeliner round her eyes, and piercings in her lip, her nose, her eyebrows, and a thick ridge of them in her earlobes. She was spikily thin; he could make out her pelvic bone under her man's suit trousers and her collarbone beneath her shirt. He tried to imagine what she would look like without her makeup and her rings, and found himself seeing a small, defenceless face, sweet and young and almost plain. They were both quite tall, like their grandmother, and had a rangy long-legged look that Peter associated, meaninglessly, with wealth and entitlement.

'Sorry.' The conker-haired one laughed. She had a lovely voice, low and clear. Eleanor's voice, he thought. 'I'm Rose, and this is Thea.'

'Esther's daughters,' said Thea. Her voice was husky. Smoker, he thought and suddenly longed for a cigarette. 'Her two youngest.'

'Of course.' He thought Rose must be a bit younger than him. Thea's age was impossible to guess; her face was blank as a pebble.

'You're becoming quite the expert on our family, I gather,' she said. He caught the whiff of patchouli oil and tobacco.

'I'm just putting things in order.'

'It's all right,' Rose said, in a kindly fashion, oddly maternal. 'We're all very grateful. I wanted to do it but Gran was insistent it should be someone from outside the family. I don't know why.'

'So what have you found?' Thea demanded. 'What skeletons in the closet?'

'Sorry to disappoint you, but nothing like that.'

'Oh surely. No one's irreproachable.' The way she

rolled out the words reminded Peter of Jonah's delivery: theatrical, ironic, self-mocking. Perhaps it was the Lee style. 'Everyone has secrets.'

'Not everyone has secrets they hide in filing cabinets,' Rose said reasonably. 'Most people's secrets are just in their heads.'

But Thea wandered off, picking up objects, turning them in her hands.

'Look, Rose,' she said. 'Do you remember this?' She held up a hexagonal brightly coloured shape, and shook it. It gave a surly rattle and she made a face. 'It's supposed to make a noise,' she said. 'It's meant to be tuneful.'

'What about these?' Rose had pulled two of the string puppets out of the box that Peter had put them in and was carefully untangling them before standing them on their weighted, lozenge-shaped feet and twitching them forward, articulated arms lifting and knees giving way with each step. Their round wooden heads with painted-on faces lolled as they clomped in tiny steps along the floorboards. 'Did we play with these?'

'I don't remember. Aren't they a bit creepy?'

'I'm going outside to have a cigarette,' said Peter.

'I'll come with you.' Thea rose eagerly, and the two of them went into the cool morning, thick and grey with the promise of rain. From where they stood, they could see Rose like a misty ghost on the other side of the glass, drifting among recovered objects of her childhood. Thea was a greedy smoker, sucking in so that her thin cheeks grew thinner, holding the smoke in her lungs and then exhaling slowly. Peter thought that there was something both bitter and childish about her.

'So. You're Gran's latest find,' she said at last, wreaths of smoke around her chalky face. It made him sound like an object that had been lying abandoned in one of those fusty antique shops, waiting for someone to pick up.

'Jonah recommended me.'

She dropped her cigarette on the ground and twisted the tip of her biker's boot on to it, as if she were killing a squirming cockroach rather than extinguishing a spark. Then she lit another one. All her movements were impatient, slightly jerky.

'It's odd that Gran is finally leaving here,' she said.

'It must be.'

'I don't come much any more. Not as much as I should. The countryside is boring, don't you think? But it feels like our childhood is being taken away. They used to have their flat in London of course, where their everyday life went on. Work and other adults and dinner parties and all Gran's political things. She used to take us on marches and demonstrations, you know. She insisted, the way other parents and grandparents insist on homework and proper nights' sleep. But this was away from all of that, and all of our lives. Far from politics and work.

A land of dreaming. We used to spend weeks at a time here. All the cousins.'

'Eight of you.'

'We'd play all day, down in those woods. Sometimes we went to the sea, of course, but often we just spent the day here. Dawn till dusk. We were one big roaming group. Our parents were sometimes here as well, of course, but we barely noticed them. Except Samuel – he was different, but then he didn't have children or responsibilities. I remember him once jumping across all those little box hedges there.' She pointed to hedges that were now tall and straggly. 'He was wearing a long coat that streamed out behind him and leaping like a racehorse. I've never forgotten that.'

'It sounds . . .'

She went on, as if he hadn't spoken, 'It didn't really matter what our other lives were like when we were here. Gran's so old now, like a relic or something, but I used to think that she and Grandpa Gil were like the king and queen in a fairy tale. When the next generation were having crises and weeping and fucking up their lives, they were steady and serene, even when Grandpa was dying. They were always so polite to each other, it was ridiculous. Sometimes I used to spy on them, to try and catch them out. I thought they must be pretending. But even when they were alone, or thought they were alone, they were respectful and kind. Perhaps they knew I was there all the time. Ear to the door. Mum says she never heard them argue. God. I can't get through a day without arguing with someone. Who will it be today? Rose probably. What about you?'

'Do I argue, you mean?' He thought for a moment. 'It has to matter a great deal and even then, I think I've learnt that you can never win an argument in a relationship. What does it mean to triumph over someone you love?'

'Oh.' Thea made a face. 'That's a bit virtuous. I love arguing. I can't stand it when the other person won't. It makes me spitting mad. Of course, I've not had many long-term relationships. Actually, I probably haven't had any. I definitely haven't had any. I have flings.'

'Do you?'

'Yes. Much more exciting. Grandpa's scattered there.' She nodded toward the hornbeam tree. 'We all came for the ceremony. Gran scattered his ashes and some of us read poems.'

'Did Eleanor read anything?'

'No. She's a very private person. I think there are lots of things she never says. She holds them inside herself. She's full of hiding places.'

For one moment, Peter thought about Eleanor's secret – though he still only had hold of the slippery edge of it yet.

'She is,' he said. 'But isn't everyone? We all have to have our secret selves.'

*

He didn't meet Eleanor during the day, though from his window he saw her walking slowly with Rose through the garden. She didn't have her stick, and was instead resting her hand on her grand-daughter's arm. The old woman looked frail and weary; her skin, thought Peter, was like paper just before it catches fire, brittle and crumpling. Her expression was sad and stern. Beside her, Rose bloomed; she was supple and smooth. Her pale cheeks glowed and her bright hair shone in the winter sun. She bent towards her grandmother, intent on her. Were they talking about how she would soon leave this place? He hated to think of Eleanor in a home, however well run it was. Sitting in one room, with all the belongings she could no longer see removed from her. Then she could only look back, at the long journey that had taken her to this resting place, this waiting room as she called it.

Now Rose had her arms around Eleanor's shoulders. Her copper locks were mingled with her grandmother's silver-white ones. Soon he would be gone and they would be like figures from a dream. He turned back to his work but his heart wasn't in it. He wanted to hear about Eleanor and Gil and this Michael from Leeds, who'd travelled on the Red Train to Spain. Peter had read several books about the Spanish Civil War. The war where poets drove ambulances and idealists lost hope and everyone betrayed everyone else. Poor Gil. How could solid kindness compete with such death-soaked glamour?

Thea and Rose, it turned out, were staying the night. He wouldn't talk to Eleanor alone, then, but he would have dinner with the three of them.

'Rose and Thea are cooking,' said Eleanor. 'I fancy that means Rose is cooking. I don't think Thea knows how. Though she used to love helping me in the kitchen when she was little.' Eleanor put her hand out flat, palm down, to indicate Thea's size.

He could smell garlic and chilli and also something sweet. Apples, cinnamon, the comfort of baking. He thought of the painting he'd seen in Amsterdam when he was there with Kaitlin. The woman pouring milk. Her yellow blouse and white kerchief, her strong hands holding and steadying the earthenware jug, the bread in its wicker basket and the white-washed walls in light that fell softly from a window that was only just in the picture. Her intense absorption in the task; her stillness and the flow of the milk. Kaitlin had stood beside him with her arms folded, gazing up. She was the Vermeer maid's antidote: restless, sharp-boned, dissatisfied, sexy. Very sexy. She had red nails and red lips and eyes that flicked from person to person, assessing, dismissing, desiring; she always knew when she was being looked at. She had taken him from the picture to a coffee house where they had smoked a joint so strong it had made his brain reel and his body melt and burn. He remembered the way Kaitlin had sat like the wick of a candle in the haze of blue smoke, hair dark golden, smile cruel and sweet.

'Peter!' Thea's voice ringing up the stairs. 'Time to eat!'

They had all changed for dinner. Thea wore a lurid purple tee-shirt, with a picture of a ladybird on it. There were words underneath, just large enough for Peter to read without seeming to stare at her flat breasts. 'More bird than lady.' Her bare arms were shockingly white and thin; her hands seemed too large; her boots too heavy for her skinny legs to lift. When she lifted a pile of plates to set on the table, her shirt rode up and Peter could see the edge of a tattoo on the small of her back. Rose had put on a moss-green shirt and tied her hair up. Her face, without make-up, was flushed from cooking. And Eleanor had unearthed a long blue dress, too big for her emaciated body and whose hem brushed the floor and sleeves came over her arthritic hands. She had looped a long bead necklace round her neck that chinked when she moved, and put on pink lipstick. She looked like a girl who'd been delving into a dressing-up box.

'Something smells good.'

'Rose has made us a three-course meal,' said Eleanor. 'We seem to be celebrating something – what is it?'

'Being here.'

'Being here. Yes. The final days.'

'Gran,' Rose said. 'We've talked about this. You know you have choices. You can live with Mum; she's all alone and lonely in a house that's too big for her, and she wants you to.'

'No. She doesn't. We would drive each other quite mad.'

'Or Quentin, or Leon.'

Why not Samuel, Peter wondered. Samuel who leapt over hedges. The one Eleanor worried about the most.

'No, my dear. Not with Quentin or Leon either. Or Samuel, for that matter,' she added as if responding to Peter's unasked question. 'I've always sworn never to let my children become my carers.' She set her hands before her on the table. 'I really would rather be dead.'

'But if people want to, then—'

'No.' Her voice was harsh.

Thea put a glass of wine in Peter's hand. He sipped it and looked at the soft fuzz of hair on the nape of Rose's neck.

'When I was young,' said Eleanor, 'I never thought much about food. I liked it, but I didn't like preparing it. My mother always did the cooking, and Merry and I just cleared the dishes, or I did and Merry frisked around, keeping us amused. Then when I was living in London, before I married, I used to eat at Lyon's tea houses or at the cheaper little restaurants. Sometimes I would just have a glass of milk and a roll with butter for my evening meal. It sufficed. Sometimes that is what I have now, when I am here alone, and then I can feel myself to be that young woman again. The past never removes itself to a distance, you know.'

There was a silence; she seemed to have stopped speaking.

'Then you taught yourself to cook after meeting Grandpa?' prompted Rose.

'Later,' said Eleanor, as if Rose hadn't spoken. 'Years later, I began to see how we all need ways of comforting ourselves and others. I used to have a certain contempt, or call it rage, for the way women darned socks and made biscuits and put flowers on the table, while the men were out in the world, making money or losing it, saving lives, getting killed or killing. Gil would come home having given men and women their faces and their identities back to them, and what had I done? Washed nappies and put plasters on grazes, cleaned the windows so that light could enter the house.'

'Sounds tedious,' said Thea. She kept hooking her lower lip between her teeth and then letting it go again.

'It probably does. It often was. I had a powerful need to be back in the world, working. But I often think of all the thousands and millions of women who've done the same, day after day and week after week, year by year. Tending. Making ends meet. Stirring the pot. Giving a rhythm and shape to the great mess of life and making it bearable. I was lucky; I was a teacher and an educationalist as well as a wife and mother. After all my children started school, I was no longer tied to the home. But even so, first and foremost, I was a wife and mother. Gil was a husband and father, none more devoted than he, but first and foremost, he was a doctor.'

She lifted her glass and swirled the wine in it gently.

'You girls are lucky,' she said. She turned towards Thea. 'It must be annoying to have an old woman to say that to you.' Thea gave a glittery smile of agreement. 'But however bad times are now, you have choices, even if your choice is to refuse, to say no. It doesn't necessarily make you happy, of course, and it can be very scary to be free. Intolerable even.' She took a sip of wine. 'I once saw Virginia Woolf, you know,' she said, as if it were a logical sequitur. 'In Hyde Park at dusk, walking alone in a grey suit. So fine, like a creature from a different world. I wanted to say something, but I was greatly in awe of her; she was almost the only person in the world I looked up to because in spite of her snobbery and her neuroses she was a noble woman and a writer whose sentences took my breath away, and so I just watched her going by. When she drowned herself, walking into the river with stones in her pockets, it was like another light going out on the horizon and the world became a little darker. Those were terrible times.'

'Gran was a heroine in the war,' said Thea cheerily.

'I was no such thing.' Eleanor's voice was sharp.

'I didn't know,' said Peter. There'd been nothing in the papers about it and for some reason he hadn't wondered about her experience of the war. He'd simply imagined her here, in this house, with horror happening far off.

'That's because it's completely untrue,' replied Eleanor. 'I did nothing at all. My girls were sent away to the country. They lodged with families. I remember the day I walked with them to the station and saw them on to the train. Some of them were quite alone – as young as six or seven and going off to some stranger. I can see their faces now, staring out from the windows. But I stayed behind. I married and had a child and waited for it all to end. Most of the time I was in the country with my mother, keeping Samuel safe. So you see, I was one of the lucky ones. There were many times I wished I was in London, helping, playing my part in the terrible drama. But once you're a mother, you can't follow your own wishes. I remained on the sidelines.'

'You sound bitter,' said Thea, rather pleased. 'I thought you were a pacifist. You wear a white poppy on Remembrance Day, don't you?'

'No, I don't.'

'Gran can be rather fierce, can't she?' Thea said to Peter.

'I was not a pacifist during that war. I believed it had to be fought.' She made a gesture, as though ending the discussion. 'Rose, what are we eating?'

'Fish. Do you like fish?' she asked, turning to Peter.

'Except skate.'

'Lucky it's not skate then,' said Thea. She managed to seem rude even when what she was saying was perfectly polite. There was a rowdy grimness about her tonight. Perhaps it was the wine that she was swigging back, or perhaps she'd taken something else as well. She prowled round the kitchen, picked up a cat and then put it down rather roughly, peered over Rose's shoulder, standing too close to her. Then she went outside for a smoke and returned in a more conciliatory mood.

They ate fish in a tomato and garlic marinade, then a soft wheel of cheese before the apple tart that Peter had smelt cooking. Thea barely ate anything. She kept dropping pieces of fish on to the floor for the cats – not surreptitiously but blatantly, wanting everyone to see. Her white face gleamed in the dim room. Eleanor ate slowly, delicately and surely spearing the food with her fork. Once a piece of fish dropped on to her lap and Peter saw the look of distress that crossed her face. Polly sat beside him and laid her soft muzzle reassuringly on his knee.

They talked about Eleanor's birthday. Samuel and Esther were going to be the main cooks. Leon and Quentin were providing the wine. Giselle would make a cake. Samuel would bring fireworks with him. He had always loved fireworks, said Eleanor, but he was not entirely to be trusted with them. They mustn't set the house on fire again now that it had a buyer. The whole family would arrive in time for the Friday evening and leave by Sunday afternoon, and during that time they would select the things of Eleanor's that they wanted to take with them. They would choose who was to have which paintings and which photographs; which books, china, silver; which of the jewellery that Eleanor no longer wore. Everything would be up for grabs. Her clothes ('though most of them are moth-worn,' she said, lifting up a fold of the blue fabric of her dress to demonstrate), Gil's beautiful suits, some of which were sixty years old but still wearable, and his many dozens of ties. Rose and Thea, it turned out, had been helping sort them all out that afternoon. The wine cellar would be emptied. On Monday a removal van would arrive for the furniture that would be put into storage. During the next week, several more of Eleanor's grandchildren would arrive to do their duty by the old woman, folding blankets and sheets, sorting crockery, climbing up into the attic to haul out old carpets and curtains that had hung in this house sixty years ago. What remained after they'd all left on the Sunday would be offered to whoever bought the house, or auctioned off after the contract of sale had been signed. Booksellers would come in on the Monday afternoon to take away any remaining volumes.

'I don't want any family feuds,' said Eleanor. 'No fierce, self-righteous, resentful quarrels over who's to get the grandfather clock or the dresser or the falling-apart book of nursery rhymes that everyone scribbled in when thcy were toddlers. No one saying or thinking that it's not fair.'

'Of course there won't be,' said Rose.

'Of course there will!' Thea brightened. 'It's never fair.'

'Don't be stupid.'

'Who's stupid? It's not the value of things, the financial value I mean. It's what they represent. That.' She pointed. 'That biscuit tin with the dented lid. I remember that from when I was tiny, and Mum says she remembers it from when she was a child.'

'It was my mother's; it must be well over a hundred years old.'

'There. I want that tin! Don't you, Rose?'

'No.'

'But there are things you want.'

'I don't care.'

'Of course you care. Gran's thin gold necklace that she always wears. Don't you want that?'

'Not if anyone else wants it.'

'I will be buried in it,' said Eleanor mildly.

'That seems a waste.'

'Does it?'

'Or that wedding photo of her and Grandpa Gil. Wouldn't you want that, Rose?'

'Of course I do, but no, not if it means falling out with everyone. Everything seems urgently important, and then a few weeks later you realize it doesn't matter.'

'Grandpa Gil's desk, with all those dinky little drawers. Everyone will want that! I can see Leon and Quentin coming to blows over it – though Quentin never comes to blows. He'll be forgiving and forbearing but sure as hell he won't give it up without a fight. I bet he gets it, in fact. People like him are very good at getting their own way while still seeming wounded and sacrificial. He'll make taking it seem like a favour to us all.'

'You make us all sound like vultures.'

'Yes! I guess Tamsin will want the hats. Marianne will want the cut glass. Giselle – hmm, let's see, Giselle will want Gran's old evening dresses and the tailored coats she wore in the forties and those lovely little button-up shoes she still has at the back of her wardrobe.'

'I am still here,' said Eleanor. 'I am still alive, you know. Ancient and blind, but still breathing.'

'Sorry.' Thea looked blithe.

'It's quite all right. In fact, it's rather a relief when

people are honest. So what do you want, Thea my dear?'

'Me? God, everything, nothing. I live in a tiny bed-sit and keep most of my clothes in a suitcase under the bed. What would I do with diamonds? Sell them for drugs? Joke, Gran!' she added hastily, although the expression on Eleanor's face hadn't changed. 'That was a joke.'

'I don't have any diamonds. I hate diamonds.'

'OK.' She drew a deep breath. 'Your moonstone ring and one of Grandpa Gil's top hats and his walking stick and that big copper bowl on the top of the piano that you put nuts in at Christmastime and the rocking chair!' She spoke so fast the words ran into each other.

'You have been thinking about it,' said Eleanor drily.

'And I would quite like that tin.'

'You shall have it. First, we must eat the crackers that are in it with this cheese. What about you, Rose – any requests?'

'Oh ho, this is going to be like that scene in Beauty and the Beast. After your wicked elder sister has asked for all sorts of greedy things, you're not going to ask for one red rose in honour of your name, are you, Rose?'

'No! I don't know what I want. I haven't thought about it.'

'I bet you have.'

'Stop it!' Her face flamed. 'I don't know why you're trying to pick an argument.'

'It's Thea's way of dealing with emotion,' Eleanor said. 'Isn't it, Thea?'

'Probably.' Thea cut a tiny slice of cheese and laid it on her plate. She didn't touch it after that. 'Will you give something to Peter, Gran? Some books, perhaps.'

'Of course, if he would like that.'

Peter thought of the purloined photographs in his room, in plain sight next to the bed so that if Rose or Thea happened to walk in they'd see them there. But of course they wouldn't walk in – though now he considered it, he wouldn't put it past Thea.

Who'd be young? thought Eleanor. And answered herself: she would.

From his room, Peter could hear the faint sounds of a piano being played; a thin, clear trickle of sound, like a stream making its way towards the sea. He pulled on jeans and an old flannel shirt and went downstairs to the living room and stepped inside. There was only a standard lamp lit, so the room was full of shadows and pockets of darkness. Eleanor sat at the piano, quite upright, her hands moving over the keys. The copper bowl that Thea wanted to inherit glowed above her. Peter wondered how her arthritic fingers could move so fluently. It was as if music released them from their crabbed stiffness.

He didn't say anything, but took a seat to one side. Eleanor played on. He didn't recognize the music, but it was plain and slow, full of repeating combinations of notes. At last, she lifted her hands from the keys and turned her head towards him.

'I didn't want to disturb you,' said Peter.

'You're not. It's nice to have you here. However tired I am, there are some nights when sleep will not come and then it's best not to lie in bed, with the hours of dread before one.'

'Hours of dread?'

'We all have them. Gil was the calmest man alive, and yet at three in the morning, oh dear. He used to call it the scuttle of crabs' claws.'

'What do you dread?'

'If I could name it, it would no longer be dread, just fear.'

'Is fear better then?'

'I think you can do battle with fear, whereas dread is more shapeless.'

'Does playing the piano help?'

'Things gradually drain away. But I find I am full of the past, which I blame on you, of course.'

14

On the train back to London after Merry's birthday
picnic, it started to rain, softly at first and then with a
violence that felt like relief, the heavy sky splitting
open and letting water splash over the parched lands.
Eleanor sat with her face to the window, staring out
at the fields and the woods that were pelted by rain.
Gil didn't press her. He said how much he had liked
meeting her family and made a few amiable remarks
about the day without needing a response. Then he
had brought out his book and Eleanor continued
looking through the streaming glass at the drowned
countryside, and then at London as it returned, with
its fumes and noise. The street lamps were just being
lit.

Gil insisted on a taxi, and then on getting out to
escort her to her front door. She didn't invite him in,
saying she was tired. She could feel the heat of the
day in her skin and her eyeballs throbbed. Gladys was
in the hall talking loudly to someone on the phone
and when she saw Eleanor she rolled her eyes and
made extravagant gestures at the mouthpiece, indi-
cating some lunatic at the other end.

In her room, Eleanor took off her hat and

loosened her hair. She stepped out of the green dress that she had liked so much that morning but that now seemed creased and stale, and pulled off her shoes. Her feet were sore. The rain stopped, and she opened the window so that the cool air slid in, filling the room with the noises of the street, and sat on the bed in her slip. The evening stretched out in front of her. Usually she loved to be alone, with a novel and a mug of tea. She never minded her own company, and sometimes had to force herself to make an effort and go out to meet friends, be sociable. One of the ways she treated herself was to eat out sometimes in the evening, sitting at a table by the window of the cheap restaurant a few minutes' walk from her rooms, eating an omelette or a lamb chop, drinking a single glass of wine. Occasionally people would try to strike up a conversation with her, sometimes trying it on of course, but often just feeling sorry for her – a young woman alone – but she politely rebuffed them.

She took delight in providing for herself. Most of the women she had met since arriving in London complained bitterly about their poverty, the struggle to make ends meet; her fellow teachers talked about finding a man who would take care of them. Teaching was the interim between growing up and getting married, having children of their own. The word 'spinster' was a comic insult, a thing to be feared. Eleanor didn't want to be taken care of; she wanted to take care of herself. She loved teaching, and she took pride in living within her means, finding the cheapest food and patching and mending clothes. She had always thought that she wanted freedom more than she wanted love. She loved Gil but she hadn't fallen for him, if falling meant losing one's head, one's heart, one's sense of self. She had remained intact and in a way that was Gil's attraction and strength. Apart from his kindliness, his steadiness, his adoration for her, he allowed her to be herself. Only during sex did he seem to want to absorb and obliterate her. Perhaps that was why she hadn't really enjoyed it: she was reluctant to let herself go. She wanted to belong to herself and not to anyone else.

But now she was in danger. She knew, as she sat on the side of the bed with the breeze blowing in from the evening outside, that her walls were crumbling. She was intensely aware of her physical self: her hot cheeks, the thickness in her throat and the looseness in her stomach, her throbbing head and heart. She almost felt sick, if feeling sick could be half-pleasurable, and she was restless but sluggish at the same time. Sitting there with a powerful sense of longing flowing and flooding through her, unable to move.

At last she rose. The water was cold because she'd forgotten to feed coins into the meter, so she just washed herself at the basin, and then put on her oldest clothes. She wanted to feel shapeless and comfy. Hidden, with no eyes on her. She stared at herself in the little mirror; her eyes glittered back at her and her face burned with a shame and excitement that she didn't want to see. She closed her eyes against herself, and pressed her forehead briefly to the glass, needing its cold solidity.

Picking up her jacket, she made her way down the stairs again, past Terence talking to himself in his room, and Gladys's closed door, out into the street. She walked briskly along the wet, gleaming streets to the restaurant she occasionally went to. It was shabby but good value, and she knew the women who worked there: the young one with a livid birthmark on her cheek, and her mother, who had a creased face and eyes the colour of wet sand. Eleanor ordered a mug of tea and a bun. Although she had only eaten a bit of a sandwich and some strawberries that day, she wasn't hungry, yet she needed something to settle and comfort her.

It was nearly empty, with just two cadaverous young men sitting in the shadows of the interior, leaning across a round table and talking in low voices like spies. Eleanor took her preferred place by the window, where she would watch the flow of life in the street outside. How she had come to love summer evenings in London, the hot stew of the day quite ebbed away and in its place air that was warm, clear, and still. Her mother hadn't wanted her to come to the city; she had begged Eleanor to find work closer to home, and she had rarely come to visit her daughter. She didn't like traffic and crowds, shrank from smoke-filled halls and pubs, was scared to walk at night past narrow alleyways and round dark corners where unknown dangers lurked. She always complained about the fog that left a dirty bloom on her skin and made her clothes unfit for wear after a single day. She didn't understand why Eleanor scrimped and saved in order to live in a poky bedsit in a loud, scary city of strangers and strangeness, rather than live in relative comfort with her family.

Eleanor drank her tea and took a few bites of the bun. Her heart was beginning to calm down and her hands no longer trembled. What had all that been about? she asked herself. Nothing. A sudden rush of turbulent longing had seized her but it would quickly recede. She needed to keep hold of herself until the danger had passed: work, read, walk through the park with Gil at her side, and remember what she most wanted from her life. She didn't want to throw herself away – the phrase rose unbidden into her mind and she considered it. It wasn't that she in any way believed, as her mother and Robert did, that young women squandered their value when they allowed themselves to have flings. (In her head she heard her mother's words hiss: 'No better than they should be . . . damaged goods.') She had read enough novels that talked about women's bloom being rubbed off if a man touched them, as if they were soft ripe peaches that could only be handled with delicacy or they would be blemished, but she had always felt scornful of such notions of female innocence and decorum. No. When she thought of throwing herself away, the image of precipitous descent came into her mind – hurtling down a fathomless cliff, disappearing from her own life. Love as self-extinction.

And anyway, it was out of the question. Of course it was. Merry had set her heart on this young man, and even if he didn't seem to have set his heart on her, Merry was her sister and she trusted Eleanor. She made up her mind that if Michael called on her, which of course he wouldn't, she would refuse to see him. When she met him next – and if he were to be Merry's beau (despite her best intentions, the thought sent a hot sizzle of jealousy searing through her) this would inevitably happen – she would be prepared and be armed against him. She would be friendly but cool. She imagined herself holding out a limp hand, offering a tepid smile and a brittle phrase, and then turning away. Soon enough, she wouldn't have to pretend.

Eleanor sipped at her cooling tea and turned her thoughts to Gil. Had anything changed? Of course it hadn't, although that afternoon, sitting on the train opposite him, she had wanted to escape him for a while, with such urgency it had made her feel dry-mouthed and desperate. She knew that Gil would ask her to marry him. Perhaps he would ask her soon, though war, like a creeping shadow, might hold him back. But if he did ask, what would she say? She imagined the scene: the tenderness and grateful delight on his face when she said yes; the way he would take her hands in both of his and press them and then gather her against his solid warmth, telling her that he would devote his life to making her happy. Then, the way his face would daze and numb and shut down if she said no. He wouldn't argue with her or be angry, but would accept her decision as just. He didn't think he was worthy of her.

Eleanor held these two faces in her mind. She had never liked anyone as much as she liked Gil; nor had she ever met anyone else who let her feel both cherished and free. Michael, he was just a quick hot flame that had leapt into life and would quickly die down again, melting back into grey ash. She finished her tea, gazed into the bottom of the mug as if she would find an answer there, set it down firmly on the table and for an instant closed her eyes. She felt sad and stern. She would say yes.

'Yes,' she said. 'Yes, I will.'

'Oh my darling. My most lovely Eleanor.' He stared at her, his face illuminated. 'You will?'

In the park where the sun poured down like honey

through the leaves and where birds sang. She could even see the blackbird in the tree above, throat pulsing rapidly as sound poured out of its sharp yellow beak.

'I will,' she said.

For a moment, she thought that Gil would cry, and was scared by his happiness. Ashamed. She took one of his hands and lifted it to her cheek, closed her eyes briefly so she wouldn't have to see the blaze of his joy.

'From the first moment, the very first second—' he began, then stopped and took her into his arms, kissing her lips, her eyelids, her neck. 'I'm happy,' he whispered. 'So happy.'

'I am too,' said Eleanor, and perhaps she was. She felt solemn and a bit shy.

Later, over dinner in a restaurant that was dark and slightly grand, with banquettes to sit on and rich red wine that made Eleanor's head feel heavy, they discussed their plans. Every so often, Gil would reach out and touch one of Eleanor's hands, as if to make sure this was real. He kept breaking off mid-sentence to stare at her and murmur endearments.

'Can I tell my mother?' he asked.

Eleanor felt a sudden spasm of panic at the thought of everything becoming public, and especially of Gil's mother hearing the news – how her tight face would pucker and become sour with barely suppressed disappointment. Later, she would probably want to talk about wedding presents and household duties, her life as Mrs Lee. Yet what was she expecting?

'Of course you can.'

'And you must tell yours. And Robert. I don't have to ask permission, do I? Or do I? Would they expect that?'

She laughed. 'Certainly not. Although they'd say yes.'

'Would they?'

'Of course! A handsome doctor – it's what my mother has dreamt of. I can't think the same is true of your mother.'

Gil laid his hand on her arm.

'She's scared of you.'

'I hardly think that can be true.'

'No. She is. She's too used to having me with her, and now she thinks you'll take me away from her. And of course you will. You already have.'

'Oh dear, that's sad.'

'That's life.'

'But still sad.'

'She'll be lonely. We won't live with her though.' He said it with a questioning note.

'No Gil. We won't.'

'Where will we live? Where would you like?'

'Oh, I haven't the slightest idea.'

Eleanor felt slightly dazed; her future was suddenly unscrolling before her. A house, a husband, a mother-in-law.

'And more importantly, when will it be?' he asked, looking at her over the rim of his glass.

'We've only just decided to get married. Shall we think about the date later?'

'I want to say it should be at once, but I think that we should wait until after the war.'

'But—'

'It will come soon. You know that, don't you?'

'I suppose so. It almost feels that people want it to come now.'

'But then it can't last long. Months only. It might be better to wait, my darling. And if anything should happen, then you'll be free.'

'You mean, if you should die.'

'Yes. But I won't die. I probably won't even go away. I'm a doctor, after all. I might be needed here.'

Eleanor thought of the young people who had gathered for Merry's birthday picnic just a few days ago, with their callow, innocent faces. How they'd bragged of their readiness for combat, looked forward to being heroes. How the young women – girls, really – had looked adoringly into their faces then. She shivered suddenly, and when Gil told her affectionately not to worry about him, couldn't tell him that she hadn't been thinking of him at all.

'Perhaps if we are going to wait, then we shouldn't tell anyone yet,' she said carefully.

'Oh?'

'We could have it as our secret, our private world, just for a few weeks more. Nobody can have opinions about us or interfere.'

'If that's what you want.'

'I think so, if you don't mind.'

'I don't mind anything any more. We know and that's all that matters.'

'Thank you.' She touched the side of his face. He had a stain on his tie and she saw he had done the buttons of his shirt up crookedly. She liked his absent-minded disregard for his appearance; she had never taken to carefully dressed, dapper men. There would always be an air of disarray about Gil, she thought – and she imagined them as old people, sitting together over a meal like this, with all their years behind them, talking about the voyage they had made together. It made her feel strange, washed through by emotions she couldn't recognize or name.

He took her back to her door but didn't come in. It was that time of the month, she told him, which was true. He smoothed her hair back from her lifted face and told her that he would never forget this day as long as he lived.

Because it was a secret, Eleanor didn't want a ring, but on the following Saturday she and Gil walked to Hatton Garden, home of goldsmiths and makers and menders of clocks and watches. In a little shop on the corner, he bought her a gold chain – so thin you could barely notice it against her skin.

'I wear it still,' Eleanor said to Peter in a voice that was soft and cracked with tiredness. She pulled at the neck on her blue dress and he saw the faintest glimmer. 'I never take it off, except once when the catch broke and I had to have it mended. I suppose, as I told Thea, that they will bury me with it. That would be right.'

With difficulty she rose from her seat and Peter came forward and took the crook of her elbow to guide her.

'I suppose I'm telling you a love story,' she said as they left the room linked together. 'And I loved Gil.'

Instead of going upstairs to her room, she insisted on going into the kitchen. She was very cold and needed a warm drink. Peter made her herbal tea in a big cup that she wrapped her jumbled fingers around, sighing as the steam rose into her face. He took the shawl that was lying on the old sofa where the cats usually slept and wrapped it round her shoulders, feeling the sharpness of her bones.

'Now I've begun,' she said, 'how can I stop?'

15

Eleanor Wright came out of the school door. She was tired after a long day and was thinking about how she would have a boiled egg for supper and then an early night with a novel. To save money, she had not taken a bus that morning but had walked to work; now her feet were hurting in their cheap black shoes. She saw that the cuffs of her white blouse were slightly grubby, even though she'd put it on clean that morning, and there was a ladder in her stockings. She would mend it this evening and if there was hot water she would wash her hair. Her skin was damp in the heat. She allowed herself to think nostalgically of the countryside, with its soft air; the mild, clean wind blowing through the branches of the old plum tree.

She started to cross the road, but then stopped because she had seen a figure on the other side, leaning against a lamppost. She raised her hand to protect her eyes from the glare of the sun, which was turning people into cut-out shapes. Yet although she couldn't make out his face, she knew that it was him. A horn blared; someone shouted at her. She tried to keep her pace steady and her expression blank as she made her way on to the other pavement, though her bones felt rubbery.

'Hello,' he said, straightening himself up from the lamppost and coming towards her. She saw he had on the same suit as he had worn on the picnic, and that it was old and worn. He wasn't wearing his public smile but was grave and quiet. His face was thinner than she remembered. 'I've been waiting hours!'

'Why are you here at all?'

'To see you,' he answered, not perturbed by her curtness.

'I haven't got time. I'm going to meet friends.'

'Perhaps I could walk with you?'

'I don't think so.' Was that her voice, so clipped and cold?

He stared at her. 'Very well,' he said. 'I've brought you something.'

She saw that he had a bag slung off one shoulder.

'What?'

'Some books.'

'For me?'

'You said you liked reading.'

'I do – but you shouldn't have gone to the trouble.'

'Here.' He was feeling in the bag. '*Grapes of Wrath.* Have you read it?'

'No.'

'And *Letters from Iceland.* I think you'll be bowled over. And also,' he pulled out the third battered volume. '*Homage to Catalonia.* It's about Spain.'

'I know. Are they your books?'

'Yes.'

'I can't take them.'

'Borrow them.'

'When will I give them back?'

'When you've read them,' he replied reasonably. 'Why can't I walk with you?'

'It's just not a good idea.'

'Why?'

'Because it isn't.'

'Are you really going to meet friends?'

'That's not your business.'

'I would like to see you again.'

'No.'

'You don't want to see me?'

'No. It was very kind of you to bring me these books—'

'Not kind. An excuse. Rather a feeble one,' he added ruefully.

'Exactly. That's why I can't see you.'

'Is it because of Merry?'

'I can't see you,' she repeated. She was walking a thin line; she knew she mustn't deviate from it for a second.

'Here.' He pushed the books into her hands. 'I'll let you go now.'

'That's best.' Disappointment tightened her throat.

'But I'll see you again soon.'

*

And there he was the following day, leaning against the same wall, wearing the same shabby suit.

'No excuse this time,' he said, showing his empty hands.

She walked past him.

That evening, she was especially affectionate to Gil. She told herself how glad she was to be marrying him, and she was. She pushed the three books under her bed, where she couldn't see them. She lay awake, hour after hour, her open eyes burning with fatigue in the darkness. She was sick with longing. Her body was soft and boneless and she imagined him touching her. She imagined herself letting him.

And the next day, Friday, he was there once more. She walked by on the other side of the road. She tried not to look at him, though it took all the will she could muster not to turn to see if he was following her. At the corner she looked back and he was gone. She made herself angry with him; fury made her body springy. He had no business to be hanging around outside her school, not taking no for an answer.

One day, she told herself as she walked stiffly away, her spine rigid with determination and her heart clattering, one day very soon, she would be beyond this and the terrible desire that chewed at her stomach and turned her legs watery would have evaporated. Then she would be returned to what was real: Gil, her work, a sense of a bounded and controlled self. She just had to keep hold of herself. She mustn't let go.

She had agreed to spend the following day with Gil, and that evening, she didn't know what to do with herself. She washed her clothes, taking extra time over the task. She drew a bath and lay in the water until it turned tepid. She tidied her rooms, although they were already tidy. She tried to read, but found that she had taken nothing in. Once, she drew out the books from under her bed and stared at them, then pushed them roughly out of sight again. Then there was a hammering at her door and her heart jolted. She sprang to her feet, arranging her hair with fumbling hands. Surely it was him. And for an instant she allowed pleasure to run through her.

But it was Gladys, who was telling her someone was on the phone.

'Did he give a name?'

'Not a he. A young lady. Mary, I think?'

It was Merry. She was speaking from a neighbour's house – they didn't have a telephone yet – and she was planning to come to London the following day to visit Eleanor. On a whim, she said: a day out with her big sister. Would that be all right?

'Of course,' said Eleanor, trying for the right tone and sounding too bright and emphatic. 'I mean, I'm seeing Gil tomorrow, but I know he'd be pleased if you were there.'

'I don't want to be in the way.'

'You wouldn't be in the way.'

'If you're sure.'

'I am. Is everything all right?'

'What do you mean? Why shouldn't it be all right?' Merry's voice was sharp.

'No reason.'

'Everything is good, thank you. I just thought it would be nice to pay you a visit. See the sights.' She gave a tight giggle.

'Lovely,' said Eleanor. Her hand was clutching the telephone too tightly. 'We'll have fun.'

Eleanor met Merry at the station. She was wearing a pale blue suit made of cheap material, whose skirt was tight enough to make her steps small and constrained. Eleanor could see the faint line at the hem where she'd taken it down an inch or so. She had tied her hair up in a chignon bun that must have taken her ages, and put on bright red lipstick – there was a tiny fleck of it on her small white teeth – and looked absurdly young, like a child dressing up in adult's clothing. She had a pair of new kid gloves, probably one of her birthday presents, which she kept pulling on then easing off again; the locket that Eleanor had given her hung around her neck. The day was already warm and there were slight beads of perspiration on her forehead. When they hugged, Eleanor could smell lavender and sweat. Merry was brightly nervous, obviously feeling out of place in the big city. But so pretty, thought Eleanor, looking at her as they crossed the road together: her heart-shaped face and her delicate features, her shining sweep of hair and clear blue eyes. And the way she lifted her eyes trustingly to one, the way she smiled so that a dimple appeared in her smooth cheek.

'So how are you?' she asked once they'd found a seat in the Lyon's bar near the station, where Gil would meet them, and ordered a pot of tea.

'Very well,' said Merry promptly. 'Don't I look well to you?'

'You look lovely,' said Eleanor. 'You always do.'

'But you look a bit pasty and tired, Ellie, if you don't mind me saying,' said Merry.

'Do I?'

'Yes. There are shadows under your eyes.'

Eleanor put a hand to her face, as if to shield it from Merry's scrutiny.

'And you look a bit thin. Have you been ill?'

'Not at all. I haven't been sleeping well. Perhaps it's the heat.'

'Hmm.' Merry put her head on one side. 'You don't want to get scrawny.'

Eleanor was surprised by the note of spite in Merry's voice, but she didn't let her face show it.

'You're right, I don't,' she said mildly.

'Gil wouldn't approve.'

'I don't think I'm trying to win Gil's approval.'

'Oh?' Delicately arched eyebrows. 'How is Gil, anyway?'

'Fine.'

And then there he was, pushing through the door carrying a hamper, one shirtsleeve rolled up and the other not, hot and beaming. He came over and kissed Eleanor on the cheek and then held out a hand to Merry.

'Hello,' he said pleasantly. 'How nice this is.'

Merry gazed up at him, that dimple in her cheek, those wide eyes, the red lips curving.

'Yes,' she said. 'Yes it is nice. I am so glad I can meet you properly at last. Eleanor has told me so much about you.'

'Really?' said Gil, delighted.

'No,' said Eleanor. 'I haven't.'

'Oh Ellie,' said Merry, and she gave her rippling laugh, throwing her head back and her white throat pulsing. 'She was always like this.'

'Like what?'

'Contrary,' said Merry.

They went to the park and Gil laid out the blanket and assembled his picnic, bashfully proud of himself. The sky was blue and the park was thronged with people. They ate Gil's sandwiches and the hard-boiled eggs while a band played on the bandstand, and a crocodile of little children went by, led by a stern woman in a long black coat.

'This is nice,' said Merry, licking her fingers.

'Not as grand as your picnic.' Gil put a cherry into his mouth and lay back. 'That was a happy occasion.'

'Did you like it?'

'Of course.'

She turned to her sister. 'And did you, Eleanor?'

'I did.'

'I thought so.'

'You were lucky with the weather.'

'Yes. Who did you talk to?'

'Oh. Well, Emma mostly. And Lily Glover, and Clive Baines a bit. Gil of course.'

'And Michael.'

'Yes, that's right.'

'What did you talk about?'

'I can't remember. I told him a bit about teaching, I think.'

'Did he mention me?'

'I don't know. Maybe.'

Gil tipped his hat over his eyes.

'What did you think of him?'

'He seemed nice,' said Eleanor coolly.

'Nice. Is that all?'

'It was a brief conversation.'

'Have you seen him since?'

'What!'

'He said he was going to London. I thought you might have seen him.'

Eleanor couldn't bring herself to tell an outright lie. 'Why on earth would you think that?' she asked instead.

'Just a thought.'

'London's a big city, Merry. You don't simply bump into people.'

'I know that.'

'I don't even know his last name. I know nothing about him.'

'Do you remember what I said to you the night before the picnic?'

'Which bit?'

'I said that I usually get what I want.' She smiled at her sister and for a moment Eleanor felt almost frightened at the harsh expression on her delicate little face. 'I won't let anything stand in my way.'

'Yes, I remember you saying that.' She hesitated, glancing over at Gil's motionless form, and then added, 'It made me anxious for you.'

'Why?' Her high trickle of laughter.

'Because no one can always have what they want. Life isn't like that.'

'My life is. It always has been.'

'I don't want you to get hurt.'

Merry gave her a thin twisting of the lips.

'If he doesn't feel the same way . . .' suggested Eleanor. She remembered his face, his piercing gaze, the way he looked at her, and her throat thickened.

'Why would you even say that?'

'I'm just saying *if*.'

Gil stirred and lifted this hat off his face. His hair was damp with sweat. He sat up and started putting the picnic things back in the hamper.

'It's time to get moving,' he said. 'I've a busy schedule planned for you, Merry, before you get on your train home!'

After Merry had left, Eleanor and Gil went to a show with Emma and her new boyfriend, Anthony, who was trying to make his way as a painter and who had a deliberately louche air about him. On the Sunday, they had dinner with Gil's mother, who was making an effort to be civil. Gil took Eleanor home and at the door he put his arms around her and kissed her and told her that he was the luckiest man in the world. She stood in the safe circle of his embrace and tried not to think of Merry's vivacious, wretched face.

16

On Monday afternoon, Eleanor came out of school and looked across the road. For a moment she felt that someone was squeezing her guts. There was no one there. So he had given up, finally taken her at her word. She should be relieved. It was over.

'It's over,' she whispered to herself softly, testing out the words. But of course, it had never begun. Merry had no need to fear any more; she herself had no need. Nothing had happened, and nobody would ever know what she had felt, what cracks had opened beneath her feet. She stood quite still, her face blank, and she didn't know what to do with herself. It seemed impossible simply to walk back to her rooms and begin the dreary round of her evening again. Work, wash her stockings and undergarments, prepare a simple supper, sit by the window. Gil would call and she would tell him about her day and he would call her 'darling' and 'my love'. She would hear Terence's cough in the room beneath.

A hand touched her on the shoulder from behind and she swung round.

'Michael!' she said, and they both heard the rush of happiness in her voice.

'Hello.' He smiled at her with great sweetness. She felt she had never been smiled at like that before – as if he were looking through all the layers of her, all her crossness and stubbornness and fear.

'You shouldn't be here.' It was her final effort. Her voice came out cracked, as though she had been running. 'You have to leave now. I'm going to marry Gil.'

Michael looked at her for a few seconds without speaking. His brow was creased in thought. If he had pretended not to know why she spoke with such vehemence or announced her engagement so abruptly, like her last defence against him, he would have put her out of danger. She could have turned on her heel and left him there. But he didn't. He just stared at her and then said, 'Shall we walk a bit, then?'

And she nodded and they started down the road together, in no particular direction, not touching or looking at each other, but Eleanor could feel his body close to hers. It was as though electric currents were crackling down her arms. She looked straight ahead of her, at the blur of the ordinary street, but knew whenever he turned his eyes on her as surely as if he had touched her. She thought her legs might not be firm enough to carry the weight of her. She tried to remember the resolution she had made, sitting over her mug of tea and bun, but it seemed too long ago and the woman she'd been then felt far off and unreal. She attempted to focus on the route they were walking, seeing its poverty through Michael's eyes. They went past Cable Street and the scene of the great confrontation, when the marchers had been turned back. She thought of saying something about it to Michael, how she'd been there, on the edge of history, but her throat felt thick and the foolish words stuck like bones. A man pushing his bike went past in the other direction and Eleanor recognized him as the father of one of her pupils. He lifted his hat and she nodded at him, tried to smile.

She thought: something is going to happen to me now. But she had a choice. She could turn aside from this and if she did not, then she would be responsible. She imagined herself stopping and telling Michael that she was going to go home this minute and that she didn't want to see him again. She could use a firm, cool voice to repel him; she heard it in her head, imagined the polite and stony expression she would have. *Leave me, if you please.* This time he would listen. It would be irrevocable. Yet still they walked on against the flow of the crowd, under a silver sky. Goosebumps pricked her arms.

'Here,' he said, and they turned off the road and into the grounds of a handsome white church that Eleanor had often passed by but never before entered. The noise of the world receded. The graveyard was large and laid out like a public park. There were rows of gravestones, some mossy and tipping in all directions, and others more recent, with fresh flowers in sunken vases at their base. An old woman was laying a bunch of violets wrapped in a large green leaf on a plot that was tiny. It must be a child, thought Eleanor. Perhaps a child who had died decades ago and this old woman was the mother who still came, year after year, to remember long after everyone else had forgotten. Her heart seemed too large in her chest. She felt elated, very scared. She could run away, she thought. She must. Before it was too late. Before she did something that she knew she would live to regret. One day, she would hate herself. Her body was sluggish and her skin felt too tender, as it had done last year when she had lain in bed for weeks with influenza.

Michael stopped at last by an ancient, knobbly quince tree with droopy leaves and the last of its floppy pink blossoms. She saw in the distance the old woman leave the churchyard, walking slowly with her shoulders stooped as if she were carrying a burden on her back.

'Eleanor,' he began.

'I shouldn't be here.' She forced herself to speak, not looking at him but away, towards the massive walls of the church and its narrow windows. 'I told you. I'm going to marry Gil.'

'Please look at me.'

'And there's Merry.'

'Please look at me.' She lifted her eyes and met his; he stared at her, into her. 'If you tell me to go, I will.'

'Then go.' The words came low and guttural. She

took a step towards him as she spoke and he didn't move. 'Go. Please go. Or there is no way back.' She stood before him and lifted a hand as if to touch him, or strike him, but then dropped it. 'Oh God,' she said in a whisper. 'Why did you come?'

'I had to.' She saw him swallow. 'Please.'

Who moved first; who kissed whom? Whose cry of pleasure is that? How can we ever let go? Now that we've started, how will we stop? What have we done?

'Are you all right?' asked Peter, concerned. Eleanor had suddenly stopped talking, breaking off in the middle of a sentence and putting her hand against her neck, holding the tiny sliver of gold. Her face was pale and her breath shallow.

'Yes,' she managed. 'But perhaps I have stayed up beyond my strength. Can you can help me upstairs?'

'Of course. Take my arm. Here.'

She tottered on her feet, and hung off him, meagre as a bag of twigs and her legs sliding under her. They made it to the stairs and he half-carried her to her bedroom, letting her gently down on to the bed where she sat curved over herself. He could see the ridge of her spine.

'Are you ill? Shall I call the emergency services?'

'Certainly not. I'm simply tired.'

'What can I do?'

'Well, I'm not going to let you undress me,' she

replied, trying to make light of it. 'Perhaps you could get Rose.'

'Rose. Yes. Don't move.'

He ran up the corridor, his feet banging in the silence, and hammered at the door of the room he knew Rose was in. There was no response, so he banged again and heard a sleepy enquiry. He opened the door. In the light that came in from the hall, he could make her out as she sat up, rubbing her eyes, her hair in a mussed tangle round her face.

'What?' she said, her voice thick with sleep.

'It's Eleanor. She'd like your help.'

'Eleanor?' She was out of bed in a flash. She was wearing pyjama bottoms and an old tee-shirt. 'Is she ill?'

'She says she's just tired.'

'Tired? Why is she awake? What time is it?'

'We were talking. I don't know what time it is.'

Rose looked at her mobile by the side of her bed. 'It's half-past three,' she said.

'I didn't know.'

He followed her into Eleanor's room. She was sitting where he had left her, but was looking quite peaceful. Her hands were in her lap.

'Gran?'

'I'm sorry to wake you. You must think me very selfish. I'm feeling better.'

'You should have been in bed hours ago. Why on earth are you still up?'

'I wanted to be up.' There was a touch of asperity in her voice. 'I was hoping you could help me off with my clothes.'

'Of course.'

'Peter! Is that you there?'

'Yes.'

'Well, go away. I don't want you here to watch me undress.'

'Sorry. Sleep well. I didn't mean to keep you up.'

'You didn't keep me up. I kept myself.'

'Sweet dreams,' he said and she raised one hand to him.

Rose left her and Eleanor lay in her bed, with the heavy pile of duvets over the top of her. She could still feel the press of Rose's lips on her cheek. Her limbs ached with such tiredness that she couldn't believe she would ever be free of it. Her bones were brittle and sore. Her stomach hurt and her throat felt as though something was lodged in it. There was a faint drumming in her head. Her cotton nightgown scraped at her skin like wire. It is tough being old, she thought, and then she thought: you have to be tough to be old. Or perhaps it's the other way round and you have to be old to be tough. The young have no idea. She closed her unseeing eyes. She thought about being young again, when her limbs were pliant and her body had none of the jagged edges and chipped fragility it had now. She thought about running down a hill, about being on a bicycle with the wind in her hair, about swimming in the river, in the sea. One by one, you lose the things you hold most dear. She would never again lie in a graveyard in the late-afternoon sunlight with that beloved, remembered face above hers, staring down at her, and life streaming through her.

She felt her old, battered, worn-out body relax in the warmth of her bed, and the sharp press of individual thoughts blur. She was in the land between wakefulness and sleep where time dissolves and the dead can return to life once more.

Be with me now. When the quince tree is in blossom, its flowers loose, its petals unfurled, that is me, that is me opening at last. The scatter of the sun through its young leaves, tumbling in petals of light on the ground. Blades of grass against tender flesh. The imprint of swallows against a sky that never stops. Appalling blue. Your eyes and I fall upwards, drowning. Do not go. Touch me now. Face, neck, breasts. Your breath, honey and spice. I taste your words, I feel your pain, touch your happiness with my fingertips. Whose skin is this, whose desire? Where do I begin and end? I hurt with joy. I have traded my entire life for this moment. I put everything in the scales but you, and you outweighed them all. Do not go. Why did you ever go?

They say that time is a river, stopping for no one, spilling its dams, sweeping everyone up in its currents. Sometimes deep and fast and clear; sometimes widening, slowing, so you can no longer see that it's moving at all. But still it is implacable. And they say that time is a one-way journey; you set off in a jostling, hopeful crowd, but it thins as you travel, and at last you realize you're alone. You've been alone all the time. You gather up burdens as you go, memories you have to carry and sins you can't dislodge, but you can't stop. You can't go back.

But they are wrong. Time is no longer a river or a lonely road; it is a sea inside me. The ebb and the flow, the tug of the cold moon that shines on its waters. Knowledge drops away; innocence returns; hope freshens. It is spring. I did not know what a long journey it would be to come home.

17

The next morning, Eleanor was not up when Peter went downstairs in his running things, and Thea and Rose were getting ready to leave. Tiredness made him cold. He put on layers of mismatched clothing, but however he bulked himself out he couldn't get warm. Winter was coming; winter had arrived. The wind blowing in from the sea had a bite to it; it gusted down the chimneys and entered the rooms. The trees were almost bare. The ground was no longer muddily soft but carved in hard grooves; leaves were crisp on the ground and the light was thin and clear. Today he could understand why Eleanor had to leave this chilly, remote place. She needed to be in the flow of the world, surrounded by the warmth and noise of other people's lives. Here she was like the last person aboard an abandoned old ship, living amid the memories of its crowded past.

After his run and shower, he went into the junk room and looked around at all the boxes and bags and piles of books and files. On an impulse, he went to the corner of the room where the paperback books were stacked in piles ready for the family to inspect them. He scanned their spines and at last found the one he was looking for. *Homage to Catalonia*. The jacket was disintegrating and some of the pages loose. No one was going to want it; they'd just put it in the skip. He put it to one side. Thea and Rose left, looking in to say a brief goodbye, and the house sunk into a silence, save for the wind against the rattling panes. But then he heard Eleanor moving around upstairs, and the rattle of pans and china in the kitchen. There was a loud voice talking dramatically: either the radio or an audio book that kept her company through all the days she was alone here. He saw the home help's car draw up, which meant that soon there would be a fire in the living room again, more food in the depleted fridge. Perhaps she would make one of her warming soups before she left.

He fidgeted through the day. Most of what was left was the miscellaneous debris, the papers and letters and bits and pieces of Eleanor's life that he'd been unable to find a category for. He considered scooping them all up and throwing them into a bag. What did it matter if a faded photograph of a woman in a severe skirt disappeared, or this group portrait taken somewhere up a mountain long ago, with its participants in breeches, carrying walking sticks was chucked carelessly away? Who would lay claim to them now? Yet there was something rather sad in the thought that people could simply disappear from memory like that: that this woman with her prudent mouth and her meticulous bun, this quaint walking party that looked as though the *Titanic* had never sunk, should be thrown on to the bonfire without even the attempt to identify them. He put them to one side, and rifled through assorted certificates: a first-aid course successfully undertaken, a swimming trial completed, a driving test passed, a stray MOT from twenty-two years ago, a parking fine, an eye test, a repeat prescription, a long-defunct pension policy, household insurance, a guarantee for a sit-on lawn-mower dating back to 1977 and for a gas-fired boiler, child benefit forms, stray bank statements from long ago. Eleanor had told Peter to put anything financial in a pile to be handed over to Leon and he dutifully added these to the box in front of him.

He felt dazed and appalled at the amount of bureaucracy involved in a life, and this was only looking at its last traces. He rarely opened letters from the bank or the student loan company, had long ago lost his paper driving licence and his National Insurance number; his mind closed down at the thought of a savings account (irrelevant since he had no money to save), and it occurred to him now that his passport was probably about to run out or had already done so. Just the idea of filling out that form and making sure the writing fitted into the boxes, that his photograph was correct, made him feel itchy. He couldn't begin to imagine himself in a life where he had a mortgage, a car, life insurance (or was it life assurance?), ISAs – he didn't know what ISAs were, in fact, and couldn't guess at what the acronym stood for, just had a vague sense that they were what sensible people invested in. They had portfolios. Stocks and shares. They followed the FTSE 100 index – what did that even mean? It was just a phrase he heard on Radio Four that made him think of jagged graphs and men in suits, shouting and waving their hands in the air like football hooligans. When his grandmother had died, she had left him £2,000. He had spent it at once, taking Kaitlin out for a ludicrously expensive meal where he had insisted, in spite of her giggling protestations, on buying a bottle of wine that cost about a pound a mouthful, and then blowing the rest on his bike. His bike was the only one of his possessions that he loved. It didn't need a tax disc, or insurance, he didn't need to pass a test to ride it, it came with no strings attached and gave him freedom.

In the early evening, when it was already quite dark, Eleanor came to him and told him she was waiting for him in the living room. The fire had been burning there most of the day and Leon had put on two large logs before he left, which were blazing in the grate, giving out substantial heat. Peter took off his jersey first and then, surreptitiously, his odd socks.

Eleanor told him to pour them both a glass of wine and they sat awhile in silence, with the companionable crackle of the fire and outside the windy darkness. The dog lay stretched between them, twitching in her sleep.

'I'll always remember this,' Peter said at last.

'That sounds rather elegiac.'

'You've been kind to me.'

'Nonsense. You've kept me company during these last days here and I've liked having you here.' She paused for a moment. 'I've liked talking to you,' she continued. 'Although to be honest I sometimes think it isn't you that I'm talking to.'

'Then to whom?'

'Ghosts. Ghosts of the past. Michael. Gil. Myself – I mean the self that I used to be. Dead selves. When you're old, time ceases to have the same meaning that it has when you are young, when it seems to run in one direction. Sometimes it feels that I'm not remembering so much as returning. That when I tell you what happened, I find myself back there, in those terrible days. Of course, all the time, I know who I am as well: old Eleanor Lee, sitting by the fire and recalling the young and foolish person she once was, like recalling a stranger. Can you drive?'

'What?' He was taken aback by the question.

'Do you have a driving licence?'

'Yes.'

'Good. I don't know why I didn't think about it before. There's an old car in the garage here. It's still insured. Sometimes the grandchildren use it and sometimes my helpers need it to run errands.'

'But why do you want me to drive it?'

'I thought we could go on a trip.'

'A trip?'

'Must you repeat everything with that note of panic in your voice?'

'Sorry. But what trip?'

'To see my sister.'

'Merry.'

'Yes.'

'Is it far?'

'About fifty miles.'

'I'm not actually sure if that's a good idea, you know. I do have a driving licence but I haven't driven for about three years, and even then I wasn't a particularly good driver. I passed on my third attempt and that was probably because he had to fill some quota.'

'You'll be fine.'

'I don't know, Eleanor. You haven't seen me driving.'

'We'll leave at about nine and even if you crawl along, we can be there before eleven. We can have a pub lunch on the way back. It's been ages since I had a pub lunch. Gil and I used to have them often, on our travels. My children seem always to take me to stuffy restaurants or respectable teashops. I can have gammon and chips and treacle tart. And beer.'

'What about my work?'

'What about it? You're nearly finished, aren't you?'

'Kind of.'

'There are no more secrets there, Peter. You've found what I needed you to find. There's nothing left to give me away.'

18

Eleanor walked back to her bedsit in a daze. She knew that she should feel guilty. And certainly guilt came down on her in curling, cresting waves, so that she could barely put one foot in front of the other and several times had to stop. At the same time she had to catch her breath not only from horror but from an exultation that rushed through her like a clean, strong wind. And then she was lifted up by a joy so tremendous and a delight so physical that she was borne forward by it, filled with a vigour that she had never experienced before. It seemed that there was some battle raging inside her and she couldn't understand how her body could contain it, and how nobody passing her by could see it. How had she never known? How had nobody ever warned her? She tried to put the scene from her and simply walk, one foot in front of the other, fast enough to feel the ache in her calves, but she couldn't prevent herself from going over what had happened. Her skin burned from his stubble and her lips were sore. Her flesh pulsed. Her stomach churned. Their time in the graveyard had been far more important than actual sex with Gil had been, labouring away in the darkness of her room. With Michael, she had abandoned herself – and a hot flush spread over her at the memory of how she had pressed her body against his and made queer whimpers and frightened, hoarse moans that were like no sounds she had ever uttered before, and how his fingers had opened up pleasure in her, sending desire gushing through her. For a few minutes, she would have done anything, yes anything, to assuage that agony of wanting. Like an animal, she thought now. If that old lady had returned, she couldn't have stopped kissing him, holding him against her, arching herself against him and letting him touch her, feel her. Oh God.

She paused for a moment and leant against the wall, trying to regain her composure. Her hair had come half-undone and when she put up a hand to rearrange it she found that there were blades of grass in it. What must she look like? She pulled her compact mirror from her bag and opened it. Her face stared at her, pale with glittering eyes and red-rubbed lips. She saw that there was a small bruise on her neck and buttoned her shirt higher to conceal it. She didn't look like herself, not the self she usually presented to the world, so in control. Her boundaries were dissolving; her surface was rupturing. His tobacco-taste was in her mouth. Everything she kept locked away and safe was spilling out. She took a few deep breaths and told herself in her mother's voice to pull herself together. Then she straightened her hair and powdered her nose. But still, she felt sure that anyone who saw her must guess. Gil would guess. But no, Gil was one of the people who would never guess, because he trusted her and was sure of her love for him. He knew, or thought he knew, that once she had pledged herself, she would always keep her word. He didn't doubt his own love and he didn't doubt hers. She had told him, not many days after returning from Merry's picnic, that she was on her monthlies, but that in any case she thought they should wait before they had sex again until after they married. She didn't feel safe with it even though he had been careful, she had explained, and also she didn't really like the secrecy of the thing, creeping past Gladys's and then Terence's doors, scared the creak of her bed could be heard. She knew she was giving too many excuses at once, each one diluting the strength of the others, but Gil hadn't noticed. He had put an arm round her and kissed her hairline, and said that of course he understood. He would wait, knowing that they would be together every night soon. He apologized if he had in any way made her feel pressured. Eleanor had laughed at him.

'How could I have felt pressured? It was me who dragged you back to my rooms, if I remember.'

'You hardly needed to drag me.'

'In any case, you can't present yourself as a cad, forcing yourself on some poor innocent woman.'

At least she had made her excuses to Gil before she had kissed Michael in the churchyard. Otherwise, she would perhaps have gone to bed with him out of guilt and self-punishment, because she didn't want to, because she hated herself.

Eleanor let herself into the house. Gladys was standing in the hall, putting the phone back on its hook.

'Eleanor!' she said. 'You've come just too late.'

She gave everything she said a roguish air, raising her eyebrows, crinkling her face into a knowing smile. She smelt of sardines and cigarettes. There was a long rip down the seam of her pink cardigan.

'Late for what?'

'That was your young man on the phone.'

The blood rushed to Eleanor's face.

'Gil?' she asked.

'Do you have other young men that I don't know of?'

'What did he want?'

'He wanted to speak to you, of course.'

'Oh.'

'Are you all right?'

'Of course.'

'You look a bit flushed.'

'Perhaps it's the walk.'

'That will be it. I told him you would call him.'

'Thank you. I'll do it later, not now.'

'You haven't had a lovers' tiff, I hope?'

'Of course not. I'm just a bit tired. I have a slight headache.'

She went up the stairs, conscious of Gladys's bright eyes on her. Gladys was fond of saying that she knew everything before it happened, and Eleanor almost believed it was true.

She closed the curtains and took off all her clothes. They smelt faintly of him. Then she washed at the sink, sluicing cold water under her arms, between her legs, over her tingling face. The bruise on her neck was clearer now. She put a finger against it and felt the throb of her pulse there.

She should ring Gil, she told herself, but she didn't know what to say to him. She lowered her head into her hands and forced herself to think. She had told Michael that she would on no account see him again. She had said that she was going to marry Gil and that her sister Merry loved him, and she didn't want to do something that she would feel guilty about for the rest of her life. This was a great mistake, a moment of madness that they needed to put behind them and never repeat. All the time she was speaking, he had gazed at her so that her voice had faltered. And then he had seized her and kissed her once more, stopping the words. But she had pulled away and left, walking out of the churchyard without once looking back at him, though she could feel him there in every nerve of her body.

*

'Hello, Gil. It's me.'

'I know.'

'How are you?'

'I am very well. I got us those tickets for the doctors' ball.'

'When is it?'

'A week on Saturday. You remember we talked about it – you can still come?'

'Of course. I'm not sure I have anything suitable to wear.'

'Whatever you wear will be lovely.'

'Hmm. I need to get a dress. Perhaps I can borrow one.'

'Will you perhaps allow me to——?'

'No.'

'All right,' he said peaceably. 'And Eleanor?'

'Yes.'

'Perhaps we can find a time when we can tell my mother.'

'Tell her what?' Though of course she knew.

'About our engagement.'

'Yes. Of course. I can't think of it just at the moment, Gil. I've got a bit of a headache.'

'I thought something was wrong.'

'Did you?'

'You sound a bit tense.'

'Sorry. It's been a long day.'

'You have an early night,' he said, tenderly. 'I'll see you tomorrow.'

'Tomorrow?'

'Yes. We agreed to see a picture together.'

'Of course. I forgot. Lovely.'

'Sleep well, my darling,' he said.

The following morning, Eleanor came down the stairs and found a letter addressed to her lying on the mat. It hadn't come with the ordinary post, so someone must have posted it by hand. She didn't recognize the handwriting but knew at once it was from him. She stared at it for a moment, as though it were a bomb that might explode if she touched it, then bent down and lifted it up. Still, she didn't open it at once. She had the sense that with every step she took a door swung open, a door clicked shut. If she threw away the letter without opening it, she was saying no. If she opened and read it, she was letting him speak to her.

Nellie, my beloved, she read, and then closed her eyes for an instant before continuing, feeling the sharp gust of pleasure at the words. *What have you done to me? What shall I do with myself now that I know you? I feel quite wild, my darling. I cannot tell if it is wild with joy or with despair. How is it that no one can tell that my heart is bursting? I want to keep you secret and deep and I want to shout your name out loud (don't worry: I won't). I have to see you again and hold you again and feel the softness of your skin and smell your clean, beautiful hair and press you to me until I don't hurt with this terrible desire. Tell me you feel the same, Nellie. You must. I know you must.*

She folded the letter in half and then in half again. Gladys's door opened and her small, inquisitive face peered out. It was too early in the morning for her. Her skin was shiny with cold cream and she had curlers in her thin hair.

'I thought I heard someone in the hall,' she said. Eleanor saw how her eyes moved at once to the letter in her hand.

'I'm about to leave for work.'

'You're ahead of yourself.' Gladys, wearing a quilted robe that looked more like a bedspread, came out into the hall. Her face was still puffy with sleep and her knobbly feet were bare on the tiles.

'I've got nothing to eat in my rooms. I'm going to stop on the way for breakfast.'

'That's good, dear. No unwelcome news I hope?'

Eleanor glanced down at the letter she was clutching in her hand. 'Just an arrangement,' she said coolly, but then spoilt it by adding unnecessarily, 'for the doctors' dance.'

'With your young man?'

'Yes. With Gil.'

Gladys put up her hand and patted Eleanor on her cheek, a playful stinging slap.

'Be good,' she said and withdrew into her own rooms.

Eleanor pushed the ridiculous, calamitous letter into her pocket and stepped out into the windless day.

He stood up from the wall on which he was sitting, dropping the cigarette on to the pavement and slinging his jacket over one arm. Eleanor looked at him. Her heart didn't roar; she felt almost calm, almost dispassionate. His shirtsleeves were rolled up. His shoes were ancient. His stubble was almost a beard and his hair was unkempt. The romance of the evening had gone from him; this morning, he looked poor and ragged. His face was too gaunt and as he came towards her with his limping gait, he reminded her of the countless men who hung around by the docks or sat in huddles in the parks during the day in their rusty work clothes, hope gradually falling from them. And as she thought this, pity ripped through her and she heard herself draw in her breath sharply. It was one thing to arm herself against his charms; another to resist his weaknesses. Later, he said his poverty had been his secret weapon. 'If I'd been middle-class and prosperous and professional, I'd have got nowhere. But think of it: a poor young man from the north who'd been injured fighting against Franco in Spain and who dreamt of becoming a writer one day.' And he'd laughed self-mockingly.

He laid these things at her feet: his homelessness, his self-hatred, his threadbare freedom, his lack of a future.

'How did you know where I live?' she asked sharply, drawing back from the hand he held out to touch her.

'I followed you.'

'You followed me! When?'

'Last night. I walked behind you and I stood right there.' He pointed. 'And watched you go inside. Then I sat and looked at the light go on upstairs so I knew which was your room. I waited until the lights went out and then I left.'

'You shouldn't have done that,' she said, her face flaming.

'I know. But what was I to do?'

'I told you I could never see you again.'

'That's impossible.' He shook another cigarette out of its packet and put it in his mouth, lighting a match behind a cupped hand. 'Don't you see?'

'No, I do not.'

'Shall we walk? I think your neighbour is looking at us.'

Eleanor glanced round and saw the curtains in Gladys's room move.

'Now look,' she said crossly.

'What?'

'You are indiscreet.'

'Indiscreet. Terrible thing that.'

She stopped and faced him. 'You're a man and I'm a woman! It makes a difference, or do you not understand that?'

'I do understand,' he answered, almost humbly.

Later, she would often find that with him: she would be roused to anger and then he would take the wind out of her sails by his ready apology, his sudden surprising meekness.

'But you must leave me alone.'

'I cannot leave you alone.'

'Come in here.' She led him into the café where she often had her breakfast, or at least a mug of tea. 'We should talk.'

They took a seat at the back of the room and a woman came to take their orders.

'What will you have?' Eleanor asked him. She saw him hesitate, his eyes scanning the blackboard for the cheapest item. She thought of saying that she was paying but knew that he would hate that.

'Coffee,' he said.

'If I have some toast, will you share it with me? I'm not very hungry.'

'No.' When the woman had gone, he leant over the table towards her. 'If you tell me that you don't feel the same way as I feel, I'll be gone at once, never fear. But you can't tell me that, can you?'

'Gil asked me to marry him, and I said yes.'

'You can't marry a man you aren't in love with.'

'Who says I don't love. Gil? I do. I love him and I like him and I trust him. He is clever and kind and the best man I ever met. He's too good for me,' she added.

'You love him but you kissed me in the church-yard.'

'I was wrong.'

'You were right.'

'I shouldn't even be sitting here with you now. Merry loves you—'

'I like Merry of course, and she has been very sweet to me at a time when I needed sweetness, but I don't believe she really loves me, not the way you mean, and I don't love her.'

'Then you shouldn't have made her feel that you did.'

'I didn't know what I felt about her until I saw you. After that, nothing else mattered.'

Their drinks and toast arrived. Eleanor pushed the plate to one side. She put her hand over his. Their eyes locked.

'It's too late,' she said. The words were a knell in her ears.

'Please don't say that.'

'I would always hate myself.'

'But you love me.'

'I don't know you.'

'You know what you feel.' He turned his hand sharply and grasped her by the wrist. He leant further towards her; she could see how long his lashes were and how there was a tiny scar on his temple, and she could see her own face in his eyes, and if she looked any longer she would drown. 'I have to be with you,' he whispered. 'I could go mad with love.'

'Ssh.'

His other hand was on her knee now, under the table.

'You are the loveliest woman I've ever set eyes on.'

'I have to go now. I'll be late.'

'You haven't finished your coffee or even touched your toast.'

'I'm not hungry.'

'Meet me this evening.'

'No. I've promised Gil—' She knew as she said it, that an excuse for not meeting him weakened her resistance.

'Then tomorrow. Meet me tomorrow.'

She pulled her hand away. 'I don't know. Michael, I don't know what to do.'

'I'll tell you what to do—'

'No!' The intensity of her refusal took them both aback. She tried to keep her voice down and speak more calmly. 'You will not tell me what to do; no one will tell me what to do. I will decide for myself.'

'You're right, of course. It's just that I'm scared that as soon as you leave me you'll push away what you feel and you'll decide against me.'

'Will you promise me something?'

'Anything.'

'If I do decide against you, will you abide by that and not try to convince me?'

Michael looked at her, frowning. Then he said, slowly: 'All right. I promise that if you decide not to see me, I will leave you alone. But please don't do that. Please.' He took her hand again between both his own and brought it against his cheek, closing his eyes for a moment. Then he kissed her knuckles and turned her hand to press his lips against her wrist, where the pulse beat. Eleanor looked at his bent head, the soft whorl of hair at his crown. Before she could stop herself she leant forward and kissed him there and heard him give a sigh. Then she stood up, leaving the toast and coffee untouched, and raised her hand in farewell.

'I remember it all with such clarity,' Eleanor said to Peter. 'I remember it as it happened, minute by minute: the words he said to me and how I felt, how the sun shone through the window, how the air felt on my skin, what it was to be young. I remember what the woman who served us that day looked like – her name was Dorothy and she had a daughter called Biddy and a husband with a weak heart. There are days, weeks, months even, that have all been swallowed up by time, gone into a fog of forgetfulness, but I remember that time as if I was back in it once more, like a room whose door I have at last pushed open and now I can simply step inside and it's all there undisturbed, undimmed.

'Sometimes I think that I will turn my head and see him standing there – blind old fool that I am – and he will be young still, and so will I, and he will call me Nellie in that way he had. Then I think my heart will break with longing, because I am back there, I am that young woman in love.'

And she placed her swollen hand where her heart was and her old, lined face wore on it a look of such sadness that Peter stood up and went over to her, crouching down before her and putting his hands on the bony ridges of her shoulders.

'I'm sorry,' he said.

'Ach. It's long ago and I've had a good and happy life. But they say that everything passes and I've found this isn't true. Or at least, there are some things that also return with a freshness that is shocking.'

Peter rose again, hearing his knees creak, and poked at the fire until the flames blazed again. He poured some more wine into both their glasses.

'I met Gil that evening,' continued Eleanor. 'We went to see a not-very-good film about a boxer and also about a young woman who was working in a milk bar, I think. I didn't concentrate. We sat in the dark and Gil held my hand and every so often I could sense his eyes on me. I could feel his happiness and love. Then we went and had a cocktail and I had a chicken sandwich, I remember. Rubbery, salty chicken. I don't think I could eat it. He asked about my headache and I said it was still there, a bit, and he said he wanted to tell his mother about us soon. He said that he could be called up soon enough, and he wanted her to have time to get used to the idea in case he had to go. I remember how he looked dishevelled and solemn and glad, and he held my hand and twisted the bangle round and round on my wrist. He was so tender and protective, so brim-full of happiness.

'I felt sick. There was an upwelling of feeling in me and I thought I would have to fall apart under its weight. In the end, I just burst into tears. Like a weak girl,' she added, disgustedly. 'He thought I was crying because the war was coming and he would perhaps go away. Although he never did go away. He stayed throughout the Blitz, tending to the sick and the dying. But he thought I was scared to lose him. He was so nice to me, so understanding – although of course he understood nothing. There were tears in his eyes too, but he said he was joyful as well as sad, because I loved him enough to weep at his going. I had thought I would tell him it was all over between us that evening, that although I knew I couldn't be with Michael, nor could I be with Gil. But I found that I couldn't, I couldn't look into his face and see it change. I was a coward. And I had never loved him as much as I loved him that evening.'

'So you didn't tell him?'

'No. I even said we would tell his mother next week perhaps. And then he took me home and saw me through the door. There were two letters waiting. One was from my mother and had been posted the day before. It was a long, rambling letter, but I only really noticed the paragraph in which she said that

Merry's young man seemed to have disappeared off the scene and that she and Robert were rather relieved but that Merry seemed wretched and on edge. They were worried about her, although in the end it was for the best. She asked me if I would come up soon to cheer Merry up and perhaps give her some sisterly advice.

'The other was from him. It wasn't a letter at all, just a scrap of a note in a gummed envelope that had been pushed through the letterbox.'

Tomorrow evening, by the quince tree. I'll be there as soon after six as I can. I will wait for you until nine xxxx

19

It started quite well. He reversed the old car slowly out of the garage without any mishap and manoeuvred backwards to the entrance of the house. Perhaps his driving had improved with rest. The car smelt musty. There was a newspaper folded in the back seat that dated back to 2002 and a bag of boiled sweets that were welded together in the glove compartment.

Eleanor was waiting. She had on a long dark-green coat with a velvet collar and a woollen scarf, deep blue in colour, and looked vigorous and purposeful as she tapped her way towards the car, refusing Peter's arm.

'This is a treat,' she said, taking off her coat and folding it neatly before handing it to Peter to put into the back. Then she settled herself into the passenger seat and fastened the safety belt. 'A day out.'

'I don't actually know where we're going.'

'I'll direct you,' she said. Peter looked at her sightless face dubiously. 'Turn left at the end of the drive.'

He revved the engine, sat forward and put the car into first, then took his foot off the clutch. The car leapt forward with a spurt of gravel under the wheels. Eleanor jerked in her seat.

'Whoops! Sorry about that,' said Peter.

'That's all right. You'll get used to it.'

He turned on to the lane rather sharply, knocking against the verge. The branch of a tree slapped the windscreen. His hands were sweating on the wheel and he felt that everything was happening a bit too fast. He swerved to avoid a pothole. The map on the dashboard slid forward and landed in Eleanor's lap.

'Perhaps you should change gear,' she remarked, not seeming at all bothered by the commotion.

'Of course.'

He changed into second and the car stopped whining so loudly.

'And again,' said Eleanor.

The car ground into third, the gearstick biting his hand.

He wanted to wipe his forehead but didn't dare take his hand off the steering wheel. He remembered that he'd left his mobile at the house: if something went wrong, he wouldn't be able to call for help.

'There's a junction coming up,' he said, and stopped abruptly several yards from the turning.

'Right here. Soon we'll be on a main road, then you'll be able to relax.'

Peter didn't think that was necessarily true. It

started to rain and he turned on the headlights and the indicators before finding the wipers.

'All right?' asked Eleanor mildly.

'I think so.'

There was a car behind him now, very close, too close. He could see the man's cross face in his mirror. He put his foot on the accelerator, surged forward, then braked to a crawl. The car bumped into them.

'Fuck,' said Peter. 'Fuck fuck fuck fuck fuck.'

There was a muffled sound beside him. He turned and put a hand on Eleanor's arm, leaning towards her.

'Are you all right, Eleanor? God, I'm so sorry. Are you hurt at all? Don't cry.'

She wasn't crying, but laughing. Her thin shoulders shook. Tears stood in the corners of her blind eyes.

The man had got out of his car. He was burly and red-faced. Peter got out too.

'Hello there,' he said.

'What did you think you were playing at?' roared the man.

'I don't know. Is there any damage done?'

'Damage! Look.'

Peter looked and could see a tiny scrape along the gleaming silver bonnet of the man's obviously swish car – though he knew nothing about cars and cared even less.

'It could have been worse,' he said. He had taken a dislike to this bellowing person.

'You shouldn't be let loose on the road.'

'Excuse me.' Eleanor's voice, steady and cool. She stood in front of them, leaning on her stick, her white hair blowing. 'You crashed into us. That seems very clear. Now you are trying to blame my young friend for your own reckless driving.'

The man stared from Peter to her, his face darkening.

'Is our car damaged, Peter?' she continued.

Peter leant forward, squinting. The car was so old and scraped anyway that one more mark wouldn't make any difference.

'I don't think so. Nothing to speak of.'

'In which case,' said Eleanor to the man, 'we will not call the police or need your insurance details. But I suggest you pay more attention next time. And,' she held up a hand to stop him from interrupting, 'don't try and bully people into taking the blame for something that was entirely your responsibility. Come on, Peter.'

They climbed back into the car.

'Wow!' said Peter.

'Off we go,' said Eleanor.

'I was going a bit too slowly, you know. I braked.'

'Go faster, then.'

'But he was a wanker.'

'Yes,' she agreed serenely. 'He was certainly a wanker.'

'Shall I drive you back home?'

'Whatever put that idea into your head?'

'I'm not sure I'm safe.'

'I feel entirely confident.'

It took them two hours to drive the fifty miles. They stopped halfway to fill up with petrol and Peter sat on the damp grass verge and smoked a cigarette to calm himself down. After that, he suddenly found driving easier, as if the road had broadened and the car had shaken off its nervy, spasmodic mood and had become obedient. He was almost enjoying himself. Eleanor made him describe what he could see out of the window: the fens, the windmill, the flat, glistening sea in the distance; the small towns with gabled red-brick houses that looked Dutch rather than English. Looking at them for her made them more vivid for him, so that many years later he would be able to recall their drive together. They passed through a large wood full of oak trees, leaves pattering down on the top of the car; Eleanor insisted they stop so that she could stand underneath the vault of the great trees and breathe in the rich smell of decay.

'Can you smell it?'

'What?'

'Mushrooms and moss and dead leaves. What's your favourite smell?'

'My favourite smell?' Sometimes she reminded him of a child.

'Yes. Coffee, mown grass, baking bread, roses?'

'I don't know.' Kaitlin after sex, he thought, turning to light a cigarette. His grandmother's face powder. Petrol. Hot sun on skin. Man-made things.

The home was on the outskirts of a small and windswept town near the coast. It was a newish complex in raw yellow brick and looked resolutely institutional in spite of all attempts to make it personal.

Peter opened the passenger door and helped Eleanor out.

'Shall I wait in the car?'

'Come in if you'd like.'

Peter hesitated. He was intensely curious to see Meredith.

'Won't she mind?' he asked. 'I mean, it'll seem a bit strange.'

'No, she won't mind. She won't know.'

'I don't know.'

'It will help me,' said Eleanor.

'All right.'

Everything was clean and new. He glimpsed through a half-open door a salon where several women were having their hair cut or curled. In another room, some kind of sing-song was going on, a young man with hefty shoulders thumping out tunes on the piano. It all seemed cheerful and purposeful, and it made Peter's spirits sink. Would this be the kind of place Eleanor would be? He couldn't imagine her here, in this bright, warm, brisk place, but then he couldn't imagine her anywhere but in her old house, sitting by the fire while the wind blew down the chimneys and rooks shouted in the trees and darkness rolled in.

Mrs Meredith Hartley had a round face and small, plump hands. With her grey hair tied back in a meagre ponytail and her faded blue eyes, she looked many years younger than Eleanor. She was sitting in a chair near the window, from which it was possible to see a snatch of sea, with a tartan blanket over her knees and a pink shawl over her shoulders. There was a miniature cyclamen on the table in front of her, and a vase of purple dried flowers on the shelf by her bed; they looked stiff and ancient. She looked at Eleanor and Peter, brightly vague, and patted her hair with one hand. She had stubby fingers whose nails were corrugated, and a deep dimple in her cheek when she smiled. She wasn't really smiling at them, but through them. The smiling was a habit, a reflex created by a lifetime of being friendly, polite and winning. She had small yellow teeth.

He watched as Eleanor crossed the room and stooped to plant a kiss on the top of Meredith's head.

'Lovely,' said Meredith. 'Golly.'

'It's me. Eleanor.' Meredith didn't react at once, so Eleanor said: 'Your big sister.'

'Sis?'

'Yes.'

'Why?'

'I've come to say hello.'

'I'm not stupid, you know.'

'Of course you're not. We've just popped in for a quick visit.'

'I'll teach you.'

'What will you teach me?' asked Eleanor calmly.

Merry giggled, a sharp fragment of laughter like someone tapping a glass once for attention.

'That would be telling. So nice of you to come. Who would have thought it?'

'And I've brought a friend with me. This is Peter.'

Peter held out his hand and Meredith looked at it, her smile widening. He wasn't sure what to do next, with his hand held out and a smile locked on his face, so he picked up her small hand and pressed it, then placed it back on her lap, but she suddenly gripped his fingers, keeping him there.

'Do you like me?' she said. 'Really like me, I mean?'

'Um, well, yes, of course. I'm very pleased to meet you. Eleanor's told me about you.'

'Silly me.' And she gave her tiny laugh, like a cracked high bell splitting its peal. 'Silly, silly me.'

'Oh no! Not at all.'

'Is Daddy here?'

'No. That is—' He faltered and threw an appealing glance at Eleanor, although of course she couldn't see it.

'Where's Daddy?'

'That's all over, Merry,' said Eleanor, standing at the side of her sister. 'That part of our life is done with. We're old, you and I.'

Meredith laughed again, louder this time.

'You would say that.' She tugged at Peter's fingers and gave a smile that was flirtatious and vicious. 'She's jealous, you see. Boys do like me. I don't know why. I could still have him if I wanted. Don't think it's not true. And Clive Baines has always been madly fond of me. Poor Clive. Quite besotted. Where is he?'

'Clive died in the war.'

Peter didn't understand why Eleanor had to tell her – surely it was kindest to pretend that everyone was still alive, still young, still in love with her. But Meredith simply said, 'Dear, dear; poor Clive,' in a comfortable tone, squeezing Peter's fingers confidingly. He had had enough of his awkward, back-stiffening bow, and now tugged his hand from her and backed away, but was stopped in his tracks by her wail of protest that grew, like a siren coming closer. Her mouth was a round hole, her sparse eyebrows were raised, her face mottled into a caricature of distress. Her plump hands made fists.

Without warning, to quieten her, Eleanor began to sing 'Twinkle, Twinkle, Little Star', and after a few husky notes, Meredith joined in, tearfully at first, and in a high, quavering voice. Peter stared at them, a feeling of grim hilarity growing, forcing its way up his throat. He gave an unfortunate snort; Eleanor pointed her cane at him warningly, but sang on. At the end, there was a brief pause. Laughter still wormed in Peter's stomach. Eleanor took off her coat and let it slither to the floor; she found the edge of the other chair and sat down on it, very straight-backed. Her face was carved with deep grooves and she seemed angry. Meredith, however, had cheered up. She giggled – there was no other word for it – and then took a deep breath and started to sing 'Silent Night'. But soon she petered out, began again, came to a final halt.

'Sing "Abide With Me",' she said. 'I like that one. Daddy sings it. You can play it on the piano.'

'I can't remember the words,' said Eleanor.

'"Abide With Me",' repeated her sister, almost petulantly. 'Oh Lord, Abide with me. Through cloud and sunshine. In my early youth.'

Eleanor frowned. She sat up straighter in her chair and began to sing, not looking towards either Meredith or Peter, but out of the window that was probably for her just a rectangle of grey light. Not tunefully, almost as though she were chanting it, she sang the hymn right through, remembering all the words and barely hesitating. Every so often, Meredith joined in and then lost the thread again. 'Change and decay,' she warbled. 'Come not in terrors.' She echoed words at the end of sentences or lines: 'sting', 'victory', 'flee'. They paid no attention to Peter or to each other; there was a locked-in quality about them both that was unsettling and distressing. The song, with all its wrong notes and echoed words, became an elegy and an incantation. They were two old women looking back at themselves and two little girls looking forward to the selves they had become.

After the first verse, Peter didn't look at either of the two women. It didn't seem right. It almost felt indecent to be in the room and he was spooked. He stared at the photos arranged on the tall chest of drawers: there were none of Eleanor. He assumed the faded full-length portrait of a chubby man in a hat and suit was her father, Eleanor's stepfather, and the head-and-shoulders tinted one with ringletted hair was Meredith herself as a pretty little girl – the girl who could still make Eleanor's face take on a sour cast. The rest were obviously of Meredith's husband, Wilfred Hartley, and her stepchildren and then their children as well.

Then suddenly Peter froze. There was a tiny, framed portrait of a young man and he knew, though how he knew he couldn't say, that it was *him*. He wanted to step forward and examine it but didn't dare move while this appalling dirge was going on. He could see indeterminate-coloured hair, wide-apart eyes, a thin face, and that was all. He took a few shuffling steps, coughing to cover the noise, and was closer. 'I need Thy presence every passing hour,' sang Eleanor, and he moved closer still. He met the gaze of the young man, hooded and enquiring. His mouth was slightly open, as if he was about to speak; his hair hung over his forehead. He looked ordinary enough, the kind of face you see every day, but he'd been loved by these two women, thought Peter; he'd loved Eleanor and lain with her under the quince tree. He'd drunk whisky by a window and been full of yearning.

'In life, in death, O Lord, abide with me.'

Eleanor stopped singing and stood up, stumbling as she did so. Peter hurried to her side and steadied her, finding her cane.

'Are you all right?'

'Perfectly. It's time to go.'

'So soon?' said Meredith in a blank tone, back to being the gracious hostess. 'Dear, dear. Do come again. Any time.'

Peter picked up the long green coat from the floor and helped Eleanor into it. He avoided giving Meredith his hand; just ducked and shuffled and said how pleased he had been to see her. Eleanor patted her shoulder and left without saying anything more.

*

272

In the pub they stopped at, she ordered half a pint of beer and a lasagne that she barely touched, though she had been eagerly anticipating her lunch out. She talked to Peter – who had a spicy tomato juice and a cheese bap in front of him – without pause, about how her mother had met Stanley Baldwin, about Clement Attlee and Harold Wilson, about her job training teachers, about the Cuban Missile Crisis, Vietnam, rationing and powdered milk, about Gil's hatred of lifts and underground trains, about picking soft fruit when she was a girl to supplement her mother's income. She described the first time she had been on an aeroplane (in 1947), and the last, eight years ago when she had been to Granada because everyone should go to the Alhambra before they died. It was the most beautiful building in all the world, she said; it was like maths and poetry combined. Peter had never known her like this: normally when Eleanor talked, it was as though she were following the secret river of her feelings and thoughts. Now she talked as though she were trying not to think or feel at all. She did not want to dip the bucket down into the well of memory, but instead was throwing out events like stepping stones over which she could cross without falling into the deep waters of the past.

All of a sudden, she stopped mid-sentence, as if she had come up against a hard object.

'What?' asked Peter, but she just shook her head slowly from side to side, as though she were trying to clear it. He was horrified to see tears in her eyes that she made no attempt to wipe away.

'Gil used to say there's no fool like an old fool,' she said, trying to smile. 'I'm an old fool.' She found her cane and planted it on the floor, rising slowly. 'Come on. Time to go home.'

20

'I will not' was the refrain hammering against her skull through the day, as she stood by the blackboard or wandered between the paired desks where the children laboured over their handwriting. She heard Lizzie's snuffling breath as she drew her thick nib down the page, or placed a forefinger between each word to make the spacing correct. She could see the nits in Mary-Jane's hair and the flea scabs on Susan's legs. 'I will not.' A fat fly buzzed. Her head ached in the heat. She opened the classroom windows and let the breeze blow through.

At six o'clock, she was standing in the grubby studio in Shoreditch that Emma's boyfriend rented, looking in a desultory fashion through the murky and depressing canvases while Emma and Anthony argued in ferocious whispers in the corner. At seven o'clock she was drinking a glass of milk in the café where she had sat with Michael just two days ago and staring out of the window at the people who flowed past. At just past eight o'clock she was in her rooms, listening to Terence's wracking cough beneath her, on and on, and wondering if she should go downstairs and see if he needed anything. At half-past eight she was washing her hair over the sink, uncomfortable trickles of water running under her collar. She looked at Michael's letter once more, though she knew it by heart: *Tomorrow evening, by the quince tree. I'll be there as soon after six as I can. I will wait for you until nine xxxx* She let herself feel once more his hand on her leg, his lips on her wrist, his eyes on her. She pushed away the memory, but it was like trying to stop a flood. It entered her through every pore. *Please.*

And just before nine, when the danger was surely past, when it was too late to change her mind, she tore out of her room, down the stairs in a clatter, past Gladys who was opening the door inquisitively as she hurtled out of the front door, hatless and coatless, her hair still damp, down to the main road. Eleanor tried to stop a passing cab but it went by without slowing. There were no buses in sight so she ran, pain sloshing in her skull and an ache beneath her ribs. Her shoes were slightly too large and kept slipping. The clock on the old church told her it was fifteen minutes past nine. He would be long gone.

And he was. The churchyard lay in its twilight, a secret garden of the dead, and she arrived at the quince tree to find there was nobody there. She gazed around her, desolate. She would never be able to find him: she didn't even know his last name, had no notion of an address or a contact for him – except for Merry, of course, who was inconsolable because he had disappeared from her life without a forwarding address or a letter to say goodbye. Eleanor let herself down on to the damp ground beneath the tree. Too late. She had done everything wrong, she shouldn't have come or she shouldn't have hesitated, and now she would never see him again. He would be swallowed up by the war that was coming. It was over and it had never begun.

She stood up and coiled her hair back on to the nape of her neck with hands that still shook slightly. She brushed the grass from her skirt and walked slowly towards the gates. A little boy in shorts that were too large for him and a snotty nose stood on the pavement crying, but when Eleanor bent down towards him he said he was just waiting for his daddy who was in the public house across the road. She felt calm at last, calm and dull, with a dazed sense that something momentous had not happened to her; she had let it pass.

But when she turned to go home, she saw a figure, tiny in the distance, yet with something about it that made her breathing shallow. A slight asymmetry in the way that it moved in and out of the shadows cast by the buildings, heading towards the cranes on the horizon. She walked quickly towards it, and then ran. For a moment, she lost it among the people coming towards her. Lost him, for now she was almost sure. A thin man in a shabby suit with a small but unmistakable limp. A cigarette in one hand, a tiny wisp of blue smoke disappearing. She didn't let herself think, just followed him and only when she was a few steps away did she slow, try to catch her breath. And then she drew alongside him and put a hand on his arm and he swung round towards her and stopped. He didn't seem pleased, just stared at her.

'You're late,' he said at last.

'I'm sorry.' Eleanor's voice was throaty and only now did she realize she was on the verge of tears. 'I'm very sorry. I thought I wouldn't, and then – I'm sorry.'

'You're sure now?' he asked.

'Yes,' she replied, though she felt only a sense of vertiginous terror at what she was setting in motion.

'You know what you're doing?'

What was she doing? Hurting Gil, betraying her sister, paying no heed to her future, putting this blind besotted love before her own freedom and autonomy.

'I know what I'm doing.'

She thought he would put his arms round her, kiss her. Instead he said, almost coldly, 'Will you come with me, Nellie?' and when she nodded mutely, he gripped hold of her hand and started walking, fast enough in spite of his dragging leg so that she almost had to run to keep up. They were heading east, into the tumbledown poverty that many of her pupils came from but which she usually avoided. Men stood in groups on the street corner, under the gas lamps that were now being lit, the day over and night-time beginning. Shapes in doorways and light spilling out from public houses, bursts of raucous laughter. A woman with a painted face leaning against a wall, and Eleanor had to look away from her gaze that was both contemptuous and beseeching. Michael didn't slacken his pace. They went down a small street with cracked paving stones. There were no lamps here, and it was suddenly darker and cooler. She was only wearing a thin blouse and she felt chilly, goosebumps on her skin. She thought of rats among the scattered rubbish and had a sudden image of Gil, sitting at his table in a newly laundered shirt, with a glass of wine in front of him. Too late to think of all that now, though for a moment his imagined expression made her stumble. They were in front of a narrow door and Michael was reaching into his pocket for a key.

'Where are we?' she said.

'My friend's. He's on nights. I'm using his room for a while.' He turned to her. 'It's not much but it's a place we can be alone.'

'Yes,' she whispered. 'That's all right.'

'Are you scared?'

'Yes.'

'Don't be.'

'Aren't you?'

'Of course.' Close to her ear. 'I am so scared and so happy I feel I could die of it.'

The door swung open on to a narrow, dank hallway. She could hear voices through the thin wall to her right: young children squabbling and a woman's high, angry remonstrating. There was a smell of meat cooking. Michael went up the stairs and she followed. Another doorway, and again he reached for the key, which was stiff in the lock. The door swung open and he turned on the light, just a bulb in the ceiling that swung slightly on its flex, sending a queasy pattern over the room.

For some reason, she'd been expecting squalor, but it was clean and quite neat: just a small stove in one corner under shelves on which stood a few tins of food and a whisky bottle, and in the other corner a single bed with a red blanket pulled over the sheets. An old bike leant against the far wall. Several piles of books stood near it, and there was a jumbled heap of clothes in the corner, next to two large, bashed-about suitcases. A woven rug covered some of the wooden boards. There was a chair near the window and a candle stuck into the neck of a liquor bottle on the sill, amid puddles of hardened wax. One of the window-panes was broken and a plastic sheet had been taped across it, which billowed in the gusts of wind.

Eleanor stood in the middle of the room and watched as Michael bent to light the candle on the windowsill, and then another that was on the wooden crate that served as a bedside table. He fetched down the whisky bottle from the shelf, pouring a generous measure into a glass and a mug.

'Here,' he said, and handed her the glass.

She took a sip, blinked, took another. It was raw,

medicinal, and it scorched its way down her throat and made her eyes water. Something loosened inside her; her terror was dissolving, her stomach softening and her throat thickening. She felt a soft, loose thud of pleasure inside her, like the insistent pulse of gravity. She finished the glass and put it down, then undid the coil of her hair.

'Eleanor,' said Michael. 'Nellie.'

'Will you turn out the light?'

Now the room had no walls or ceiling; it was just a guttering space, everywhere and nowhere, now and for ever, and she could see the shine of his eyes and the paleness of his torso when he took off his shirt. Someone was shouting outside in the street, just beneath their window, but that seemed a long way off. Here, they were cocooned by candlelight and the quiet rustling of their clothes, the unsteady rasp of their breath. He unbuttoned her blouse and put his face into her newly washed hair and between her breasts, and she put her arms around him and felt the bumped ridge of his spine and the sharp cage of his ribs. He tasted of whisky and tobacco, unfamiliar. He was a stranger – and she was a stranger too as she lay back on the narrow bed, the blanket scratching at her bare skin. She watched herself turn into a woman who lifted up her arms, twisted her body; she heard herself give a high moan of pleasure. His face between her thighs, and her own face burned. Then he was inside her with a violence that shocked her;

she pressed her mouth against his shoulder to stop herself from crying out. When she looked at his face, it was screwed up in a kind of bitter anguish that made her want to gather him against her. This felt almost like despair, she thought: this urgent blind striving.

Afterwards they lay close together on the bed. He raised himself up on one arm and pushed her hair away from her face, staring at her intently, then closed his eyes and lay down again, his fingers tracing her jaw-line, trailing down her throat to her neck as though he were memorising her. After a while, he got up and poured them both some more whisky. She looked at his bare back with the sharp shoulder blades, like wings, and his pale narrow buttocks, his legs with muscles that tautened as he moved. He turned and his penis swung between his legs. In spite of her times with Gil, she had never seen a man naked before, not really, and she found him beautiful and strange, almost sinister. Had he really laid that pale body over hers? She pulled on his shirt and went to the bathroom, which was out on the landing. The children had stopped wailing and the mother shouting. She washed her face and between her legs. Her body ached. The face in the mirror was someone else's – the woman who had thrashed on the bed and uttered animal cries, not Eleanor Wright the teacher. Not Eleanor Wright the fiancée of Dr Gilbert Lee.

When she returned, Michael, still naked, was sitting

on the bed smoking a cigarette and knocking the ash hissing into a chipped mug. He watched her as she crossed the room and she was acutely conscious of her own nakedness under his thin shirt. She felt appraised. She had become an object, like someone in a painting. Woman after Making Love. With Gil, sex had been toilsome and untransforming. He had, it seemed, left her intact, even as her blood spotted the sheets. She had still been herself when she had risen from the bed: Eleanor Wright. Now she wasn't so sure. She felt that she had been pierced and ruptured by passion. She had lost herself, cried out with a voice that wasn't her own, let waves of desire sweep through her inner spaces. Her body ached, her skin was sore and she herself felt fragile, knocked about and close to tears. She didn't even know who he was and yet he had seen her as no one else ever had, writhing and arching on the bed as his fingers found her out.

She sat on the floor and put her back against his legs. He leant forward to kiss the top of her head, then slid his arms around her and pulled her closer. She took a gulp of whisky and handed him the glass.

'What now?' he asked. She twisted her head to look at him. 'I mean, what will you do?'

'I will tell Gil it's over. I was going to anyway, even if—' She didn't finish the sentence. She thought of Gil's face, his world, the lovely familiarity of him. 'But it's hard to make someone unhappy,' she added. 'It's very hard.'

'One of us was going to be unhappy.'

'But you're stronger than he is.'

Her words surprised her, and yet as soon as she had spoken them she knew them to hold a truth. There was something about Gil that was passive and already defeated. He wouldn't defend himself against blows that were aimed at him; he wouldn't be angry with her or even try to win her back. He would simply let her go and suffer.

After a silence, Michael said: 'Do you love him still?'

'Of course.'

'And me – do you love me?'

Eleanor twisted and knelt, looking at him with a bright, fierce gaze.

'I'm here,' she said. 'I chose you.'

He pulled on his trousers and cooked for them – at least, he emptied a tin of watery, salty stew into a pan and heated it, carved hunks of stale bread, made a pot of tea in a tin teapot with a cracked spout that they drank bitter and strong, without milk. He asked her questions about her dead father and her living mother, always wanting more detail than she gave, trying to strip away outer layers of her self-protecting story and go in deeper, darker, stranger. He listened intently, trying to hear what she wasn't saying. He wanted to know the things that she never told anyone, to ferret out her secrets and to make crooked and shaded the things that had seemed straight. She felt that she was learning a new language, one that made her feel giddy with possibilities.

She didn't want to talk about Merry, but he made her. He said they should look at what they were doing full on, not bury anything. 'It will return to haunt us if we don't,' he said.

'When we're old together,' he said, and at that she took his face between her hands and kissed him and felt his mouth smile under hers.

He made her talk about her and Merry as girls: her resentment and the sense of being overlooked, and of losing her mother, somehow, to this new family with the kind husband and adorable, winsome daughter. 'It made me feel sick at myself,' she said and he nodded. 'I was someone I didn't want to be: mean and jealous.'

'And what about her – did you make her mean and jealous as well?'

'She didn't need to be. She was the princess in the fairy tale, remember: she always got everything she wanted.'

Then she put a hand over her mouth.

'Do you think that's why?'

'No, of course it isn't.'

'Am I that cruel?'

'No, Nellie.' He was round to her side, holding her. 'No. But you have to look at it clearly; you have to see it from all sides.'

'What are you talking about?'

'Before I go away.'

'I don't understand.'

'I want us to think about this together,' he said patiently, 'so that when we're apart you won't be filled with doubt and guilt.'

'Doubt and guilt.' She repeated the words as though their taste was in her mouth.

'Because you can't leave me,' he said. 'Not any more. Not for any reason.'

He talked of himself, too – offering things up. He told her about the poverty of his childhood, the cockroaches on the ceiling and the privy in the yard, shared by six families. How he used to hear his mother crying at night, when she thought everyone was asleep.

'She looked worn out by thirty-five,' he said. 'She was pretty when she was young; a little thing with curly hair and a smile like spring. But being poor isn't good for the looks. At the age when rich women still look young and strong, she'd lost half her teeth, her hair was thin and her skin bad. Five of us and two that didn't survive, in that little house with damp coming in through the walls. My father was a disappointed man. He could have been kind in a different life, but he'd come back from the public house fighting-drunk and you could hear him in their room, going at it for all he was worth, like a bloody piston engine, and then he'd despair when she fell pregnant.'

He'd been good at school. He couldn't afford university but after his Highers he'd gone to night school, working during the day at any job he could turn his hand to. He was always ardent for books and learning, he said. He talked of education with a kind of reverence that Eleanor had encountered in some of the parents of her pupils: not just as the thing that could rescue them from the life they were born into, but with an almost religious sense of its virtues. He was a member of the Left Book Club; he read about science and politics and history, whatever he could lay his hands on. He knew he was a mixture of the ignorant and the oddly well informed. He had learnt the Greek alphabet and had taught himself rudimentary Spanish before going to Spain. But Spain, he said, was going to hell in a handcart. He pulled books out from under the bed and found a pamphlet that he read passages from. It was a poem about Spain – Eleanor later discovered it was by Auden, but at the time, all she knew was that the words rang out in that little room like a curse. He liked marches and protests and impassioned meetings; he knew more about what had really happened during the anti-fascist march in Cable Street than she did, even though she'd been there; he had strong feelings about the divorce bill; he thought women should rise up in righteous anger. He didn't believe in the monarchy;

the abdication crisis had been an irrelevance; who cared? He pulled her closer to him; his mouth against her throat. She could feel the painful beating of her heart. He didn't believe in any kind of God. He didn't believe in marriage but he'd marry her if she said the word. He'd do anything for her. He thought they should live abroad, or perhaps in Scotland. What did she think of Scotland, once the war was done with? Or even America, land of the free. He lit a cigarette and the acrid smoke stung her eyes. He kissed her and she tasted blood on her lip, and whisky. He told her they had found each other. She felt she was being drawn into a whole new world that was dark with danger and bright with joy.

They briefly slept and when they woke they made love again, dreamily, while outside in the street the sounds of early morning were starting up again. Summer rain pattered against the window; the blanket was scratchy against her skin; her lips were swollen and she hurt between her legs. Her breasts felt tender. There was a bruise, purple against the milky paleness of her thigh; she didn't know how that had got there but she probably had others she couldn't see. Her whole body felt bruised. Her heart too. Any touch could hurt her, yet when he pressed his fingers into her flesh she was glad. She wasn't really sure how she had got here. Yesterday evening seemed a dream now, and last night unreal, not occupying time or space.

At last Michael got up and made coffee. He filled a bowl with the rest of the hot water from the kettle and dipped a thin cloth into it, then washed her. She let him, standing in the middle of the floor with water streaming off her body. He was good at it and she thought: he's done this before; but it didn't matter. She put the clothes from yesterday back on. They were slightly grubby, creased; a button had gone missing; her stockings had a ladder. She looked like what she was, she thought: a woman getting dressed after a night of sex and almost no sleep. She had no comb (she had nothing in fact; she'd run out as she was, without even a coat). But he got a fork from the drawer and she tried to tame her hair with that, tugging it through knots and her eyes watering.

'I need to go home before I go to school,' she said. 'I can't be seen like this.'

'I'll take you.'

'Take me?'

'On the bike. We'll have plenty of time.'

He lifted the bike down the stairs and she followed, conscious of a face looking at her from behind a half-opened door. He helped her on to the thin seat and she gathered up her skirt with one hand and put her other hand on his waist and he stood up in the pedals and cycled her back towards Islington. She could see the effort in the back of his neck. Her skin stung in the damp breeze.

'You'd better let me down here,' she said. 'I don't want anyone seeing me.'

He stopped and she dismounted.

'I'll wait outside your school this afternoon,' he said.

'No. Let me tell Gil first.'

'When?'

'This Saturday. After the dance.'

'That's days away.'

'I have to tell him before I see you again.'

'Will you come to me then?'

'Yes.'

'Saturday.'

'Yes.'

He pulled her into the shadows and kissed her, long and hard, his hand against the small of her back and her body soft with desire again.

'I'll be waiting,' he said, and she turned and walked up the long street, knowing he was still there, watching her until she was out of sight.

Gladys let her in because she'd forgotten her key. Eleanor felt the woman's bright, canny gaze take in her swollen lips and disordered hair and stained, creased blouse. But she didn't say anything.

'She always knew everything,' Eleanor said to Peter now. 'She didn't have to see things to know they were going on. She knew everything before it even happened.'

'Then what?' asked Peter, bumping the car up the drive, over the potholes. The lights were all off and the house looked abandoned.

'Then I told Gil.'

The dance was over, the band had packed up and departed. Gil walked Eleanor home along the deserted streets. It was raining, and he tucked her arm through his and held his large umbrella above them both. She wore her borrowed gown that was slightly too large for her; Emma had fastened it with pins, but she had to hold up the skirts with one hand to prevent them trailing.

'So,' began Gil cheerfully, 'what did you make of—?'

'There's something I have to say,' cut in Eleanor. Her voice sounded sharp, almost rude.

'What is it?'

'I have made a mistake.'

'A mistake?'

'I cannot marry you.'

For a moment, everything continued as it had been. They walked at the same pace, under the dome of the umbrella; Gil's arm remained tucked around hers; the expression on his face didn't alter, but remained genial. Then he slowed and his arm slackened. His face slackened as well.

'I don't understand,' he said at last, stopping and

turning towards her. Eleanor could hear the rain dripping on the umbrella's canvas and see it streaming off the edges. 'I don't understand in any way. We've just been dancing and you've met my friends and talked with them. You were a bit quiet but everything seemed all right, and now you tell me that you cannot marry me?'

'I thought it was what I wanted, but I was wrong. I have behaved very badly towards you, Gil.'

'You cannot marry me,' he repeated. 'Why?'

'I'm not ready to marry anyone.'

'Those are words a woman would speak to a fool,' he said. 'To let him down gently. I'm not a fool.'

'I don't have the words,' she said wretchedly. 'I just know that I made a mistake.'

'A mistake,' he repeated, dragging out the words. 'Which bit? The loving me, or simply the agreeing to marry me?'

'I don't want to marry you. That's all I can say.'

'Then I can wait. I can wait as long as you want.'

'Gil—'

'We don't have to tell my mother or anyone else. We don't even have to get married, if you don't want to marry. We can just be together, as we were.'

She made herself look into his face. 'It's not that.'

'What are you saying? Are you saying you don't want to be with me?'

'I am saying that it's over. I have made a terrible mistake and I am very sorry. Sorry for the pain.'

'Pain.' His voice was dull. 'Sorry for the pain. I don't understand you. Why?'

'It's me,' she said. 'You couldn't have been nicer or kinder or better to me. It's just me.'

'But what's happened?'

'Nothing.' For she couldn't tell him.

'But I thought we were happy.'

She didn't say anything.

'Weren't you happy, Eleanor?'

'I was. But it's over.'

'I was happy,' he went on. 'I was so happy. Happier than I've ever been in my life. Until this very moment, and these words. Where do they come from?'

'I have thought about this a great deal, and—'

'How can you have been thinking about it when you haven't said anything to me?'

'I'm sorry,' she repeated miserably.

'When did you start thinking this? When?'

'I don't know.' She thought back to the picnic, the last fresh days of spring. 'It's crept up on me and now I know I just need to be single for a while longer.'

'All right. All right. You can be single. We don't need to be married yet. We were going to wait anyway. But you don't really mean you want to end it.'

'I do.'

'There's someone else.'

'It's not that.' She couldn't lie outright.

'So it's just me.'

'No – it's just me, Gil.'

He shook his head slowly from side to side. 'No,' he said. His face looked heavy and his body bulky with wretchedness.

'I am so sorry,' she repeated. She felt that at any minute she would have to break free of him and run through the wet streets, just to be away from the expression on his face and the terror that was engulfing her at what she was doing.

He stared down at her. 'But I love you. Don't you love me?'

'I do,' she replied, and at that moment she wanted so badly to take him in her arms and comfort him that she could feel her body straining to do so. She clenched her fists. 'I love you very much. But not the way you want.'

'This is really happening? This is the end?'

'I'm sorry,' she said once more.

'You mean, we're going to part and I won't see you? We'll go our separate ways?'

'Oh Gil.' She suppressed a sob; she would not weep when she was the one who was hurting him. 'It would be better not to see each other.'

He insisted on walking her home, holding the umbrella carefully to shield her from the rain. He waited at the door until she had found her key and unlocked it. He lifted her hand to his lips and kissed it, his dark messy hair falling forward. She would have much preferred his anger or his contempt to this terrible kindness.

That night, she sat for many hours in her chair near the window. She wasn't really thinking, though thoughts drifted through her, and she wasn't really feeling, though emotions clutched at her and then let go. It was more as though she were keeping vigil, saying goodbye to her old life, before entering the new one.

When she pictured Gil she felt pain, like a toothache sending electric throbs through her whole body, surprising her by its sharpness. And when she let herself imagine Michael, waiting for her in that little room, she felt a dizzying fear. Vertigo. She didn't know him; she didn't know his world; she no longer knew herself. She was stepping over the edge, into darkness.

At last she shivered and rose from her chair. The stars had faded and there was a faint rim of light on the horizon; birds sang from the plane trees. The sounds of the street were filtering into her room. She was exhausted but fully awake, and quite emptied of desire, of hope, of love even. All she knew was that there was no returning to the old familiar ways.

She did not go to Michael that day, although she knew that he would be expecting her. She wandered through the streets for hours, letting her feet take her: past houses where families were sitting down to their Sunday lunch, into little parks, along the canal glinting brownly in the sunlight. At one point, she found herself by the churchyard where she and Michael had met but she did not go into it. That frenzy of desire seemed like a dream now. Her body was placid. Her bruises were fading, her lips losing their chapped soreness.

She went into a tea shop and asked for a glass of milk which she drank sitting on the stool at the far end of the counter, feeling it coat the inside of her mouth and slide smoothly down her tired throat. The sun came in spears of gold through the clear glass at the top of the door and spread out over the floor, but where she sat in the recesses was dim and cool, like a cave or like the little church at home where she'd been christened and confirmed. She thought she could sit here always, not going back into the bright hot clamorous world.

When she arrived back at her bedsit, it was early evening. The blue sky was turning silver. She climbed the stairs and opened her door, stared in at the tidy space. What should she do now? She stood in front of the fly-blown mirror and re-fastened her hair. She washed her face in cold water. She put on a clean blouse, seeing as she did so Gil's gold chain round her neck. Perhaps she should return it. Her eyes filled with unexpected tears but she blinked them away.

Then she left once more, closing the door quietly so that Gladys would not hear and put her head round the door, observe her with those inquisitive knowing eyes of hers, and walked through the dusk, towards the place where Michael was staying. She had been there only once, and that was in the dark and dazed, but she found she knew the way. She ignored the stares of the men standing in groups on corners. She felt as though she were making her way towards a place that might not be real; that the building would have disappeared or that nobody there would know who she meant when she asked for Michael.

And indeed, when she was let in, going up the stairs to the room, the man who opened the door at her knock wasn't Michael at all. He was older, with grizzled dark hair, a pitted face and a crease between his brown eyes.

'Yes?'

'I was looking for Michael.'

'He's not here.' He must have sensed her anxiety, for he added quickly, in his gravelly smoker's voice. 'But he'll be back soon. You're to step inside.' And he held the door wide open, standing back to let her through.

'I'm sorry?'

The man smiled. 'He said if anyone turned up I was not to let them leave. I imagine he meant you.'

'Will he be long?'

'No. He has barely stepped out for a minute these last two days. Waiting, he was, though he wouldn't say. Standing at the window smoking and looking out. Pacing the room. Scribbling things and then tearing them up. So I'm guessing he won't be long. I am leaving in a few minutes myself. You can stay here till he comes. Please.' And he gestured again into the bare, neat room.

Eleanor went inside. The man lifted clothes off the chair and she sat. He was big but slow and graceful; she saw his calloused hands and his frayed shirt cuffs. He offered her a cigarette and she shook her head. He held up the whisky bottle – the same one she and Michael had drunk from – and she shook her head. She didn't know what she would do if she had even one sip of alcohol, what would happen. Everything seemed misty and immensely far off; when she lifted her hand to smooth her skirt, it was like the hand of a stranger.

The man – she would never discover his name – handed her a mug of tea, stewed and bitter, and she sipped it. He was sweeping the floor, pulling the covers over the bed, putting on his jacket, whistling to himself softly. Then he stood before her.

'Goodbye,' he said.

She rose. 'Goodbye. Thank you.'

'Good luck,' he said. Her eyes filled with tears. She smiled at him and he put a hand on her shoulder and turned and left.

She sat down once more. At last the door opened and Michael stepped inside, slim and jacketless, carrying a bag, his hair swept back from his face. It was twilight outside now and the room was dim and full of shadows. He didn't see her at once, sitting silently to one side. When he did, his face became illuminated for a moment. But then – making out her expression and her upright, withholding posture – he stood quite still, staring down at her, not smiling but searching her face for answers.

'You told him then?' he said at last.

'Yes.'

If he had tried to embrace or kiss her, she would have pushed him away. But he did not. He just looked at her.

'I bought us some supper, in case you came,' he said. 'And some wine. Do you like wine?'

'Yes.' But how would she put food or wine into her body?

He took two tall candles out of the bag and screwed them into empty bottles, then struck a match to light them.

'Are you cold?' he asked.

She nodded and he took the cover from the bed and draped it over her shoulders and on to her lap, careful not to touch her. It was hard to believe they had ever lain naked together, mouth to mouth and body to body.

She watched him as he moved about the room in his stockinged feet, noiseless and deft, putting a cold roast chicken on to a plate, unwrapping a piece of cheese, cutting slices of bread, easing the cork from the bottle of wine, laying two apples and two yellow pears out on the window sill. Only when everything was prepared did he turn to her.

'Was it very bad?'

'I don't know. He was—' She flinched under his gaze. 'He was very kind.'

'I see. And now you're wondering what on earth you're doing here, with me.'

'Yes.'

'But you came.'

'I came.'

He poured purple wine into two tumblers and handed her one. She took an experimental sip. It was harsh and sour, not like the elegant wines Gil ordered in restaurants or served up in his polished and airy dining room. Michael sat on the edge of the bed and rolled himself a thin cigarette. The smoke made her eyes sting.

'You look tired.'

'I didn't sleep.'

'Eat some food.'

He stubbed out his half-smoked cigarette in a saucer on the floor and stood to carve her some chicken. He laid it on a small plate with a forget-me-not painted on its rim, alongside a slice of bread, cut off a wedge of cheese. She saw how he tried to arrange them to look appetising.

'I have no butter.'

'It doesn't matter.'

She took a bite. She was suddenly ravenous, trembling with hunger and exhaustion. She pushed bread into her mouth and chewed, took another mouthful of wine.

'All right?' he asked her.

She nodded. She finished the food and he quartered a pear for her and she ate it slowly, its sweet juice running down her chin. And then he took his own sheets from under the bed, laid them across the ones his room-mate used, and gestured.

'Try to sleep,' he said, adding quickly: 'Don't worry. I'm just going to sit in the chair awhile.'

She was too dazed to argue. She took off her shoes and her skirt, and then climbed under the sheets. She closed her eyes and felt herself being sucked under, sinking down into a thick darkness of dreams.

When she woke, she opened her eyes to see him sitting at the small table, writing in a notebook by the light of the guttering candle. He had a glass of wine in front of him and his hair fell over his forehead. He was frowning in concentration. Her body felt soft and sluggish with sleep. She could taste the wine she had drunk. She closed her eyes again.

The next time that she woke, he was still in the chair and the candle was still flickering, nearly burnt down to its base and throwing strange lights. But he was asleep, his head tipped to one side and resting on the wing of the chair, his hand half-curled. The notebook had fallen to the floor. She sat up in bed. She no longer felt tired and her confusion had lifted, the way a mist burns off. It was very quiet; she could not hear any sounds from the street, or from the other occupants in the house. She slid her legs out of the bed and stood up, going over to where Michael sat. He had long eyelashes, she thought, spiky on his cheek in the candlelight, and under the lids she could see his eyes move rapidly. He mouth was slightly open. She could see the rise and fall of his breathing through his thin shirt. She bent and picked up the notebook, put it back on the table, and he frowned and murmured something, sounding distressed. She put a hand very gently on his shoulder and he surged awake, like a swimmer thrashing towards the surface, coming to his feet in one movement before his eyes were properly open.

'It's all right,' she said. 'You're all right. We're all right.'

'Oh.' His arms were slack by his side. 'I was having such a dream, Nellie.'

'You're awake now.' They weren't touching but were very close.

'Yes.' He rubbed his face and looked at her. 'But why are you? I thought you would sleep till morning.'

'Come to bed.'

'But—'

'Come to bed, Michael. Just to hold each other, keep off the nightmares. We can talk later.'

He nodded. She unbuttoned his shirt, his breath on her cheek. He unbuckled his belt and stepped out of his trousers. How thin he was, she thought. Thin and strong: her breath caught in her throat. Half-clothed, they lay in the bed, a sheet over them, her head in the hollow of his neck and his arm around her, their legs tangled. He smelt unfamiliar.

'Sweet dreams,' he said into her hair. 'Sweet dreams, my dearest Nell.'

The following morning, early, he went out and bought eggs and boiled them two each, which they ate sitting in bed, dipping bread into the yolks and salt, drinking coffee that he'd made in a pewter jug.

'Will you tell me?' he asked at last.

She shook her head. 'There's nothing to tell. I told him it was over. I had to repeat it several times. It was as if he couldn't make sense of the words.'

'Did you say anything about—?'

'I couldn't. I didn't know if it would be cruel, for no reason – or perhaps I simply couldn't bring myself to say the words and see his face. And any-way—' She stopped, licked her salty fingers, looked into Michael's face. 'Anyway, I can't tell anyone until I've told Merry.'

'When will you do that?'

'I don't know. I can't decide what is the right thing. I mean, right for her. And then, I want—' She stopped.

'What do you want?' asked Michael, after a pause.

'I want us to be secret, safe from the eyes of the world. I don't want people talking about us or making judgements.'

'Does it matter what other people think?'

'We're causing pain and distress.'

'We don't have a choice, Nellie.'

Eleanor looked at him with something like wonder.

'Of course we have a choice. I am choosing my own happiness over Merry's.'

'I was never going to be with Merry; you know that.'

'I know. But that's not the point. All her life Merry has been sure of her loveliness, her charm, her capacity to captivate. And all her life I have been her audience, admiring and applauding her. She's like an actress on the stage, performing the only part that she knows, and we have stood in the wings. It's not that she will be upset, Michael – it's that her whole sense of who she is will be threatened. Her sister going off with the man she has set her heart on. I know that; I have to be honest and clear-eyed with myself. I can't pretend it's not a betrayal. We come to each other out of a fearful tangle of other people's distress.'

'But we do come together.'

'Yes.' It felt strangely domestic and unsettling to be sitting having breakfast together. 'We do come together.'

22

'So then you told Merry?' asked Peter after a long pause.

They were sitting by the fire again after eating supper.

'It was rather more complicated than that.' Eleanor's tone was dry, almost harsh. 'I wanted to put it off as long as I could. It seemed that the whole country was waiting for the war to properly begin, like a storm to burst. I was waiting too – for the war, of course, and for my own private resolution. I don't know. Perhaps deep down and hidden even from myself – I had the thought, and this is still hard to admit, all these decades later – that I should wait to see if Michael survived the war before I told Merry. That perhaps there wouldn't be the need.'

'You mean, because he might die?'

'That's what happens in wars. Young men die. And I perhaps let myself imagine telling Merry, causing such damage, for no reason. This must sound cold-blooded. It didn't feel that way. It was more like a succession of thoughts and images that whirled through my mind during those tumultuous and heightened times.

'I saw him as often as I could over the weeks that followed. We knew that he would soon be sent to training camp and then he would go to fight. Everything was too intense; war and love became indistinguishable. Once or twice, I smuggled him into my rooms when we couldn't go to his friend's place. Or we went to horrible cheap hotels where we had to sign ourselves in with a married name.' She smiled suddenly. 'Mr and Mrs Ramsay, after Virginia Woolf's novel, which we had talked of the first time that we met. Damp walls and stains on the floors, flickering bulbs. It didn't matter. Once, we made love in Epping Forest. We could hear families nearby. He put a hand over my mouth to stop me crying out loud. My nails made marks on his back that he carried for weeks. I was in love. I was so in love that I felt sick and ill with it: ashamed, exultant, consumed. Very scared.

'We listened to war being announced on the wireless together. The whole country was listening, I think, everyone gathered round their set, a silence lying over cities and towns. We didn't say anything. He got up and made us both a mug of tea and we drank it in silence. I knew—' She stopped.

'What? What did you know?'

'I knew this couldn't last. These days, our secret life, my secret self. But still I could not bring myself to tell Merry. I told myself it was out of kindness, but it was cowardice that prevented me. I didn't want to see myself the way she would see me, after she knew what I'd done. And the thought of what my mother would feel was too much for me. And Robert, who had always been good to me, would hate me. So for a short while I existed in a no man's land, after the deed but before the confession; something done but not yet discovered. My own ticking bomb.

'It all happened too quickly. Suddenly, we were at war; of course, it was inevitable but at the same time it was shocking. Every man between the age of eighteen and forty was called up. They didn't go at once but it was the beginning of the end. I thought that perhaps Michael would be exempt because of his leg. But it was just a small limp; not enough to stop him killing men or getting killed.'

Gladys called up to Eleanor from the hall: there was a call for her from her mother. Sally still wasn't used to speaking on the phone, and she was stiff and formal, talking too loud and artificially separating each word.

'Are you coming home for my birthday this weekend?'

'I don't think I can. Sorry. I should have said.'

'Why not? You always come. We've been expecting you.'

'It's hard to get away. What with everything.'

'Hard to get away.' Sally's voice was flat. 'What makes you so special?'

'What?'

'Just because you live in the great city now, it doesn't make you better than us.'

'Of course not!'

'And just because we're at war, doesn't mean family no longer matters. It matters more.'

'I know. You're right.'

'So come and see us.'

'Mum—'

'Come and see us or we'll think you're avoiding us. Are you avoiding us?'

'Why would I do that?' She held the receiver tight and felt the jolt of her heart.

'I don't know; why would you? I'll make up your bed.'

'News from home?' asked Gladys, head to one side like a tipsy little bird.

Eleanor was uncomfortable with her neighbour nowadays, who knew when she wasn't at home, who saw her creeping back at dawn, and whose shrewd gaze took in the change that Eleanor could see in the mirror.

The days leading up to her visit home were filled with an ugly anticipation. Eleanor felt cold and shivery; there was a tight knot in her stomach. She tried to imagine what she would say, sitting round the little table and making light conversation, lying in bed beside Merry and listening to her confidences. She felt clotted with deceit.

'Don't go,' said Michael. He turned from the open window, where he was smoking a cigarette, and stared at her. She could feel the way his gaze took her in, her nakedness under the thin sheet, the sweat still on her body.

'I have to.'

'No.' He stubbed the cigarette out on the window-sill and let it fall to the pavement outside. 'No you do not. You can stay. We have so little time. I go for training in four days' time. And then—' he gave a small sharp wince, 'Then I will be sent to fight. Who knows when we will next meet? Stay with me until then.'

'I'll be back tomorrow.'

'How do I know that?'

She tried to laugh, although she too was full of a kind of foreboding.

'You know because I'm telling you. Don't you trust me?'

'No,' he said. 'Not in this.' He knelt by the bed. His hand was between her thighs that were still sticky. 'You want to do the right thing.'

'Don't you also want to do the right thing?'

'No. I just want you. I would sell my soul for you.'

She wanted to say that some things are more important even than love or happiness, but his mouth was on hers and the words were blotted out.

*

Robert met her at the station and drove her to the house. Even the weather seemed uneasy and full of foreboding. The sky was a dark, ominous brown and wind whipped at the tops of the trees. A few large drops of rain fell. A storm was brewing.

Even before Eleanor was in the car, he had told her that they were worried about Merry.

'Why is that?' asked Eleanor, staring out of the window at the road running towards them, the corn in the fields on either side. Her voice was tight and cool. Surely he must hear.

'I don't know.' He sighed. 'All the spirit seems to have gone out of her. It's that dratted young man of hers. I always knew he'd be trouble, from the moment I set eyes on him.'

'Did you?' Eleanor repeated, turning her face from her stepfather so that he wouldn't see the shame written on it. There was no way of speaking in a manner that sounded normal. Her words, her light, brisk tone, her pretended ignorance, grated on her own ears.

'I saw what he was like. And I was right, wasn't I? He courted her and made her fall for him and then just disappeared off the face of the earth.'

'Mmm.' What else could she say?

'She's not like you. She's delicate and emotional, ruled by her heart. She thought she would marry him. She still thinks so.'

'You mean she still thinks she'll marry him?'

'She insists that he's coming back. She says that she

312

knows he loves her and it's just this war that's keeping him away. She says she trusts him and gets very angry if we say anything sympathetic. She's proud, you see.'

'Yes.'

'I knew as soon as I set eyes on him.'

'What did you know?'

'I knew no good would come from him.'

They sat at the table and ate boiled fish with potatoes from the garden, whose skins were slightly bitter. It was a beige meal, thought Eleanor, moving it round the plate with her fork. Beige and soggy, dispiriting somehow. Robert drank beer and the three women water, and they talked of the war as everyone, all over the country was doing – it was that strange time of limbo, when the country was at war but nothing was happening. Sally lit a stub of candle and there were wild flowers that she had gathered in a jug. Eleanor had bought her a pair of smart suede gloves that Sally said she'd never have occasion to wear. She was still making out that her daughter had become too grand for their country ways. Outside the wind strengthened, until it sounded like a waterfall through the trees.

Merry was wearing a loose dress made of soft dark material and her hair was scraped up on the top of her head, making her face look smaller than usual, her blue eyes larger. She looked like a waif, thought Eleanor; perhaps that was the point. There was something slightly artificial about her manner, as if she was in a melodrama, and her eyes glittered. She reminded Eleanor of cracked glass, through which the light shone crookedly. Her voice was brittle, her laugh high, unsteady. She couldn't seem to keep still, shifting in her chair, fidgeting at things with her hands, picking up her tumbler and then putting it down again untouched. Robert and Sally were very solicitous towards her. They kept praising her and asking Eleanor to agree with them – which of course she did. It was like a strained and worn-out version of the way things had always been.

After their meal, Merry suddenly stood up and said to Eleanor: 'Will you take a walk with me before we go to bed?'

'A walk! But it's raining,' said Sally, alarmed. 'You'll both get pneumonia.'

'It's hardly raining yet. Just for a few minutes, in the garden.' She spoke directly to her sister, her face white and pinched with determination. It was as though Sally and Robert weren't in the room with them. 'There is something I need to ask you.'

'Why not use the parlour?' asked Sally.

Eleanor stood up. 'All right,' she said to Merry. 'Before the rains start.'

'I'll clear up.' Robert rolled up his shirtsleeves, revealing his pale freckled arms. 'Go on, the two of you, but not for long. We don't want to send out the search parties.'

So they put on their coats and stepped outside, into the damp and gusting wind. Merry tucked her arm through Eleanor's and matched her step to her sister's. Eleanor tried to think of something to talk about, but her mind was quite blank. She waited to see what would happen.

'Ellie,' said Merry at last, as they crossed the grass together. 'Will you promise to do something for me, please?'

'What?'

'You're supposed to say yes. If I ask you for a favour, you're supposed to agree before even knowing what it is. Because you're my only sister and we love each other—' she paused, and then added, 'unconditionally,' separating out each syllable so that the word sounded nonsensical. 'So if I say that it means everything to me, will you do it? I would for you.'

'I would never ask you.'

'You mean you won't?'

'What is it you want from me, Merry?'

'I don't understand why you're so cold with me.'

'I do not mean to be cold.'

'You know that he's gone?'

Eleanor didn't pretend not to understand. 'Michael?' she said. 'Yes.'

'Will you bring him back?'

'How can I do that?'

'Will you?' Her fingers pressed Eleanor's wrist.

Eleanor stopped and turned, took her sister by the shoulders.

'Listen, Merry,' she said, trying to keep her voice level. 'How can you want someone if he does not want you? Let him go.'

'I can make him want me. Look at me!'

She pulled away from Eleanor and stepped back, flinging out her arms and turning in a circle, her dress ballooning out and her hair coming untied in the wind. As she whirled, she let out a small, hysterical yelp that sent a shiver through Eleanor.

'Merry, please don't. Come inside now.'

Merry stopped suddenly, her arms dropping to her sides. Eleanor could smell the fear on her, a sharp high odour of distress.

'You've always been jealous of me.'

Eleanor considered this. 'I don't think so,' she said at last, gravely. 'Or not in the way that you mean.'

'I won't let you get away with it. I'd rather die.'

'You don't know what you're saying.'

'I'm not a child.'

'I know that.'

'I can ruin everything for you.'

'Can you?' She felt tired to her bones now. 'Perhaps.'

'Don't think I won't.'

Then all of a sudden the rain started in earnest, as if the stretched and swollen sky had split and water was at last gushing through. Merry ran inside, shouting something, but Eleanor stood for a while, welcoming the heavy downpour and the scouring wind.

When she returned to the house, soaked to the skin and cold, only Sally remained in the kitchen.

'What have you said to Merry?' she asked.

'Nothing.'

'She doesn't seem to think so.'

Eleanor took off her coat and hung it from the hook on the door. She towelled the ends of her hair and then said, 'There's something you should know.'

'What's that?'

'I have left Gil.'

Sally stared at Eleanor as though she were a stranger.

'Why would you go and do such a foolish thing?'

'Because I've fallen in love with someone else.' Eleanor tried to keep her voice calm. She could feel the drunken galloping of her heart.

'No,' said Sally. 'You mustn't. You just mustn't—' As if it hadn't happened yet.

'I've told Gil it is over between us.'

'No!' her mother said again, more urgently. 'It won't be too late. You can make everything right again. He'll take you back.'

'I don't want to be taken back. And it is too late. I've committed myself, and there's no going back.'

Sally actually lifted her hands to ward off the blow.

Eleanor could see that her mother knew what she meant. She came from a different world and thought her daughter had brought shame on the family and on herself. She was spoilt, a damaged fruit.

'I don't want to hear this. I don't want to know anything else.'

'I thought I could tell you,' said Eleanor. 'I wanted to talk to someone about it all. I need to. You're my mother. Perhaps you can help me. I don't know who else to talk to. Please.'

'You should have thought about that before,' said Sally, her mouth in a thin, grim line. 'I thought you had more sense. I must say I am disappointed in you, Eleanor.'

'When I had children myself,' Eleanor said to Peter now, 'I made a pledge that I would never say such a thing to them. Anger is a hundred times better; it's clean and honest. Disappointment is all about the other person; it's a form of emotional blackmail. Anyway, even if I had been going to, it was quite impossible to tell her about Michael after that – and maybe that was her intention, for I don't know to this day if she guessed. Perhaps she knew and didn't want to; or perhaps she had no idea. What I understood then, however, was what I already really knew: that I could look for no support or understanding in that quarter.

'Years later, when she lay dying, there was a

moment when I thought we would talk, and I would ask her – but what? She was a stranger to me as I was to her. She had become as thin as a skeleton so that all her features looked as though they were too big for her, as if they belonged to someone else, and I could barely recognize her. She was very scared. Robert was long dead and I was the only one to sit at her bedside and hold her hand and see her over the threshold. My children came, but not at the end. She didn't want them. I think they made her realize her time was drawing near and she didn't want to know. I sat in that hospital and I thought about when I was a little girl and it was just the two of us looking out for each other. I don't know what she was thinking about. What do people think about as they lie dying? I imagine I will find out before long, when my children are round my bed, holding my hand. I wonder if I'll be scared.'

'Are you scared now?'

'I don't know. We shall see.'

'What happened next?'

'Well now, Peter. Listen.'

Eleanor sat for a long time in the kitchen, by the dwindling fire, her wet clothes gradually drying on her. She could hear movements in the rooms above her and then it was silent inside the little house, while outside the clamorous roar of the wind and rain swept round it, shrieking in the eaves and banging at the thin panes of glass in the window so that Eleanor thought they would break. She thought of Merry's words – 'I can ruin everything for you' – and of her mother's implacable refusal to hear her out. She thought of Michael waiting for her, wanting her, and of the war ahead, the darkness into which they must all go.

At last, when it was late, she stood and went up the little stairs to the room that she and Merry had shared, the twin beds. The air was slightly sour, and she could hear the rasp of Merry's breathing in the close darkness. She was asleep, or pretending to be, and at least they would not have to talk. Tomorrow she would rise before her sister woke and leave on the first train; she didn't know when she would return. This was no longer her home.

She felt exhausted but also janglingly awake, and could not bring herself to lie in the narrow bed, just a few inches from Merry. She unlaced her boots and eased them off, untied her hair and sat in the chair beside the bed. She pressed her cold fingers against her scorching eyes under their closed lids and listened to the moans of the wind, the creaking of trees and the rustling of their leaves.

She must have fallen asleep. When she woke, like a swimmer plunging up to the surface, she had no sense of how long she had slept or of what the time was now. All she knew – and how she knew, she could not say – was that she was alone in the room. She stretched out her arm to Merry's bed and found only a jumble of sheets over a patch of vague warmth where a body had lain. She rose, feeling her way blindly, catching her ankle, knocking against furniture, and made her way down the stairs. Past the dull embers, pushing her feet into boots that were too large for her, and out into the streaming wildness that took her breath from her as she ran.

Her mind was a whirling chaos, but her feet carried her. Her body knew where Merry had gone and what she had set out to do. Rage and despair gave Eleanor power: she sped over the sodden ground and through the thickets, barely minding how they tore at her clothes and hair, how her skirts wrapped round her legs. Fury so strong it was almost euphoric lifted her from the bank of the river in a leap that carried her to the surging centre of the river. As she hung in the air waiting for the fall, she realized that the storm had died away, that stars shone in the great sky above her, that an owl was shrieking nearby, the loneliest sound, that she didn't want to die. For a moment, she thought not of Merry, nor Michael, but of her father and his brave wide smile. What a short stretch of life he had had. How sad he must have been to go.

When she had been rolled over and over by the surging river until she was nothing but bursting lungs and flailing arms, when she had dragged Merry to the bank and hauled her inch by inch out of the flooding river on to the muddy grass, when she had pumped her chest and blown breath into her lungs and seen her sister turn her face to vomit a thin trickle of river water on to the earth, seen her eyes flutter open, Eleanor lay back and stared at the great bowl of soft darkness above her. She felt nauseous herself, and cold gripped and cramped her limbs. Her body was spent, like a discarded object that had served its purpose and now had no meaning or function left. She knew that she should get Merry home before she died of hypothermia, having been saved from drowning, but for a moment she couldn't bring herself to move, or to stir herself to any kind of action. Particularly not for this sister of hers, who had played her trump card. She thought of the panicky flurry her arrival would cause, all the explanations and recriminations. And she thought of what lay beyond, the wasteland where her hopes had been. Better just to lie on the grass, feeling the tilt of the earth beneath her, and stare at the beautiful impersonal sky and listen to the wind blowing the last of itself out in soft sighs.

Merry gave a moan and a liquid cough. Eleanor forced herself to sit up. She looked at her sister, illuminated by the moon so that she looked like a figure out of a Gothic illustration, with her hair spread out around her and her torn white nightgown. There was vomit over her chin, and her lips were bloodless. Her eyes flicked open and gazed sightlessly.

'Right,' said Eleanor. She stood up and collected her sodden skirt and boots, putting them on with difficulty, then considered. A fireman's lift, that was it: the head and upper body slung down the back. She bent down and seized Merry by her shoulders, pulling her into a sitting position, feeling how the head lolled. She smelt of sick and mud, and her skin was cold and rubbery. But she was breathing in shallow, panting gasps and making odd sounds. Eleanor hauled her half-upright in a strange embrace and struggled to pull her body over her shoulders. She was like a rag doll, but surprisingly heavy for such a slender creature, her arms bouncing around and her legs dragging at the ground. At last Eleanor had her in position. She grasped her upper legs firmly and started to walk home. She could hear Merry groaning and making little exclamations, and hear too her own ragged breathing. Her back ached and pain tore at her arms. She tried to think of nothing – not what had just happened, nor of what was to come, not of Michael, just one step in front of the other over the meadow, through thick brambles and thin, whipping branches, back on to the road. How long ago had she run along here with her hair streaming behind her like a banner? Her throat hurt, her eyes hurt, her head was thick. Her ankle, where she had turned it, throbbed at each step. Merry's head banged against her back. It must hurt her, too. Good. She imagined letting the body crash to the hard surface and leaving it there.

At last she was home, standing on the threshold with her burden. She couldn't open the door and when she tried to call out she could only croak, so she simply kicked hard and repeatedly at the wooden panels until at last Robert was there in front of her in his plaid dressing gown and his bleary, freckled face.

'What—?' he began before his eyes took in Eleanor, ripped and wild and streaked with river mud, and then the body slung like a sack over her shoulders with the blonde hair streaming down, heard the burbling sound coming from it. He gathered Merry from her, making crooning noises as though she were a baby bird. Eleanor stood just inside the door, dripping muddy water on to the newly washed floor, shivering. She watched as Robert pulled her wet clothes off Merry and heaped blankets on top of her. Then he started to blow the embers back into life, puffing specks of ash over his own face in the process. Now Sally was there too, her hair in curlers, her face greasy with cold cream and her mouth in an almost-comical 'o' of dismay. Her hands flew up to her lips. She turned on Eleanor.

'What's happened?' Her voice was a terrified hiss. And then: 'What have you done?'

The doctor came, irritated to be called out on such a night as this but quickly reassuring. Milk heated with honey and whisky, a hot fire, bricks warmed in the oven and put at Merry's icy feet, more blankets over her until she was a thick, soft mound with her face emerging from the top, small and pinched. She slept and she woke; she smiled at the three of them. Eleanor went upstairs and took off her skirt and blouse and undergarments, pushing them into the basket; she wouldn't wear them again. She pulled on the old robe that was left on the hook for her use and went downstairs again. Merry was propped up on her pillow now with a mug of sweet tea. Her face had more colour in it and she seemed almost contented. Perhaps triumphant. She darted smiling glances at Eleanor every now and then.

'What happened?' Sally asked again.

'Merry went down to the river and fell in,' Eleanor replied, aware of how nonsensical her words were.

'Went to the river? In the storm? And you went with her?'

'Not exactly.'

'What? You went down to the river too?'

Eleanor looked at her mother's sharp, frightened face and at Robert, silent and bent towards his daughter at a crooked, uncomfortable angle. His ginger hair stood up in little peaks and tufts and he was white around the eyes.

'I woke to find her gone so went to find her,' she said. 'I saw her in the river and pulled her out.' That terrifying tussle that had seemed to go on for half her lifetime but must have lasted just a few minutes. 'You'll have to ask Merry why she was in the river in the first place. That's for her to say, not me.'

They were talking about Merry as if she wasn't there – and indeed, she seemed largely absent, with her vague expression and wandering eyes.

'But you suspect—' began Robert. He lifted his face towards her and she saw how utterly bewildered and frightened he was; all his sprightly optimism had drained away and he looked old and frail.

'She fell,' interrupted Sally, her voice harsh and loud. 'Of course she fell. She's had a lucky escape.' She turned and tutted comfortingly to Merry. 'How stupid to go out on a night like this. What were you thinking.' It wasn't a question; she certainly didn't want an answer. She wanted a story: two young women running into the storm for a dare, for a jaunt.

'Stupid,' said Merry, her voice like a chime. 'Stupid.' She gave a laugh, a spiteful, tinkling sound. And silence fell. The three of them stared at her; Eleanor felt that someone had taken her heart and her guts in a great hand and twisted them.

'Silly me,' Merry said again, in a shriller tone. And she smiled at Eleanor, showing her small white teeth. Eleanor saw the tip of her pink tongue and the dimple that appeared on her cheek. Sally used to say that an angel had put a finger there – Merry had liked that.

Robert gave his daughter a perplexed stare and

patted her where he thought her knee must be under the pile of covers.

'Are you all right?' he asked Merry.

'Right as rain,' she replied, lightly, with another liquid, bubbling giggle, as if the river had entered her.

Eleanor saw the slight lopsidedness of her sister's mouth; the strange expression on her face and the way her eyes darted around and then rested on random objects. What if—? She thought and then stopped herself.

'What if?' asked Peter, after a long pause while Eleanor stared into the twisting flames that threw strange shapes over the room.

'What if there was something wrong with her, of course,' Eleanor replied matter-of-factly. 'What if she was brain-damaged in some way.'

'And was there? Was she?'

'Yes.' Her voice was clear, ringing out into the room. 'She was never quite the same again. Or no, that's not right. She was almost too the same, too like a caricature of the old Merry, as if she had been arrested – or drowned – into a version of herself.'

'That's—' Peter hesitated. 'That must have been very hard. For you, I mean.'

'Because it was my fault, you mean?'

'No. Of course it wasn't your fault. She did it to herself, and to you – but you already felt guilty.'

'Guilty, oh yes. For the rest of my life. And so

angry – with her, with myself. The blight.' She gave a deep sigh and repeated the word. 'The blight.'

'But she married?'

'What's that got to do with anything?'

'I just thought – well, she couldn't have been so bad if someone wanted to marry her.'

'You think so?'

'Or at least, of sound mind.'

'Sound mind? I have no idea what that means. All I know is that she was like a girl for the rest of her life. A sweet, flirtatious girl. In my experience, that's what lots of men want in the women they marry.'

'I suppose so.'

'You've met her; she's still like a girl.'

'Yes.' Peter remembered the old woman smiling up at him and grasping his hands as if they shared a secret together.

'I knew it wasn't my fault, but I also knew it was. For the rest of my life, not a day went by that I didn't feel guilt about Merry. And I hated her for that even while I looked after her and did my duty. And she hated me, smilingly, insidiously, implacably. My sister is a good hater. Though neither of us ever said a word after that terrible night about Michael, nor about what she had tried to do. Nor did Sally and Robert. It was unmentionable, unforgettable. It was a secret that flourished in the silence and the dark. I have never told anyone until now.'

'Thank you.'

She made her familiar gesture, palms upwards. 'I'm not sure it's a gift I'm giving you.'

'Didn't you tell Michael?'

Eleanor stared into the flames, no doubt seeing the past in that indistinct brightness.

'Oh. Michael . . .'

23

Eleanor returned to London the following afternoon, in borrowed clothes and with a sprained ankle. Like Michael, she thought with desolation: now we both limp.

As she turned into her road she saw him, sitting where he'd sat before, on the low wall across the road from where she lived. He had his back half-turned to her, but she recognized him at once from the shape of his back, the cut of his shabby suit, the way he was smoking, a ghost of smoke rising up in the bright air. She stopped as abruptly as if she'd been struck, and for a few seconds she didn't move. If he had turned then to see her, she didn't know what she would have done. But he didn't turn, only dropped his cigarette on the ground and put one foot on it to extinguish it, then straightened up again, watching for her but in the wrong direction.

Eleanor ran, hobbling, back from where she had come. When she was out of sight she stopped to catch her breath. She didn't know what she was feeling, she only knew that she couldn't meet him. Not now, with the memory of last night crouched behind her like some ghastly hobgoblin and the image of Merry as she'd last seen her – her fixedly smiling face and her thin sing-song voice – hovering in front of her.

She stood for a while in indecision, then made up her mind and walked to Emma's flat, her carpet-bag empty of clothes swinging beside her and her sprained ankle throbbing with each step. She welcomed the pain; it prevented her from thinking or feeling.

Emma opened the door and took in the sorry sight of her with a single, sweeping glance.

'Gin,' she said, taking Eleanor by the elbow and tugging her into the damp little hall. 'That's what you need.'

They drank the gin, which Emma kept on her window sill and was slightly warm, with water. Eleanor sat on the bed, her back against the wall, and felt the clear slightly greasy liquid wash through her. The room was pleasantly untidy. The sharp contours of the day dissolved. She was blurred and sad now. She looked at the wavering face of her friend.

'Do you want to tell me?' Emma asked.

'I don't think I can.'

'Is it Gil?'

'Oh, Gil. No, that's all over.'

'For good?'

'Yes,' said Eleanor. 'For good.' Good seemed the wrong word in the circumstances. She could scarcely remember Gil's face now, but she could remember, vividly, the shape of his hands and how warm and strong they had felt, clasping hers.

'He was nice,' said Emma.

'Yes. He was. Is.'

'Why then?'

'I fell in love with someone else,' said Eleanor. Her words dropped from her lips and she heard and considered them. How insubstantial they sounded.

'There's no arguing with that,' said Emma. 'What fools we are.'

'Yes.'

'Who did you fall in love with?' She spoke with a mild, unobtrusive curiosity.

'That doesn't matter now.'

'Is it finished with, then?'

'Yes.'

'Was he a rotter?'

'No.'

Oh God, if she could hold on to him one more time, his stubble against her cheek and his fingers pressing her flesh. For a moment she thought she would howl out loud.

'Oh well,' said Emma. 'Our world's ending anyway; we're all going to hell now, one way or another. More gin?'

Eleanor held out her tumbler.

'Can I stay here tonight?'

'Of course.'

'Thanks. And Emma, if I write a letter, do you think we can get someone to deliver it?'

'Where to?'

Eleanor shrugged and Emma didn't press her.

'The boy downstairs has a bike and he does errands for me sometimes,' she said. 'I can ask him.'

'I don't have any money on me.'

'You can owe me.'

'Thanks.'

Emma went out for food and Eleanor wrote a letter, the pad of paper on her knees. The gin loosened her normally neat copperplate handwriting and the pen slipped between her fingers in the heat.

Dear Michael, she wrote, then stopped, crossed out the words, tore the paper from the pad.

I cannot see you again, she began once more. *Merry tried to drown herself in the river. We have done too much damage and I cannot live with myself if we continue.* She halted for a few seconds, considering. A headache was starting up, pressing against her eyeballs. *You have meant everything to me,* she continued. *But everything is not enough. I always knew it but did not want to see. You will be angry, I know, and think I am a coward. Perhaps I am. I don't know anything any more, except I can't continue. It would destroy me and that would destroy us, everything we've been together. But I will always—* She stopped. She couldn't say that she loved him, not while she was telling him goodbye. *I will always hold you in my heart.*

Not a minute will go by, she didn't write, that I will not think of you and want you and miss you.

She told the boy with the bike to take it to her road in Islington.

'There will be a man waiting across the road from number 57. Give it to him.'

'A man?'

'Young, thin, wearing a suit that's held up by a tie, maybe smoking a cigarette.'

'Does he have a name?'

Eleanor hesitated. She was reluctant to identify him even to this boy whom after today she would probably have nothing to do with.

'Michael,' she said at last in a low voice, as if someone might overhear her.

'And I just give him the letter?'

'Yes.'

'Do I wait for a reply?'

'No.'

She stayed with Emma for three days, knowing after that Michael would have gone north for his training and wouldn't be able to find her. When she returned to her bedsit, there were two letters from him in the hallway – a thick envelope and a slimmer one. She picked them both up and took them outside. An old man with a cigarette in his mouth walked past and she asked him if he had a light. When he produced one she lit the corners of both envelopes and held them till they were burning well. Then she dropped them to the ground and watched until they turned to ash. It was the only way she knew of keeping to her resolve. Gladys told her, for once tactfully turning away from Eleanor and speaking in a casual tone, that there had been a man outside the house, waiting. But he had eventually gone, she said. There was no need to worry.

She was as unhappy as she had ever been, but she pushed the feeling deep inside her and would not give it the light and air of thought. She met friends and she worked and read and every day she took long walks through a city that was gradually emptying itself of its young men. She was tight and hard with grief. She didn't cry; she thought that she would never cry again. She felt that her life was over almost before it had begun. In a single summer.

Her pupils left clutching bags and wearing their best clothes, their hair washed and combed. Eleanor went to the station. She watched them board the train. Some were sobbing and others looked jubilant. The older ones held the hands of their younger siblings, trying to be more grown-up than they were. They didn't know where they were going; they waved handkerchiefs out of windows or pressed their faces to the glass, noses squashed and eyes wide. They left her with a letter saying goodbye that Peter found more than seventy-five years later. Eleanor signed up for the Women's Voluntary Services. She wanted to be part of history, swimming in its currents. She was alone, without Michael and without Gil, without her family.

Winter arrived, hard and terrible; one of the coldest winters anyone could remember. She didn't go home; she thought perhaps she didn't have a home any more and she didn't mind.

At the beginning of March, coming back to her bedsit in the twilight, with damp wind blowing against her face, she saw him and for a moment she thought it must be a waking dream: a shifting, unreliable glimpse of the face she had tried not to picture and had come to believe she would never see again. She stopped. She couldn't work out what she was feeling. Terror perhaps, or was it joy? Something frozen melting and something hard crumbling, like the coming of spring at last after a long winter. He was waiting, as he had waited so many times before, opposite her rooms. He was no longer in his thin shabby suit, but wore a uniform. As she drew closer, she could see that his soft hair was cropped so that she could almost make out the scalp beneath. And as she approached him and they stood face to face, she noticed that he had a broken blood vessel in one eye. She put her hand to her heart as if to prevent its painful beating.

He made no move towards her. She understood that she could walk past him, into the house, close the door behind her, and he wouldn't pursue her. He didn't smile or speak, just waited to see what she would decide. And as she stared into his eyes, she felt that she was looking into a desolate landscape of the hidden self and she knew that as long as she lived she would remember the moment when he let her see everything he was.

She took the last two steps that separated them and put up one hand, touching his cheek with the tips of her fingers very lightly. Still he didn't move, though a small writhing crossed his face.

'I never knew,' she said at last softly. Never knew how deep it could go; how much love could hurt. Looking at his face, she felt scoured by the feeling. 'Come with me.'

'Wait.' It was the first word he'd spoken. 'You won't leave again?'

'I won't leave again.'

'Not if—'

'Not if anything.'

She took his hand and led him across the road and through the door. Gladys came into the hall at the sound of the door closing, but Eleanor didn't let go of Michael's hand as she took him up the stairs. She couldn't remember why they had ever bothered to hide themselves before, like a dirty secret from the light, like a squalid fling that would run its course and need never be mentioned to the snickering world.

He had chilblains, new callouses on his hands, new lines on his face. She hated to see him so. She took him in her arms and held him against her breast; whispered words into his ear that made him groan.

He had a few days' leave before being sent abroad; he had managed to borrow a small cottage in Norfolk for three days, on the chance she would come with him. She told him she would come with him, anywhere. In those few days, love seemed so grievously powerful and the self so fragile and porous that even speaking was hard. They used low, soft tones with each other and chose their words with care.

They travelled by the slow train to the coast, stopping at empty stations, not saying very much, staring out of the window and then back at each other. He was still in his uniform, which was a bit too large for him. The house was square, plain, very small and barely furnished, half a mile from the sea. It stood alone in marshy, windswept fens, with the great sky above them and the wrinkling sea in the distance. They felt that they were quite alone, and for that brief period the war stood far off, just a distant rumbling, a faint shadow. The days were cold and bright, and the wind that swept in from the North Sea took their breath away. They walked for miles along the vast, deserted beaches, the wet sand shining and the seabirds stepping delicately through the shallows or borne aloft on the currents of air, calling; and they hunkered down behind the dunes and felt for each other through layers of clothing, Eleanor's hair blowing into his face and sand on their lips. They found shells on the beach and Eleanor took some home with her and kept them with her father's cuff-links. In the evenings he would build a fire and she sat beside him and watched as he stood at the stove, making their dinner from the supplies they had brought from Eleanor's rooms. She played songs on the battered piano in the living room, some of whose notes were missing. Decades later, hearing them, they would bring back those days by the sea but she never played them again herself. They made love and tasted the salt on each other's skin. They drank whisky and tasted it in each other's mouths. They woke in the night and reached out for each other.

On the last day he dressed once more in his uniform. Naked, she watched him from the bed as he buckled his belt, buttoned his jacket, tied up his laces, until he looked camouflaged, diminished. He turned, feeling her gaze, and came towards her. And she unbuttoned the jacket and pulled it off; knelt and unlaced his heavy boots. She took off his trousers and laid him down on her bed, pale and slender, with his shorn head and his unsmiling face. She leant over him and kissed him. She lowered herself on to him. It could never be enough.

'Don't go,' she said afterwards.

'You know that I have to go.'

'Don't die.' She hated the words even as she was saying them: they were the words Merry would have spoken.

'I've no intention of dying. I'll be back before you can miss me.'

'I miss you already.'

'How can you miss me when you have me?'

'How can I have you when you're going?'

'Because you always have me,' he said. 'It doesn't matter where I am, how far from you; you have me. I'm leaving my heart in your care.'

'I'll take good care.'

'Do that. It won't be long, Nell. Will it?' he added, and she saw he was scared.

'No. No, of course it won't.'

'And then we'll have the rest of our lives.'

'But it was long and we didn't have the rest of our lives. We just had those few snatched, secret months.'

Peter got up and closed the curtains.

'And then what——?'

'Enough of me,' said Eleanor. 'Enough of the past. Time to talk about the party.'

'Party?'

'My birthday party. Most people get presents for their birthday – I will give presents. Lots of presents. Everything I've got. Wine and jewels and pictures and furniture and books. A great free-for-all. What will you have?'

'Me!'

'Yes. Take your pick.'

'I couldn't – I don't want anything.'

'Surely. If it makes it easier for you, you can choose after they've all gone. There'll be plenty left.'

'I plan to go before they arrive.'

'Which would be a pity. But in that case, you'd better choose now.'

'Perhaps just a couple of photographs,' he said. Then he could take the photographs he had already put beside his bed.

'That doesn't seem quite adequate, after all you've done.'

'I've liked being here. This has been my halfway house. My safe place.'

'I'm glad.' She briefly laid a cool, dry hand over his.

'And now it's nearly time for me to go.'

'Me too,' said Eleanor. She was smiling at him and he smiled back, although he knew that she couldn't see.

24

In May, Michael was killed in the Siege of Calais. Eleanor didn't hear of it directly: she had only one scrap of a letter that he had posted before embarking, and then nothing. Michael's mother was officially informed and she told family and friends, although gradually. Merry heard of it from the aunt and uncle with whom Michael had been staying when she had met him; they knew of their nephew's past involvement with Merry but not that he had left her. They thought she was still his girl and came to the house especially to tell her, even though they themselves were stumbling in their grief. They held her hand and treated her like the dead man's acknowledged sweetheart and it gave her solace. She did not tell them she had heard nothing from Michael for very many months, and she wept in their embrace. She was very pretty and delicate. Her eyes were red-rimmed. She told her friends of the death, and then after a day or two of sobbing she wrote a letter to Eleanor. She put a great deal of care into the letter and wrote it several times before it satisfied her. She was laying down a version of events that she felt confident Eleanor wouldn't contradict. Although she could never admit it to herself, she was glad that Michael had died; now he could belong to her again. Eleanor would never have him. In the end, Eleanor had lost and she had won.

Dearest Eleanor, I have some tragic news and I wanted to give it myself, before you heard from Daddy or Sally, though they've been very kind to me. Everyone has been kind. You've always tried to protect me but you can't protect me from this. My darling Michael has been killed. You understood how much we meant to each other; I know how you stood up for us with Daddy and Sally. I will remember him and love him until the day I die. It is a dreadful waste of his life and our happiness. I have written to his mother and I think I will go and visit her soon. We will be able to talk about Michael and perhaps that will give both of us some much-needed comfort.

I wish you were here, Eleanor. I am trying to be strong but it is very hard when I feel so weak and unhappy. But at least I know that he died fighting bravely for his country and what it is to have been truly loved.
Your ever-loving sister, Merry

At first, Eleanor didn't take in the contents of the letter that she crumpled in her hand. Her hand was trembling but her brain was still and empty. There was a sour feeling in her throat, as if she had been sick. She opened up the letter and stared at it, trying to make sense of the words. *My darling Michael has been killed*. That meant *her* Michael had been killed, her darling and her love, who had found her out and made her real. Has been killed. Was dead. Is dead. Was, is and ever more shall be dead. But still, her brain didn't process the fact; she simply went on staring at the writing, girlishly round and neat, the way Merry had always written since elementary school. Eleanor could see her sister as she was then: the end of a plait in her mouth and a puckering frown on her pretty face. Triumphant.

It is a dreadful waste of his life. As if he'd been crumpled up and thrown away. She imagined Michael limping towards battle. No, she couldn't imagine it. She refused to imagine that she would never see him again. *I know what it is to have been truly loved*. Merry's easy, lying, self-deceiving words – words she would repeat until even she believed them – but did she, Eleanor, know what it was to have been truly loved? No; for they had only just begun. He had told her, that last anguished time that even now made her body lurch with a kind of remembered, hopeless desire, that a lifetime would be too short.

He died fighting bravely. What did Merry know, what did any of them know, about how Michael would have died? This trite phrase, *died fighting bravely*, was just a sticking plaster over a gaping hole where the heart used to be. Perhaps he had died bravely, thinking of King and country, thinking of England's hills and fields, or perhaps he had died slowly, horribly, lying in the mud like an animal in pain, and alone, no one to hold him and look into those eyes of his and say his name.

They would not grow old together. She would grow old alone.

She put her hand against her heart to feel it beating. She felt the weight of her breast, soft and full against the heel of her hand, and then she laid a palm flat against her belly. She closed her eyes and let the knowledge enter her.

She was sick, but even after there was nothing left she still retched, stinging bile splattering against the toilet bowl. Then she washed her face with cold water and cleaned her teeth and put on fresh clothes. She felt dizzy, clammy, cold, dark. So cold and dark although it was bright summer.

Dearest Merry, she wrote, and then stopped. Her pen slipped in her hand. There were birds singing outside in the dusk, perched on the plane tree. She took another piece of paper and began again. *Dear Merry, I am so very sorry for your loss.*

They were words she could have written to a stranger. This was to be the lie that Merry would build her life on: that Michael had died loving her; that she was the best beloved. This was how she could survive, her frail but steely self kept intact.

And how would she, Eleanor, survive? What was her story to be? *These are terrible times,* she wrote, *and I hate to think of what you must be going through.* She knew it was her task to say something about the comfort to be drawn from having known love, but she couldn't. *I am glad that you are being cared for and of course I will come and see you very soon. All my thoughts are with you, Eleanor.*

It was insufficient but it was all the generosity that she could manage for now. She took the letter to the postbox and then she walked all the way to the churchyard and the quince tree. She sat in its dappled light and remembered him.

She was sick again in the night, but the nausea wouldn't leave her. There was a nasty taste in her mouth and it was as if she was poisoned. Her breasts felt uncomfortable and her skin prickled. Perhaps she was ill – but of course she knew that she wasn't ill. She had known for days, weeks even, as she leant over her wireless listening to the news, or sat in the little hall up the road planning evacuations and mobile canteens, chatting with the other women who all had husbands or brothers or sons abroad, or ate her buttered roll in the little café and heard everyone talking of the war. How long had it been? She counted back to their last time together in the small house near the sea, the tender frenzy. They hadn't taken care. Now she didn't know what to do or who to tell. There was no one in the world she could tell and there was no one who could tell her what to do.

Once, she had been engaged to Dr Gilbert Lee: anticipating a church wedding with white satin and bridesmaids, family heirlooms, a house with windows through which the light fell over polished floors, a disapproving mother-in-law, theatregoing and concerts and days flowing past like a broad steady river. Now she was on her own in a city in danger, and Michael was dead and she was in trouble.

At last, she told her friend Emma, who lived a rackety kind of life with her artists and penniless poets. Emma regarded her with excited horror, a hand over her mouth.

'Oh my gosh. You poor thing,' she said. 'Gin. Castor oil. Hot baths.'

'Or I could try falling down the stairs,' suggested Eleanor drily.

'There are things you can take. Someone said putting elm bark up you. I don't know. I've never . . . but I can ask people.'

'Thank you.'

'Who——? Was it the man who you——?'

'That's not relevant,' said Eleanor, cutting her short. 'Someone I'm not going to see again.'

*

Suddenly, the roads seemed to be full of pregnant women, of women pushing babies in perambulators. They had wedding rings on their fingers. They had husbands. She hid in her room with the curtains drawn, repelled by the glare of the sun. Its heat seemed hostile. Everything seemed dirty, infested, rotten. Her skin felt smeared, however much she washed. Food made her stomach heave. Even the thought of the rich yellow of an egg yolk or the blisters of blood on meat flooded her mouth with bile. She could smell what Terence was cooking in his room. Sardines. Corned beef. Sour milk. Fried eggs. Beer. She could smell the garlic on Gladys's breath. She heaved the contents of her stomach into the toilet when she woke and still couldn't get rid of the nausea that coated her insides.

She lay on her bed in her slip and felt the squashy softness of her breasts against the pillow. It was just a collection of cells, no bigger than a fingernail or a broad bean or something. Yet though her face had become thin and pale, purple shadows blooming under her eyes, and her collarbone seemed sharp as a blade, her spare body was swelling and ripening, as if one day it must split like a purple fig, a melon spilling its seeds. She was like a piece of food herself, slightly rotten. She thought she could smell her own disintegration.

*

Across the street one day, near Oxford Street, she caught sight of Gil. He was walking with a woman. She only glimpsed them for a few seconds, but she could see that the woman was small and full of vivacity and she was laughing, her head tipped back. She had her arm through Gil's and was laughing into his face. She couldn't see his expression but she imagined it to be solemn and happy, the way it used to be with her. She turned quickly away and stood with her back to them, her face pressed to some shop window, pretending to be gazing in at the wares. But she couldn't see anything beyond her own reflection. She stood like that until they were gone and she was safe from being seen.

Gladys knocked at her door, put her small face round it.

'Can I come in?'

'Yes.' Eleanor struggled to a sitting position and pushed her hair back from her hot face.

Gladys sat down on the edge of Eleanor's bed, folded her hands in her lap.

'You're not well,' she said.

'No. I think it's a sickness bug.'

'Mmm.' Eleanor could feel Gladys's bright, restless eyes travelling over her body. 'How are you going to get better?'

'I don't know what you mean.'

'Your young man—'

It was a relief to talk about it. 'He died.' For the first time, Eleanor's eyes filled with hot tears; she could feel grief unlodge in her stomach. She looked away and swallowed hard. 'He died in France.'

'Oh my dear.' For some reason, she didn't mind Gladys's sympathy. 'So you're in a tidy bit of trouble now, aren't you?'

'I fear I am.'

'Have you thought of what you will do?'

'Do?'

'About your troubles.'

It seemed odd to Eleanor that neither of them said the words out loud: *pregnancy*, *baby*, *illegitimacy*, *disgrace* . . . They just said 'troubles', delicately skirting around the thing itself.

'I don't know,' she said, biting her lip, looking towards the window.

'There are chemists, you know.'

'Chemists? But it's not allowed. What would I ask for?'

'The ones that can help often have signs.'

'Signs?'

'"Cures for all blockages", "Treatments for all ladies' ailments". That kind of thing. Once you start looking, you will see them.'

'And then I just ask for – what do I ask for?'

'Say you haven't been getting your monthlies and you need help.'

'And they'll just give me something over the counter, as easy as that?'

'I don't know if it's easy. It can be nasty and then, whether it will actually work . . .' And she gave a little shrug.

Eleanor wanted to ask her if she'd ever been in the same situation, but she didn't know how.

'Thank you,' she said instead. 'I appreciate it.'

'We women should help each other.'

'You're right. We should.'

Gladys got up and gave Eleanor one of her friendly nudges.

'You come and find me if you want something.'

'Thank you.'

'Let me know how you get on!' As if it were a job interview or a date.

'I will.'

It was the third chemist she went to. By now she was stiff with a kind of furious embarrassment. She lurked among the shelves until there were no other customers, sure as she did so that they all knew anyway. It was written all over her: in her breasts and belly and skin. She hated the middle-aged man behind the counter and the way he seemed to eye her with a mixture of contempt and curiosity. She caught him looking at her ring-less fingers and her stomach and he hardly bothered to look away. His arch politeness thinly disguised his distaste, and there was something else in his voice and his eyes as well – lechery perhaps? She was a fallen woman. She had given in to her desires, or someone else's. A man's hands had travelled over her body; he had been inside her. She imagined swiping violently at the glass bottles neatly lined up, looking so decorative, knocking them to the ground with a shattering of glass, coloured pills rolling on to the floor.

He gave her a bottle and instructions as to dosage. He called her 'Madam' and wished her a return to her health as if he were mocking her. Or perhaps, she thought later, he was quite sincere but her paranoia poisoned everything.

She hadn't known how ill she would feel. After the first day, she simply lay in bed with the curtains closed and the sheet pulled over her, shivering and appalled. Her body was like an alien object. Horrible things were happening to it; strange obscene sensations. Her skin crawled and pain uncurled and blossomed in her guts. There was a dull, heavy ache in her lower back and whichever position she lay in, she couldn't find a place of comfort. She drank tumbler after tumbler of water, but remained thirsty, her mouth parched and tasting of metal. Was this what was meant to happen? Did this mean it was working? She had no idea. She was violently sick and worried that she had vomited up the medicine as well. She had diarrhoea too. She had turned to foul liquid. Everything was spilling out of her except the thing itself. No blood, except for a few spots after the third day.

Gladys brought her chicken soup and sat by her to make sure she swallowed it down. She tried. It tasted of rubbish. There was nothing that wasn't polluted. She remembered Michael, the way he had been those last days, but the memory was defiled. He had died and left his life inside her, and now she felt like a corpse because of it.

It wasn't working. She had one pill left and nothing was happening. She was washed up and grey and empty of everything except the baby. The foetus. Gladys had told her she must never call it a baby; that was to make it alive in her imagination. The foetus then, curled up inside her. She thought she had felt it move – like a feather tickling at her. Sinister little feather. She looked at the pair of knitting needles on the top of her chest, pushed into a ball of blue wool with a few inches of some garment strung along one of them. She had been going to knit Michael a scarf; that's what women did, they sat at home knitting for their men at the front. She picked up the free needle and looked at it, running her fingers along its edge to the point. But she had read that's what desperate women did: heated a thin metal knitting needle and pushed it deep inside, although how did the hand not tremble, slip? She twisted her face at the thought of it. She pictured squatting on the floor, legs apart, and sinking her body down so that the needle pierced her, like a monstrous inversion of the act of love. Could she do that? She put down the needle. Nothing could make her slide a thin hot blade in between her legs.

The war seemed far off. She heard of Dunkirk on the wireless, and in the street outside her window everyone was talking about it. Gladys was full of it when she came to check on her. A flotilla of boats bobbing on the sea. It was like a fairy tale of rescue; it didn't seem real. People had gas masks, ration books; every evening they put up their blackout curtains. Trains full of baby-faced men in uniforms were pulling out from stations. Men were dying in their thousands, bombs dropping, buildings toppling, but her world was shrinking to this room, this bed, this toxic, swollen body.

She dreamt she was swimming. That was the whole of her dream: naked and swimming all alone across an expanse of clear water, seeing her limbs white and strong beneath her. But she knew that she was lithe and free and she woke with a feeling of gladness in her throat that gradually slipped from her as she remembered.

*

It hadn't worked. She was still pregnant. With child, that was how the Bible put it. Yet this morning, now that all the pills were done with and the poisoning over, she felt better, stronger. She got out of her bed, wobbling as she stood up, the room tipping. She took a bath and washed her hair for the first time in more than a week. The water was cold. She put on clean, loose-fitting clothes and tied her hair back in a single thick plait. She was no longer disgusted by her body, although it felt as if it belonged to someone else entirely. When she looked at herself in the mirror, her face shocked her: it looked older, thinner, with a greyish tinge, as if her skin were slightly dirty. There was a cold sore on the side of her mouth. No one would call her beautiful now, but she couldn't care less about that. She pulled open the curtains to let the summer day into her sour-smelling room. A lilt of gladness caught at her. She put her hand against her belly and kept it there. She had a sudden and ludicrous picture of herself living in a little cottage in the country, pegging sheets out on the line and a baby in a basket beside her. A stupid fantasy from a child's picture book of motherhood, all about clean living and simple virtue: an escape from the noisy, crowded, soiled world of London, where people of all ages and colours and creeds rubbed against each other and the gas lamps chased the night away. But what was she going to do?

She went downstairs slowly, gripping the banisters, still weak and slightly dizzy, and out of the front door. She hadn't eaten a proper meal for many days and now she made her way along the street like a convalescent. Familiar things seemed as new as when she had arrived in London for the first time with her cardboard suitcase, her ill-cut fringe and her bulky black shoes. She went to her usual café. It was emptier than normal. She took her seat by the window and asked for a pot of tea and a toasted fruit bun with butter, and didn't mind that she was spending money she should be saving up. She ate it very slowly, tearing off tiny mouthfuls. She almost cried at the goodness of it, and of the hot tea trickling down her parched throat.

She sat there for a long time, while the light faded and a moon appeared above the chimneys, shining faintly through the foggy darkness. She felt quite placid now. She would let the baby grow inside her; she would see what happened. Of course, she wouldn't be able to continue teaching afterwards. They didn't allow married women to be teachers, let alone unmarried mothers.

She ordered herself a poached egg and another cup of tea so that she didn't have to leave this cosy space. And at last, sitting looking out on to the streets with people flowing past, she let herself think of Michael. She pictured his dear face – the secret face no one knew but her. She let herself remember him as he promised her that he would soon return. And she pledged to herself that however long she lived and whatever happened along the way, she wouldn't forget him. She would keep him alive in her memory long after everyone else had forgotten him: his curiosity, his quickness, his loneliness, his anger, the terrible strength of his hope, the way he would read a book as if he were devouring it; the way he laid his love at her feet; the way he had chosen her. Her lost love, her dearest heart, with his limp and his shabby clothes and his pale torso and his strong arms that would never, not ever, hold her again. His eyes that would never gaze into hers again, and the unnerving way that he looked at her as she took off her clothes, making her doubly naked, as if her soul were stripped. The way that he said her name, called her Nellie. No one would call her Nellie again. No one would ever make her lose herself again, not like that. How she would miss him, down the corridor of years. How she would be sad for him, that he had missed life. She would return to being Eleanor. Even as a single mother with the world judging her – she instinctively put her hand on her belly – she would be Eleanor. Self-possessed, in control, defended against the world and all its gifts and curses; nobody would know her secret life.

She drank her tea and ate the egg, mopping it up with white bread. She would think of what she should do tomorrow. Tonight, she would sleep and perhaps she would dream of him. Perhaps she would even be able to cry at last, for him and for herself.

But when she finally returned to her bedsit, Gladys met her in the hall. Her little face was alight with a scared kind of glee.

'Someone's here for you,' she whispered, jerking her head upwards towards Eleanor's room. 'He came an hour ago and wouldn't leave.'

For a moment, Eleanor thought that she meant Michael and she felt quite giddy, as if a world had opened up inside her and underneath her and there was no firm ground anywhere. She put a hand against the wall to steady herself. Gladys saw her expression.

'Oh no dear,' she said. 'It's your Dr Lee.'

'Gil.'

'I said I didn't know when you'd be back but he insisted on waiting for you. He said it was important. You left your door unlocked so I let him in. My room isn't really fit for visitors. Is it all right?'

'I suppose so,' Eleanor replied dully. The sudden elation had drained away, swilling through her heart and then running out of it, leaving her feeling dusty and drab. 'I'll go up.'

'That medicine that made you so badly—' Gladys hesitated.

'It hasn't worked.'

'Oh dear.'

'But I feel well again.'

'I suppose that's something,' Gladys said doubtfully.

'Yes.'

She mounted the stairs. The last time she had seen Gil, he had been walking with that other woman, who was pretty and who gazed up at his face with the kind of love he deserved. The last time she had met him, she had danced with him and then, at the end of the evening, told him it was over. She remembered his face under the umbrella he held over them both, blank and heavy with disbelief.

She hesitated in front of her door and then pushed at it. He was sitting at the small table by the window and stood up as she entered, his face serious but not grim. He had lost a bit of weight and looked older. His untidy hair had been cut short. He wasn't in uniform but he looked like a soldier on leave. All young men looked like soldiers on leave nowadays.

'Hello Gil.' She went forward and gave him her hand as though she were some lady out of a Victorian novel. He took it and pressed it, then let it go.

'Eleanor,' he said.

His eyes were on her and she felt sharply conscious of the change that he was seeing in her. Her face was thinner and her figure fuller. Her skin had lost its radiance. She was no longer the woman he had fallen for.

'You've been ill,' he said. It wasn't a question.

She nodded and turned away. Her bed was unmade; there was a faint smell of illness in the room.

'I'm sorry.'

'Oh.' She made a gesture of indifference. 'Men are dying all over Europe. I've just been a bit unwell.' She turned towards him again. 'Why have you come, Gil?'

'I've come to ask you something.' But he paused.

'Yes?'

'I hope you won't feel I'm—' He put his hand up to his face. 'I know you told me that it was over.'

'Gil—'

'Perhaps I should have argued, tried to hold on to you. But that's not my way. I took what you had said and tried to get on with my life. I did get on with my life. I told myself that it was the end. But now, now I've come to ask you if you will not change your mind. Will you please marry me, Eleanor?'

'Why?' she said, staring at him almost aghast. 'Why are you asking?'

'Because I love you, and—'

'No! Why are you asking me now? Why are you here?'

'I thought perhaps things might have changed for you.'

'Changed. You need to say the words out loud, Gil.'

'I thought perhaps I could help you.'

'You saw me the other day, in the street.'

He nodded. 'I did see you.'

'And you realised I was in trouble.'

'I thought you might be.'

'How?' She was horrified. 'How can anyone know?'

'I don't know. It came on me in a flash: the way you looked. Your shape ever so slightly changed.' His cheeks flushed. 'And you had your hand laid on your stomach, the way expecting women do.'

'Of course, you're the doctor.' She nodded. 'So you've come here to do the gentlemanly thing – although it's not you who has got me into trouble.'

'I've come here because it would make me very happy if you would consent to be my wife.'

He was talking in a jarringly old-fashioned way. Shyness made him stiff and awkward.

'You were with another woman that day.'

'Yes.'

'She looked nice.'

'She is very nice.' He considered for a moment. 'Her name is Annie and she is a nurse.'

'And she also looked as though she liked you. You looked happy with her.'

'Did I?'

'And yet you're here asking me to marry you

because you think I need your help. I don't want your charity, Gil.'

He sat down suddenly on her unmade bed, the bed they had lain in together once. He had deep eyes and his hands had felt inside bodies. Eleanor instinctively put her own hand against her stomach, then just as quickly removed it. Her cheeks were burning with shame.

'The truth is,' Gil said, speaking now in the quiet and simple way she was familiar with. 'The truth is, Eleanor, that after you left me I was in a bad way. I don't know if others saw it, but it was an effort for me to get through each day adequately. The zest was gone from everything. I was in the shadow. It lasted a long time, this feeling of dreariness and absence. I worked, I ate and drank, I slept, I saw people, I played several games of tennis and of course war doesn't allow you to be too turned in on yourself, even those of us whose duty lies here at home. And then I met Annie, who is so sunny and optimistic. I thought I had survived you, until I saw you in the street, forlorn and alone, and I realized that I was still in love with you after all.'

'Poor Annie.'

'That's as may be. It hadn't gone far between her and me. We were just in those early days. Not like with us. I don't give myself easily, Eleanor.'

'I know.' She wanted to say that neither did she, but stopped herself.

'So that's why I've come, because I want to marry you. I know you're in trouble, but that's not why I want to marry you – that's why I think you might agree to marry me.'

'I'm in love with another man,' she said.

'I understand that.'

'How do you know I'm not going to marry him?'

'Are you?'

Eleanor looked out of the window. Her eyes stung with tears.

'He's dead,' she said, adding, 'but I still love him.'

'And you are carrying his child.'

'Yes. In spite of all my best efforts.'

'Merry's young man.'

'How did you know?'

'I didn't know until this moment, but I saw the way it was between you at that picnic.'

'You never said you suspected. Even at the end.'

'What would I have said? I trusted you.' He paused, clenching and unclenching his hands. 'I believed it was the only way I could keep you: by trusting you, by waiting for your feelings to return to me. I thought your passion for this other person would die down again and I would still be there.'

'Poor Gil. I felt that too, for a while. I tried to make that true. But you see, you were wrong to trust me. I betrayed you.'

'You followed your heart. I just wish it had led you to me, not him.'

'Why are you being so dreadfully forgiving? It's – it's horrible. The better you behave, the more I become the abject sinner. Don't you see that it's impossible, Gil. It would be like that always – you forgiving me, and me, unworthy, being forgiven by you.' She grimaced. 'Impossible!'

'No!' He stood up in agitation. For a moment he didn't look like himself, but a man Eleanor didn't know yet: the colour was up in his cheeks, his fists were clenched and his eyes glowed. 'I'm not like that. If you accepted me, I would always be grateful that you gave me a second chance. That in spite of everything, we had endured this and come through. I could make you happy, I know I could. It would be my life's work.'

'Oh, Gil. You're quite mad. But the fact of the matter is that I'm not in love with you. I'm in love with him. With a dead man.'

'I know that.'

'Which means that however much trouble I'm in, I can't marry you.'

'I've thought it all through. We could marry at once, before you begin to properly show – show to the outside world, I mean. And then—' He faltered momentarily. 'Then we live together as friends. I won't ask you for anything you don't want to give me.'

'You mean, no sex?'

'Until – or unless – you wanted it.'

'You'd end up hating me.'

'Never that.'

'Yes. You'd think of her – Annie – who loved you, looked up at you. And you'd curse me, and you'd curse him, too.'

'You can say his name, you know.'

'Michael,' she said. 'His name was Michael.'

'I know.'

'Of course. But isn't it odd that you are the only person I can speak to about him? The one person with whom out of common kindness and decency I should remain silent.'

'You can if you want,' he said. 'If it helps you.'

'There is something terrifying to me about your goodness,' said Eleanor.

'Please.' He gazed at her, his face working. 'Please don't say that. I'm not good. I have been wretched and angry and jealous and torn by ugly emotions. But I can do this. We can do this. We can make it work.'

'I loved him,' Eleanor said softly. 'I left you for him. You shouldn't make do with being second best.' He didn't reply and she continued. 'Then the baby would come and perhaps it would have Michael's face, Michael's ways. It wouldn't be your child, Gil; it would be his. Whenever you looked at this child you would remember its father.'

'Perhaps. But I would look after it and protect it and give it all my affection. If you would let me.'

'Let you?'

'If you would let me be the father. I would never say or feel anything but gratitude. I would consider myself the lucky one, the one who is saved from himself.'

Eleanor, looking at his impassioned face, thought of what this life would be. She and Gil and this child that was growing inside her, in a well-ordered house, with money enough, security, kindness, comfort. And behind her, the figure of Michael would stand, a lonely figure in the apocalyptic landscape of war. And behind that figure, those nights and days they had spent together, when she had given up her world for him, given up herself, let him inside her body and her soul in a rapture of loss.

'I don't know,' she said at last. 'I think you are noble and reckless and I don't—'

'Don't say anything just now,' he urged. 'Think about it. I've got to be away for a few days. Let me call on you when I return. Tell me then.'

'All right.'

'But say yes.'

'You're a romantic, Dr Lee.' And she smiled at him.

He wrote to her, setting it out once more.

My dear Eleanor,

You're wrong: I didn't speak lightly or recklessly, and I am not particularly noble or even romantic, except perhaps where

you are concerned. I loved you from the moment I set eyes on
you and that has never changed, nor will it do so. I wouldn't
be taking you on, you'd be taking on <u>me</u>: my melancholy, my
cautious and solitary nature, my lack of charisma and elo-
quence. I am, as you know, a dogged kind of fellow, not a
star. I am a doctor, not a hero. I am a rationalist and not a
poet. Anything I have achieved has been done through patience
and determination but I have come to believe that these are
not secondary virtues. Their roots go deep. I believe you can
trust me. I think you know by now how much I care for you
and how I will never cease to work for your happiness.

I will call on you when I return next week.
Yours in hope and love, Gilbert

'And so you said yes,' said Peter after a long silence.

'Not at once. You have to understand that I wasn't
so very terrified of being a single mother, although
my mother would have been mortified with the
shame of it. I knew it would be hard, but I didn't
mind that. I almost welcomed the thought of hard-
ship – as if I needed to prove and punish myself. I
think there was part of me that wanted to proclaim
to the world that I was bearing Michael's child. I liked
Gil as much as anyone I'd ever met; indeed, I loved
him. I respected and admired him, and trusted him
implicitly. I knew that he would never go back on
what he said to me during that meeting, take the
moral high ground or remind me of what he had
done for me. And he never did, not once, in all the

years we had together. He was the most generous of men; one of his obituaries used my word "noble" to describe him and I think that's not an exaggeration. What's more, I believed that if I made up my mind to accept him, we could be happy together and have a good, equal, affectionate marriage. But—'

'But?'

'But I was, as he himself had said, in love with a dead man. As much if not more in love as I had been when he was alive. Put all of the many good and sensible reasons for marrying Gil in one side of the scale and that single fact in the other side, and the scale still tipped towards Michael. Even though Michael was no longer there.'

'So what made you change your mind?'

'I think it was my father. He had died before I was even born, and my life had in some ways been shaped around his absence. I didn't want my own child to grow up like that. It was almost as if I was giving myself a second chance. Does that make sense to you?'

'I'm not sure,' Peter said. 'Perhaps.'

'I went for a long walk the night before I gave my answer. I walked down past the school that had become a centre for war efforts, down the street I had walked with Michael that first night we had spent together, past the house where he had taken me. I walked and I remembered and I thought. I had to face what I would be giving up if I became a wife to Gil: the Eleanor who had been so wildly in love, who had been reckless, lost and free. The Nellie whom Michael had adored. The independent spirit. The new woman.'

'But then you said yes,' said Peter softly and almost regretfully, watching the expression on the old woman's face.

'I said yes. Yes, I will. I do.'

25

The following day Samuel turned up. Peter didn't hear him arrive and never found out quite how he'd got there – certainly not by car. But when he went into the junk room after his breakfast, he found him sitting cross-legged on the floor, surrounded by photographs. His feet were bare and he was only wearing a thin shirt. He was in his sixties but he looked like a boy.

'Peter!' he said, rising to his feet in a single graceful motion. 'Hello.' As if he had known him always.

He held out a hand. Eleanor's piano-playing hands, thought Peter, though Samuel didn't resemble his mother in other ways. He was not tall, and was slender and light on his feet as a cat or a tightrope walker. Peter remembered Thea talking about her uncle jumping over the garden hedges with his coat flying out behind him. He had an androgynous air, a youthfulness in spite of the grey hair and the weathered face. Named Samuel after Eleanor's father, whom she had never known. The one she always worried about. Michael's child. Flesh of my flesh, she had said.

'Hello.' Peter took the hand.

'I'm Samuel.'

'I know.'

'Of course you do. But look, it's a beautiful day out there. Why don't we have a walk in the woods and you can tell me.'

'Tell you what?'

'Whatever you want.'

It was a beautiful day, still and cold and clear, though Samuel, tipping his head back as though he were sniffing the air, said that it felt like snow must come soon. They went through the garden. Samuel had pulled on an old but lovely coat and a soft hat and pushed his naked feet into boots. He pointed out plants and birds as they went, exclaimed over the state of the fruit cage, plucked a withered yellow rose.

Peter was uneasy at first. He knew things about Samuel that Samuel didn't know about himself. But gradually he relaxed. At first Samuel asked soothing questions about the work Peter had done. Then he talked himself, moving easily between subjects. Peter learnt that he lived in Cornwall at the moment, but he was always on the move. He felt he had no anchor but he didn't mind that; it was what he had chosen. He didn't own a house and hated the idea of having property or of settling in one place, one life. He was a musician of sorts – he played the violin, the accordion and the piano. Eleanor had been his piano teacher. Gil had taught him to love nature; he missed his father with a freshness that surprised him. He occasionally played in folk bands, but for many years he had given private lessons to make ends meet. He liked walking and would walk for many miles rather than taking a bus or a taxi. He liked being rootless and yet he dearly loved this house and sometimes he dreamt about it. The idea of Eleanor in a home made him feel almost ill; he had wanted her to live with him but she had refused.

Peter found that he was saying things as well, things he hadn't meant to say – about books he loved, about his own mother, about playing the flute but never making the sound he heard in his imagination, about the gap between what you strive for and what you achieve. Fragments of his life he lifted from his mind and laid before this son of Michael's. Samuel listened, nodded, and once he laid a hand lightly on Peter's arm. Was this what Michael had been like too, full of an elusive mystery and charm, both intimate and yet elusive?

Then the two of them returned to the house together and Samuel left later in the day without saying goodbye. Peter saw him go, walking into the afternoon darkness. Eleanor played the piano for longer than usual, the rippling notes of a Chopin étude, and at dinner she was quiet and softer than usual.

He said: 'When you were married, Eleanor, did you—?'

But she held up her hand.

'No, Peter,' she said, not angry but severe. 'There is nothing left to say. The story I've been telling you is over. I married Gil; I became Eleanor Lee. When Samuel was born I held him in my arms and I promised him that I would protect him from everything. Even the truth. Of course, it was impossible. You cannot protect people from life, or even wish them happiness. For what is happiness, after all? Everyone must suffer, in their own particular way. I lived through the war. So many people died. Robert died, swerving in his beloved car to avoid a cyclist. Emma died, in the Blitz, and I miss her still; sometimes I think about the things I want to tell her and how she'll laugh mockingly at me. And Gladys died in the Blitz too. I never knew what happened to her beloved cat. Poor Clive Baines died, with a photograph of Merry in his breast pocket. All those eager young men. So many of my schoolchildren; I never knew how many. But here I am, full of years, four children, eight grandchildren. A begetter.'

She lay in bed between clean sheets. Her limbs felt frail, her bones brittle and her skin thin. Her heart was full. She thought that tonight she could just catch the sound of the sea, like a person breathing in a neighbouring room. The wind in the trees and the waves on the shore, the bats in the sky, the last leaves falling in the woods where her children used to play.

She could almost hear their voices now. Often as a mother she had to run away from their terrible, importunate love. Their needs. Their desire to have the whole of her. There were many times when she had escaped from them all, pretending she was at work, but in fact simply roaming the city. Such pleasure in sitting in cafés, or in empty cinemas, quite alone and unaccounted for, no one knowing where she was, no one wanting something from her. Or walking for hours by the sea, her footprints dissolving into the wet sand. Or simply sitting in the garden with a book, blocking out their voices and warding off their sticky, clutching hands, trying not to see Gil's affectionate glances. The necessity of being just herself, briefly untrammelled by the ropes of duty and desire. Eleanor Lee. Eleanor Wright. Nellie. Nell.

There are days when the younger self accuses you. Is this who you wanted to be? Is this the life you wanted to live? What had happened to the books she had dreamt of writing, the journeys she had planned to take, the person she had thought to become? What had happened to that quiet, stubborn, fierce girl who promised herself freedom and adventure and who thought she could do anything? If eighteen-year-old Eleanor Wright had met forty-year-old or sixty-year-old or ninety-four-year-old Eleanor Lee, what would she have thought of her? She wouldn't have even recognized her. If she had read about her life – the good marriage, the children whom she had cared for and worried over and loved, the steady, worthwhile work, the days filled with purpose, the secrets untold – would she have admired it or thought that something had been lost?

Of course something had been lost. There is always something lost. Hopes and dreams and possibilities. Shadow lives and shadow selves. Roads not followed, loves not taken, doors left closed. In the end you have to choose who you will become. You are your life's work. Every moment of every day makes you. Only at the end, when your story is over, do you know what you have created.

She could have said no. No to Gil, to motherhood and serene family life, to safety and happiness and love. She could have said no to Eleanor Lee. She almost did, in spite of everything. But I do, she said in that little registrar office in Marylebone, a few weeks after Michael had died. I do, in her little cloche hat and her loose dress, with the stubborn life tickling her under the ribs and her mother crying with happiness and relief and old Mrs Lee's mouth set in disapproval. I do, to the man whom she was to tend for the rest of his life, laying his blue scarf beside him in the coffin, kissing his high forehead. What is love, after all? Not just the cries of anguish in a small house by the sea, but the daily knowledge, the small kindnesses, the garnering of memories year by year, the endurance of it. They had done well, the two of them. They had had a fine journey together.

She knew, of course, that if Michael had lived, he would have become just a man, flesh and blood, thinning hair and dodgy joints and daily needs and habits that would come to irritate and entrap her. Instead he had been the flame inside her, the quick bright ghost in her unimpeachable life. Ghost of her other self. Ghost of her youth and her impossible dream of freedom.

Never spoken. She had never spoken of him to anyone. She had never said his name out loud, after her engagement to Gil. It had been an unspoken contract. Even when Merry had talked of him, increasingly garrulous and exaggerated – her great lost love, the man who would have returned from the war to marry her and become the father of her children – she hadn't repeated his name, just fixed her face in meaningless sympathy, retreating into herself. Even when Samuel was born with Michael's eyes and his melancholy and she had held his squashy sweetness against her and breathed in his sawdust smell, she had remained silent. She had tried not to think of him, and when he came to her in dreams and in solitude, she would push him away. No, not away; she would press him down into herself, into the deep dark room inside her that no one else knew of. We all have secret rooms.

Now she had opened the door. He was in the world again, on her tongue, in her mouth, in the air. The syllables reverberated. He had stepped out of the shadows, flaring with love, and the room was full of him, her life was radiant with him again; his soft brown hair and his wide-set eyes and his old suit and his quick limp and the way he said her name and found her out. An old woman foolish with passion. Him, Gil, her mother, her father whom she had never met. All dead and all living still. If she closed her blind eyes, she could see them.

'It's been such a long time,' she said out loud. She reached out a hand towards the absence beside her. 'I've waited for so long.'

26

Peter had intended to leave well before Eleanor's ninety-fifth birthday party, but somehow he had lingered. There was always just a bit more to do – what had Jonah called it? The snagging. He didn't want to be around when everyone arrived, the great pushy mass of family bursting in through the door and filling the house with noise and bustle and a rightful sense of belonging. But he didn't want to go either. His little room in the roof, the woods at the end of the garden, the fire that he and Eleanor sat by in the evenings, held him.

Days speeded up. People came and went, bearing away carloads of things. Boxes of wine and of china, smaller pieces of furniture, rugs, cushions. He met Quentin, the one who had fallen out with Leon over religion. He didn't seem fanatical to Peter, just distracted, slightly fraying round the edges. He met Tamsin, the grand-daughter whom Thea said would want Eleanor's hats. She was in a friendly rush, dashing from room to room and talking too quickly. Giselle came, without Leon. She perched on the rocking horse and chatted to Peter about how he must go to St Petersburg, to the Hermitage. She couldn't believe he'd never been. She gave him a slice of apple and cinnamon cake and kissed him goodbye when she went, leaving the red shape of her mouth on his cheek. Esther came with another young woman in tow. Her hair had been cut shorter and she wore glasses perched on the end of her nose. A man arrived in a large van and took away all the garden tools and the sit-on mower.

In the midst of all the movement, Eleanor seemed to become stiller, like a rock in a river. She sat for many hours at the piano, while people edged sideboards and coffee tables past her. Or retreated to her room, where they could hear her audiobooks playing. They no longer had their evenings together – but perhaps there was nothing left to say. In this version of her story, she had disappeared into marriage and become invisible, the way that women do in Trollope's novels. Or perhaps, he thought, she had become visible, had become her public self.

It was very cold now, a snap in the air and a crunch underfoot. The sky became blank and white. The house's heating was inadequate. Peter sometimes wore his coat when he worked; he wished he had fingerless gloves and slippers. The cats had taken to sleeping on his bed and he welcomed their warm weight on him.

Two days before her birthday, he went to Eleanor

where she sat in the kitchen at lunch, eating scrambled eggs on burnt toast. The room was full of smoke.

'I will leave tomorrow,' he said.

'Nonsense. Stay for the party at least. The last hurrah,' she added drily. 'Stay for the bonfire. You can't leave before the bonfire. My life going up in flames.'

'It's just your family.'

'Gail and her little boy are coming. And Christy, the gardener. And Mrs Monroe up the road. Family means whatever I want it to mean. It's as you wish, of course, but you'd be part of the family and I'd be glad of your company.'

'Really?'

'If I didn't want you here, I wouldn't ask you. Haven't you understood that yet?'

So he remained, ringing his mother to tell her he'd be home after the weekend, in time for Christmas – though their Christmas was a paltry affair, like a threadbare imitation of festivity. At the start of the New Year, he was going to move out of her house, he told himself. He would start again and was ready.

He sorted the last papers, helped Leon pack books into boxes and write labels on to them and then put Gil's medical photographs into cardboard folders. Then he was enlisted by Eleanor to collect grandchildren and their partners from the station he had arrived at himself just a few weeks ago. He took Rose to the shops in the nearest town for food and pushed the trolley down supermarket aisles while she tossed in food, consulting the list she'd made: aubergines and red peppers, couscous, walnuts, bags of salad, cream, paper napkins. Giselle was making a giant pavlova. Leon and Quentin were in charge of the wine and Marianne would bring the cheese. Samuel turned up with a sack of fireworks. Peter went round the garden with him, collecting fallen branches to make a bonfire. Thea smoked roll-ups in the woods.

Young people Peter only recognized from photos were suddenly in the house. A baby with a bald head cried loudly. A toddler sat under the piano while Eleanor played. Three children kicked a ball through the garden, smashing plants. A couple argued in the rose garden, thinking that no one could hear them. There were flowers on the window sills and mantelpieces. Pictures were removed from walls, leaving clean squares on the grubby paintwork; Peter helped fold them in bubble wrap and carry them to cars. The rocking horse was put in the hall. The piano would stay for the new owners, and all the beds. Someone found the puppet theatre, in its constituent parts, and took it reverently to Samuel who stared at it for several long moments, his eyes bright. Thea took the copper bowl and the biscuit tin she coveted into the room she was sharing with her sisters. The skip that Leon had arranged filled up: so much was being thrown away. Everyone crowded into the junk room and rifled through the piles of books, exclaiming over the ones they'd known as children, arguing about who should have what. They divided up photographs; Peter thought of the three he had pilfered, but he didn't return them. They went through Eleanor's clothes and jewellery, trying things on, standing before the mirror in Indian shawls and velvet coats with unravelling hems. They made numerous pots of tea and toasted crumpets at the fire. Late arrivals came in with damp hair and cold cheeks and everyone hugged everyone else and there were groups in corners exchanging news, whispering secrets and warnings. Jonah came. His beard was gone; he brought a bottle of whisky and a bag of figs. Sometimes a fault line cracked; voices were raised, doors slammed. Polly was no longer Peter's faithful shadow. She ambled peacefully from person to person.

'Where will she go?' Peter asked Rose.

'Polly? With Quentin. He like dogs and he lives in the country.'

'What about the cats?'

'Mum's taking them.'

Quentin's son David arrived with Merry. Someone had dressed her in a pink skirt and a lavender jersey, like a sweet pea. She was vague, flustered, patchily vivacious. She clutched at people as they passed, and she asked for her father. 'Daddy,' she kept saying. 'Where's Daddy?' Marianne sat her by the fire in the living room and put a cat on her lap and she bent over it, pressing her face into its neck and murmuring words no one could hear. Sometimes she gave her unnerving laugh.

It started to snow, thinly at first, small separate flakes that dissolved on the hard earth, then with a thick, blinding certainty. The world became obscure. The shabby garden, the fruit cage and the unpruned roses were beautiful and strange. In the swirling distance, the bare trees stood like ghosts. Peter walked towards them, hearing the creak of his feet, the muffled sounds.

Inside, everything was disappearing. The house was being stripped. Rooms began to echo. Dust balls swirled and cracks were exposed. Cobwebs hung in corners. Eleanor walked to the hornbeam, leaning on Samuel's arm. She stood there for several minutes in the flurries of snow, her white hair catching the white flakes. Peter, heaving armfuls of twigs and old leaves on to the bonfire, watched her. What was she thinking? Who was she thinking of?

He helped Rose and Tamsin carry a second table into the kitchen, and then they set places for twenty-eight. The best china (they'd pack it away the following morning) augmented with chipped plates that would be put on the skip, silver candle-sticks, glasses of all shapes and sizes, paper napkins, flowers along the tables, in jam-jars because the vases had all been put in boxes. Mis-matched chairs along the sides. Eleanor would be at the head of the table, of course. The fire was lit. It felt snug and safe, snow outside and inside the fire, the smell of baking. Someone had brought Christmas crackers. Samuel and Esther prepared the food: they were very serious about it, their faces shiny with sweat. They were to have a vast fattee, layers of flat bread, cinnamon rice, chick-peas and aubergines, studded with walnuts and pomegranate seeds, daubed with yoghurt. Rose assembled smoked salmon blinis. Steam filled the room.

The snow stopped falling. At six o'clock, the bonfire was lit and sparks flew up into the black sky. Grandchildren pulled bin bags full of papers out-side and started to feed the flames, slowly at first but then a kind of wildness took hold. Peter stood to one side and watched as the blaze gobbled up let-ters, photographs, drawings, bills, school essays and university dissertations, certificates, notebooks, doodles, first drafts, architectural plans, contracts, qualifications, proofs, queries. The air was filled now with swirling petals of ash. Sticks of unwanted, broken furniture were thrown in. Firelight fell strangely on faces. Rockets and Roman candles were lit and with soft splutters and sharp cracks they exploded into the night. Flowers opening, dying, falling.

Peter looked at Eleanor and she stared into the leaping flames. Her skirt blew round her legs and her shawl flapped. Her face gave nothing away.

Merry sat on one side of him, Gail's son Jamie on the other, fidgeting – Peter remembered that the last time he'd seen him, he'd been climbing the kitchen stool over and over again. His small body squirmed with impatient energy. Merry determinedly held Peter's hand so that he could only use his fork. He kept dropping chunks of aubergine and pieces of walnut into his lap. She herself ate with her fingers, rather expertly he thought, lifting slushy balls of rice and chickpea into her mouth; her lips were greasy and her cheeks had spots of excited pink on them. Sometimes she called him Clive and sometimes she called him Gordon. She told him that she was getting married soon. When she laughed, her little cracked peal, like a damaged bell valiantly ringing out, he thought she might be about to cry. She was wearing a lopsided yellow crown from her cracker. Peter's was purple. He'd got two large dice from his cracker as well.

'Can I have those?' asked Jamie.

'Sure.' He pushed them over.

'Is your hair gold or orange?'

'What do you think?'

'Mummy says orange and I say golden brown.'

'A mixture then.'

'Do you like football?'

'No.'

'Oh.' The boy looked at him. 'Do you like Tiny Wings?'

'I don't know what that is.'

'Do you like chocolate then?'

'I suppose so.'

'What's your favourite colour?'

'Green. What's yours?'

'Blue, I think,' Jamie replied seriously. 'Or red.'

'Mine's yellow,' chimed Merry. 'Like my hair. Daddy says it's my crowning glory.'

Jamie nudged Peter with his sharp elbow and said in a loud hiss: 'What's she on about? Her hair's dead grey.' He frowned. 'What's your favourite food?'

'Um. Brie, cherries, brown shrimps. What about you?'

'I like cucumber and pies and eels.'

'Eels?'

'Strawberries,' said Merry into Peter's ear. 'Sweet red strawberries. Hmm?'

'This is horrible.' Jamie prodded his food. 'Why are you here?'

'Here in this house you mean?'

'Why are you sleeping here?'

'I've been working for Mrs Lee.'

'Is she going to die soon?'

'She's very old,' said Peter. 'She's ninety-five today. But I don't think she's going to die very soon. She's strong.'

'Her face is ploughed up.'

'I'm sorry?'

'Can you do headstands?'

'I don't think so.'

'Or cartwheels.'

'Definitely not.'

'What can you do?'

'That's a good question.'

'Why?'

'What?'

'I'm glad you've come back,' said Merry to his left. 'Very glad indeed, my dear. Have you missed me?'

'Well,' said Peter, playing for time, taking a large gulp of wine. 'Where have I been?'

'Where indeed? Some people don't know which side their bread is buttered.'

Opposite, he could hear Leon talking about drones. Further up the table, Rose was saying in her soft carrying voice that making bread was a form of therapy and Eleanor said something about how Virginia Woolf loved to bake. Out of sight on his side of the table, Thea gave a loud and dirty laugh.

'Were you shot in the face?' asked Merry. She touched his scattering of freckles with her greasy fingers.

'No.' Then before he could stop himself he said, 'Do you remember Michael?'

'Michael? Michael?' Her eyes were suddenly blue and hard. Her mouth pursed. 'You don't deserve me,' she said. She pointed at Jamie. 'And you should stand in the corner.'

Jamie's eyes grew round. Then he stuck his tongue out at her and turned back to Peter.

'I rode on the back of a motorbike. A thousand miles an hour.' And he slithered from his seat and disappeared under the table. There was a yelp.

Leon chinked a knife against the side of his glass and slowly the room fell into silence.

'Eleanor said no speeches, so this is really just going to be a toast,' he said, looking round the room. He was clearly used to this kind of thing. 'We are gathered together to celebrate the—'

'Please Leon,' said Eleanor, 'that sounds suspiciously like the start of a speech.'

'All right.' He smiled, disappointed. 'Please raise your glasses to our mother, mother-in-law, sister, grandmother, great-grandmother; to our wonderful Eleanor.'

Everyone drank. Someone called out for a speech from her. She rose, grasping her cane.

'I just want to say this.' Her voice was thin and clear. 'This is a house of memories. Memories of childhood and of growing up; happy times I hope, but also difficult and painful ones. But memories which I believe make us who we are. Even when we have left here and new owners have moved in and put their own mark upon the place, pulled up the trees we loved, knocked down walls, painted over cracks and blemishes, the memories will remain. Do not drink to me. Drink to our memories; our house of memories.'

27

Peter pushed Merry to Quentin's car in her wheel-chair. She was kicking her legs with their swollen ankles and little slippered feet out in front of her girl-ishly, and every so often she laughed politely as if someone had told her a joke she didn't entirely under-stand. Under her thick coat she wore last night's lavender outfit, which she had spilt food down. Her hair had been brushed and tied into a loose plait: that would be Rose, thought Peter. She had put her great aunt to bed last night and probably got her up this morning. He felt a moment of pity and affection for the young woman with the chestnut hair whom everyone turned to.

Quentin wasn't there but the car was unlocked. Merry, smiling, lifted up her arms like a child to be picked up. Peter hesitated then bent down and picked Merry up in his arms and she held him round the neck, tightly. She was surprisingly light, as if her bones were made of balsa wood. Her cheek was pressed against his and he smelt talcum powder and soap. Her breath was on his skin.

'My dear,' she said tenderly and contentedly as he

placed her in the passenger seat. 'How handsome you are.'

'Thank you!' He leant across her for the safety belt.

'What about me?'

Peter looked at her, then glanced behind him to make sure they were alone.

'You're very pretty,' he said.

'Mirror, mirror on the wall, am I the prettiest of them all?'

Her face, surprisingly unlined, was plump and soft like dough. She took his hand. Her mouth was slightly askew and her teeth yellow and even. Her blue eyes were scared and imploring. Peter thought of Eleanor, gravely mysterious, lustrous and strong. *Pretty* wasn't the word for her.

'You'll always be the prettiest,' he said seriously. 'You should know that. Don't be sad.'

'I have been sad. I have,' she said wonderingly.

'I know. But it's all right now. Everything's all right.'

'What about Ellie?'

'Don't worry about that any more.'

'Why did you leave?'

'Everyone leaves in the end,' he said.

'Everyone leaves,' she repeated in her thin silver voice. A single tear ran down her cheek, fat and round, and then dissolved. 'Oh dear, oh dear.'

He thought of these two old women, bashed and scarred by life, rolled over by it, and yet in whom the torrents of the past still ran so clear and strong. In their nineties and both still bound together and still haunted by a young man who had died over seventy years ago.

He bent down and kissed her on the top of her head, then stood back.

'Goodbye,' he said.

'Goodbye, Peter,' Eleanor said.

He took her crabbed and liver-spotted hand, with its thin silky skin, and remembered their first meeting. Polly came softly up beside them.

'Goodbye, Eleanor.'

They were in the living room that was almost empty now. All around them the house rang with activity. The morning after, and those who were up early were practical, energetic, lifting last boxes, stripping sheets. Esther and Rose were in Eleanor's bedroom, packing the bags that on the following day would go with her, first to Leon's house for Christmas and then to the home. 'A home,' she had said to Peter once. 'Not my home.'

'I wish you luck.'

'Thank you,' he said. 'For everything.'

'It's me who should be thanking you.'

'I will never forget you.'

'Oh.' She gave a soft, blurred laugh. 'I will fade.'

'No.' He was urgent.

'I don't know why I talked to you the way I did. Quite out of character.'

'I'm glad you did.'

'My secret life,' she said, smiling. 'Be careful what you do with it.'

'I'll carry it with me.'

'What are you going to do next?'

'I don't know yet. Something.'

'Let me know.'

'Really?'

'Of course. Now I had better go.'

'Sorry. I'm keeping you. I'm very bad at saying goodbye. I can never bring things to an end.'

'I, on the other hand, am very good at it,' she said. She touched him lightly on the shoulder. 'Take care, Peter. Reach out for life.'

And she turned and walked from the room, tall and straight.

He didn't want to say goodbye to anyone else. They were all too busy – or, like Thea, still asleep. He pulled on his coat, his gloves, his woolly hat, and picked up his bike panniers. Outside, the wind was blowing away the last of the morning mist. The snow was thick and clean. Above the deck of clouds, the sky was clearing. He made his way to his bike. Polly trotted after him. He turned back and looked at the old house. Almost every window was lit up. In the garden, Samuel was standing beside the smouldering bonfire, his head bent. He looked deep in thought.

Peter put the panniers on his bike, checked the tyres were blown up. He was putting the moment off when he would wobble up the gravel drive and out on to the road.

'Goodbye,' he said to the dog. She regarded him with her mild brown eyes and he felt tears start up, a great lump in his throat coming loose, sobs gathering under his ribs.

'Peter! Wait!'

It was Rose, running towards him.

'Hi.' He turned slightly from her so that she wouldn't see his distress – but of course she could see it. She had her grandmother's instincts.

'You're leaving without saying goodbye?'

'I thought it was best to just go.'

'Perhaps. But Eleanor wanted to give you this.' She held out a small sealed envelope.

'Thanks.' He took it and put it into his coat pocket.

'I hope we meet again,' she was saying. 'Ring me when you're in London and we can have a drink. With Thea, Jonah perhaps.'

'I'd like that.'

'Give me your number then.' She handed him her mobile and he entered his details.

'Well.' He was ready to leave now, with his bike leaning against him and the cold wind in his face. 'Bye.'

She reached up and gave him a quick kiss on his cheek.

'Be happy,' she said and was gone.

Polly trotted after her, tail swinging. In the far distance he could see Samuel. Behind windows, shapes moved about, indistinguishable. Curtains were drawn open. Were those piano notes he could hear?

He took out the envelope and slid it open. Inside was a collection of small shells. Shells that Michael and Eleanor had found on their beach, in those last days. They lay like teeth in the palm of his gloved hand.

Then he got on his bike and left and didn't look back at the house of memories.

28

Eighteen months later, on a breathlessly hot summer day, Samuel Lee opened the door to the bike shop, the bell jangling. A young, heavily bearded man behind the counter nodded at him.

'Can I help you?'

'I'm looking for Peter Mistley; I was told I could find him here.'

'He's in the workshop. I'll call for him.'

He didn't move, simply leant forward slightly.

'Peter,' he roared. 'Pete! Visitor for you.'

There was a muffled acknowledgement that came from somewhere behind them, then a few moments later Peter came into the room, carrying a bike wheel and with oil on his hands.

'Oh!' he said on seeing Samuel.

'Hello Peter.' Samuel raised a hand in greeting. 'Rose told me I could find you here. How are you?'

'I'm well.'

'You look it.'

Peter leant the wheel against a wall, underneath a rack of helmets and bike lights.

'But that's not what you're here for, is it – to ask me if I'm well?'

'No.'

'She died.'

'She's in a coma.'

'So why are you here, not with her?'

'The hospital's nearby. I needed a break. I've been there for days and it could last days more. We have a rota.'

Peter, looking at him properly for the first time, saw that Samuel was exhausted, little veins ticking, hollows at the temple and purple under the eyes.

'I'm very sorry,' he said.

'I watch her lying there, very peaceful, and I ask myself if she knows that she's dying. If she's scared. If she's ready. She's ninety-six, after all — seventy years older than my father when he died.'

It took a few seconds for what Samuel had said to sink in. Peter felt as if someone had punched him in the stomach.

'What?' he managed eventually.

'That's why I'm here in fact. Eleanor gave me something to pass on to you.'

Samuel handed him a small padded envelope; Peter opened it and pulled out a faded, dog-eared photograph. A thin face looked at him, wide-set eyes and a wing of hair falling over his forehead. Not smiling, but perhaps slightly amused. Watchful.

'She said it was for you, but I was hoping you would give it to me.'

'I don't understand.'

'Don't you?'

'How long have you known?'

'Some years.'

'But how? I thought – I mean, Eleanor said . . .' He stopped.

'Eleanor never said anything to me.'

'Was it Gil?'

'No. It was my aunt.'

'Merry.'

'Yes.'

'So she knew everything, after all. Even that.'

'I have no idea what she knew and what she suspected. Her memory was going and she was rambling and not making sense. A young man who was head over heels in love with her – and a story of betrayal. She was sentimental, then vituperative. When she talked about Eleanor she actually bared her teeth, like a horse. I hadn't known she had so much anger stored up. I always thought she was sweet but when she was going into her fog I suddenly saw her as someone who was full of passion and fear and pain. It made me like her more. She showed me his photo – the one she has now in her room.'

Peter nodded. He remembered it.

'I looked at it and it was like looking at a photograph of myself as a young man. There was no mistaking it.' He tapped his chin. 'We even have the same little cleft here.'

'Yes.'

'I knew, like a flash of lightning illuminating the landscape. My whole life stood clear and cast in a different meaning.'

'Were you upset?'

'I was more – electrified is the word that comes to mind. Startled with a new awareness. I did the maths. The large gap between myself and my siblings which I had just put down to the war. The dates of Eleanor and Gil's wedding and my own birth: why had it not occurred to me before? And then the way that they were with me.'

'How were they?'

'Solicitous. Careful.'

'But you never talked to Eleanor about it?'

'If she didn't want to tell me, I didn't want to know. And I can understand why she never spoke. But it must have been a heavy weight on her, to keep silent all her life. Why did she tell you?'

'Because I'm a stranger, someone who didn't matter, someone who it wouldn't matter to.'

'Like a priest.'

'Oh no.' Peter felt almost shocked. 'She didn't want absolution. She just wanted to tell her story at last, before she died.'

'But not to me.'

'I'm sorry.'

'It's hardly your fault.'

'Of course you should keep the photograph.

399

Perhaps I should tell you that when she talked of Gil, she was very—'

'No.' Samuel held up his hands, palms upwards. 'I don't want you to tell me anything of what she said. The only person who could ever tell me would be her, and now that's not going to happen. Her story will stay with you and die with her. She was always very insistent that everyone had to have their private space. She never tried to find out our secrets and it would seem quite wrong to try to find out hers, especially as she lies dying. I've never talked to anyone about it myself, above all not my siblings. Half-siblings, as it turns out. There has always been something mysterious about my mother. Something none of us could get at, however loving she was.'

The doorbell jangled and a young woman entered. Her face warmed as she saw Peter, whose own face lit with pleasure. He smiled across at her and held up his hand. Samuel looked at him, pleased.

'I should be going,' he said.

'Is Polly all right?'

'Polly is quite contented.'

'I hope—' Peter stopped. For what did he hope? He thought of Eleanor moving slowly and lightly towards the death that she had told him when they first met that she no longer feared. A long journey ending. 'That it's peaceful,' he finished.

'Thank you. She was fond of you. Do you have a message for her? In case she can still hear what we say?'

What do you say to a dying person? 'I don't know. That I think she is very fine. That as long as I live I won't forget her.'

'I'll tell her.'

He rested his hand on Peter's shoulder for an instant, gave his curious little bow, and left the shop.

'Who was that?' asked the young woman, going up to Peter and taking his hand between her own.

'Someone I met when I was still in my darker days.'

'You both looked very solemn.'

'Yes. But it's all right. It's good.'

29

He was very close to her this evening. She could see his face and feel his body, not far from hers. She could feel his eyes watching her and because he was watching her, she was beautiful again and full of fresh, fast joy.

'You've come at last,' she said. 'I knew you would.'

'I've never been away, Nellie.'

'Sometimes I didn't know that. Sometimes I couldn't see you.'

'It's all right. It's always been all right. Everything.'

He was so tender tonight. His eyes were deep and full of love. He took her hand. He said her name. She didn't need to pretend any longer. She didn't need to try any more.

'I never forgot,' she said. 'Not a day went by. Not an hour.'

'What's she saying?' Esther bent closer. 'She's saying something but I can't make it out.'

'I don't know.'

'Are the others coming?'

'Yes. They'll be here soon.'

'I wish I could make out what she's saying. It could be important.'

Samuel took hold of his mother's hand once more, the bunch of thin sharp bones, the crooked fingers with their ridged nails.

'Hello,' he said. 'We're all here. We're with you.'

'Be with me now, at the twilight hour. When the light fails.'

'I'm here.'

'Tell me.'

'What shall I tell you?'

'Tell me about us, when we were young. What was it like? What was I like then?'

'A summer day. The sun throbbed in my eyes. I was going to see my new sweetheart and try to forget, but my leg hurt and my mind was full of grim thoughts that I was unable to shake off. A group of people gathered; young men; women in pretty frocks, like flowers. I saw you standing apart in a green dress. Your shadow slanted across the road. You had soft dark hair and grey eyes and a slow stare. A door opened in me.'

'A door opened in me,' she repeated. 'Yes.'

'Mother. Eleanor. What are you saying?'

Leon had arrived. He pulled up a third chair and sat close to her. He put his thumb on her wrist to feel for the reedy quiver of her pulse, professional, then leant forward and kissed her on the forehead.

'We can't make it out. We think that perhaps she's trying to tell us something.'

'She doesn't seem agitated,' said Samuel. 'She's smiling. Look.'

'Should we call the nurse?'

'What for?'

'How long will it be?'

'They said not long.'

'Eleanor,' Samuel's voice was low. 'We're with you and Quentin will be here soon. Your children. We aren't going to leave.'

'No.' Esther clutched at Eleanor's hand. 'We won't go away. We want you to know how much we love you. We all love you. I'm sorry we used to argue. I took things out on you, but I always loved you. I hope you know that.' She wiped the back of her hand across her eyes. 'I wish I knew if she could hear me. That it's not too late.'

'And it was too late. Everything else became muted and insubstantial. The rest of the world fell away. I just felt your gaze on me. Merry led me across to you and told us we were obliged to get on and you said, "Hello Michael. I'll do my best." You gave me your hand and I took it in mine, like this. I don't remember what I said.'

'You said, "I'm sure you will, and so will I."'

'And we did, didn't we?'

'Yes. We did. We have. We are.'

'We sat by the river.'

'The river.'

'I tried to talk to them all. I tried to laugh and there you were, with your shapely legs and your smooth throat and the way you turned your head. I could drown in you.'

'Yes.'

'We talked about books.'

'Virginia Woolf. I remember. I remember it all.'

'She's thinking about Virginia Woolf!' Leon gave a bark of sudden laughter. 'How like Eleanor is that! To be thinking of Virginia Woolf on her deathbed. Can you believe it?'

'It's making her happy.'

A nurse came in. Her shoes clacked across the floor. She picked up the chart at the foot of the bed and looked at it. She stood by Eleanor, examining the monitors above her bed. She felt for her pulse. The family sat quietly and waited for her to leave again. She smiled at them. She was thinking of what time she could get away. She had promised her daughter she wouldn't be home late, but she felt she ought to stay and see this one out. It couldn't be long now.

'Do you think she is scared?' Esther asked Samuel.

'I think for some time she has been ready to die.'

*

'Have you ever felt so in love that you almost wanted to die?'

'Yes.'

'And you can't tell if you're feeling happiness or grief?'

'Yes.'

'You need to hold and be held. You need to lose yourself and be lost.'

'Ah yes.'

'Is she in pain? Does it hurt?'

'I don't know. I don't think so.'

'And it hurts.'

'It does hurt. Like loss. An absence.'

'You act out a self in the world. You talk and eat and smile and listen, and all the time you long for the other.'

'I have felt these things. You know I have.'

'I would have traded my entire life for a day of you.'

'Such a short time.'

'When you were mine.'

'When you were mine.'

Quentin rushed into the room, out of puff, stopping on the threshold and looking at the huddled group around the bed, the motionless figure barely disturbing the sheets.

'I'm not—?'

'No. She's still here.'

'Good. Good.'

He lifted the chair from the side of the room. He sat and laid his hand on Eleanor's body and closed his eyes for a moment. Leon glared at him suspiciously: was he praying for her mortal soul? Eleanor wouldn't like that. For a moment, hostility pulsed between them.

'Has she said anything?' Quentin asked.

'Yes, but we haven't been able to understand much of it. Just snatches.'

'She mentioned Virginia Woolf.'

'Virginia Woolf! That's typical.'

'And we think she said it was a short time.'

'You mean a short time until she dies?'

'We don't know.'

'She looks as if she has found peace.'

'Yes.'

'I found you.'

'Found me.'

'I held you. I kissed your eyelids and your mouth and your throat and I heard you cry out. My love. My love. In the churchyard.'

'Under the quince tree.'

'Did she say quince tree?'

'I think so.' They were whispering now, watching

407

her and solemn. Like a feather, she could be lifted away at any time.

'Isn't it strange? I wonder what is going through her mind.'

'She always loved quince trees.'

'Do you remember the quince jelly she would make every year? We used to help. The smell of honey filled the house.'

'The sun was like honey. The leaves were bright. You lay in my arms. Birds sang. Everything was opening, everything was dissolving. You said yes.'

'I said yes. I do.'

'By the sea. In our house. Such anguish and such love. To hold you one last time. To say goodbye.'

'Don't go.'

'Nellie.'

'Please don't leave me.'

'Of course we're not leaving, Mummy.'

'Mum, it's all right.'

'Eleanor.'

'We won't go. Shush now.'

'We're here.'

'All of us.'

'Don't be scared.'

'Don't be scared, my love.'

'Without you.'

'I'll come back.'

'I can't. All alone.'

'Nellie. Nellie.'

'I never forgot.'

'I know.'

'I loved Gil. I loved my children. But not a day. Not an hour.'

'She's talking about Gil.'

'Yes.'

'Do you think she knows she's dying?'

'I don't know.'

'Don't be upset, Esther. Sad of course, but not upset. She's very old.'

'So young. On the bank of the river. Under the quince tree. Beside the great sea.'

'Listen. Her breathing's changed.'

'Does that mean——?'

'I think so.'

'Ah no. No.'

'Hush now. It's all right. She needs to let go. It's her time.'

'Time. It's time. They say that time is a river, stopping for no one, spilling its dams, sweeping everyone up in its currents. Sometimes deep and fast and clear; sometimes widening, slowing, so you can no longer see that it's moving at all. But still it is implacable. And they say that time is a one-way journey; you set off in a jostling, hopeful crowd, but it thins as you travel, and at last you realize you're alone. You've been alone all the time. You gather up burdens as you go, memories you have to carry and sins you can't dislodge, and you can't stop. You can't go back. But they are wrong. Time is no longer a river or a lonely road; it is a sea inside me. The ebb and the flow, the tug of the cold moon that shines on its waters. Knowledge drops away; innocence returns; hope freshens. It is spring again. I did not know what a long journey it would be to come home.'

Like a feather lifting. Like a petal falling. Like snow melting. Like a touch on the door, which opens.